"I wish it, Seth," I assured him. "Truly."

But the words had scarcely left my lips when I saw his expression change. It was a shadow—he'd thought of something troublesome—and it covered over the gleam of his eyes as markedly as a cloud obscuring the sun. I was stricken with fear. "My wishing it is not enough then?" I asked.

He swallowed, nervous as a boy. "Does this mean you've outgrown Peter Mason?"

"Outgrown?" I stiffened. The very word sent a stab of fury right through me. "That word presumes that my feelings for him were childish," I said, deeply offended. "Now that I believe he's surely dead, or gone from me forever, I am ready to begin a new life."

Seth winced. "That's not what I wanted to hear," he mumbled miserably.

"I know," I said. "I'm sorry. I would like to say I love only you. Perhaps, one day . . . All I can say now is that I think I would like to live my life with you. If you don't find this to be enough, then I shall consider myself refused."

Rachel's Passage

PAULA REID

HarperPaperbacks
A Division of HarperCollinsPublishers

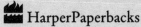

HarperPaperbacks
A Division of HarperCollinsPublishers
10 East 53rd Street, New York, NY 10022-5299

This is a work of fiction. The characters, incidents, and dialogues
are products of the author's imagination and are not to be
construed as real. Any resemblance to actual events or persons,
living or dead, is entirely coincidental.

ISBN 0-06-101362-5

HarperCollins®, ■®, and HarperPaperbacks™,
are trademarks of HarperCollinsPublishers, Inc.

Cover illustration: © 1998 by Jon Paul

First printing: December 1998

Printed in the United States of America

Visit HarperPaperbacks on the World Wide Web at
http://www.harpercollins.com

❖ 10 9 8 7 6 5 4 3 2 1

To my daughter, Wendy,
who reads everything I write
and tells me exactly what she thinks.

Acknowledgments

There are two books for which I feel particular gratitude: *Women in American Law,* by Marlene Stein Wortman, where I first learned about self-divorce; and *A History of American Law,* by Lawrence M. Friedman, which helped a layman deal with the intricacies of legal practices in Jeffersonian America. Grateful thanks to Cynthia R. Snyder, site supervisor of the New Castle Court House, who generously provided me with material about Delaware law and who took me through the courthouse that is so integral to my story.

To the gifted playwright Terryl Paiste, who painstakingly read all the revisions and gave me invaluable advice and assistance; to my editor, Laura Cifelli, who demanded the best of me; to my agent Tory Pryor, a wise counselor who has been unflagging in her support of my work; and to Lyda Rochmis, Paula Klein, and Ethel Buc, who read early versions of the book and helped with criticism and encouragement; to my attorney-son David for some basic legal understanding, to my husband who gave me constant reinforcement, my most heartfelt thanks. Without them, a poorer story and a poorer life.

May you have a lawsuit in which you know you are in the right.
> —*Old Gypsy Curse*

Prologue

Mr. William Galliard, attorney-at-law, considered himself a mild-mannered man, but when his clerk poked his
head in the office door for the third time in half an hour,
Galliard lost his temper. He'd been struggling with a
brief dealing with a complicated property dispute, and it
was exasperating to be interrupted by a clerk who
became nervous and anxious at any minor provocation.
"For God's sake, Harry," Mr. Galliard snapped, "what is
it now?"

"I . . . We . . . have a problem, sir," Harry Ferguson
said in a voice that trembled even more than customar-
ily. "M-may I come in?"

Galliard glowered at him. "Can't you see I'm busy?"

"Yes, sir, but—"

The attorney cut him off. "I said I'm busy!" With a
disgusted grunt, he waved his clerk away and returned
his attention to the brief. After a moment, however, not
having heard the door close, he glanced up again. Sure
enough, his clerk's head was still stuck in the doorway,
a doleful expression on his face. Galliard sighed in res-
ignation. "Damn it, Harry, come in if you must."

"Thank you, sir," the clerk whispered as he entered, closing the door carefully behind him. "Sorry to interrupt, but you see, the lady insists on seeing you."

"What lady?" Galliard asked absently, his mind still absorbed by the brief.

"Why, Mistress Mason, sir," Harry said, blinking at him through his spectacles, "Rachel Mason. The lady you were expecting. The one you told me to send packing."

He remembered. It was a case of criminal conversation that his cousin in Delaware had referred to him. That deuced referral had quite annoyed him. In his experience, cases of criminal conversation—in plain English, adultery cases—were sordid. He had no wish to earn a reputation as an advocate for people of unsavory character. The fact that his cousin believed him to be highly qualified for cases of that sort only added to his annoyance. He'd ordered Harry to dispense with the matter of Mistress Mason by returning the papers to the lady when she called at the office and informing her that he would not take the case. It was a simple enough task. "Didn't you tell her I won't represent her?" he demanded.

"Yes sir, I did. But you see, she's weeping."

"*Weeping*?" Galliard's irritation grew to full-blown anger. "Blast it, Harry," he exploded, "can't you deal with a few tears?"

"I'm. . . not at all s-skilled at that," Harry admitted helplessly. "And this lady's tears are a bit . . . well . . . heartrending."

"For goodness sake, man," Galliard barked, "don't kick up a dust about a simple task. In dealing with females a man must learn to ignore their tears. Just say you're sorry, *totidem verbis*, and show her the door."

"*Totidem v-verbis?*" Harry stammered, confused.

"'In so many words.' You merely say 'Sorry, ma'am.' As simple as that."

"*Me?*" Poor Harry peered at his employer for a moment, the eyes behind his spectacles looking as frightened as a rabbit's—a trembling little rabbit who's heard an unexpected growl in the underbrush. "M-me? Show her the door?"

"Yes, *you*, damn it!" the lawyer shouted. "What am I paying you for?"

"Y-yes, Mr. Galliard, sir." The poor fellow's voice cracked with wounded feelings.

Galliard winced. He didn't like to admit that he was as annoyed with himself for being so short with the fellow as he was with his clerk for being such a ninny. To avoid facing his own guilt, he tried again to return his attention to his papers.

The clerk turned to go. "If it's so simple," he muttered under his breath, "why don't you do it yourself?"

Galliard threw down his pen. "*What* did you say?" he asked furiously, though he'd heard every word. But before Harry could reply, the lawyer was struck with a feeling of shame. He was *bullying* the fellow. And what was worse, he was pushing an unpleasant task on his assistant that clearly he was reluctant to do himself. "Never mind," he said quickly, getting to his feet. "You're right. I'm sorry. I *will* do it myself." And he strode past the relieved clerk to the outer office.

The woman in question, Rachel Mason, was seated on the settle near the door, her head lowered, dabbing at her eyes with a handkerchief. Her dress was ladylike, of a plain gray material in a thick weave, but not so thick that it could disguise the slimness of her form. The modest shawl of dark green wool that covered her shoulders seemed to him an inadequate covering for so cold a day. He felt a twinge of pity for her. He could not see her face, for, with her head thus bent, the brim of her bonnet hid it from his view; nevertheless the picture she made was both pleasing and pathetic. He could already see why Harry had found it difficult to treat her with dispatch.

But William Galliard was no Harry Ferguson. When it came to handling women in states of high emotion, the lawyer considered himself to be quite efficient. He had a spirited wife and three almost-grown daughters, and as head of such a household, he was as expert in such matters as any man. So he took a deep breath and cleared his throat. "How do you do, ma'am?" he said firmly. "I'm William Galliard. I regret, Mistress Mason, that I am unable to—"

She looked up then, and the words froze on his tongue.

The sight of her changed everything. As he later told Harry, it was not her beauty that affected him so strongly, although she was certainly lovely. It was her expression. There was something of such sweetness in the way she looked at him that he was utterly disarmed. He'd often noticed, in women of outstanding beauty, that by the time they reached adulthood the admiration they'd received gave them a self-assurance—an arrogance, almost—that he could not like. But this lady had none of that. There was an unaffected modesty about her, a hesitancy of demeanor that instantly charmed him. Not only that, but there was in her eyes the shining clarity of pure innocence. No one looking at her would ever doubt a word she said. Those eyes, that look, revealed a person who could not lie.

While he stood gaping, she fixed those eyes on him.

Then she held out her hand. "Mr. Galliard," she said softly, "I thank you for at least agreeing to see me. I could not go, you see, until you told me why."

"Why?" the lawyer echoed, too stunned by his reaction to this appealing creature to think clearly.

"Why you are not taking my case," she said.

"Oh. Yes. Umm . . ." His mind stumbled about to find something sensible to say, for he was momentarily at a loss. *Could this woman possibly be an adulteress?* he wondered, already questioning his determination not to represent her. "Well, you see, ma'am," he mumbled, "your case, from what I can determine from the rudimentary notes my cousin sent to me, is . . . well, it's a very weak one."

"Yes, I suppose it is." She stood up and looked him directly in the eye. "Are you saying, then, that you take only strong cases—the ones you are certain to win?"

Whether or not she meant the question as a censure, it was a criticism that hit its mark. His eyes dropped from her steady gaze. "Well, I . . . I . . ."

"Is that how an attorney gets a reputation for brilliance?" she persisted. "By taking cases that are strong to begin with?"

Galliard had to smile. "You, ma'am, have the makings of an attorney yourself. Your questions have the quality of adept cross-examination."

She was startled. "Was I cross-examining you? Oh, dear! Please forgive . . . I didn't mean to . . . I'm dreadfully sorry."

"Don't apologize, ma'am, please. Your questions were quite justified. The only answer I can make is an evasive one: that if I have a reputation for brilliance, it is completely unwarranted."

She studied the lawyer for a moment and shook her

head, rejecting his self-denigration. "Brilliant or not, Mr. Galliard, you must not refuse me." Her eyes clouded with inner turmoil. "I need your help. Desperately."

Since Galliard had already mentally reversed his earlier decision, he had no problem in agreeing. "Very well, ma'am," he said, taking hold of her elbow and leading her toward his office, "come this way. You need to tell me a great deal more about this case if I'm to be of any help, brilliant or otherwise."

Harry Ferguson, standing in the office doorway, raised his eyebrows as his employer ushered the lady over the threshold. "I thought you were going to show her the door," he whispered, gloating, as Galliard passed. "Weren't you merely to say 'So sorry,' in so many words? *Totidem verbis?*"

Galliard glared at him. "Mr. Ferguson," he said loudly, "be good enough to bring our *new client* a cup of tea. Right now. *Totidem verbis*, hop to it!"

Harry made a quick exit while his employer ushered his new client to a chair beside his desk. "Sit down, ma'am, please. I have many questions I must ask."

"Yes, so I surmised." Mrs. Mason sat down with graceful ease, but the lawyer noticed that she twisted her gloved fingers nervously. "Before you ask your questions, Mr. Galliard," she said earnestly, "you must permit me to express my gratitude to you for—"

"For taking the case?" He put up a hand to stop her. "Time enough for thanks when I have won it for you."

Her expression brightened. "Do you think you *can* win it for me?"

"How can I say? The information I have here in this referral letter is very sketchy." He reread the letter, giving her the opportunity to study his face. Then he leaned back in his chair and studied hers. "I wonder, ma'am, if you could assist me by telling me in detail all the facts of this case."

The lady's self-assurance faltered. "In . . . d-detail?"

"Explicit detail, yes. I can't defend you if I am in ignorance of any of the facts. It could be disastrous if the opposition is in possession of information that I'm unaware of."

"But the details, sir"—a blush rose from her throat and suffused her cheeks—"the details are very. . . intimate."

"Yes, I assumed as much, from the nature of the case. But I assure you, ma'am, that anything you tell me is privileged."

"Privileged? What does—?"

"It means that anything you say is kept strictly between ourselves. No one can force me to reveal a single word."

She did not seem comforted by this. "I don't believe . . . I'm afraid, Mr. Galliard, that I . . . I could not speak openly of such details to a . . . a stranger."

Galliard, familiar as he was with the female mind, quite understood her reticence. "Yes, I do sympathize, ma'am." He rubbed his chin, nonplussed. In a moment, however, he thought of a way to break through her reserve. "Then, instead of *speaking* them, do you think you could *write* them?"

Her eyes widened. "Write them?"

"Yes. In that way you need not even see my face as I read. But I do need you to write all the facts that are relevant to the case."

She bit her underlip worriedly. "But, sir, half my life is relevant to the case."

"Then you must write an account of half your life. Do not look so frightened, ma'am. Just write your story as if you were telling it to a friend. A very good friend. For that is what I shall be to you."

There was a tap at the open door, and Harry entered with the tea tray and set it down. "Is there anything else, sir?" he asked.

"Yes, Harry, clear the desk in the little room down the hall. When we've had our tea, Mrs. Mason will be doing some writing. In private."

But Mrs. Mason shook her head and stood up. "Thank you, but I shall forgo the tea if you don't mind. And your little room. Since I think this task may take a long time, I should leave at once and write it in my hotel room."

"Perhaps that would be best." Galliard rose and, motioning Harry aside, he himself escorted her to the outer door. "Remember, ma'am," he said, lifting her hand to his lips, "that you must write everything, fully and freely. I assure you that I am the soul of discretion. You can trust me."

She drew in a trembling breath. "I *must* trust you, sir," she said, meeting his eyes with a steady gaze. "I shall be putting my life in your hands."

PART I

Rachel's Story

PART I

Rachel's Story

I

*E*ven now, I can shut my eyes and see myself standing on an overturned rain barrel peering into the side window of the taproom of Hansen's Ordinary, under the sign that reads BEER AND BEDS, with the rain falling heavily down and mixing with the tears streaming down my cheeks. It was the day I was watching my sister Clarissa being tried for criminal conversation.

Until that day, I'd never heard those words. I was only fourteen—the trial occurred in 1795, more than a decade ago—and I had no idea why my sister was being brought to court. Those two words puzzled and frightened me. *How could mere conversation be a crime,* I wondered? It made no sense.

Yet when I dared to ask what the trouble was, I was shunted aside. My brother Simon, who was eighteen then, refused to explain anything. My mother, Sarah Weller, would say not a word about it in my presence and refused to let me attend the trial. But when she and Papa—my father, Josiah Weller—went to court, I stole out and followed them.

It was the fall session of the New Castle, Delaware, County Court. Since the courthouse roof was being repaired, the proceedings were being held in Hansen's tavern. Because of the salacious nature of the case, the taproom was packed full with people who'd come to hear and leer. I slipped in among them, trying to stay out of Mama's sight.

The first words I heard shook me into a state of trembling terror. The speaker was Abel Becker, the lawyer for my sister's accuser. (Yes, the very man who will be arguing against you in my case.) "This good man, George Epps," he was saying in a loud, clear voice, "left our town for the Western territory for the single and admirable purpose of finding a way to increase his fortune for himself and his beloved wife, only to return and discover her living *in flagrante delicto* in the home of Jacob Hooper——" Here he paused, slowly letting his eyes roam over the faces of each of the jury members before adding in ringing tones, "——and pregnant with his child!"

Again he paused dramatically while everyone gasped in titillated horror. Now, more than a decade later, I can still remember exactly how he concluded: "Since there's no question of the paternity of the still-unborn child— Mr. Epps being absent for the past three years!—it is obvious that Jacob Hooper and Clarissa Weller Epps have been living in a state of criminal conversation!"

The judge pounded his gavel ferociously against the wooden bar but could not silence the ensuing uproar.

I felt the blood drain from my face, reacting more to the tension in the room than any new understanding of what was meant by the words "criminal conversation." Mrs. Frisch, the linen-draper's wife who stood in front of me, didn't understand either. I heard her ask her husband. He eyed her in disgust. "It means adultery, you goose," he muttered. "Adultery."

My heart dropped down to my shoes. Adultery? It couldn't be! I'd heard the sin spoken of often enough in church, but I'd never before heard of it in connection with anyone I knew. And certainly not in connection with Clarissa! *Adultery!* How could that dreadful word be linked to my own beloved sister?

I peeped over Mr. Frisch's shoulder, wanting to see the faces of the principals in the case. Though I was familiar with all of them, they seemed like strangers now. Clarissa sat at one of the two tables in front of the bar, with Mama and Papa on one side and her husband, the defendant, Jacob Hooper, on the other. Clarissa, usually a lovely, spirited woman who carried herself with self-confident charm, was now looking quite unlike herself. Her eyes were red-rimmed, her face was ashy, and her usually bouncy, dark-red hair now hung down in limp neglect. Her shaking hands roamed nervously over her swollen belly. I noticed that Jacob made a hesitant effort to grasp one of those twittering hands, but Clarissa, too tense to be consoled, pushed him away. Jacob's usually cheerful face was now the picture of misery.

Seth was sitting on Jacob's other side. (Yes, the same Seth Trahern who is the plaintiff in the present case.) I barely knew him then. All I knew was that he owned the print shop and put out our town newspaper, the *Newcastle Register*. He was a tall, gangling fellow, quite pleasant-looking despite having a scar across his cheek that I'd heard he'd acquired fighting with George Washington against the British. He had light eyes, more gray than blue and rather piercing, and a slow smile that was infrequent but unquestionably warm. My parents had chosen him to speak in Clarissa's defense.

Abel Becker sat at another table with his client,

George Epps. George—a small, swarthy man I'd never really liked—sat in stiff-lipped, unmoving silence throughout the proceeding. His cold, detached gaze was fixed on a point on the wall behind the judge, as if none of what was transpiring had anything to do with him.

In my fourteen-year-old eyes, Lawyer Becker made a ludicrous figure, with his black, tailed coat straining across his generous midsection, his shoulder-long, wiry, graying hair pulled back from a high forehead and tied at the nape in formal style, and his heavy chin forced into a double fold above his tight, starched collar. I realize now that he was—and is—a very good lawyer. But that day he seemed dastardly to me.

When the judge's gavel finally quieted the crowd, only Clarissa's choking sobs continued to disturb the silence. Seth Trahern turned in his chair, patted her on the shoulder, and rose to speak for the defense. Everyone knew that Seth was no lawyer, but the reason Papa chose him was obvious: As writer and publisher of the town's newspaper, he knew how to use words. He'd been educated at college in Pennsylvania, a claim no one else in the town could make. Even though he was rather shy and reticent as a speaker, my father must have believed he was the best man available to talk my sister out of this trouble.

In his quiet, slow pace, Seth explained to the judge that Epps had disappeared without telling his wife he was leaving. Clarissa Weller Epps, now Mrs. Hooper, he said, would testify that she'd had not had a word from George Epps for three years. After two years and two months, she'd made a public declaration that she was no longer his wife and, with the agreement of her parents in particular and the society of New Castle in general, had wedded the defendant, Jacob Hooper, in a ceremony witnessed by more than a dozen citizens. "This type of separation and remarriage is not uncommon," Seth said, reading from notes, "and is generally considered a socially acceptable expedient for setting marital inequities to right. If the court should frown on this one, it would set a precedent that might taint many other contented households with the stain of illegality."

Several of the spectators nodded their agreement.

After those opening remarks, Mr. Becker began to make his case. He called a witness, Lemuel Lonergan, an unkempt, bearded fellow who looked uncomfortable in his shabby Sunday clothes. Mr. Lonergan testified that the plaintiff, his dear friend George Epps, was the best of men. Furthermore, he declared, Epps had informed him in no uncertain terms of his intention to return from the frontier to the arms of his wife. "If he tol' *me* he was comin' back, he fer sure tol' his wife," the man concluded. "I wouldn't call that no desertion."

Then Seth approached him. "You say that you're certain Mistress Hooper knew Mr. Epps would return?"

"You bet. If I knew, she knew," Lonergan insisted.

"How can you be sure of that?" Seth pressed. "Did you ever speak to her about Mr. Epps's intention to return?"

The witness frowned. "Well, no, sir. I couldn't do that. I on'y has a noddin' acquaintance with the lady."

"A nodding acquaintance? You didn't *nod* the information to her, did you?"

The spectators tittered at Seth's little sarcasm. It was the first time they'd laughed. The bearded witness frowned uncomfortably and muttered, "I guess not."

"She didn't tell you she knew, did she, by nods or any other means?" Seth asked.

"No, 'course not."

Seth Trahern shrugged. "If you didn't tell her, and she didn't tell you, you can't know for sure whether she knew Mr. Epps's intentions or not, can you?"

The witness scratched his beard. "No, sir," he admitted, "I s'pose I can't."

The point being made, Trahern took his seat. Abel Becker then called a second witness—I can't remember his name—who made the same claim: that he'd been told by Mr. Epps that he fully intended to return. Mr. Trahern, in cross-examination, asked if the witness had ever come forward to inform the lady that her husband fully intended to return. The witness merely shrugged.

"A shrug ain't no answer," the judge said testily. "Did you inform the lady or didn't you?"

"I didn't," the fellow admitted.

"Why not?" Mr. Trahern inquired.

"'Tweren't no business of mine," the fellow said defensively.

"Strange that it wasn't then, but it is now," Mr. Trahern snapped.

"Objection!" Abel Becker cried.

"Sustained," said the judge. "Just questions, Trahern, just questions. Save your comments for the summation."

When Abel finished with his witnesses, Seth called Clarissa herself to testify. Heavy-footed and ungainly, she shuffled up to the bar, never once lifting her eyes. After taking the oath in an inaudible whisper, she seated herself on the witness chair. She tearfully declared—in her resonant, if quivering, contralto—that she'd had no inkling of her husband's intentions nor of his whereabouts for the past three years, and that she'd been completely convinced he had deserted her.

"Ma'am," Mr. Trahern asked after she'd finished

relating the agonizing details of her bewilderment, her destitution, and the necessity of returning to her parents' support, "how did you come to the decision to divorce Mr. Epps in the manner you chose?"

"Mr. Hooper proposed the plan to my father. He'd known of several cases in Pennsylvania of what's called 'self-divorce.' We even asked Mr. Becker there about it. He said he believed it was acceptable."

Abel Becker promptly objected. "I said it was acceptable only if both parties agree. Or the husband had truly deserted the wife," he explained loudly.

"You'll have your say in due time, Mr. Becker," the judge said. "Proceed, Mr. Trahern."

"Thank you," Seth murmured and turned to Clarissa. "In the three years of his absence, did you ever get any financial support from Mr. Epps?"

"No, sir."

"Did any sort of message ever reach you—by letter, by word of mouth, by so much as a smoke-signal—that Mr. Epps was going to return, or that he was even alive?"

"No, sir, not a word or sign."

Seth paused for a moment and took a deep breath. "Tell me, ma'am," he asked in a suddenly gentle voice, "now that Mr. Epps has returned, do you regret having taken the action to divorce him?"

"No, I do not," Clarissa said, lifting her eyes at last and speaking firmly. "For three years Mr. Epps gave no thought to my situation. Mr. Hooper was the one who concerned himself with my loneliness and destitution. In my heart I have only one true husband. He is Jacob Hooper."

I felt like applauding. Everything in Clarissa's declaration I knew to be true and sincere. Not only Clarissa's words but her trembling voice, her large eyes wet with fear, and her awkward posture—the clumsy, full-bellied, knees-apart way that a woman sits in late pregnancy—were persuasive. I was sure she'd won over the entire court to her side.

But when I looked around, I could detect little sympathy in the disapproving faces around me. "Where was *God's law* in all this?" I heard a female voice demand loudly. It was the Widow Rowse, the leader of the ladies' circle at church and the most self-righteous woman in town. Though the judge glared at her, pounding his gavel in disapproval, her words seemed to echo in the air.

And later, the judge's instructions to the jury destroyed what little was left of my optimism. I can still bring to mind his exact words: "The law is perfectly clear," he intoned, "as to a separation and subsequent cohabitation with another, that it *must be after an agreement between both parties.* Since the plaintiff in this case was not a party to the agreement, the only way that a finding for the defense can be supportable is if you conclude that his absence was *proven* to be a true desertion and that said desertion therefore constituted a tacit agreement to separation."

The men of the jury rose and shuffled out to the back room. The spectators began to mill about, exchanging views. Mistress Rowse, the woman who'd spoken aloud, argued furiously with anyone who would listen that divorce for any reason was an affront to the Lord. I looked about in the hope of spotting someone who would stand up against her. That was when Simon, who'd been standing at the side of the bar near Clarissa's table, caught a glimpse of me. I was certain he'd give me away to Mama, but he just circled the room till he reached me, grabbed me by the ear, and, without a word, dragged me out into the rain. "Go home," he ordered tersely, "before Mama spots you."

Of course I did not go home. That was when I ran round to the side of the tavern, upturned the rain barrel, set it below a window and climbed up. I was already in position when the jury filed back into the taproom.

Though I couldn't hear, it was plain to see from the reaction at Clarissa's table that the verdict was against her. (I learned later that they'd decided that desertion had *not* been proved. Thus Mr. Epps, the plaintiff, was awarded one hundred and seventy-four pounds in damages.) As soon as the decision was announced, Mr. Epps rose, nodded once, looked over at his one-time wife in sneering satisfaction, and stalked from the room. Clarissa sagged against Jacob in despair. Mama stood up straight and tall, but I could tell, by the set of her mouth, that she was hit hard. Poor Papa was so stricken he swayed on his feet and had to clutch Mama's shoulder for support. The sight of their despair made my tears begin to flow.

I watched the spectators slowly disperse. Despite the drenching rain that continued to fall, a small crowd gathered outside the tavern door waiting for Clarissa to emerge. I climbed down from my perch and peered at them from the corner of the tavern, wondering what their intentions were. When Clarissa came out the door on Jacob's arm, they shouted out curses.

"*Adulteress!*" the God-fearing Rowse woman spat out as my poor sister tottered by. Mama had to be restrained from striking her.

I understood at that moment, with the impact of a blow, that life for Clarissa would never be the same. I hid myself, shuddering from cold and misery, while the family climbed into Papa's trap and rode off. Suddenly someone touched me on the shoulder. I wheeled around in terror. It was Seth, who'd come out a side door. "You're Rachel, Clarissa's sister, aren't you?" he asked me. "Why are you standing here in the rain?"

I gulped and blinked guiltily up at him, not knowing what to say. Like me, he had neither hat nor umbrella. Raindrops were dripping from his flattened hair and running down along the scar on his cheek. "I . . . I . . . couldn't . . . They wouldn't let me . . . watch," I stammered after a pause.

"'Twas not much to see," he said ruefully. "I lost her the case."

"Will they . . . Do you think they'll always call her names like that?" I asked him.

"Some will, I suppose. There are always those who only feel upright when they have someone to look down on."

I smothered a groan. It was dreadful to realize that my sister would forever have insults flung at her face and slurs whispered behind her back. "And is her marriage to Jacob Hooper no longer a . . . a . . . ?"

"A legal contract? No, child, I'm afraid it isn't." He put his arm about my shoulders and led me down the street to his curricle. I was hardly aware that he was taking me home. I could only think of Clarissa. My poor sister would live forever under a cloud of shame. Her child would be a bastard. It seemed to me, in my fourteen-year-old naïveté, that Clarissa had been condemned to a living hell. The prospect was devastating. Imagining myself in Clarissa's place, I wondered if such humiliation could be borne at all.

Seth, lifting me up onto the carriage, must have seen the agony in my eyes. "Don't look like that, little

Rachel," he said with a kindly smile as he put me on the seat and jumped up beside me. "'Tis not the end of the world. When your family and I planned for this trial, we considered the possibility that we might lose. We discussed what choices would be open to Clarissa and Jacob under those circumstances. I believe they've decided to go to Canada and start a new life. No one there will call them adulterers nor consider their child a bastard. I hope that gives you some consolation."

I suppose it did. Nevertheless I remember turning away from him and clasping my hands together at my chest. *Please, God,* I prayed, *let not such tragedy befall me! Not ever! If it did, I fear I'd die!*

Yet here I am, about to face the very tragedy I dreaded and still alive.

2

Four years later, at age eighteen, I met Peter. I was, I fear, still quite an ignorant girl. It was at that time—November of 1799—that I overheard my father say I was foolish about men.

The words shocked me. I now realize, of course, that I was naive for my years, but since naïveté is not a quality one recognizes in oneself, I believed until that moment that I was as knowing about men as most girls my age. It hurt me to discover that Papa did not agree.

I'd begun to wonder, at that time, if I was pretty. I feel shame to admit that the question of my appearance was a fascination to me. I knew it was not a proper subject to think about, much less to speak about. Sinful, rather. As the daughter of a God-fearing, hard-working farmer with modest acreage, I was not permitted to pay mind to such things as looks. I was kept too busy with chores to dwell on frivolities like my appearance. I plaited my hair to keep it out of the way; my clothes were homespun and home-sewn, designed for utility and long wear, not to show off my shape; and even my feet were hidden by clumsy shoes, or, more often than not, thrust into shabby boots that my brother Simon had outgrown. I could not have been a pretty sight

dressed in that way. Yet I was aware that men sometimes watched me with a certain strange intensity when
I walked into town. I didn't understand why.

Despite my sense of the impropriety of the subject, I
couldn't help dwelling on it. I was not so naive that I
didn't realize how important a girl's appearance was to
her future. I knew a girl had to make a good marriage,
and that her looks are her best asset in that regard. My
mother, however, never reassured me about my appearance. She was the daughter of a schoolmaster, and she
constantly stressed the fact that she'd given me as good
an education as she could, a better one than she'd given
my brother, and certainly better than any other girl in
our town. I wondered why Mama made me more skilled
at speaking and penscript than she did Simon, and I concluded that she thought my looks were not good enough
to win me a husband, so she'd provided me with the asset
of an education.

I was, therefore, not confident of my appearance,
despite the glances men cast at me. There was only one
mirror in our farmhouse, two feet square in a scarred
wooden frame, the silvering badly eroded. It hung in
my parents' bedroom. Occasionally I would peer into it
to try to envision what others saw when they looked at
me. I would squint at the one large dark eye looking
back at me (there was not enough silvering between the
black streaks to see both eyes at once) and wonder if I
was pretty enough to win myself a passable husband,
but the mirror gave back no useful information. If this
makes me appear dreadfully vain, I hope you will at
least feel a bit of sympathy for a young girl who had
never had a real glimpse of her face.

At about that time, I asked Simon to tell me if I was
pretty. He was twenty-two then, married and the father

of three, so I thought he surely ought to know about such things. But he merely raised his brows and threw me a look of such scorn that I knew he thought the question simpleminded.

"No, please," I insisted. "I want to know."

"Too pretty for Mama's comfort, I bet," he muttered and walked away. I puzzled over that a long time, but I couldn't make sense of it.

Then, in late August of that year, Papa hired Peter Mason to help with the harvest. I was shaking out my counterpane from the dormer window in my attic bedroom when I first laid eyes on him. He was hoeing a row in Mama's vegetable garden. Even from the back he was good to look upon. He had broad shoulders and slim hips, and the rolled-up sleeves of his shabby homespun shirt revealed a pair of shapely, muscular arms. I was eager for him to turn around, so that I might glimpse his face. I flapped the quilt noisily. He evidently heard, for he turned and looked up. I actually felt my chest constrict at the sight of him. He was the handsomest young man I'd ever beheld. He had a beautiful abundance of hair, a pair of dark, brooding eyes, and a dimpled chin. The only flaw in his face was a slight downward twist to his mouth, but I liked even that because it brought a bittersweet touch to his smile.

We stared at each other for a moment before he dropped his eyes and returned to hoeing the row. I watched for a bit, hoping he'd turn around again, but he kept resolutely at his work. When he'd finished hoeing, he shouldered his rake, threw one glance in my direction, and marched off toward the barn. In a moment, I realized, he would turn the corner and be out of my view. Truly entranced by the look of him, I leaned farther and farther out the window to keep him in sight.

And then—I am humiliated to have to admit it—I almost tumbled out! I gasped, dropping the counterpane to the ground. I had to clutch at the window sash to save myself. Peter heard the sound I made and turned around. "Are you all right, miss?" he asked, dropping his hoe and running back in my direction.

I felt myself flush red. "I . . . er . . . d-dropped the quilt," I stammered.

"So I see," he said, grinning up at me. He picked it up, rolled it into a ball, and tossed it up.

I caught it and clutched it to my chest. "Th-thank you," I said, very aware of my flaming cheeks. "That was g-good of you."

"'Twarn't nothing," he said as he picked up his hoe. "Ain't like it was a cannonball, you know."

"Cannonball!" I exclaimed with a little laugh. "I could never have caught that."

"I could never've throwed it. So don't you be dropping one of those!" He chuckled as he shouldered his hoe and, with a nod to me, marched off. From that moment I was completely besotted.

For several days afterward we eyed each other in passing without so much as exchanging a nod. Then, one hot day, Mama sent me out to the field with a bucket of small beer for the men to drink. (She brewed small beer herself; weaker than true beer, it was refreshing without being intoxicating.) I found Peter at the edge of the west section, dozing under a tree. He woke at my footstep and jumped up, flushing in momentary embarrassment. Then, snatching off his brimmed hat, he grinned brazenly. "Except for being stony broke, Miss Rachel," he said, "I'm a true gent. Like a gent, I enjoy taking a nap in the heat of the day."

It was cheeky, but in truth I admired his manner. Any

other man caught napping, I thought, would have stuttered some excuse. I handed him the dipper without comment, unable to meet his eyes, but I could feel him staring at me while he drank. I managed to throw him a small smile before I ran off.

Each day thereafter, when I brought him a drink, we talked a bit . . . very awkward, silly exchanges. "My friend Timmy Styles says you're the prettiest girl in town," he'd say, taking a strand of my hair and twirling it round his finger.

"Does he?" I'd ask, blushing and pulling my hair from his hold. "And what do you say?"

"I tell him he's balmy. I say you're the prettiest in the whole state. In the whole country, far as I know."

"Then perhaps you ought to wait until you see the whole country before you say such things," I'd retort and run off.

Then one day, after an innocuous exchange like this, and without a bit of warning, he pulled me to him and kissed me. I'd never before been kissed. It tasted as sweet as sack wine. I trembled all over with the thrill of it. And I could feel him trembling, too. His air of brazen confidence deserted him completely, and, stuttering like a smitten boy, he declared his love and said I was beautiful. Not just pretty, he said. *Beautiful.* At that moment I believed, with a certainty I cannot explain to this day, that we were meant for one another.

We kissed a great deal when we had the chance. Later, because I permitted him some timid little attempts to explore my body, we considered ourselves betrothed. We spoke of marriage, but he had no money, no connections, no prospects. The only hope we had for an imminent wedding was the possibility that Papa would help him, give him some land as a dowry, perhaps, or take him on permanently at a decent wage. I feared that Mama wouldn't approve of him (I thought she'd consider him vulgar), but I hoped Papa, being a blunt, down-to-earth farmer, would see a likeness between them.

However, before we announced to anyone that we were in love, Papa found him napping just as I had done. He lost his temper and gave Peter the sack at once. He would have found any suggestion of a likeness between them an insult. There was no hope now that he would approve of my choice any more than Mama would. Peter and I, utterly devastated, thought it best to keep our betrothal a secret until Peter found work and could come to Papa with something to show for himself.

But autumn passed without Peter getting any work except odd jobs, and November came in with a spell of bitter weather. Winter was almost upon us, the season I usually detested. That year, however, promised to be different. To be in love, and to have that love reciprocated, was a joy beyond any I'd experienced, despite our difficulties. During the cold nights I spun happy plans for my future. Those dreams warmed me even when the fire in my little hearth turned to ash. Come spring, I told myself, when Papa had forgotten his anger at Peter, I would announce to my parents that I was betrothed, and they would permit us to be married.

But my bubble of joy was abruptly pricked that November afternoon when I overheard my father speaking of me. I'd been visiting Annette—Annette Coudray, my best friend, with whom I shared every secret thought—but I cut the visit short when I noticed that the wind had turned icy and a heavy snow had begun to fall. I quickly hurried home. Entering by the side door, I paused in the lumber room to shake the snow from my boots. That was when I heard my father. "For a clever girl," he was saying, "our Rachel surely is foolish about men."

I remember how my insides stiffened. Foolish about men? *What on earth*, I wondered angrily, *did he mean by that?*

3

I froze in the act of removing a wet shoe, shocked into immobility. I wanted to hear more, to understand what my father meant. It was eavesdropping, I knew that. And I truly believed that eavesdropping was dishonest, sneakish, and contemptible. Furthermore, I was quite familiar with the saying that eavesdroppers never hear good of themselves. All the same I stood there behind the door and listened.

"Joss Weller, how can you say such a thing?" I heard my mother ask. I was surprised to hear Mama take my side against him. It was wonderful, I remember thinking, how Mama echoed my feelings. I let out a silent breath of gratitude.

"I can say she's foolish on the subject because it's God's truth," Papa declared. "She knows better how to pick a horse for herself than a man."

"Rachel's never picked a man for herself in all her life," Mama argued. I nodded in agreement, peeping with one eye through the space between the door and the jamb to watch them.

"Is that so?" Papa snapped. "I suppose Peter Mason don't count?"

I felt myself stiffen. How—and what—did they know about Peter?

"Of course he doesn't count," Mama said calmly, pouring boiling water into Papa's mug of tea. "'Tis nothing but girlish calf-love."

"You can call it girlish. I call it foolish. That boy'll never be worth a bean." He took a mouthful of tea, made a gurgling sound, and spat it out. "Are you tryin' to burn me, woman?"

Mama, holding her mug in her two hands to warm her fingers, showed no sympathy. "If you'd sip 'stead of gulping, you wouldn't be burning yourself. And as for the Mason boy, he's naught to take seriously. Girls find that sort handsome when they're young. She'll get over him."

"Handsome? Peter *Mason*?" Papa snorted in disgust. "Looks like a haberdasher's dummy to me. When will she get over him? The girl's eighteen. Old enough to have some sense when it comes to men."

"How can I say? It depends."

"On what?"

"On who else comes along."

"Why do we have to wait till someone comes along? There's a perfectly good man wants 'er right now."

Mama cocked her head like a curious sparrow, a gesture I felt myself making in the identical style there behind the door. "Really?" she asked. "Who?"

Yes, who? I also wondered, fascinated in spite of myself.

"Seth Trahern, that's who," Papa said.

I almost groaned aloud. My mother, on the other hand, lit up like a just-filled lamp. She put down her cup excitedly. "Seth? He asked you for her?"

"Well, not in so many words," Papa hedged. "He ain't

the sort to speak of such things outright. But I could tell."

"How?" Mama demanded.

"What do you mean, how?"

"If he didn't ask in so many words, I'd like to know how you, of all people, could tell."

"See here, woman," Papa said, slamming down his cup and jumping up angrily, "think ye I'm too thick to sniff out the way the wind is blowin'?"

Mama snorted. "You couldn't sniff out that sort of wind if it swept up over you and pulled you out to sea."

"Is that so? That shows how little you know me after thirty years of wedlock. I sniffed it out right enough."

"What did Seth actually *say* that made you sniff that particular wind?" Mama prodded.

"He asked if she was promised to the Mason boy, that's what! Is that good enough for you?"

Mama eyed Papa speculatively as he sat down again. "Yes, I'd say that was a wind right enough. If Seth even took *notice* of her interest in Peter, it's a sign."

"See?" Papa grinned in triumph. "I told you so."

"Then speak to him," Mama said, leaning forward and reaching out across the table to grasp his hand. "Seth Trahern is too good a catch to ignore. Speak to him tomorrow! And don't beat about the bush. Say it outright that we're willing to see him wed to our Rachel."

Oh, Mama, no! something in me screamed. I had to bite my knuckles to keep from crying those words out loud. They *couldn't* mean to wed me to Seth Trahern, I thought. In my foolish view I considered him old. He was thirty at least! And such a gawk. He always seemed to be far off somewhere, his pale grayish eyes bemused, thinking of something that had nothing to do with the here and now. My father admired him because he compiled the town newspaper and filled it with political diatribes.

But I cared nothing for his writings. To my way of thinking, a mind preoccupied with politics was not necessarily an asset in a husband. As far as I was concerned, the most important quality a man had to have was charm, and Seth Trahern had none that I could see. He hardly ever smiled, and he always seemed stiff and awkward. He could *write* words well enough, and I remembered that he spoke impressively that time in court, but at church socials he'd always seemed to me to be tongue-tied when it came to speaking to women. What was it, I wondered, that made my mother think he was a catch?

Of course, the man was steady, sober, and certainly prosperous by Mama's standards. Our farm was not large, and thus, to my mother, Seth Trahern's printing business and two-storied clapboard house meant, if not actual wealth, at least real substance. That was what had won my mother, I supposed. But Mama wouldn't have to *bed* him.

My feelings were in turmoil. An image of Seth Trahern getting into bed beside me leaped into my mind. I had not, before this, thought badly of his looks. He was, I'd believed, a fine-looking man. Even the scar on his left cheek had not seemed to me particularly disfiguring. But now, imagining him reaching for me, I found him frightening. I imagined a pair of large hands, with their ink-stained fingers, touching me, . . . a face—with the scar suddenly red and huge—coming close, . . . a mouth, leering in lechery, almost upon mine! Ugh! I shuddered in revulsion. *Let Mama marry him,* I cried inside myself, *but I never will!*

Stifling a sob, I threw off my other wet shoe, thrust my feet into my brother's old boots and reached for my still-wet shawl. I couldn't just stand idly by and let my parents ruin my prospects! I threw the shawl over my head and made for the door, shaking from head to toe. I had to tell Peter. At once.

I must have made a sound. "Rachel? Is that you?" I heard Mama call from the dining room.

I didn't answer. I opened the outer door and fled, running headlong into the swirling snow and the deepening dark with heedless desperation, as if my life depended on it.

Oh, would that I had stayed home!

4

In spite of my brother's ill-fitting boots, I covered the two miles between Papa's farm and town in less than half an hour. The bell in the steeple of Immanuel Church chimed six just as I came onto Delaware Street. Every road and turning, usually so familiar, looked strange in the gathering dark under the covering of snow. I shivered and hurried on down the street to where the light from the tavern windows spilled out onto the snow and lit Hansen's wooden sign. Peter was inside, I was sure of that. But I couldn't go inside. A tavern was a man's place, or a whore's. I needed to find someone, a boy perhaps, to go in for me.

Fortunately, I could see a man coming toward me from down the street. His head was lowered against the blowing snow, so he did not see me. I asked myself if it would be very dreadful to accost a stranger on the street and ask him to do me the favor of taking a message inside. But as the man drew closer, I saw that he was not a stranger. It was my brother, Simon.

Just as I was about to call out to him, the tavern door burst open and out rolled two bodies locked in tight combat. "I'll knock yer damned block off, ye double-damned Tory!" shouted one of them as they rolled, arms flailing, down the three steps leading from the tavern door. I recognized the voice of my brother's good friend, Charlie Lund, who owned the town's livery stable.

"Not before I split your stupid head open, you idiotic Republican!" retorted the other man, gasping.

I hid myself behind the corner of the tavern as Simon ran over to the writhing bodies. "Charlie Lund, you fool, are you at it again?" he grunted as he tried to pull the men apart.

At the same time Mr. Hansen, the tavern-keeper, came hurrying down the steps. "Charlie, for the love of God, let him go. Fisticuffs ain't goin' to prove who has the right of it."

Simon and Mr. Hansen separated the combatants, and I saw that the other man, the smaller of the two, was Courtland White, the town's wealthiest citizen. He'd evidently had the worst of it, for his nose was bloody. Pulling out a handkerchief, he held it to his nose and stalked away, throwing a last imprecation over his shoulder at Charlie. "We need Hamiltonians to run this country," he shouted as he stalked off into the whiteness of the swirling snow, "if only to prevent fools like you from mucking it up."

"What was that about?" Simon asked the tavern-keeper, as the two followed a stumbling Charlie Lund up the steps.

"What do ye think?" Mr. Hansen responded. "Courtland said a good word about Mr. Alexander Hamilton, and Charlie went off like a firecracker."

They were up the steps and about to enter the tavern. I waited until Mr. Hansen had gone inside before I hissed, "Simon!"

My brother whirled about in surprise and peered down through the snowy mist. "*Rachel?* Is it you?" Still squinting, he clumped down the stairs and came toward me. "What in hell are you doing out here alone?"

"I can just as well ask you the same question," I retorted, annoyed that he'd not thrown me so much as a word of greeting.

He glared down at me. "I ain't a green girl. I'm *allowed* to go out at night alone."

I studied his face in the dim light. Simon was not yet twenty-two, but his face was becoming as weathered as Papa's. I'd noticed that his wife, too, was beginning to show her age, with her hair already graying, her forehead wrinkled, and her waist thickened by having given birth three times in three years. "I suppose Abby made no objection to being left at home alone with your babes," I said nastily.

"My wife and her objections ain't no concern of yours," Simon said, irritable and brusque. "A man's entitled to a draft or two after a day stuck in a barn whittlin' shingles."

"And to have a bit of fun creating a fracas over politics?" I sneered.

"Yes, if it comes to that," he said defensively. "Politics is important for all our lives. If you weren't such a goose, you'd take an interest in what's going on in the world. Politics can affect even you, you know."

"Oh, pooh! As if the doings of Mr. Hamilton and Mr. Jefferson would ever have anything to do with me."

"But they do, Miss Featherbrain, they do. If Hamilton and his Federalists have their way, those damn aristocrats and rich landowners like Courtland White will be making all the decisions, and the Republican-Democrats—ordinary fellows like Papa and me—won't have a word to say to protect our rights. Then where will we all be, eh?"

I only shrugged. "I don't know. Things generally work out for the best, don't they?"

"No, they don't!" he barked. "Not by themselves."

"But they would, if you men didn't treat everything like a sporting event. You all behave as if politics is one enormous boxing match."

He rolled his eyes in disgust. "Why, oh why," he asked the sky, "am I standing here in the snow talking politics to an idiot girl?" And he turned to go back to the tavern.

I caught his arm. "Wait, Simon," I begged, knowing I'd better be conciliatory, "do me a favor. If Peter Mason is in there . . ." I felt myself flush.

"Well?" Simon prodded. "What about him?"

"Will you . . . send him out to me?"

He looked at me closely. "You've come out to meet the Mason fellow?"

"Yes," I admitted.

"Does Papa know you're out here in the dark and the snow to meet a man?"

I dropped my eyes in shame. "No."

"Hmm." Simon regarded me speculatively. "He don't like Mason much, does he?"

"No, he doesn't." I looked up and met his eye. "But I do."

"A lot?"

"Yes."

Simon expelled a long breath that misted in the air. "You're a fool, y'know. You could do a whole lot better than Peter Mason."

"You're a fine one to talk," I snapped, suppressing an urge to defend my choice. "Mama says you could've wed Inger Olsen and had two hundred prime acres and lived in a tall house with dormers on the second story."

Simon broke into a reluctant laugh. "Right. It would've been grand. I'd've had a tyrant for a father-in-law and a brood of kids with crossed eyes and thick necks."

"There you are, then," I pointed out. "You married the one you fancied. That's what I want to do."

Simon's smile died. "Not that it matters much in the end, you know, Rachel," he said, his voice taking on a bleak earnestness. "After a few years, it don't seem to make much difference who you marry. It's all disappointments and drudgery."

Those words touched me to the core. "Oh, Simon!" I cried in sudden sympathy, and I threw my arms about him.

He hugged me tightly before pulling away. Then, recovering from the emotion that had momentarily overwhelmed him, he peered at me from under his dark brows, now thickened and whitened with snow. I thought for a moment he would refuse me. But then he shrugged and nodded. "All right, I'll send the fellow out. You may as well have a bit of fun out of life while you can. It ain't no business of mine to bridle you."

He went inside. A few seconds later, Peter came out the door, his step unsteady. "Rachel?"

"Peter?" I couldn't see clearly through the thickly falling snow, but I thought he stumbled. "Oh, God! Please don't be drunk. Not now, when I need you to be sharp!"

"No, of course I ain't drunk. I only had a porter. For the warmth." And he held out his arms.

Relieved, I ran to him. "Oh, Peter!" I cried and flung myself against him.

He put his arms about me but remained tense. "What is it? What are you doing out on such a night? And why do you need me to be sharp?"

I remember gazing up at him. I loved his cleft chin even as it was then, shadowed with the soft stubble of unshaven whiskers. I loved his full-lipped, expressive mouth, and the way his dark, unruly hair fell over his forehead. But most of all I loved the gleam in his wonderful darkly burning eyes. I loved him so much that I tried to ignore the smell of ale on his breath. "Peter, do you love me?" I asked urgently, grasping the lapels of his thin coat. "Do you love me really and truly?"

He cupped my face with one hand. "You know I do. You didn't have to come out on this hellish night to ask me that." He held me tightly against his chest and kissed me, hard and sure.

"Then we must be wed," I whispered when he let me go. "Right away."

He dropped his arms and gaped down at me with knit brows. "Why?" he asked, alarmed. "You're not—! We never—! I barely ever touched you!"

I didn't, at first, understand what he was suggesting. Then, when I did, I shook my head impatiently. "No, no! Don't be daft," I explained. "It's Papa. He wants to marry me off to Seth Trahern."

"*What?*" Peter stiffened in fury and shock. "Mr. *Trahern?* That's . . . absurd! It's the most bean-headed, rumdumb thing I ever heard tell! Doggone it, the man's thirty-five if he's a day!"

I could but sigh helplessly. "I suppose thirty-five is not so very old to Papa."

He stared at me for a moment, nonplussed. Then he turned and marched about, stamping his feet in frustration and making a messy circle in the snow. When his anger had somewhat abated, he glanced back at me worriedly. "Is it all arranged?" he asked.

"No, not yet. But I'm afraid—"

He stomped back to me and pulled me into his arms again. "I won't let 'em do it to you," he said loudly. "They'll have to kill me first!"

I clung to him, ignoring the strong wind that was causing us both to shiver. Murmuring endearments, he drew me to the shelter of the side of the tavern. "I won't let 'em take you from me," he muttered almost tearfully.

I wished with all my heart that we could run off somewhere and marry right then. Yet even in my desperation I knew that it was an impossibility. He hadn't a penny to his name.

He seemed to read my mind. "Aye," he said in glum despair, "what good are wishes?"

"What *can* we do?" I asked hopelessly.

There was no answer. I slipped my arms about his waist as if to hold him fast and dropped my head on his shoulder. "I'll die," I croaked from a tightened throat, "if I have to bed with Seth Trahern."

"I'll kill him first," Peter swore through clenched teeth.

We held each other in miserable silence. "They're signing up men for the *Brandish*," he said at last. "Timmy Styles told me. I told him no. I didn't want to do it. It's a three-month voyage. Three months away from you . . . I didn't believe I could bear it. But now, damn it all, I'll have to. I'll just have to."

"No," I cried, "you can't go to sea and leave me behind! Three months asunder is . . . is forever!" A vague premonition of disaster seemed to be clutching at my insides. I gripped his shoulders so tightly that he winced.

"It's the only thing to do," he said. "The pay is good. A hundred twenty dollars. It'd be a start for us."

"No! I couldn't bear it. *Three months!* 'Tis an eternity!"

"No it ain't." He lifted his head and spoke with a determination and maturity I hadn't heard in his voice before. "Three months is but a season. It'll pass." He took both my arms and held me off, studying my face with a glittering intensity. "I'll be back by spring. Meanwhile, you have to be strong. Can you hold them off till then?"

There was something in those burning eyes that overwhelmed me. My knees grew weak. As I stood there with him, the heavy snowflakes eddying around us, curtaining us off from the world, I felt that my body and soul would dissolve with love. There was nothing he could ask that I would not have given him. "With every breath in my body," I vowed, throwing my arms about his neck. "As long as I know you're coming back to me."

"I'll be back," he promised. "By spring."

5

A week went by. I believed it was the worst of my
eighteen-year existence, for it was the week
Peter left for Philadelphia. After saying good-bye to
him, I felt utterly bereft. My misery was so great I did
not take note that Mama was making preparations for
something special. She was kneading bleached-wheat
dough for a special bread, ironing her favorite table
cloth, and setting me to scrubbing and dusting as if for
spring cleaning. I didn't ask what was afoot until I saw
her trimming the crust for her delectable oyster pie, a
delicacy she prepared only for holidays. That piecrust
opened my eyes. At last I asked what these preparations
were for.

"Mr. Trahern is coming for dinner tonight," Mama
said, her eyes alight with excitement.

I stiffened. *Heavens,* I thought, *Papa must have already
spoken to Seth about a match!* I should have been expecting
something of the sort, but not so soon! *So, Papa,* I said to
myself in despair, *you're offering me over to Seth as if I were a
malformed calf you want to rid yourself of.*

I wondered what sort of bargain he'd made with
Seth to induce the man to offer for me. I had no idea
what kind of dowry the important Mr. Trahern would

consider adequate to agree to take me on as wife. But what difference did the dowry make? I was heartsick no matter what Papa had agreed to pay.

I was not prepared for this catastrophe. My parting with Peter was too new and raw for me to even think of betraying him by sitting down to dinner with another suitor. So, instead of handling the matter with calm good sense, I flew into a spoilt-child rage and instantly declared that I would not—*never, ever, Mama, even if you beat me with a switch!*—come down for dinner with Seth Trahern. Bursting into rebellious tears, I clattered up the stairs and slammed my bedroom door behind me.

Mama, surprised by the violence of my reaction, hurried up the stairs after me. "Rachel Weller," she demanded as she burst into my room, "what's wrong with you?"

I was lying face down on the bed. "I know why you're making this dinner," I cried from the depth of my pillow. "You want me to wed Seth Trahern!"

"Yes, I do," she said, "but how did you guess?"

"Never mind how! What matters is that you wish me to marry an old man!"

This shocked her. "Old man? Seth?"

I lifted my head. "I hear he's thirty if he's a day," I threw at her.

"Ah, I see!" Mama suddenly caught a glimmer of the matter from my viewpoint. "Twelve years older'n you, then." Not that she summoned up much sympathy for me; to reject a man like Seth because of numbers must have seemed ridiculous to her. "You're too young and silly," she said, "to understand what really matters in a marriage."

"A difference of twelve years in age must matter," I argued.

"The age difference is considerable, I admit." Mama's voice was gentle as she sat down on the edge of the bed and smoothed the top of my head. "But your father is nine years older'n me, and it never mattered a whit. Twelve doesn't seem to be that much worse."

"It *is* worse!" I threw off her hand and cast myself face down into my pillow again. "Mr. Trahern is a . . . a . . . croaker!"

Mama sat up in rigid disapproval. "I don't like your tone, miss. And I don't like that word, whatever it may mean."

"It means he's . . . solemncholy. You know, a gloom-spreader."

"Solemncholy!" Mama exclaimed, rising to her feet. "I never heard such flimflammery! Sit up at once and behave like a creature of sense."

"It's not flimflammery," I pouted, sitting up and wiping my cheeks as I warmed to the subject. "He never smiles."

"Nonsense! I've always found the man to be perfectly pleasant and agreeable."

"Agreeable? How can you say that?" I felt very brave, setting myself against my mother for the first time in my life. "He has no conversation. All he ever does is talk politics. He doesn't laugh or dance or—"

"Or carouse, is that what you were about to say?" Mama interrupted in disgust. "No, I don't suppose he does. He's not a drinker. Unlike your precious Peter Mason, who, I hear tell, goes reeling home from the tavern every night of the week."

"That's not *true!*" I cried out in offense. "'Tis filthy gossip." I swung my feet over the side of the bed and stood up to face Mama, my whole body trembling. "I can't believe it of you, Mama. You don't usually spread gossip. How many times have you warned me not to repeat such . . . such malicious flimflam?"

"Very well, perhaps it *is* only gossip. But you never hear such rumors about Seth Trahern. As for his conversation, he talks politics because that's what everyone wants. He knows so much. Why, he has more mother wit in his little finger than your Peter Mason has in his whole head!"

"So you say," I muttered under my breath.

But Mama heard me. "Yes, so I say. And I also say that you may just as well stop this foolish spluttering here and now! It won't do you any good to ride rusty with me. Wash your face, put on your Sunday dress and make yourself ready."

"But—!"

"But me no buts!" I could see from the way Mama strode to the door that I'd upset her more than she would ever admit.

Nevertheless I would not give up. "It's only his *substance*," I threw after her desperately. "He has substance, that's what I heard you say to Papa. I know what substance means—money. If he weren't well-to-do, you would not thrust him at me this way!"

Mama stopped in her tracks. She turned around slowly and peered at me in sincere disappointment. I'd truly hurt her. "If that's what you think, Rachel Weller, you're misjudging me as much as you misjudge Mr. Trahern," she said, her mouth tight. "You have been my daughter for eighteen years. I would hope you'd know me better. But I shan't waste words defending myself. I will only say one thing: You've taken leave of your senses if you don't appreciate the honor that man does you. And until you regain those senses, Miss Mulehead, you will do as I say. You will greet our guest with all the politeness that's been bred in you. Do you hear me?"

I lifted my chin to object, but the hurt in my mother's eyes stilled my tongue.

"Rachel," Mama snapped, "I asked if you heard me."

That look of anger, hurt, and disappointment melted away the last of my courage. "Yes, Mama," I mumbled.

"Good then. I know you will correct your thoughts before dinnertime. No one will ever say that Sarah Weller raised a numskull."

6

I dressed and came down to dinner as Mama had ordered me to. But I felt angry and sullen. Mama looked quite nervous as she showed Seth Trahern into the dining room, for she must have feared that the prospects for the success of her dinner were bleak. I don't think she'd said anything to Papa about our quarrel; she must have felt that there was no point in alarming him. One of them needed to be comfortable and loose-tongued if there was to be a bit of pleasant conversation over the oyster pie.

It was no surprise to me that the dinner turned out to be a stiff, formal affair. I was unsmiling and distant. I said not a word except to answer direct questions in a manner that veered on the farthest edge of politeness. Seth, never garrulous at the best of times, seemed positively tongue-tied. Mama felt too uneasy to speak freely, but after Papa ran out of words she spoke up in desperation. "You seem very silent tonight, Mr. Trahern," she stated flatly. "I hope nothing's amiss."

"I did learn sad news today," Seth admitted. "Mr. Washington died last week. The seventh of December. 'Tis a date for history."

"But not surprising," Mama said, trying to prevent

the evening from sinking in gloom. "We've been hearing for weeks that the man was ailing."

"Still, it's sad news indeed," Papa sighed. "We won't soon see his like again. Mr. Adams ain't no way his equal."

"Mr. Adams is a good man," Seth said.

"Yes, yes, I know what you wrote in the paper last week. He kept us from an out-and-out war with France." Papa eyed his visitor in disapproval. "You ain't sayin' you're goin' to vote for him this time just for that?"

"No, I didn't say that," Seth said, a small smile showing itself in the corners of his mouth. "As editor of the *Register*, I'm trying to remain impartial."

"Impartial, my ass," Papa spat out.

"Joss Weller!" Mama cried. "There are ladies present!"

Papa shrugged. "Sorry, my dear. Forgot myself. But if Seth Trahern ain't a Jefferson man, I'll eat his damn impartial paper from first page to last."

Seth laughed. "With this wonderful appleleather pudding in front of you, Joss, I'd say you were pretty foolish to eat paper."

Mama leaned back in her seat, relieved that politics had broken through the awkwardness. After the pudding and the cups of tea had been consumed, she glanced at Papa with a meaningful look—a warning to go along with her machinations—and said loudly, "Rachel, my love, it grows chilly in here. Take Mr. Trahern into the parlor where there's a nice big fire. Mr. Weller and I will join you in a few moments."

I threw my mother a look of desperation, but the glance I got in return was so quelling I rose to my feet at once. "This way, Mr. Trahern," I said as pleasantly as my emotions permitted.

He could easily have found his way himself, for the

parlor was not more than four steps away, in the very next room. Our house was a modest size. It was sturdy, neat, and always in good repair, but it was in no sense elegant. The entire household consisted of only five rooms, three on the main floor—the dining room where we'd just been, the parlor beyond, and my parents' bedroom beyond that—and two tiny rooms upstairs in the attic. The kitchen was merely a kind of shed, built as an extension to the dining room and sharing the fireplace with it. So was the lumber room just inside the back door, used merely as a storeroom for odds and ends. There were no hallways; one simply crossed through the door of one room to get to another. The front door opened directly into the dining room. I would get to my bedroom by means of a narrow stairway just to the right of the door, abutting the east wall. All the rooms were small and low-ceilinged. Seth had to stoop to get through the doorway to the parlor.

In the parlor, I sat down on a wooden rocking chair and made a motion to Seth indicating that he should take the high-backed chair opposite me. He sat down awkwardly, all long-legged angles and elbows, like a boy in his teens. Since he was not looking at me, he didn't see me eyeing him.

There was a long, dreadful silence. When I could bear it no longer, I started to speak. "I'm not very—" I began.

But the silence must have become unbearable for Seth, too. "I wonder, Miss Wel—" he began at the same moment.

We both stopped, and I gave a hiccuping laugh. "Sorry," I mumbled. "You were saying?"

He shook his head. "No, you. Please."

"It was . . . nothing."

"Please go on," he insisted. "I wasn't going to say anything important."

"Nor was I. I was only going to say that . . . that I'm very sorry but I . . ." I took a deep breath for courage and looked straight into his eyes. "I'm not very interested in politics."

He threw me a gentle smile. "I didn't suppose a young lady like you would dwell on the subject."

"No, I don't. I admit it. I don't dwell on it at all. I don't know anything about Mr. Adams saving us from a war," I burst out in a rush of words, "or about why Papa dislikes Mr. Hamilton so much, or why he didn't think you should have defended the president, or anything else of the sort. I'm a very stupid girl. So we shall probably not find anything to talk about."

He looked uncomfortable. "You know you're far from stupid, Miss Weller. There must be something other than politics we can discuss."

"What?" I said, purposely challenging him. "Name something."

His discomfort increased. "I don't . . . I haven't given any thought . . ."

I knew I was being rude. I should have been trying to put him at ease. But putting him at ease was the last thing I wanted. "It shouldn't be necessary—in an ordinary conversation like this—to prepare a topic in advance, should it?" The question was asked spitefully; I was perfectly aware that there was, in my tone, a suggestion of a sneer.

He did not miss my intent, and it devastated him. "You're right," he mumbled. "It shouldn't be necessary . . ."

The helplessness in his voice made me glance over at him. He was looking down at the floor, his fingers clenched. *Why*, I thought in surprise, *the man is awkward as a boy, uncomfortable and utterly miserable!* I could hardly believe it. This was Seth Trahern, the most respected man in the community, yet here he was, completely overset by having to converse with a mere girl. Without any real effort on my part, I'd made him wretched.

My own anger and misery melted away, swept aside by a sudden and unfamiliar awareness of my female power. *I* was in control of this interview, not he! Despite the fact that he was years older than I, and a man of considerable (to fall back on my mother's assessment) substance, I'd somehow reduced him to boyish incompetence.

This sense of power was strangely pleasing. I felt deliciously wicked. I leaned back in my chair and extended my legs with the relaxed sensuousness of a stretching cat. "I hope you've thought of a subject," I murmured, soft-voiced and teasing. "Mama surely expects us to be conversing."

I think my feline emanations reached him all the way across the space between us, and you may be sure they did nothing to ease his discomfort. He must have realized that more was required of him than he felt capable of. This situation required skill in parlor talk . . . in flirtation. He needed self-assurance, and he had none. "Perhaps we could talk about books you've read," he suggested lamely.

"Books?" I raised one of my eyebrows in a manner I felt certain was contemptuous. "Mama might like that subject, I suppose."

"But you don't?"

"Well, I don't come by many books these days. I've read all the books that Mama brought with her when she married Papa years ago. I do enjoy reading novels when I come upon them—I recently read *Children of the*

Abbey and cried through all six hundred pages—but I'm certain that the books I read would not interest you."

"I wouldn't say that," he objected gently. "I could interest myself in anything that interested you."

It was sweetly said, I had to admit. But his sweetness distressed me. If I succumbed to it, I might actually like him a little, and I was determined not to find anything likeable about him. I forced myself to eye him coldly. "But I don't care to discuss books at this moment," I said.

"I see," was the extent of his reply.

I was making a clod of him. Any man with a grain of sense, I thought, ought to be able to find a topic for casual conversation.

"Sunday's sermon, then," he offered in desperation. "I thought Reverend Phillips was very . . . er . . . eloquent about how a lie creates an ever-increasing circle of greater and greater falsehoods—"

"Goodness, Mr. Trahern," I interrupted heartlessly, "do you really find reviewing sermons an entertaining subject for conversation?"

He stared at me for a moment. "If you're looking for entertainment, ma'am, I'm afraid I'm at a loss." He sighed and rose. "Most gentlemen in these circumstances," he mumbled, crossing to the fireplace and staring down at the flames, "would entertain you by paying you compliments, I suppose."

"But you are above such things?"

He threw me a bewildered look over his shoulder. "I just . . . don't know how."

"'Tis not so difficult, Mr. Trahern," I said, aware that I was cruelly taunting him but unable to stop myself. To speak the truth, I was fully enjoying this unfamiliar but heady game. "All you have to do is find something to praise. It can be my gown, the curl of my hair, the shape of my fingers, the size of my shoe, anything. Simply declare that you admire it. You, who have such an easy way with words in your newspaper, can certainly invent something about me to admire, can't you?"

"In my newspaper I deal with facts, not invention," he responded gloomily.

I gurgled. "Are you saying that you find nothing to admire in the 'facts' of me?"

He turned about slowly and looked down at me. "I find everything about you admirable, Miss Weller, or else I wouldn't be here. But it seems that *you* would have to be inventive to find admirable qualities in *me*. Under the circumstances, then, I'd best cut this interview short. If you'll excuse me, I'll take myself out of your way and back to town."

He turned away so precipitously that I was startled. I hadn't expected so abrupt an end to the exchange, especially now when I was beginning to enjoy myself. He, however, was wise enough to see that there was no reason to prolong the interview; it was obvious to him that it was my parents who wanted him, not I. There was nothing for him now but to escape. He strode from the room with a firm step, trying to keep some semblance of pride, but even in this he was frustrated, for he stumbled over the threshold in a final humiliation.

I followed out some distance behind him. In the dining room, he came face to face with my parents. Their faces showed immediate alarm. "You ain't leavin' so soon?" Papa asked.

"Yes, I am."

"But . . . did you already ask her—?" Mama inquired nervously.

"No. This was a mistake. I'm the last man in the world she wants. I'm sorry."

Mama grasped his arm. "Wait, Seth," she said urgently. "Don't be hasty. The girl hasn't had a chance to know you. If you want her to want you, you've got to court her a little."

"Court her? I wouldn't know how." He made Mama a little bow. "Please, ma'am," he said, "let's not pursue this matter. 'Twas a blunder we shouldn't prolong. I'm much obliged to you for the excellent dinner, of course, which was a treat for a bachelor like me." He said all this as he backed to the door, reaching hastily for his outdoor clothes as he passed the coatrack. "Thank you both, and goodnight."

Mama and Papa followed him to the doorway and watched as Seth strode quickly away into the darkness. "Wonder what went wrong," Papa asked Mama in disappointment.

"I'll tell you what went wrong," Mama said furiously, wheeling about and striding into the house. "Your daughter turned him down, that's what!"

She stormed across the dining room toward me, Papa at her heels. "What on earth did you say to him?" she demanded of me.

"Nothing," I said in quick defense, feeling guilty nonetheless. "Nothing at all."

"Don't tell me that," Mama snapped. "You must have said something. The man looked . . . crushed!"

"As if he'd been kicked in the belly," Papa added angrily.

"But I didn't say anything," I insisted. "We were trying to find a subject for conversation when he suddenly up and left. Just like that."

"Just like that? Without makin' you a marriage offer?" my father wanted to know.

"Marriage?" The very word made me stiffen. "We

never got anywhere *near* the subject of marriage."

"He must've had *some* reason to stalk off like that," Mama said.

I shrugged. "He mumbled a few mystifying words . . . about my having to invent something admirable about him . . . and then he suddenly excused himself."

"Having to invent something admirable? What did he mean?"

"I can't imagine," I insisted dishonestly.

Mama squinted at me through narrowed eyes. "You said or did *something* that drove him off, and you know it. Even at the table you were churlish. Sitting there with that Friday face! Never offering him a kind word or a smile. It was disgraceful! I'm shamed that you're my daughter."

"And you've probably lost your best chance," Papa said in disgust, turning away and stalking off to his bedroom. "All my efforts . . . gone for naught."

"He's right, you know," Mama sighed as she gazed after him. "It has all been for naught." She turned back to me, now more saddened than angry. "I know you don't think so now, Rachel Weller, being too young and silly to know what you've lost, but whoever you wed after this, he'll not be the equal of Seth Trahern."

7

I have been trying to write this as I might have told it to my best friend, Annette Coudray. Annette and I always spoke together in the intimate way women do who know each other well. I hope, Mr. Galliard, you will not be shocked at the way we young girls conversed about those things.

Annette and I were always frank with each other. I remember vividly how we first spoke about Seth. That conversation may have been the reason I began to think of him differently.

In those my innocent years I badly needed Annette's advice. I went to her often in my troubles, and at the time of which we speak, my troubles seemed immense. The atmosphere at home seemed colder than the winter outdoors. The only place I found real warmth was in the Coudrays' kitchen. There we two young women could be alone, free to exchange intimacies without fear of parental interruption. Annette's father, like mine, was always busy in the barn or stable; and her mother, a woman whose French refinement made her too delicate for what she called "*la grossiereté de la vie Americaine,*" often took to her bed for days at a time. Annette thus often found herself mistress of the kitchen, where she could entertain me in delightful privacy.

It was in that kitchen that I unburdened myself of my secret unhappiness. "My parents," I complained as we sat beside a large barrel shucking dried corn, "don't have the slightest concern for my feelings. I can't understand them. They were young once. Do they not remember what it was like to love someone?"

Annette was a very pretty girl, with a ripe figure that was the joy of her betrothed and the despair of her mother, who thought she was too plump. She listened to my complaints with real sympathy. "Perhaps they never were in love," she said. "I don't think my Maman loved Papa. Their marriage was, you know, of their parents' arranging."

"But at least yours permitted you to become engaged to Martin Knudsen, the man of your choice. They didn't try to arrange yours, to push you to wed an old croaker like Seth Trahern."

Annette's eyebrows rose is surprise. "You think Mr. Trahern is a croaker?"

"Don't you?"

"No, I don't. I think Mr. Trahern's rather nice. *Distingué*, you know?"

"*Nice?*" I gave a scornful laugh. "You can't be serious! I suppose, if you were in my place, you'd wed him?"

"In your place I most certainly would."

I refused to believe her. "What rot! He's past thirty!"

Annette shrugged. "What does that matter? Think of the honor of it."

"Honor? What honor?"

"The honor of being Mistress Seth Trahern, the wife of the publisher of the *Newcastle Register,* the cleverest man in town."

"Seems a doubtful honor to me," I said.

"Not a bit. Everyone would respect you."

"Who cares about respect when you're alone in the bedroom with him," I exclaimed with brazen honesty.

Annette considered the matter for a moment. "I can't imagine anything wrong with him in the bedroom," she said, her lips curling mischievously. "I'd rather enjoy testing him."

"Would you indeed?" I giggled at Annette's boldness, despite my astonishment that a girl of her sophistication found Seth Trahern attractive.

"Yes, I would." Annette's naughty smile widened. "I like the leanness of him, don't you? Did you ever notice the way only his hips swing when he walks, while not a muscle moves above his waist? A bit . . . er . . . stallion-ish, you know, with a ripple underneath. Mmmm." She wriggled in her chair. "Makes me itch just thinking of it."

"Ann*ette!*" I, prude that I was, forced myself not to laugh. I felt that I should not encourage Annette in these shocking ways. I remember giving her a look of disapproval. "You're just saying those things to tease me."

"Perhaps I am," Annette admitted, returning to her work. "'Tis because you're such a prig sometimes."

"Is it priggish to wish not to bed someone you don't love?" I demanded in self-defense. "I suppose you'd prefer the 'stallionish' Mr. Trahern in your bed over your Martin."

"I'm not saying that," Annette argued. "I care for Martin dearly, you know that. And I mean no disloyalty to him by what I'm saying. But if a man like Mr. Trahern would offer, I'd be hard put to turn him down." She paused in her work, her eyes fogging over with speculation about the entrancing possibility of a tumble in bed with someone other than her intended.

"Goodness, Annette, what are you saying?" I cried in outrage. "I thought you *loved* Martin!"

"I do. And I can't wait to be wed to him. He's my reality, the other not even a dream. After all, it isn't I who Mr. Trahern wants. But if I were you I'd be very tempted to say yes. For many reasons."

"What other reasons," I asked, "besides his stallionish hips?"

"Well, for one thing, your parents would positively gloat, especially after the shame of your sister Clarissa."

This was an unexpected turn in the conversation. It brought me up short. "What are you talking about?" I asked, surprised. "It's been more than four years since the trial. Do you think my parents still feel shame?"

Annette resumed her shucking. "I think the shame of it will never go away, at least not for your mother."

"Why should she feel shamed? She was not the one accused."

"But she's the mother. Mothers feel more for their children, you know, than they do for themselves."

"Not my mother," I muttered bitterly.

Annette threw me a look of scorn. "*Ooh la la*, you are to be pitied indeed!" She knew full well how much my mother truly cared for her children. "I suppose if *you* were ever accused of criminal conversation your mother would merely shrug."

"She wouldn't feel shamed. She'd only feel anger. She would probably cast me out into the snow," I retorted, but I remember shuddering inwardly at the thought of the humiliation. "She would! After delivering a thundering scold on my having broken one of God's commandments."

"She did not do so to your sister," Annette pointed out reasonably.

"You're right," I had to agree. "I suppose I haven't been fair to Mama in my thoughts."

Annette patted my hand forgivingly. Then she sighed. "Your mother surely suffered dreadfully after the trial. It must have been terrible for her!"

"Yes, but how very much worse for Clarissa!" I said, remembering the appalling scene on the street after the trial.

"There is no question that Clarissa suffered. But it must have been as awful for your mother as for her. And afterward, it was perhaps even worse for her. She lost her daughter, the pleasure of seeing her grandchildren grow up, and the reputation of the family."

"You may be right," I said, thinking about Mama's feelings for the first time. "I've never discussed it with her."

"That's the selfish prig in you," Annette said with her usual bluntness. "She'd probably have spoken to you of it if you'd asked."

I felt ashamed of myself. My heart suddenly ached for Mama. Annette had made me realize how thoughtless I'd been about her pain. "That blasted trial was so unfair!" I said bleakly.

Annette sighed. "Yes, that's true. But as Papa always says, life itself is unfair. *La vie injuste.*"

I sat there with my head lowered, lost in thought. I wondered, as I'd done so often since the trial, how such injustice could happen to women. The words *criminal conversation* sounded again in my head. What dreadful words they were! They were stones thrown into a lake of shame, sending ripples of suffering out to the ends of time.

But there was nothing I could do about it now, I told myself. I had a different problem at present: Seth Trahern. Somehow Annette and I had gotten away from the subject. I firmly brought us back again. "But Annette," I said, "I don't see why you think that if I made a marriage with Mr. Trahern, it would make any difference to Mama's life."

"At the very least," Annette pointed out, "it would improve the family's reputation."

"Reputation, pooh! Who cares for that?"

"All right, then, if you don't believe your mother cares," Annette said, shrugging, "then you needn't consider marrying Mr. Trahern for that reason."

I remember stiffening up and glowering at my friend. "I won't consider it for *any* reason, so you may as well stop trying to change my mind."

Annette gave a taunting laugh. "You must suit yourself, of course. But if you think Mr. Trahern is a croaker, Rachel, *ma chere*, something in your upstairs must be a bit unhinged."

8

The year ended and a new century dawned. It was 1800. Seth Trahern's newspaper had an editorial about the exciting prospects of the new century and our new nation that drew admiring comments from everyone in town. Mr. Hansen cut it out and pasted it in the tavern window. It was even reprinted in a newspaper in Philadelphia. Papa made sure to read it to me. But I didn't care. I was too steeped in gloom, for I'd had no word from Peter for more than a month.

Two more months came and went. March burst in with an early spring. Crocuses peeped out from melting patches of snow. Glimmerings of green showed themselves on the branches of the trees. Spring was on its way, but there was no sign of my betrothed. He'd been gone for four months. Every passing day made me wonder if Peter Mason was ever coming back, or if, like my sister, I had been deserted.

New Castle is not a port like Wilmington or Philadelphia, so news of shipping was of little interest there. No one in town had heard of the *Brandish,* much less shown any concern about its whereabouts. There was not a single soul to tell me what had happened to Peter. His only friend, Timmy Styles, had also gone to sea. No one else seemed to care if he were alive or dead.

Never in my life had I been so miserable. Something inside my chest ached constantly, as if a huge hand were squeezing my heart in a tight clutch. Day and night the pain was with me. To add to my misery, there was no one in whom I could confide. Annette was by this time happily immersed in her own wedding plans, and I did not wish to dampen her spirits. My brother Simon seemed too weighed down with his own problems to have the energy to deal with mine. And Mama and Papa didn't seem to have forgiven me for the disaster of Seth Trahern's 'courtship'; it seemed to me they no longer showed me the affection they once had. My life was empty, joyless, and drab, nor did I see any prospect of improvement.

The lowest point occurred on a particularly lovely, warm March morning. I stepped out of doors shortly after sunup to find myself confronted with a landscape of breathtaking loveliness. A luminous sky, glowing like a sapphire crystal, spread a radiance over the fields lying before me. At my feet every green sprout of Mama's vegetable garden sparkled with early-morning frost, and beyond it my father's field of winter barley stretched out to the horizon in lush profusion. The tops of the plants, growing heavy with seeds soon to be harvested, undulated in the morning breeze like gentle waves in a golden sea. The breeze itself, wafting in from the not-so-distant bay, smelled of ocean salt. It was a morning of such beauty my aching heart could not bear so great a contrast to my misery. I had to turn away from the scene.

Remember that I was still in my eighteenth year. I fear girls of that age (at least the foolish ones, as I was) tend to wallow in their misery. They have not yet learned that the misery one wallows in is not severe. When one suffers true misery (as I've learned since), wallowing in it is the last thing one wants to do. But I, inexperienced in real pain, believed I was truly suffering. I ran down to the root cellar in the mistaken belief that hiding myself in the dark, away from all that beauty, would be in some contrary way comforting. It was not.

A little later my mother came down to discover her daughter weeping disconsolately in the dank shadows. "Is this how you spend your time?" she demanded, arms akimbo. "Hiding away in the dirt and the dark, steeping yourself in self-pity?"

I was furious. I jumped to my feet, dashing the wetness from my cheek with one hand and brushing off the floor dirt from my skirt with the other. "'Tis an added bitterness," I said, choked, "when a girl gets no touch of sympathy from even her mother."

"If I thought sympathy would be useful to you, I'd show you some," Mama said, turning me around by my shoulders and propelling me toward the stairs.

"Perhaps it wouldn't be useful, but it would at least be kind," I retorted as we started up the steps.

Mama did not soften. "I've heard Mr. Philips warn in many sermons that a prudent cruelty is better than foolish pity."

"Very well," I said as I came up blinking into the sunlight, "be cruel and prudent if you wish, though I don't see how it makes anything better."

"I've no wish to be kind if it's Peter Mason you're crying over," Mama said heartlessly.

I swung about to face her. "You *are* cruel! He's a human being, whatever you may think of him. It can't be right that you care nothing if he's alive or dead!"

"I don't wish him ill. Never did. I just didn't want him for you."

"But *I* wanted him," I insisted, tears welling up in my eyes again, despite my determination to hold them back. "Have my wishes no standing with you at all?"

"No, not when you act so witless and absurd." Nevertheless Mama lifted a corner of her apron and dabbed at my cheeks. "If you're bound to learn what happened to the boy," she said more gently, "whyn't you ask Mr. Trahern to find out?"

"Mr. Trahern, Mr. Trahern!" I cried out in disgust. "Can't you ever think of anyone else? What can he know about Peter?"

"He prints the newspaper, doesn't he? He'd know how to make inquiries."

Goodness, but that was true! I remember thinking. He *would* know how. But I wouldn't admit that to Mama. "I don't need any help from Mr. Trahern, thank you." With that, I turned on my heel and set off for the barn.

"Pigheaded as always," my mother called after me. "If you'd not been so pigheaded this past December, Rachel Weller, you might be readying yourself for a wedding at this moment instead of weeping over what might have been."

"I'd likely be weeping all the more," I retorted over my shoulder.

She would not let me have the last word. "Would you? I'd not be so certain, Mistress Woeful, if I were you. You'd have been better acquainted with Seth Trahern by this time, and even you, mule-brained though you are, would've learned to appreciate him."

I kept on walking, pretending I was too far off to hear.

9

Mama was right, of course. If there was anyone in New Castle who could learn something about Peter's ship, it was Seth Trahern. After thinking it over for several hours, I pulled off my apron, snatched up a bonnet and shawl and marched off to town. When I approached the Trahern print shop, however, my courage began to fail me. How could I face the man to whom I'd been so dreadfully rude and have the temerity to ask him a favor?

As I neared the shop, my resolve weakened even more. I was not accustomed to entering a place of business as impressive as the print shop. It awed me. The brass plate on the door had a newly made shine, and the huge front window, with its four eight-paned rows, gleamed as if it had just been washed. The words Trahern's Printing were spelled out across the two middle rows, one letter in each pane of glass. I stared at the words, wondering if I had the courage to go in.

Then I noticed someone standing in the shop window right under the letter H in Trahern's. It was Billy Shupp, Seth's printer's devil in those days—a red-headed, good-natured boy of fifteen or so who, whenever he saw me, had a way of peering at me with a sort of . . . of wince, as if the sight of me gave him pain. This day, when he caught my eye, he did not wince. Instead, he gawked in surprise.

That look unnerved me, and I turned on my heel and started back home. I'd not gone three steps, however, when I changed my mind again. I know I sound a thorough dunderhead, which is perfectly true. I scarcely knew what I was about. But I thought, *If I don't do this today, I shall never learn what's happened to Peter,* so I turned about again.

As I approached again, I saw Billy back away from the window as if he were terrified that I might actually go in. I supposed this was because newspaper work was a man's business. Men came and went quite freely through the door of the *Newcastle Register,* but a woman transacting business there was a rarity. This thought somehow managed to stiffen my spine. I felt rebellious. *Women,* I told myself, *have a right to enter a shop as freely as men!* So I pushed the shop door open and crossed the threshold with a firm step.

Billy, gaping at me, backed to the desk where Seth sat writing. "Goodness!" he exclaimed, poking at Seth's shoulder nervously. "Mr. Trahern, look who's here!"

"Hmm?" Seth murmured absently, not looking round. He was so completely absorbed in the composition of an article for the newspaper that he hadn't even heard the bell jangle. "How does this sound, Billy?" he asked, and he read aloud something about Mr. Hamilton being lost to good judgment for criticizing President Adams for making peace with France. Then, not waiting for an answer, he resumed his writing. Billy poked him again, but Seth didn't take notice.

Billy desperately took matters in his own hands.

"Good afternoon, ma'am," he croaked, his voice break-ing. "Come on in an' have a seat."

"No, thank you," I said awkwardly, not knowing what to do to attract Seth's attention.

"Wh-what can we do for you, M-Miz Weller?" the boy stuttered.

Seth's head came up at once, and he dropped his pen. "Miss Weller!" he gasped, stumbling to his feet.

I dropped my eyes in embarrassment. "Good after-noon," I mumbled.

"Yes, good afternoon." He seemed as ill at ease as I. "Is there . . . er . . . something—? I mean, did you wish any assistance?"

I forced myself to look at him. "I . . . I need to ask a . . . a favor of you, Mr. Trahern."

"Of course. Anything."

It was very kindly said. I was grateful. But I couldn't go on, not in front of the boy. I threw Billy an uneasy glance.

Seth saw the look. "Here, Billy," he said, tossing the boy a coin. "Go to Hansen's and get yourself a mobby."

Billy looked curiously from him to me before nod-ding. I knew that a mobby—one of those sugary brews whose tang comes from distilling sweet potatoes and peaches—was invariably a young boy's delight, but I could see that Billy would have preferred remaining right where he was and listening to the conversation. Another glance at his employer's face, however, con-vinced him to do as he was told. With a shrug, he pulled his cap down from its hook near the door and took his reluctant departure.

By the time the door closed behind him, Seth's dis-comfort had passed. "What is it, ma'am?" he asked gen-tly.

I went right to the point. "Do you remember a young man who used to work for the farmers round about? Named Mason?"

Seth's expression seemed to tighten. "Yes, I do. Peter Mason. Why?"

"This past December he sailed from Philadelphia on a ship called the *Brandish*, and no one's heard of him since. At least no one that I know of."

"I see," Seth said. "And—?"

"I thought . . ." The sudden lack of warmth in his voice frightened me. I had to clench my fists to make myself go on. "I wondered if you could find out something . . ."

He looked for a moment as if he were going to turn away, to dismiss the matter, and me, from his mind. But almost immediately his expression softened. "The *Daily Mail* in Wilmington carries shipping news," he told me. "I'm acquainted with the printer. I suppose I could make inquiries."

"'Twould be most kind of you," I said. "Most kind." And before he could say anything in response, I fled.

For more than a week I heard nothing. Then one morning, while I was upstairs at my bed-making, I heard Mama answer the door. "Mr. Trahern!" I heard her exclaim. "What a pleasant surprise. Come in, do!"

I clutched the pillow I was plumping to my breast and went to the bedroom door to hear more. "I have some information for Miss Rachel," he said to Mama, his tone formal enough to indicate to her that he had no other purpose in making this visit. "About her friend Peter Mason."

Mama snorted. "Ah, I see. She went to you for help after all."

"I beg your pardon?" Seth asked, not understanding.

"'Tis naught," Mama said. "The girl's upstairs doing the beds. I'll get her." She started up the stairs.

But I couldn't wait. I raced to the stairway and started down, but when I caught Mama's eye, I slowed to a dignified walk. I edged past Mama without looking at her and went down to Seth. "It was good of you to come," I said in breathless greeting.

"Not at all," he murmured.

"You have some news for me?"

He nodded, but spying Mama still standing there on the stairs, he did not say anything more.

"You can speak," I assured him. "Mama knows about this."

"Hmmph," Mama grunted from her post up above, "you might first take the man into the parlor, you goose, and offer him a chair and a glass of our brew."

I felt myself redden. "Yes, of course. Come this way, please, Mr. Trahern." Seth obediently followed me across the dining room to the parlor. Mama did not follow. To my extreme embarrassment, I became aware that I was motioning Seth to the very chair he'd sat in during his last visit. However, I was too tense with worry about Peter to trouble myself about my past misconduct. Nor did I remember to offer a drink to this man who'd gone so far out of his way for me. I merely stood like a gawk before his chair, studying his expression for signs of what was to come.

Seth, after a quick glance at my face, did not wait for me to sit, nor did he bother to exchange pleasantries. He promptly removed the letter he'd received from Wilmington from his coat pocket and unfolded it. "The news is not good, I'm afraid," he said bluntly. "There has been no sighting of the *Brandish* since January, when it was seen from a great distance by the *Redoubtable*. The captain of the *Redoubtable* reported that from that distance the *Brandish* seemed to be engaged in a battle with another ship whose flag he could not make out. There was so much smoke, you see."

My knees gave way, and I sank upon the nearest chair. "Then how could he know it was the *Brandish*?" I asked, unable to keep my voice from trembling.

"He was familiar with her outlines. He knew the *Brandish* well. My friend writes that the captain had been mate on her a few years ago."

"Oh, I see. What happened then?"

"He tried to sail to assist her, but a fog came up and the winds were not propitious, and by the time he got to the spot there was no sign of either ship. He surmises the *Brandish* was either sunk or captured."

I felt my heart sink like the ship. "I don't understand," I said, shaken. "By whom would the ship have been captured?"

"The British, I assume, since President Adams has made peace with the French."

"I thought we were supposed to be at peace with the British, too," I said angrily, filled with resentment toward men and their everlasting wars. "Did not Mr. John Jay sign a treaty with them about respecting our neutrality in their stupid wars with the French?"

"Yes, he did. But the British have not been honoring that treaty, I'm afraid. They continue to harass our ships every chance they get."

I slumped down upon the vacant chair. "So you believe it was the British who sank the *Brandish*?"

"Yes, I fear so," he said gently. "'Tis the most likely explanation."

I felt myself shudder. "And the men?"

Seth shook his head. "'Tis not known. The

Redoubtable spotted neither wreckage nor survivors."

The heart in my chest clenched with pain. "No survivors?"

"They did not see any."

We fell silent. There was no other information. Seth rose to go, but my spirit was so bruised I could not even look up at him. He went to the door, but there he paused. My look of misery must have touched him. "That no survivors were seen does not mean there were none," he pointed out. "In such cases, many do manage to survive."

I looked over at him. "Do they?" I asked, seeking any possible ray of hope. "How?"

He sighed. "There's no use to offer you platitudes, ma'am. It would be best for you to know the facts. The captain of a ship that captures an American vessel, whether British or French, usually impresses the survivors."

"Impressment?" I was startled at the suggestion. My eyes flew up to his. "Oh, God! Then Peter is either dead or impressed?"

"Those are the most likely consequences."

"I see," I said, the little flicker of hope dying. I'd never heard of an impressed seaman coming home.

"I'm sorry," he muttered awkwardly.

I did not—could not—answer.

Seth remained in the doorway for a moment of indecision. I think he wanted to comfort me somehow. But then he turned away and left me to my grief.

IO

A few weeks later, in mid-April, my dear friend Annette was wedded to Martin Knudsen. The wedding was, Annette's father said, the happiest occasion ever held in the Coudray home. Forty-two guests crammed the downstairs rooms, stuffed themselves with delicious samples of French cookery, drank huge amounts of whiskey, rum, and gin, and danced all night long to the music of three fiddlers, one bass player, a piper, and a drummer. The bride, wearing a silk gown in a soft brown (her mother called it *cachou de Laval*), looked lovelier than I'd ever seen her. She was radiant; and the groom—a brawny, cheerful fellow with ruddy cheeks and the straight blond hair of a Viking—did not need liquor to enhance the shining glow of his smile.

It was a wildly festive affair, for not only was this a marriage of which everyone approved, but it was being held after a long, cold winter. Since the warm, wet spring foretold a good crop, every member of this hard-working farming community was in a mood to celebrate. The alternation of eating, drinking, and dancing was carried on all night. Even the older women (the "hens," Papa liked to call them) stayed on till dawn, sitting on the sidelines chatting, laughing, and clapping their hands to the music.

Only Madame Coudray was elegantly restrained. She'd emerged from her usual seclusion for this occasion looking charmingly French in a high-waisted gown of blue peau-de-soie she'd brought with her from Paris years ago, but she declined to dance or carouse. She played her role as hostess and mother of the bride by sitting on a high-backed chair against the wall opposite the parlor door and receiving every visitor with an extended hand, a tremulous smile, and an apology for not getting up. "So weak, you see," she explained over and over in her charming accent, "from affliction to ze nerves, but I make ze effort for my beloved Annette, who looks so. . . so. . . *tres charmant, n'est-ce pas?*"

And Annette did look *tres charmant*. I, on the other hand, felt drawn and pale. "Positively scrawny," Annette cried when she saw me. Since Martin's brother and I made up the entire wedding party, Annette declared that such pallor would not do. "'Tis necessary for my only bridesmaid to make a good appearance," she insisted, so she rubbed some rouge on my cheeks, piled up my hair at the top of my head, and ripped off the lace tucker from my Sunday dress of blue-green taffeta, leaving my neck and shoulders bare. As a final touch, she took a sprig of white anemones from the spring wildflowers of her wedding bouquet and made me place them in the cleave of my breasts. Then she studied me from head to foot and smiled approvingly. "You know, *ma chere,* that—with the exception of the groom himself, who'd best have eyes only for me—there isn't a man in the room whose eyes won't be attracted to those flowers and who won't think Rachel Weller the loveliest creature here."

"Except for the bride, of course," I laughed, hugging her.

The wedding ceremony itself was simple and brief, the bride and groom seated on chairs facing the seated minister and holding hands. The assemblage was dutifully silent during the ceremony, but the moment the groom kissed his bride, the music and the roistering began. Though I felt far from lovely, I was asked by several of the men present to dance. I obliged the first three or four, but after a while I went to sit beside my mother. Glad as I was for my friend's happiness, I couldn't seem to rouse myself from a lethargy that was my almost constant condition. Though I longed to feel the happy abandon of the other guests, my spirit could not shake itself from the weight of the depression that had overwhelmed me since I'd learned of Peter's disappearance.

I noticed that Seth Trahern did not join in the dancing either. He stood on the sidelines with Abel Becker and the few other abstainers, sipping at his whiskey and smiling at the energetic gyrations of the dancers. I was surprised that none of the ladies present had inveigled him into dancing, since he was the best looking man in the room. Yes, I had to admit it! How strange, I thought, that I'd never judged him so before.

After awhile, the dancers asked for a "longways." As they lined up, I realized that the tune being played was "The Old Maid's Last Prayer." Since I was certainly one of the few old maids present, I gave a silent thanks to the good Lord that at least they weren't singing the dreadful words.

At that moment Annette tossed me a teasing glance, crossed the room to Seth and pulled him in the line opposite her. He could not, in those circumstances, refuse a request from the bride. As soon as he stepped out with her, all the onlookers crowded round to watch and laugh, for he was well known for avoiding the dance floor.

He surprised everyone (and himself, too, I expect) by how well he did as the bride's partner in that dance. He knew the steps well enough, and when he was uncertain, he followed the fellow next to him. What he lacked in finesse, he made up for in enthusiasm and a natural grace of movement. When the dance ended, everyone cheered.

The musicians next played a cotillion, a dance newly imported from France. Charlie Lund shouted out for Abel to join the dancers, knowing full well he'd refuse. "If these deuced French pigeon-hoppings don't suit Mr. Hamilton," Abel retorted loudly, "they most assuredly don't suit me."

Annette, with an impish twinkle, turned to Seth. "If you were a true Jeffersonian, Seth Trahern, you'd show where you stand by asking a lady to dance the cotillion with you."

"Yes, you're right," Seth agreed, bowing to her. "It's as much a political statement as an editorial."

I knew that Annette expected him to ask me; I reddened, and my pulse began to race. But Seth turned in the opposite direction. He approached Mme. Coudray and asked her to stand up with him. To the astonishment of all present, Mme. Coudray agreed. A cheer rose up in the air for Seth, for the crowd knew that no one else could have managed to tempt the oh-so-delicate Frenchwoman to her feet and engage her in so energetic an activity as a dance. When it was over, several fellows slapped Seth on the back in approval, while others ragged him unmercifully on his success.

Apparently he fully enjoyed this unaccustomed triumph, for the next thing he did was seek out *my* mother's hand for a quadrille! Mama had not danced since her own wedding, for Papa preferred drinking and roistering with the men to cutting a figure on the dance floor. When Seth asked her, Mama blushed like a girl, jumped up eagerly, and took his hand.

Annette came up beside me. "Your mother has more sense than you," she whispered as we watched Seth swing Mama in a lively turn around the floor. "If you're not a complete jackass, you'll dance with that man when he asks you."

But Seth did not ask me.

By the party's end, Seth had participated in six dances. I'd surprised myself by actually counting them. For one of those dances, he'd stood up with Miss Lucy Harper, a prim, somewhat bucktoothed spinster whom some of the older women had glanced at nervously when the fiddlers had played the Old Maid song. Miss Harper was generally considered past her last prayers, so this pairing caused a great deal of tongue-wagging and giggling among the old hens. She was certainly "available"—the only single female that Seth had danced with—and it set them all to speculating on the possibility that Seth Trahern might be looking to take himself a wife at last. I have to admit that the sight of the pair of them dancing together upset me.

"See? I told you so!" Mama said to me in the wagon on the way home. "He'll wed that horsey-faced Harper woman, and you'll have lost your best chance."

"Mama, please," I begged wearily, "let us not speak of Seth Trahern any more."

"Yup, woman, stop your tongue-waggin'," my very drunk father agreed. "What's done is done. Ain't no use naggin' at the girl."

So Mama clamped her mouth shut, and we rode the rest of the way in silence. Wishing to banish my mother's words from my mind, I tried to bring Peter's face to memory as a defense, but I couldn't quite remember how he looked. Even more confusing was the fact that Seth Trahern no longer seemed to me to be quite so old and undesirable as he had when he'd come courting me. It surprised me to realize how good-looking he'd suddenly become in my eyes. I began to wonder if I'd made a dreadful mistake by rejecting him.

The sun was shining brightly into my bedroom when I at last shut my door on the world. I remember that, as I took off my Sunday dress and folded it carefully into the chest at the foot of my bed, I felt quite miserable. I'd hoped, when this evening began, that Annette's wedding celebration would be a happy night for me—a night in which I would forget my own troubles and concentrate on my friend's good fortune. I wanted to come home with wedding music ringing in my ears. Instead, the only sound in my head was the echo of Mama's dire prediction. Wrapped in despair, I drew the curtains against the brightness of the day and threw myself upon my bed. *Was Mama right after all?* I asked myself. Was Seth Trahern really interested in Lucy Harper? Had I, Rachel Weller, really lost my best chance?

II

*P*eter was not coming back. That was a fact I had to face. In the week after the wedding, I willed myself to face it. April was almost gone. Five months had passed since his departure. He was probably dead. As Annette was constantly warning me, "If you're ever to have a husband, *ma chere*, you must give up dreaming of Peter's return and begin to be practical."

Now that Annette was married and settled (a "matron," she called herself), her next goal was to see me settled, too. "You don't *like* being a spinster, do you?" she asked me at every opportunity.

I assured her that I wanted a husband, I truly did. I would soon be nineteen. I did not want to spend the rest of my life like Lucy Harper, who lived with her parents, who was undoubtedly lonely, and who must have been stingingly aware that everyone laughed at her behind her back. Everyone in town, young and old alike, treated spinsters with scorn and pity. I dreaded being called "old maid." Those two innocent words, when put together, somehow give off sparks of offense. They become a sneer toward a woman simply because her female parts are not in use. An aging virgin. To me at that time the phrase spelled failure, the failure of the "maid" to accomplish the one thing she'd been trained for since the age of twelve: to find herself a husband.

"You know, Rachel," Annette said to me one day when we sat together in the parlor of Martin's rustic farmhouse, sewing a comforter for the newlyweds' bed, "you *could* find yourself a husband if you put your mind to it. I know a few unmarried fellows who'd be interested."

I looked at her dubiously. "Who in particular?"

"Thomas Rowse, for one," she replied promptly.

The suggestion made me start in surprise. Young Rowse was the son of the righteous Widow Rowse, who still looked on all my family as godless. Though young Rowse had once confessed to Simon that he had a "yearn" for me, I did not believe the feeling was strong enough to entice him to oppose his mother. Not that I wished for him to do so. "No, please, do not consider him," I begged Annette. "He has such a foolish grin. And a laugh that starts out like a snort and ends with a squeal. The very sound of it makes me shudder."

"Then that disposes of Thomas Rowse." Annette finished the seam on her side of the comforter and shook it out as if shaking off the dismissed Mr. Rowse. "But there are others."

"Who else?"

Again Annette did not hesitate. "There's Courtland White, of course. He's generally considered a good catch."

She was right about that. Courtland was a gentleman of sorts who was financially very snug, who'd been to college in Virginia (although he'd never finished), and who'd inherited four hundred acres of prime land and what in New Castle was considered a mansion. But he was one of the highest of the High Federalists, so enam-

ored of Mr. Hamilton that he approved his every statement. "If I should ever encourage a High Tory to court
me," I said, laughing at the very suggestion, "my father
would have conniptions."

"Come to think of it, so would I," Annette admitted,
pausing in her stitching to envision the unlikely pairing.
"He's too twitchy-nosed and shivery."

It was quite true. The man was small-boned, bucktoothed, and highly nervous. Marrying him would be
like wedding a cotton-tailed rabbit.

And thus the second prospective candidate was summarily dismissed.

But Annette had not yet exhausted her list. "What
about John Odell Junior?" she suggested. "Martin has
hinted more than once that, if you smiled at him
encouragingly, he'd willingly come calling."

I considered the suggestion. John Odell Senior
owned two grist mills and a distillery, and John Junior
was therefore said to have "prospects." Of all of the eli-
gibles, the younger Odell was probably the one my parents would approve. "He's a good man, I suppose," I
said, "solid and sturdy."

"Ah?" Annette, her needle stilled, looked across at me
with eyes alight with a matchmaking gleam. "Then shall
I ask Martin to suggest—?"

I shook my head. "Frankly, Annette, John Odell
Junior is as exciting to me as unsalted soup."

Annette frowned at me in disgust for a moment
before emitting a hopeless sigh. "Your mother's right,
you know," she said at last. "You made a mistake turning down Seth Trahern. He was the best of them all."

I dropped my eyes from her face. Those words upset
me, for the truth of them was becoming more obvious
to me every day. Seth Trahern *was* the best of them all. I

found myself wishing now that I'd not been so dismissive when he came to court me. I reluctantly admitted to myself that if he came calling now, I'd accept him like a shot.

But just as my pride would not let me admit that to my parents, it did not let me admit it to Annette.

12

The ladies' circle of the church had long been planning a picnic supper to follow a Sunday afternoon service. The date they chose was the second Sunday in May, should the weather be favorable. Fortunately, the appointed day dawned so clear and warm—more like July than May—that the ladies were convinced heaven itself had sent its blessing on their plans. They arrived at church that morning with their curricles, traps, or wagons loaded with provisions. Mama herself brought enough salt pork and smoked ham to feed half the congregation.

The pastor kindly made his sermons short. It was only a little past two when the afternoon service was concluded. The men promptly set out tables and benches on the grounds at the side of the church, while the women busily began preparing platters of sliced meats, bowls of potato savory, baskets of hoecakes, and pitchers of ale and sack wine. Every female, even very young ones, took part in the preparations. There was so much laughter and woman-talk while this was going on that none of us was aware that the men had vanished from the area.

Annette, looking around for Martin to sample her

bean-and-tomato salad, was the first of the women to notice. "Where do you suppose the men have gone?" she asked me.

I had no idea. But a sudden burst of cheering from behind the church answered her question. The other women, enjoying this rare opportunity for female socializing, were too engrossed in their chatter to pay mind to the sound, but Annette and I were curious. We laid aside the dishes we were holding and quietly slipped away to investigate.

We heard more cheering and shouting as we made our way toward the rear yard. Before leaving the shelter of the building, we paused and looked round the corner. The sight that met our eyes shocked us. The men were standing about in a circle, forming a little clearing in the center of which two men, stripped naked to their waists, were engaging in fisticuffs. One of the boxers was Charlie Lund. The other was Seth.

The peculiar behavior of the fighters made it clear to me at once that this was not explosion of violence but a sporting event. A boxing match. I'd never in my life seen one. The two fighters, their skins wet and gleaming in the sun, were hopping about, dodging and weaving, and only occasionally swinging their fists. Abel Becker, obviously the referee, was carefully circling around them. Charlie Lund, much heavier than Seth and massive in his arms and shoulders, was throwing blows more frequently than his opponent. Seth was taller, leaner, and seemed to me quite adept at evading Charlie's blows. He seemed to enjoy making Charlie miss the mark.

The observers, watching the fighters intently, evidently enjoyed the evasive tactics too, for they cheered approvingly every time Charlie missed. And between those cheers, they shouted out what seemed to me to be strange encouragement. "Use your left, Charlie, damn it," someone yelled.

"Come on, Seth, don't hold back. Let 'im have it," came another voice.

Every time a blow was actually struck, the crowd cheered even louder. I could not then—and still cannot—understand the pleasure that men take in watching two fighters maul each other.

I had just time enough to take in the scene when Charlie landed a blow to Seth's chin, and he went down. I couldn't help it; I gasped. But Seth was evidently not hurt, for he got up at once and continued to fight. However, a man standing nearby heard the sound I'd made and turned around. It was Martin. As soon as he saw us, he grinned guiltily and loped over.

"Good God, Martin," his wife demanded, "what is going on?"

"Just a little boxing match," he said, shrugging. "The fellows got into an argument about what was better in boxing, weight or skill. We're testing it out. Charlie has the brawn, but Seth learned boxing at college. I've got a wager on his skill."

"Wagering on a *Sunday*?" Annette exclaimed. "Have you no conscience?"

"Don't take on, m'dear. 'Tis for a good cause. We're going to put the winnings in the poor box. Even the pastor placed a bet."

There was a loud cry from the crowd. Seth had landed a blow that rocked Charlie almost off his feet. Annette and I exchanged worried looks, for we were sure the noise would bring the other women round, and there'd be a to-do. At that moment, Seth swung again, a swift, powerful blow to Charlie's chin. The sound of the impact was dreadful to me. Charlie went down backward and lay spread out on the ground, unmoving.

As a few women came up behind us, gaping, Abel Becker began counting over the fallen Charlie. Charlie sat up on his elbow at the count of six, shook his head as if to recover his senses, and put a hand to his jaw. "Enough," he said.

While the crowd of men shouted their approval or disapproval, depending, I suppose, on their wagers, Seth gave Charlie a hand and pulled him to his feet. Poor Charlie tried for a moment to get his equilibrium, but he tottered, turned away, and vomited into the grass.

"Damn it, Charlie," Abel said, offering him a handkerchief, "I told you not to drink so much ale before a fight." Then he turned to Seth, took his hand, and held it aloft. "Gentlemen," he said to the crowd, "I give you our proof of skill over brawn, the winner, Seth Trahern."

The cheering was loud with enthusiasm. Seth acknowledged it with a little bow. "Speech, speech!" someone yelled.

Seth put an arm about Charlie and faced the men gathering around them. "I owe this victory in part to skill, in part to Charlie's thirst for ale, but mostly to my mother," he said, grinning. "She gave me what I needed to beat this brute: a pair of large hands and"—with an affectionate pat on Charlie's belly—"a good digestion."

The men laughed. Even Charlie joined in.

The women were crowding in by this time, demanding to know what was going on. The Widow Rowse, of course, was loudly berating everyone in earshot. "This is an act of sinfulness," she cried, "especially on the Lord's day!" It took the best efforts of the minister himself to calm her down.

Seth, as soon as he realized that there were women watching, hurriedly picked up his shirt from the grass and pulled it on. As he was tying his neckcloth, his eye fell on me. It seemed to me he turned quite red. But because I immediately looked away from him, I could not be sure.

That night, lying sleepless in my bed, I could think of no one but Seth. His appearance this afternoon during the boxing match had surprised me. He'd seemed younger, stronger, more vital than I'd ever imagined a man of thirty could be. In truth, the sight of his bare arms and shoulders, sinewy and gleaming with sweat, had pleasured my eyes. Why had I ever thought him too old for me? And why had I said to Mama that he was a croaker? There certainly had been no lack of charm in the man this afternoon when he'd spoken to the crowd.

But it was more than that. In the few short months since he'd come to ask for my hand, my feelings for him had undergone a complete reversal. *What had made the change?* I asked myself. Was it loneliness? My mother's nagging? Annette's admission that he made her itch? My growing sense of his quiet yet manly dependability? Perhaps it was all of those things.

His calmness, his confidence, the respect others showed to him, his easy smile, his unpedantic intellect . . . all these qualities I had somehow learned to value. I still believed I would never love anyone but Peter, but Peter was gone. The fact was that the only other man in all of New Castle with whom I could bear to spend my life was Seth Trahern.

It was not so wrong—was it?—to consider him a possibility. After all, he was not yet wed. The rumor that he might pursue Lucy Harper had died quickly, for he'd done nothing since that one dance at Annette's wedding to feed it. Of course, there wasn't much hope that he still had some feeling for me, not after the dreadful way I'd behaved. But hadn't he blushed this afternoon when he met my eye? That could be a good sign.

Perhaps, then, it was not too late to correct my mistake. But I didn't know how to convince him to renew his suit. I couldn't ask Papa to speak to him again, not after all the objections I'd made. Besides, in spite of all their nagging, my parents had never suggested the possibility of reopening the negotiations. They'd both made it plain that they considered the matter closed.

I tried to think of other ways to make my feelings plain to Seth. I thought of asking Simon to speak to him in Papa's place, but it is not something done by a brother when a father is still alive. I even thought of using Annette to intercede for me . . . or, better, Annette's husband Martin, who considered Seth a friend and often spent evenings at the print shop with other men debating political issues. But it would be too humiliating to even discuss such a subject with Martin. These were ideas born of desperation. They did not hold up to close scrutiny.

So, there in my bedroom in the dark, I made the most desperate decision of all. I would ask Seth myself.

13

I debated with myself for another day. Then, dressed in my best blouse and a skirt of dark brown dowlas—coarse, everyday stuff, but the skirt had a flounce on the bottom that fluttered when I walked—I set out to ask Seth to wed me. The flutter of my heart was, I hoped, invisible.

As I approached Seth's establishment, resolved to do or die, I saw Billy Shupp standing outside the shop washing the windows. When he saw me, he dropped the washcloth into the bucket and dashed inside. It was not an act designed to bring confidence to my spirit, which was already wavering in fear and indecision. But I'd already debated for long hours on the foolishness versus the wisdom of offering myself to Mr. Trahern, and I'd concluded that it was, in the long term, wise. If he were to refuse me, I would of course suffer humiliation. But that would pass. If, on the other hand, he accepted me, I would not have been foolish at all. So I ignored Billy's disconcerting action and continued on my way.

But the sight that met my eyes when I entered the shop was even more disconcerting. There had been some sort of accident. Seth Trahern was smeared with black ink. His hands were so badly covered with it that it looked as if he were wearing a pair of torn gloves. And a huge streak of it had been spread across his nose and forehead. A besmirched inkpot was leaking the ugly stuff on to the table, and there was a large pool of it on the floor at Seth's feet. And Billy was staring at the mess, wide-eyed.

I gaped from Seth's streaked face to Billy's and back. "Oh, dear," I muttered in embarrassment, "has something happened? Have I come at . . . at an awkward time?"

Seth shook his head and threw me a sheepish grin. "No, not at all," he assured me. "A little carelessness on my part. It happens all the time."

Billy blinked. "All the time?" he asked in astonishment. "I ain't *ever* seen you slop the ink before."

But Seth waved the remark aside. "Is there something I can do for you, ma'am?" he asked me. He sounded breathless, as if he'd been running at a great speed down the street.

"Well, I . . ." I began, but I realized that what I had to say could not be discussed before Billy.

Seth understood my hesitation. He put a dirty hand in his pocket, smearing his britches. "Billy, here's a quarter-dollar. Why don't you—?"

The boy sighed in frustration. "I know. Run over to Hansen's and get myself a mobby."

"Yes," Seth muttered, not taking his eyes from my face.

Billy evidently didn't want to go. "Don't you want me to mop up that mess first?"

"No," Seth said firmly, making a head-gesture toward the door. "It'll keep."

The boy knew when to give in. He left at once.

"Won't you sit down?" Seth asked me, indicating the bench near the stove.

I shook my head, trembling with fright. "May as well say what I've come to say standing. So if I'm refused, I can run away faster."

He peered at me for a moment before saying, "I won't refuse you anything, ma'am."

It was a kind thing to say, I thought, and I looked at him gratefully. But then I lowered my eyes. "I wouldn't wager on that," I said. "I've come to . . . to ask you . . ."

"Yes, ma'am?"

". . . if you . . ." It was going to be harder than I thought. I threw another quick look at him.

"If I what?" he prodded.

"This is very difficult," I mumbled. "I'm positively quaking in my shoes."

"I can't imagine why. Am I so very forbidding?"

"It's not that. It's just a . . . a very *intimate* question."

"Is it, indeed? You've certainly piqued my curiosity, ma'am. It's not often that young ladies come in here with intimate questions."

"You are not making it easier for me, Mr. Trahern, by ma'aming me to death," I burst out.

He grinned at that. "I'll gladly call you Miss Weller if that will make it easier."

"It will not. There's nothing intimate about 'Miss Weller.'"

"Rachel, then. Why don't you ask it flat out, Rachel, and get it over with?"

"Yes. Yes, I will. Mr. Trahern, what I want to know is . . ." I expelled a nervous breath and then proceeded in a rush. ". . . do you still want to wed me?"

He blinked at me as if he didn't quite hear. "What?" he asked.

I had not expected that response. It seemed flat and cold. I felt my lower lip began to tremble. "See? There *are* some things you'd refuse me." I took a backward step and turned to run away.

But he grasped my hand and pulled me back. "Wait!" he demanded. "What, exactly, have I refused?"

"My proposal," I said bluntly, finding it easier to admit now that the matter was out in the open. "I asked you to marry me."

"Did you?" He shook his head in disbelief. "How is it possible that I didn't hear that?"

I looked down at the hand he held, now marked with a black smudge. "Perhaps I didn't say it very well."

He looked, too. "Oh, drat, look at what I've done to you," he muttered.

"'Tis naught."

"'Tis not naught. You'll have to scrub for weeks with strong lye soap."

That made me laugh. "For weeks?"

"It'll seem like weeks. Just my luck to be covered with ink the one time in my life a beautiful young lady makes me a proposal."

Beautiful. He'd called me beautiful. My heart gave a tiny leap in my chest. If he truly thought me beautiful, things might go well after all. It is indeed wonderful, is it not, how a woman is soothed by a little compliment? I remember smiling up at him and thinking that he looked rather charming besmirched with ink. "You do look a sight," I said, putting a timid finger on the smudge on his cheek.

He took that hand, too, and peered down at me earnestly. "Are you certain you mean this, Rachel? I thought you found me a bore."

"I never said—"

"You said I had no conversation."

"Did I?" I'd been a stupid child that day when I'd taunted him in the parlor. I shook my head ruefully. "If you are going to throw all my foolish remarks in my face, Mr. Trahern," I countered, "we shall never get to the point."

"But it *is* the point. I told your father I'd be the happiest man in the world if I could wed you. But only if you wished it. *Do* you wish it, girl?"

I had to drop my eyes from his face. "Why else would I be here?"

"Because your parents sent you, perhaps?"

"They don't know anything about this."

"Then look at me, ma'am, and—"

"You're ma'aming me again."

"Then look at me, Rachel, and tell me to my face that you wish it."

I met his gaze. What I saw surprised me and lifted my spirits more than had seemed possible a few moments earlier. His eyes were glittering with excitement . . . and something more. And that something could not but please me.

I'd known he had been interested in wedding me, but that had been many weeks ago. Could it be that he wanted me still? If the look in his eyes meant what I thought, this man—a man admired and respected by everyone I knew—loved me a great deal. Loved *me*. I was an ordinary, unlearned, foolish girl, and yet he actually looked happy at the prospect of giving over to me the power to affect his comfort, his happiness, his very life! There was nothing fearful about surrendering my freedom to someone who cared for me so much. How could it be wrong to wed such a man? "I wish it, Seth," I assured him. "Truly."

But the words had scarcely left my lips when I saw his expression change. It was a shadow—he'd thought of something troublesome—and it covered over the gleam of his eyes as markedly as a cloud obscuring the sun. I was stricken with fear. "My wishing it is not enough then?" I asked.

He dropped his hold on my hands and turned aside. "Before we go further," he said, not looking at me, "there's something I ought to ask."

"Ask, then."

It was obviously something he was reluctant to ask. He swallowed, nervous as a boy. "Does this mean you've outgrown Peter Mason?"

"*Outgrown?*" The very word sent a stab of fury right through me. How could he ask that? The question threatened to spoil everything. I clenched my fists, confused, pained, and angry. "That word presumes that my feelings for him were childish," I said, deeply offended. "The truth is that there was nothing childish about them."

Seth turned and looked at me, his mouth tight. "You still love him, then?"

I bit my lip. *Mama would advise me to lie*, I thought. *If I speak the truth, I will lose him.* But Seth was too upright himself for me to lie to. It would not be right. "I think I will always love him," I admitted.

"Then, for God's sake, woman," he burst out angrily, "why are you here?"

I had gone so far in revealing my feelings that I was now unable to say anything but the truth. "I've faced the fact that he's surely dead. I'm ready to begin a new life."

Seth winced. "That's not what I wanted to hear," he mumbled miserably.

"I know," I said. "I'm sorry. I would like to say I love

only you. Perhaps, one day . . . All I can say now is that I think I would like to live my life with you. If you don't find this to be enough, then I shall consider myself refused."

He shook his head. "How can I refuse? I was able to walk away from you once, but not now."

"Why is it different now?"

He looked down at me, his eyes revealing both his hurt and a gentle, forgiving affection. "Because you came here to me, all by yourself, offering yourself to me. No one else made you do it. That's too precious a gift to be refused, even if you must hold some of it back."

An emotion I'd never felt before, one that I could not name, burned in my throat. "Thank you, Seth," I croaked, "that was . . . kind."

"Kind?" He gave a bitter laugh. "I don't feel at all kind."

"What, then?"

"I don't know. Confused. Angry. Grateful. Frightened."

"Yes, I know. Me, too. But you mean you'll *do* it, then? *Marry* me?"

"Yes." He shut his eyes, as if the word pained him. "Oh, God, yes."

His tone of voice made me shiver. I was awed at the emotion he revealed. I didn't deserve it, I thought, but I swore to myself that I would try to be worthy of his regard. "I hope, Seth," I said, choked, "that you'll not come to regret this."

He smiled at last, as if he'd overcome some inner struggle. "How can I regret it?" he said. "What I feel most of all is fortunate. More fortunate than I ever expected. Or ever deserved." His smile widened, and he took a step toward me. "You realize, don't you, that these inky hands are the only reason I am not crushing you in my arms."

I came up to him, stood up on tiptoe, and kissed his one clean cheek. "There! Will that do?"

"I suppose it will have to. I think, Rachel, my girl, that this is the strangest betrothal in history. Not even a proper embrace to mark the moment."

I laughed in joyous relief. "'Tis not yet a betrothal," I pointed out. "You must come to the house and ask Papa for my hand in the traditional way."

"Oh? Must I?"

"Of course. You don't want to shame me by telling the world I offered myself to you, do you?"

"No, of course I don't. I'd be happy to ask for your hand in the proper way. And *then* may I expect the traditional embrace?"

I giggled and went to the door. "Of course. On one other condition."

"Another one? And what, Rachel, ma'am, is that?"

I opened the door and stepped over the threshold. "That you clean yourself up first," I grinned back at him over my shoulder as I ran off. "One scrub with strong lye soap on my skin is quite enough."

14

*I*f Seth had second thoughts about his agreement to be a second-choice husband, he never, to my knowledge, expressed them aloud. As arranged, he appeared at our house the very next evening dressed in fine style, sporting a striped waistcoat, a frilled neckcloth, and a cheerful expression. When I answered the door and took my first glimpse of him, I felt a glow of pleasure. Not only was I relieved to see him (for I'd worried all day that he might change his mind), but I thought his appearance just right for the purpose for which he'd come.

He removed his hat—a tall, black castor that made him look like a politician—and bowed. "Good evening, ma'am," he said, moderating his formality with a surreptitious wink at me. "I wonder if I might have a word with your father."

I curtseyed meekly. "Of course, sir. If you'll wait in the parlor, I'll—"

But Papa heard our voices and came up behind me. "Seth!" he greeted with outstretched hand. "What brings you way out here? Come in, come in."

Mama, clearing the supper dishes from the table, looked up in surprise. "Good even, Seth," she exclaimed, taking his hat, "how good to see you! Will you sit down at table? 'Tis not too late for a bite. My pork roast is still warm."

"No, thank you, ma'am," Seth said. "'Tis very kind, but I've already supped. I've come to have a word with Joss, an' it please you."

"Oh." Mama's smile changed to a look of puzzlement. "Of course. Take him into the parlor, Joss."

Papa led the way. "Can't be you're wantin' my opinion on some news item, can it?" he asked, closing the parlor door behind him.

Mama stared at the closed door, her brows knit. "What on earth can he be wishing to speak to Papa about?" she asked. "The way he looked, all smiles and dressed to the nines, one might imagine he was going to ask for—" A shocking idea dawning, she turned and eyed me suspiciously. "Look at me, Rachel! Has anything passed between you and Seth?"

"Passed?"

"Yes, passed. Don't give me that innocent look, miss! You know perfectly well what I mean." She took a step closer to me and studied my face, a look of delight dawning in her own. "Rachel Weller! Don't tell me you've changed your mind about—"

But before she could finish the sentence, the parlor door opened and Papa, looking stunned, emerged. "Sarah, you'll not *believe*—" he began.

Seth, following him out, put a hand on the older man's shoulder. "Permit me, Joss," he said and turned to Mama. "I asked his permission to wed Rachel, but he won't give it without speaking to you first."

Mama's eyes flew to mine, her question to me still hanging in the air. I lowered my head, but I could feel a blush suffusing my cheeks.

"Oh, my God!" Mama's hand flew to her breast, as if to keep her breath steady. But, quite unable to steady her shaking knees, she sank down upon the nearest chair. "Oh, my God!" she repeated breathlessly.

Seth, smiling broadly, knelt down beside her chair and took her hand. "Come, Sarah, say yes. You were willing once to see your daughter wed to me. Why not now?"

Mama put a shaking hand to her forehead. "Why not, indeed. But 'tis not I to whom you should be kneeling."

"Yes, it is," Seth insisted. "You, it seems, are the last obstacle to my happiness."

"Am I?" Astounded and confused, Mama leaned forward, took his face in her hands and gave it close scrutiny. "I see that this is not the same look you had the last time you asked," she said. "Can it be you've knelt like this in front of Rachel before coming here tonight?"

Seth looked over at me, asking with his eyes how he could answer without giving away what he'd promised to keep secret.

I stepped forward. "I . . . Well, Mama, all I need say is that I . . . I knew he was coming tonight. And why."

"Rachel!" Papa exclaimed in delight.

Mama jumped up from her chair. "Are you saying, girl, that there's an understanding between you?"

"A complete understanding," Seth said, getting to his feet.

Mama swung round and beamed at him. "Then of *course* we say yes," she cried. Flinging herself at him, she enveloped him in an enthusiastic embrace.

What followed was a scene of general rejoicing. Mama shed tears of happiness. Papa shook Seth's hand and slapped him on the back at the same time. Then he took out a precious bottle of arrack that he'd kept locked away for just such an occasion, and poured four drinks. "It's an honor to have you in the family, Seth Trahern," he intoned, raising his glass.

"And a joy," Mama added. "And as for you, Rachel Weller, it does my heart good to see you come to your senses at last."

The bottle was passed around many times, and our small house rang with laughter. It was the first time in many years that the Weller house was a scene of celebration.

When at last Mama cleared away the glasses and ordered Papa into the kitchen to help her wash them, Seth put his arm about me. "Have you noticed," he murmured into my ear, "that my hands and face are scrubbed clean?"

"I noticed," I said, blushing again.

"Then I have the right to exact your promise." He pulled me close and kissed me, long and hard. It was a moment for which I'd braced myself, half dreading it. The kiss would not be like Peter's, that I knew. But, as it turned out, there was no need for dread. I liked the taste of Seth's lips on mine, the feel of his muscled chest against my breasts, the way his hands moved along my back. It was so pleasurable I felt unfaithful to my memory of Peter. I was shaken to my core.

When Seth let me go, he grinned down at me. "Now that," he said, "is what I call a proper betrothal."

I walked with him to his trap. I was still trembling and dizzy. I didn't know if it was the kiss, the arrack, or my guilt that so greatly flummoxed me. Seth did not seem to notice my discomfiture. He was as composed as always as he kissed my hand and wished me goodnight. Then he climbed up onto the seat. "I can hardly wait for summer," he remarked, picking up the reins.

"Summer?"

"Our wedding. August. Before the harvest. I arranged the date with your father."

I was surprised. "Do you *wish* to wait till August?"

"Not I. I thought you would."

"Oh." I didn't understand. I'd expected him to be more eager than that.

He waved and started off. I turned away, wondering why his last bit of news disappointed me. He'd arranged to wait three months to wed me when he could have set the date within a sennight. Why? I pondered the question as I started back to the house. He'd said it wasn't for himself he'd set the late date, but for *me*. Then the answer burst upon me: he wanted to give Peter Mason a last chance to make a reappearance!

I turned and watched his little trap disappear down the road, a lump in my throat. If that was his reason, I could feel nothing but gratitude. Mama had been right all along. This person I'd agreed to marry was a very good man indeed.

15

This prolonged engagement period turned out to be a pleasant interim, all things considered. Seth called at our house every few days, and in the warm spring weather we "walked out" together. On these strolls I learned how to converse comfortably with this man I was pledged to marry.

I wanted to learn everything I could about Seth. I prodded him to speak of his childhood and his family. I wished I could converse with him about politics, but I was woefully ignorant on that subject. Although I encouraged him to talk about what he was writing in his newspaper, I still couldn't imagine the intensity of his interest in those matters.

That understanding was brought home to me one day when Mama sent me into town to deliver a strawberry-rhubarb pie she had baked especially for him. Seth and Billy stopped their work when I came in and welcomed me warmly enough, but when they sniffed what I'd brought in the towel-wrapped pie tin, they hooted with real excitement. "I shall love your mother forever," Billy sighed in ecstasy, hovering over me as I set the tin down on the worktable.

"I think," I complained, "that the pie is receiving a more eager welcome than I did."

"We're always delighted to see you, my dear," Seth assured me, "but we are, after all, two bachelors for whom such culinary treats are a rarity."

"The mere smell makes my mouth water," Billy exclaimed, gazing down hungrily at the pie that I was now uncovering. The sight of Mama's flaky crust, with the red, tangy-sweet filling oozing out of the tiny holes in the top, was indeed a cause for wild delight. The pie, they insisted, had to be eaten at once.

Billy pulled a couple of plates, forks, and a knife from a cupboard and asked me to cut slices for them.

"Good-sized ones, too, my dear," Seth instructed. "Not the sort of thin slivers you ladies like to carve for yourselves."

They both hung over my shoulders and watched as I cut. I cut one section and was sliding it, dripping with reddish succulence, onto one of the plates, when we heard the sound of rapidly clattering hooves just outside the window. Surprised, we looked up to see a horse go racing by, his mane flying. Before we could blink, a rock came hurtling through the window with a terrible crash, wrecking the window frame, shattering several panes of glass, and missing Seth's head by a hair.

I screamed. Seth, with amazing presence of mind, immediately pulled me into his arms, his chest and shoulders protecting me from the flying debris. Shards of glass flew hither and yon, spraying the walls, the press, the desk, and crashing to the floor. The brittle sound of splintering glass was frightening.

As we stood there in shocked immobility, the hoof-beats clattered off into the distance.

There was a moment of frozen silence before Seth asked, "Are you hurt?"

I shook my head. "Are you?"

"No," he said. "Billy?"

The boy shook some fragments from his red hair. "I'm fine," he assured his employer.

We brushed glass splinters from our shoulders, expelling relieved breaths that we'd miraculously escaped injury. Then Seth looked about to assess the damage. The framing of several windowpanes was broken, and five of the glass panes were destroyed. A confusion of broken glass and debris was scattered all about the shop, with several evil-looking splinters lying on Mama's beautiful pie. "It's now completely inedible, I fear," Seth said, emitting a long, sad sigh.

Billy let out a string of curses completely unsuited to a lady's ears, but Seth was too preoccupied to reprimand him. He was searching about for the rock that had done the damage. He found it lying on the floor near the stove. A piece of newspaper was tied round it with rough string. Seth untied it and spread it out. "Yesterday's editorial," he said to Billy after a quick glance.

"What?" I asked in disbelief. "Yours?"

Seth merely sighed another deep sigh and nodded. Billy growled in disgust and went for the broom.

I looked from one to the other in dismay. "I don't understand. What on earth does it mean?"

"It means," Seth said slowly, staring down at the gallimaufry on the floor, "that someone doesn't like what I wrote."

"Who would do such a thing?" I asked, appalled. "I didn't think you had an enemy in the world."

"It must have been some loony Hamilton man," Billy offered as he began to sweep.

"What did you write, Seth, to make someone so angry?"

Seth ran a troubled hand through his hair. "I wrote that Mr. Hamilton should be ashamed of the insulting lies he's been writing about President Adams, who is, after all, a Federalist himself and the head of Hamilton's own party."

"Do you think it was Courtland White?" Billy asked, looking up from his work.

"Don't be a cod's head," Seth said calmly. "He'd never do anything so foolish. There are other Federalists in the vicinity who read the paper."

"Then who do you think it was?" the boy asked.

"It doesn't matter who. What matters is the atmosphere that seems to prevail these days. The campaign is becoming too vicious."

"What campaign?" I asked stupidly.

"What *campaign*?" Billy asked in surprise. "You been *sleeping* through the year, ma'am?"

Seth glared at the boy, the look promptly silencing him, and then turned to me. "It's the campaign to elect a president," he explained matter-of-factly, as if my question had been perfectly ordinary instead of utterly idiotic. "The election is months off, yet the arguments are already shockingly savage."

"That may be," put in Billy bitterly, "but that don't excuse throwin' stones."

"No, it doesn't," Seth agreed, "but that's what happens when tempers get too short."

I stiffened. "Is throwing rocks what you men do when your tempers are short?" I demanded.

"Not all of us," Seth said, flashing a comforting grin at me. "Don't look so frightened, my dear. It's only broken glass. No one was hurt."

"Yes, but if times are as bad as you say—"

"We shall live through them."

Seth set about the business of putting up boards over the broken window, while I began to assist Billy in cleaning up the mess. But I felt strangely unsatisfied. "I don't see, Seth, what was so awful in what you wrote," I ventured after a long silence.

"That's just the point. It wasn't awful. Actually, it was quite reasonable. You see, the arch-Federalists who follow Alexander Hamilton have broken with President Adams and are vilifying him in scurrilous public statements. Even Mr. Jefferson is disturbed by the Hamiltonians' unfair accusations. I felt I had to write an objection." He stepped back and stared at his boarded-up window and sighed. "With the mood of the country so quarrelsome, I suppose I should have expected something like this."

"Expected rock-throwing? Just because of some mild words in a newspaper?" I demanded.

"Party politics, that's what it is," Billy muttered in disgust.

"I still don't understand. I know you'll say I'm an ignorant girl, Billy Shupp, but I don't know what party politics *is*."

Seth explained. "When Mr. Washington was president, he thought the government could function without political parties. He knew how ugly the fights in England could be between Tories and Whigs, and he hoped we could avoid it here. But it seems that human nature requires enmity. We are seeing the beginnings of adversarial parties in America after all."

"Not *human* nature," I muttered. "*Men's* nature. If women were permitted to run the country, we would not be so adversarial. And we would certainly not throw stones."

He smiled down at me and took my chin in his hand. "If you ran for president, my lovely Rachel, you would certainly get my vote." And noting that Billy had turned away, he leaned down and kissed my cheek.

After that day, my interest in matters of politics grew by leaps and bounds. I wasn't sure why. Perhaps it was the prospect of being Seth's wife. I suddenly felt a need to learn. I could not allow myself to remain so uninformed. It would not do, I told myself, for the town's most perceptive citizen in political affairs to be ashamed of his wife.

I asked a great many questions after that day. Seth was pleased when I asked them. He said—kind fellow that he was—that they were intelligent and to the point. I think he was looking at me with eyes of love. I didn't even understand the true difference between those antagonistic parties he'd spoken of: the Federalists and the Republican-Democrats. "Papa says that the Federalists are the rich man's party and the Republicans for the ordinary man," I admitted to Seth, blatantly exposing my naïveté, "but I imagine the difference is more complicated than that."

"You're right, it is," Seth said. "The Federalists are a party split in half. They are often spokesmen for the more prosperous among us, but the moderates in their group have sensible principles. The arch-Federalists, however, follow Hamilton's theory that only the aristocrats are fit to govern. The Republican-Democrats tend to favor the ordinary man. Mr. Jefferson, for example, puts a good deal of faith in the common sense of ordinary people. I hope he's right."

That cleared the matter for me enough to venture an opinion. "I think, if I could vote, I'd be a Republican," I decided. "Mr. Hamilton seems arrogant to me."

"That may be, but I think that even if the Republicans

win, they must learn to accept certain basic Federalist principles, like sound fiscal policies at home and a wary eye on the French abroad, all of which Jeffersonians oppose."

I remember being surprised at that. "Are you a Federalist, then?" I asked.

"I like to think I'm neither. When I write my editorials, I like to fool myself into believing I'm a journalist, and journalists should be impartial."

I ignored his unjustified modesty and went to the real point. "But you write strong opinions, don't you? You take stands. Just the other day you wrote a strong diatribe against the Alien and Sedition Acts. How can that be impartial?"

He smiled at me fondly, proud, I think, that I was trying to learn. "You're right again. It's not impartial. But I take my stands on particular issues. I don't follow any single faction in making up my mind."

"Perhaps that's the best way for a journalist to be," I said.

He took my hand, and we walked on in congenial contentment. But the congeniality did not prevail on one particular topic, a subject that Seth tried assiduously to avoid—the situation between Britain and the United States on the high seas. That subject threatened to bring to mind a certain missing sailor whose name had become unmentionable since the day I'd proposed at the printing shop.

Only once did the subject come up. It was when Seth told me about a piece he was writing about the intractability of Britain in the execution of the John Jay treaty. "I wrote that Britain is guilty of hostile inflexibility," he remarked casually, "but perhaps I shouldn't have been so strong." He did not anticipate where this innocent remark might lead.

I couldn't help it. On matters of British impressment of sailors, I had a personal reason for my feelings against Britain. "Of course you should have been strong," I declared firmly, "Britain *is* inflexible, is it not?"

"Perhaps, but perhaps not actually hostile."

"How can you say so?" I demanded angrily. This was one topic on which I had strong opinions of my own. And I'd concluded, as had most Americans, that Britain was high-handed in its dealings with Adams' government. "The English stop our ships and impress our free men and call them British deserters! How can we sit idly by and let them do it?"

There it was, the impressment topic. The moment the words were out of my mouth, I was sorry I'd said them. The subject of impressment inevitably brought Peter to mind and was therefore a topic to avoid. But Seth couldn't avoid it now. "There's no question that the British are infringing on our liberties at sea," he said slowly, "but they have a rationale. A good number of British seamen are deserting and finding their way onto American ships, where conditions are better. Shocking as this may seem, as many as twenty-five percent of our seamen are British deserters. The British know we encourage the desertion and even, in some cases, give the deserters false citizenship papers. It makes good Englishmen furious."

"Isn't that too bad for them!" I scoffed, unable to stop myself.

"But, you see, the British have a rule. It's called 'indefeasible allegiance,'" Seth pointed out.

"And what does that mean?" I asked belligerently.

"It means that an Englishman's allegiance to England is not voidable. Once a British citizen, always a British citizen."

I was outraged. "That's a *terrible* rule! Does it apply to emigrants as well as deserters?"

"Yes, it does. I don't say I approve of the rule. I'm only using it to demonstrate—"

"That the British have a rationale," I cut in. "Yes, I heard you. But I don't give a fig for their rationale." I dropped his arm and stalked away from him.

He caught up with me in three strides. "You're becoming quite a vehement politician, aren't you?" he asked, grinning down at me with ill-concealed pride as he tucked my arm back in his.

His good nature touched me and made me ashamed for having intruded Peter into our thoughts, though his name had not been mentioned. I gave him a half-hearted smile and lowered my head. "No, not really," I admitted.

We walked on a little while in silence. After awhile I decided to speak openly about it. I glanced up at him askance. "You think my opinions are too personal, don't you? That I'm thinking of Peter."

His step slowed. "Are you?"

"I suppose I am. I can't help myself." I shot him a quick, guilty look. "Are you disgusted with me?"

"How can I be? My attachment to you is too strong to break now, no matter how we may disagree."

Something in me grew warm at those words. "An indefeasible allegiance, is it?" I quipped.

He threw his head back and laughed. "As indefeasible as it is possible to be," he said, and he caught me up in his arms and swung me about in delight.

My tiny verbal riposte had saved the moment from stinging us both, but we were again made aware that the shadow of Peter Mason was always hanging over us.

16

My betrothal time, though pleasant, was not without flaws, the most troublesome being the absence of physical interplay. Seth and I indulged in none of the love-games that betrothed couples engaged in. Bundling was often indulged in by "promised" couples—I knew that Annette and Martin had done some "tarrying" when they were engaged—but Seth made no attempts in that regard. Even kissing was something he seemed to avoid. The kiss he'd given me the evening when Papa approved his proposal had been thrilling, but he'd not done it since. I admit that I was perfectly willing for him to do it again, but I didn't know how to tell him. My reticence must have been dampening to him.

After that first kiss, he rarely did more than kiss my hand or peck at my cheek when saying goodnight. Once or twice he took me in his arms in a spontaneous embrace, in the manner in which he'd swung me about when I'd joked about his indefeasible allegiance, but he didn't kiss me in the way he'd had that first time. I stupidly could think of no answer when I asked myself why.

As the day of the wedding approached, my tension grew. Once we were married, I supposed, he would

surely require my indulgence in the physical require-
ments of wedlock. My mother had told me years before
about what I was to expect in the marriage bed. But
what she couldn't explain was how it would feel. Would
I be revolted? Would I feel disloyal to Peter? Could I
bear it? The questions were troublesome, and I had not
the courage to discuss them with either Mama or
Annette. I told myself that, like most other girls, I would
have to discover the answers for myself.

Sometime during the week before my wedding, I had
a dream in which Peter Mason, resplendent in a blue
uniform with gold buttons and enormous epaulets, came
storming into the parlor just when the pastor was asking, "Should anyone amongst us have knowledge of any
just impediment, public or private, to these nuptials, let
him that knoweth it speak it now or forever after hold
his peace." The intruder, not bothering to voice objections, lifted me into his arms and carried me to the door,
while Seth opened his mouth and emitted a cry so piercing that it wakened me. I trembled in alarm for several
minutes afterwards. Now, trying to recall the details of
the dream, I can bring to mind the triumphant look on
Peter's face and the agony on Seth's. But I have no recollection of what my own feelings had been.

The wedding was held on the tenth of August in the
year 1800, as planned. It was held in the Weller parlor,
with about a dozen guests present: an overjoyed Mama
and Papa, of course; the pastor of the church, smiling
benignly; an ecstatic and pregnant Annette with her
husband Martin and her father (her mother was too ill
to attend); my brother Simon and his worn, pale-faced
wife; a scrubbed and polished Billy Shupp; Seth's
housekeeper, Clara Gruenwald; and Abel Becker, who
stood up with Seth.

It was a subdued affair, with no dancing. And, although I glanced nervously at the door every few minutes (the dream having had a long-lasting effect on me), no Peter Mason appeared to claim his beloved.

After a wedding supper had been consumed and toasts drunk, Seth handed me up into his rig and drove me off to his house in town. All during the ride, I kept my hands clenched in my lap. And the muscles in my throat were so tight I could barely breathe.

It seems to me that I use the words frightened and terror-stricken very often in this narrative. I am ashamed of all the times that I was too timorous to act. If I had had a modicum of bravery at that time, much of what I've suffered would have been avoided. My only excuse is that I was nineteen and dreadfully inexperienced. In the five years since my wedding to Seth, I have lived a lifetime. I trust that the pain of those years has at least given me some stiffness in my backbone. My fondest hope is that I've managed to acquire a little more courage to face—and fight against—the blows that are still to come.

But that courage was sadly lacking on my wedding night. When Seth's carriage pulled to a stop in front of his house that night, I was hard put to hide the panic in my breast. Seth jumped down and lifted me from the seat. He carried me over the threshold and up to the bedroom, where he set me down, kissed my cheek, and started toward the door. "Where are you g-going?" I stammered in surprise.

"I have to stable the horses," he said. "Don't wait up for me. I'll sleep in the room down the hall."

"But . . . why?"

He gave me a level look. "I don't think you're ready yet for me to share your bed."

"I'm not?"

"Do you think you are?"

"I . . . don't know."

He drew me to him, holding me tightly with one arm, and tilted up my face to look at him. Then, slowly, he kissed me. I wanted to respond, to press my breasts against his chest, to throw my arms about his neck and hold on for dear life. But something—yes, that deuced, girlish fearfulness—held me rigid and unmoving, and after a moment he let me go. "So, you see?" he asked.

I turned away and dropped my head in my hands. "I never wished . . . I did not intend, when I asked you to wed me, to withhold . . ."

"I know. But I can't bring myself to bed a reluctant bride."

"I am not reluctant, Seth," I said.

"Not ready, then."

I turned and faced him. "But when will I be ready?"

He smiled down at me, a patient, understanding smile that both irked me for its condescension and hurt me by the suffering it revealed. "When it happens, we'll know," he said.

"Both of us?"

"I think so." He crossed over the threshold before adding, "I hope so." And he gently closed the door behind him.

I remember that I stood there staring at the door, a long breath escaping from my chest. It was a breath of relief, I was sure of that. What I wasn't sure of was why there were tears coursing down my cheeks.

17

I have been writing all night without pause, like someone possessed. I can't seem to help myself. Incidents . . . conversations . . . bits of my life that I didn't know I remembered are leaping into my head, and something impels me to write them down. I think I must do this to justify myself, not so much to you, my advocate, but to me. If I relive it all, perhaps I will understand what I've done. And be able to forgive myself.

But back to my story: those early days with Seth.

There were many wonderful, if unfamiliar, accoutrements in my new home, but the most interesting to me was the mirror. My delight in it must indicate an unseemly, superficial nature, but I've sworn to be truthful, so I must paint myself as I truly was. The mirror was a small one, and it hung over a chest of drawers in my bedroom. But its silvering was flawless, so I was able to see all of my face and a good part of my upper body. It was a new experience to see my reflection, but it was hard to believe it was myself I was seeing. The woman in the glass was not the Rachel I'd imagined. I appeared smaller and thinner than the sturdy woman I'd supposed myself to be. I'd imagined I'd see a younger version of

Mama, but the woman in the mirror was more . . . more delicate; she seemed to me too vulnerable to the blows of life. I could not accept the mirror image as a true reflection of the real.

Married life, too, didn't feel real. My life had become so different from what it had been a short time before that it seemed a dream. I expected to wake at any moment and find myself in my little bedroom on my father's farm.

There was something unsettling about this new life. I was now mistress of a fine house, one of the finest in town. There was a carved settee in the front room—much grander a room than the parlor at home—and real paintings on two of the walls. And all the windows were covered with draperies, whereas at my mother's house only her bed was draped. Most impressive of all, in addition to the settee, there were six chairs in the parlor alone. Since the number of chairs in a household was a way of calculating its value, that one number was enough to prove to me how rich I'd become.

The unsettling part was that, although the house had eight rooms—three more than my parents had—I had less work to do. Seth had insisted I keep his house-keeper coming to clean every day. For years, since the death of his mother, Seth had employed Clara Gruen-wald to clean and cook for him; he would not hear of letting her go now. For her part, Frau Gruenwald, who lived with an invalid husband in a section of the city called Germantown and kept her own small household going on the wages she received from Seth, was deter-mined to continue to earn her keep in spite of the new mistress in the house. In her strongly accented English, she soon made it clear that I was not to lift a finger. I often felt like a spoilt princess, especially when Frau

Gruenwald would wrest a broom from my hand or push me away from the pot I was stirring.

The one chore the housekeeper couldn't keep me from doing was bed-making. In order to keep the hired woman from knowing that my husband and I slept in separate rooms, I made sure the beds were made and all telltale signs hidden before Frau Gruenwald arrived in the morning. The fact of separate bedrooms was a shame to me, and I kept it secret even from Mama and Annette.

Other than that, there was no reason not to be happy, I told myself. No demands were being made on me that I could not fulfill. Nothing was denied me that I asked for. Then why was there a little knot of . . . of *unease* lodged somewhere at the bottom of my chest? I could not call it discontent, for it wasn't as strong as that. Unease was the right word.

But I was not raised to sit about and dwell on something as insubstantial as unease. Especially since the feeling had no rational basis. I had to be up and doing. With so little housework to do, I busied myself with the one task I'd had little time for before—making clothes. The farm clothes I'd brought with me from home were too shabby for living in town. Dressmaking, therefore, was a useful occupation.

I made myself a new walking gown the very first week of my married life. It was of a soft green kenting, linen that my mother had taken from her trunk of treasures and given to me before the wedding. When it was finished, I put it on and promptly went out to show it off. I felt like a great lady when I walked down Main Street to Seth's shop, the new skirts swishing round my ankles. When I came in, it seemed to me that Seth's eyes lit up. I know I blushed with pleasure.

That night Seth came home with a package under his arm. It was a bolt of jaconet cotton in a rich, dark red, which he said was for another new gown. It was a lovely gift. I would have two new gowns at once! It was all too much!

It took almost a week to make the dark red dress, because I took special pains. The little ruffled collar at the neck was the prettiest I'd ever made. For once I had ample time to cut and trim little half-moons along the edge. I put shirring at the waistline, because Annette said it would emphasize the female shape above.

When it was finished, I was delighted with it. Because Seth had bought the fabric for me, the dress was precious. I had to show it off to someone. In the absence of anyone else, I ran downstairs to find Clara. "No, I must call her Frau Gruenwald," I reminded myself as I sped down the stairs. The housekeeper permitted Seth to call her Clara, but she'd made it clear from the outset that I, her new young mistress, must give her the respect of her full title.

I discovered Frau Gruenwald mixing dough for bread. "What do you think of my dress?" I asked eagerly, whirling around.

The housekeeper looked up, studied the dress from top to bottom and smiled one of her rare smiles. "*Sehr niedlich,*" she said in approval. "Very nice."

With my own opinion thus seconded, I pulled a shawl from its hook near the door and ran out to show myself off to my husband. I entered the shop with a dancing step, but stopped short when I discovered only Billy Shupp on the premises. "Where's Mr. Trahern?" I asked, disappointed.

"There's a meetin' at the church, to choose an elector," Billy said. "With Courtland White holdin' out for the Federalists, it's likely to take all afternoon."

"Oh," I sighed, deflated.

"Of course, it might not take as long as that. Y'never know," the boy said encouragingly. "Whyn't you wait a bit?"

With nothing better to do, I nodded agreement and sank down on the bench. Billy returned to his work. The room was silent for several minutes.

I looked over the paper, but since I'd already read most of it, I found myself watching the boy at his work. He was standing in front of an angled table, fitting little pieces of metal into a hollowed-out strip of wood. "What are you doing, Billy?" I asked curiously.

"Settin' type," the boy said. "I'm puttin' the letters into this composin' stick, see?"

I got up and watched over his shoulder. "You certainly are quick, Billy. How'd you learn to pick out the letters so fast?"

"Been doin' it for years," the boy said, blushing with pride. "Mr. Trahern says I've become the best he's seen."

"Well, good for you."

The boy shrugged. "It's gettin' to be a wearisome chore these days. I'd ruther be layin' out the pages."

"Laying out?

"Lockin' in the print into the frame. That's real interesting. You have to take the lines of type, see, an' place 'em proper in the galley, with—"

"What's a galley?"

"It's a tray, like this here. See, you put in the sticks of type till you've got a page, and then you add the blocks an' quoins and ornamental rows to fill in the spaces an' make a nice design. For that you need a little . . . well, Mr. Trahern calls it artistry."

"Does Mr. Trahern do that?"

"We both do it. But Mr. Trahern says that one day he's gonna hire another devil to set the type an' promote me. Then I'll get to do the galleys all the time, an' we'll have an extra hand with the press. It'll give him more time to do the writin'."

I stared at the boy for a moment, for my brain was suddenly alight with a radical idea. "Billy," I asked after a moment, "do you think I . . . ?" Then my courage deserted me, and my voice died away.

"What, ma'am? Do I think what?"

I took a deep breath to make myself brave. "That I could learn to set type?"

"Anyone can learn," Billy said carelessly. "But why would you want to?"

"To be useful. To be able to help here in the shop."

Billy gaped. "*You*, Miz Trahern?"

"Yes. Me."

"But . . . you're a lady."

"Yes, I suppose I am, now that I'm wed."

He looked at me as if I'd turned demented. "You was always a lady, ma'am. An' I ain't never heard of no lady settin' type."

"I'd wager you've never heard of a lady pushing a plow either, but I've helped Papa with the plowing many times."

Billy looked nonplussed. "I don't know if Mr. Trahern would want me to . . . to . . ."

"He wouldn't object. I'm sure he wouldn't. Let's start right now. What are these four big cases, and why are they tilted?"

"They're the fonts, ma'am. Metal letters, see? Mr. Trahern says they're the most valuable things in the shop. They come from Holland. These two cases hold the letters we call Roman, the up-and-down type. And those two are italics. The letters are slanted, like. The upper cases hold the capital letters and the lower cases are the small ones. And the tables're tilted like that so you can see the letters better."

I peered into the Roman lower case. "I don't see how you can tell which is which. They're all backwards."

"Reversed. Like in a mirror. That's so they'll read the right way when they're printed. You get used to readin' backwards after a while. If you're really serious about learnin' this, ma'am, you'll soon—"

"Oh, I'm serious all right. In fact, I'll start today. But first I'm going home to change this dress. I remember being dirtied with that ink before. I don't want to have to wash this new dress with lye soap."

18

*I*t took several weeks for me to be proficient at type-setting, but at last I was permitted to set a real arti-cle. The first piece I set all by myself was Seth's weekly editorial, to appear on page two. The headline read: Are The People's Wishes To Be Ignored? and then:

> As the date for the election of our next president draws near, the possibility of a huge injustice appears to be looming. Although all indications from our sixteen states show that the popular vote favors the election of Mr. Jefferson by a large majority, the electoral vote will be close—so close, in fact, that there exists a distinct possibility that the people's choice will be overridden in the electoral college, thus causing a—

I was setting the type from his written copy fairly well until this point, but here I needed help. I looked over my shoulder to where Seth sat writing at his desk. I hesitated to disturb him. Billy was working the press, so I didn't want to interrupt him either. *I'm still too new at this work*, I remember thinking worriedly.

I'd been spending a part of each day at the shop, taking

instruction from Billy. Seth had made no objection. Neither did he interfere. He let his two "apprentices" proceed on their own. I soon learned that the worst thing an apprentice could do was to drop a composing stick, causing the fonts to be spilled—"pied" Billy called it—in a mess on the floor. I dropped it more than once. When it happened, I would look across at Seth in alarm, but he would pretend not to notice. Billy would do the scolding, but his scolds were very mild. I was aware that Seth sometimes eavesdropped on our exchanges, a slight smile of amusement on his face, but he never interrupted or corrected. He evidently wanted us to manage on our own.

Seth glanced up at me at that moment and caught my look of confusion. "Something wrong?" he asked.

"Excuse me for being a bother, Seth," I murmured diffidently, "but I can't make out this word."

"You are never a bother," Seth assured me as he rose and came to look. "Perversion," he said and promptly turned back toward his desk.

I nodded and carefully set the next line:

—perversion of the popular will.

Here I paused again. "What does that mean, perversion of the popular will?" I asked, barely realizing I'd spoken aloud.

He was just about to sit down, but he paused to explain. "The legislatures in most of the states are Federalist. Despite the fact that their populations are strongly Republican, they've chosen to make all their electoral votes for Adams for president and Pinckney for vice president."

"But how can they do that?" I asked, incensed.

"They can, and they will. It's the legislators in each

state who choose the electors, not the people. And several states have the unit rule. Take New Jersey, for example. Despite the fact that the majority of their voters prefer Jefferson, all seven of their electoral votes will go for the Federalists." He frowned and ran his fingers through his hair, a gesture he often used when he felt helpless. "Seems a definite perversion of the democratic ideal to me."

"You really shouldn't read what you're settin', ma'am," Billy put in. "I tol' you it on'y slows you down. Just make yourself see letters and spaces. Try not to read the words."

"It's all right, Billy," Seth said. "I like her to read what I write."

"That ain't what you tol' me when *I* was settin' type," the boy grumbled.

Seth laughed. "Sorry, boy, but you're not my wife. In her position she gets certain privileges."

"Then may I have the privilege of asking another question?" I asked, my cheeks hot with a pleasurable embarrassment.

"As many questions as you like."

"You said a good newspaper publisher should be objective in what he writes. Doesn't this show a partiality toward Mr. Jefferson?"

"Yes, it does. But damn it, Rachel, I can't be impartial in this matter. The Federalists are setting themselves above the will of the people in this election, and they're using every trick they can devise to keep themselves in power. I find it dastardly. The Hamiltonians think they were born to govern, that only they are capable of running the country. They sometimes sound like the very sort of leaders we fought a revolution to be free of. It's no wonder Jefferson's won such popular support. He has confidence in the common sense of the common man. That's the sort of belief that gave us our liberty, and I'll be damned if I'll print a word in disagreement."

"Hear, hear!" Billy applauded. "You should be writin' that down."

"Yes, Seth, you should." I beamed at my husband proudly. "You are very convincing when you're aroused, you know."

Now it was Seth's turn to blush. "Balderdash," he said, taking his seat and lowering his head over his work. "I'm only saying what everyone knows."

I studied the back of his head, a feeling of warm propriety sweeping over me. This wise, modest, good man was my very own husband. It had been a good thing to wed him. The best thing I'd every done. My mother had been right about that.

It was not only his grasp of politics and the respect that everyone seemed to feel for him that impressed me; it was the essential kindness and honesty that defined his character and that influenced the way he lived his life. In large ways and small he was always kind and just and generous. I had not realized, in my foolish girlhood, how important those qualities were.

Just the night before, I'd experienced an instance of his generosity. My friend Annette had had her baby—a rosy, healthy little girl—and I'd knitted a sacque for her. It was of soft wool I myself had carded three times over before spinning so there would not be a stiff fiber left to scratch an infant's skin. Finally I was ready to trim the garment. I wanted to edge the hood with pink ribbon and sew little rosetted ties down the front instead of buttons. But the ribbon I saw at the linen-draper's was more costly than I'd expected . . . so costly, in fact, that I was a bit frightened to tell Seth the total.

"I've a shop-note from the draper's," I'd said in a timid rush when we sat across the table from each other at dinner. "It's for ribbon for Annette's baby's sacque. Twelve shillings a yard, and I needed three. I hope you won't be cross with me. I let him cut it before I asked the price, and then it was too late to change my mind."

Seth smiled at me over the candles in that gentle way of his and assured me I could buy whatever I wished at the draper's and at any other shop I fancied.

"Without asking you?" I'd gaped at him, amazed, for Mama had always had to seek permission from her husband before spending actual cash.

"Without asking," Seth assured me. "I'll let you know if I think you're becoming extravagant."

I'd gulped and dropped my eyes to my plate. My husband's kindnesses always touched me with emotions of both gratitude and guilt. Now, standing in his shop with the composing stick forgotten in my hand, those same feelings returned. *I don't deserve such kindness,* a voice inside me said. I was not a true wife to him. He demanded nothing of me, yet he gave so much. It was not right.

"Ahem."

The cough was from Billy, who was looking at me in reproach. A good worker, his look said, does not stand about daydreaming. I put my thoughts aside and returned to my typesetting.

That night, lying alone in my large bed, my thoughts returned to Seth. I wondered how and when I could tell him what I felt . . . that I wanted to be a good wife, in every way. I was ready for him to share my bed. The prospect no longer revolted or frightened me. To be truthful, I was eager for it. The only problem was shyness. I was too shy to tell him what I felt. And if I was too shy for the words, wouldn't I be too shy for the deed? Again, fearfulness was inhibiting my will to act.

I wished I could ask Annette what married love was like, but I didn't even have the courage for that. I'd tried once or twice, but I could never bring the matter to my tongue. If I asked so naive a question, Annette would guess that Seth was not sharing my bed. I didn't want anyone—not Annette, not my mother, not anyone—to know that. My continuing virginity filled me with shame.

I scolded myself for these feelings. Annette never seemed ashamed of anything. Annette's baby—a healthy, bouncing, eight-pounder—was born in October, less than seven months after her wedding. Since there was no question of its being premature, there had been some derisive gossip, but when Annette heard of it she only laughed. It did not seem to trouble her that everyone knew she'd indulged in lovemaking outside the sanctity of wedlock. After what had happened to my sister, I knew I could never have faced the gossip that circulated about Annette. But since she and Martin were now properly married, the baby's early birth was not a matter for serious concern, not even among the gossipers. The scandal-mongering did not trouble Annette. She didn't care what others thought of her. Oh, how I admired that sort of courage! But, alas, I did not possess it.

The next day, the baby's sacque finished, I wrapped it in the lovely, thin silver paper that the linen-draper had given me with the expensive ribbon and, dressed in my new red jaconet, took myself off to visit my friend. It was Martin himself who greeted me at the door. "She'll be so glad to have company," he said as he led me to the back of the little house where the bedroom was. "The midwife says she must stay abed another three weeks. New mothers must rest fully so that their strength will return. But that doesn't keep her from ruling the house-hold in her usual manner." And, smiling proudly, he threw open the bedroom door.

Annette was nursing the infant, beaming down at the suckling babe in deep contentment. She glanced up at me only briefly, though her smile widened. "Come in, *ma chere*, come in," she said, complacently continuing to nurse until the baby, sated, fell from the nipple in a deep sleep. Annette rested the child on her shoulder and grinned up at me. "Isn't she beautiful?" she asked.

"Indeed she is. And I see a bit of yellow hair," I mur-mured, bending over the baby to admire her more closely. "Like her daddy's."

"I call her Nicole," the proud mother said.

"A lovely name. As beautiful as she is."

Annette patted the side of the bed. "Now, Rachel, sit down here and tell me everything that's passed," she ordered, setting the sleeping babe on the pillow beside her.

"Nothing much to tell." I perched alongside the baby and let the infant curl her tiny fingers about one of my own. "You're the one with the news."

"You're already becoming acquainted with my news. Isn't she clever, holding you like that even in her sleep? But never mind the baby now. You must have a great deal to tell me." She cocked her head and studied me shrewdly. "Wedlock seems to agree with you. You are blooming. In a new gown, too. Very grand."

"Do you like it? Truly? Seth bought the goods. 'Tis not a color I'd have chosen."

"It's most becoming. Gives a flush to your cheeks. I hope you're as happy as you look."

My eyes fell. "Well, I . . ." I felt an almost overpower-ing urge to confide in my best friend the problem that was most pressing on my mind. But, as usual, my courage deserted me. The subject was too humiliating. Besides, if Annette should mention the separate beds to her husband, and the word spread, it would be most embarrassing to Seth. I could not chance it. "I am happy indeed," I said. But even as I uttered that lie, I felt a pang of pain. The closeness I'd always felt toward Annette in our girlhood was slipping away as we progressed to maturity.

Annette's brow knit in sudden suspicion. "Rachel Weller!" she said in sharp reprimand. "I mean, Rachel *Trahern*, don't tell me you're still pining away for your Peter Mason?"

"No, of course not!" I said quickly. Then I sighed. "Hardly ever," I added honestly.

Annette glared at me. "You're a fool."

I threw her a sheepish grin, relieved to be back on terms of intimacy. "I don't think of him often, truly I don't," I insisted. "And I *am* happy with Seth. In fact, marriage is spoiling me."

"Is it indeed?"

I nodded. "It's strange, Annette. I have nothing to *do*! Frau Gruenwald cooks and cleans for us, and I am like Curly-locks in the children's rhyme who sits on a cushion and sews a fine seam."

Annette laughed. "Enjoy it while you can. Soon enough everything will change, and there won't be hours enough in the day for all you'll have to do."

"Change? In what way?"

"In what way do you think, you goose? You'll be with child."

"Oh." I felt a hot blush rise from my neck to my cheeks. "Yes, of course. With child."

19

*M*y brother Simon had told me once that politics could affect my very life. I didn't believe
him then, but the election of 1800 was to prove to me
how true that was.

In those first weeks of my marriage I did not dream
how important that election would be to me. I did realize, however, that the more I learned about the subject,
the more I learned about my own nature—and Seth's.
And most of what I learned was discovered in his shop,
for it was there he thought about, wrote about, and
talked about the things that most concerned him. I
hadn't known, before I began to spend time in the shop
setting type, what a popular meeting place the print
shop was for the men in the town who cared about politics. Especially in the late fall and winter, after darkness
had forced an end to farm chores, and after their suppers
had been consumed, a number of men would gather
around the stove in the center of the shop to discuss the
current happenings. There were three, in particular,
who were almost always present: Abel Becker, of
course; Charles Lund, the young hothead who ran the
livery stable; and Courtland White, the quiet mother's-
boy who'd been to college. Billy Shupp called them "the

regulars." But other men dropped in also, especially when the news excited them. Papa was one of them. He used to come occasionally before the wedding, but now that Seth was "family," he made the trip in from the farm at least twice a week.

The first time I stayed at the shop for one of those meetings was when Seth told me Papa would probably come that evening. I wanted to send a message to Mama, so I waited for him. That's when I overheard for the first time how politics was argued among men.

It was an argument right enough—loud, boisterous, and vituperative. At the time of which I speak, late in October of 1800, matters were becoming tense, because the electoral college was due to meet on December 7th to choose the next president, and the voting was still not decisive. Most of the men in the circle around the stove (on this evening the regulars and Papa were joined by the two John Odells, father and son, and Martin Knudsen, Annette's husband) were Jeffersonians, and that night they were objecting violently to the fact that the electors to the electoral college were appointed by the state legislatures. "The people's votes don't count if the legislature can appoint any elector it wants," Charlie Lund declared. "It ain't democratic."

Abel Becker was the most outspoken voice for the Federalists. "It's as democratic as is useful," he answered promptly. "The people vote for the best men they can find to represent them in the legislature, and then it's up to *them* to make the decisions—decisions the ordinary citizen is too busy or too indifferent or too ignorant to make for himself."

"Spoken like a true Hamiltonian," Papa retorted. "Always thinking that the ordinary people are ignorant."

Seth was busily scratching away at his desk, writing

another editorial on the election. I always admired his ability to concentrate on his writing, even when others were talking loudly. And the voices were getting louder every moment. But this time, Seth looked up. "I wonder how the split between Hamilton and Adams will affect the Federalist cause," he remarked.

"Won't make a bit of difference," Abel declared firmly. "No Adams man hates a Hamilton man enough to switch over to Jefferson in the end."

Several voices rose to disagree, but Papa stilled them. "He's right," he said in disgust. "They'll stick to their own when push comes to shove."

John Odell Senior threw up his hands. "Don't seem right," he said with the authority of a prosperous mill-owner and distiller. He'd come out tonight because he was a devout Jeffersonian, and he loved to argue politics. On the other hand, his son, John Odell Junior, just sat there on the bench and gaped at me. It discomposed me at first, but when the argument heated up, I forgot him. The other men took no notice of me at all.

"What don't seem right?" Charlie Lund asked.

"This whole election don't seem right. I hear that in Massachusetts more people voted agin the Federalists than for 'em," Odell Senior explained. "But all their votes go to the Feds. Is that fair? How many votes do they have, Seth?"

"Massachusetts?" Seth looked round from his place at his desk. "Fourteen."

"Don't seem right. Why don't they split up the votes fair?"

"Some states have the damn unit rule," said Charlie. "That's the most unfair part of the system."

"We here in Delaware have the unit rule system," Abel reminded him.

"That don't make it right," Papa put in. That was just what I wanted to say, although I knew better than to contribute to the discussion. Women's opinions on politics were neither respected nor welcomed by most men.

"You don't like it because our three votes are going to the Federalists," Abel said, settling himself comfortably on the bench and lighting up his pipe. "I don't hear you complaining about the unit rule in Virginia, where all their nineteen votes are going to the Republicans."

"I've been keeping a score," said the usually quiet Courtland White, the only other Federalist among them, "and I figure that if Maryland splits, as is likely, and South Carolina goes for Jefferson, there's going to be a tie in the electoral college."

"That's a lot of ifs," Martin Knudsen laughed.

"My figures agree with Courtland's, I'm afraid," Seth said.

"What happens then?" Odell Senior asked. "If there *is* a tie."

"It goes to the House of Representatives," Abel chuckled, "where it's one state, one vote."

"And that makes you happy?" Papa demanded angrily.

"Yes, Joss, it does. Happy as a clam at high tide, as the Marylanders like to say. The House majority is still Federalist. That gives us a chance."

"Damnation," ranted Charlie Lund, "don't you sit there an' tell me that the House is goin' to vote Federalist when most o' the people plainly want Jefferson."

"They'll vote their convictions, which is why the voters sent them to Congress in the first place," Abel Becker said.

Seth shook his head in disapproval and stood up. "They're *representatives*, Abel," he argued. "Shouldn't they represent the voters' views?"

"In an ideal world, I suppose they would. But you know as well as I do, Seth, that the views of the rabble can change like the tide. What's an elected representative to do? He can't represent all the shades of opinion in his district all the time. He has to act as he thinks best."

Charlie Lund walked toward him. "Who're you callin' rabble?" he asked menacingly.

"Oh, sit down, Charlie," Martin said mildly. "He's only expressing his blasted aristocratic views."

"Yeah? Well, he ought watch his damn tongue." But Charlie obeyed Martin's suggestion and sat down.

The elder Odell stroked his chin. "Seems to me, Abel, that you're talkin' more like a Tory than your hero Hamilton. Since when did you start thinkin' it right for our representatives to take stands against the wishes of their constituencies? If they do that, what's the point of voting?"

"Maybe there isn't any point to it," Abel answered smoothly. "Most voters don't know what they're doing anyway."

"Is that so?" Charlie was on his feet again. "Are you sayin' we shouldn't have the right to vote?"

"Of course he isn't saying that," Papa said reasonably. "Can't you see he's baiting you?"

But Charlie was beyond being placated. He planted himself before the still-seated lawyer and leaned over him. "Listen, you tub of lard, is that what you and your Tory friends are fixin' to do—get a nobility back? Is that what you want, eh? You want us to get down on our hands and knees and ask His Majesty King George to forgive us and take us back so you won't have to worry about the rabble voting any more?"

"Watch your tongue, Charlie," young Odell warned

with a glance in my direction. "Can't you see there's a lady present?"

Charlie Lund looked at me and blushed. "Sorry, ma'am," he muttered.

"You don't have to be an Anglophile to worry about the wisdom of the ordinary voter," Courtland White said dryly. "If the voters have their way, we'll have a godless atheist as president, the French swarming over us, and our women in danger of pillage and rape. Begging your pardon, Mrs. Trahern, for the language."

This raised a enraged cry of objection from almost everyone. "Come now, Courtland," Seth said calmly, holding up a hand for order, "you don't believe any of that nonsense, do you? The war fever is over. The only ones who still speak of it are the War Whoopers, and everyone knows how insane they are. As for Jefferson's atheism, he's no more godless than you are."

"I'm only suggesting possibilities," Courtland said, backing down. "One reads those things in the press all the time."

"Then the press should be ashamed," Odell Senior said.

"The press has no shame," Seth admitted with a shrug as he returned to his desk.

"I'll tell you one thing," my father said with dire conviction. "If the House votes the Feds into the presidency, there'll be hell to pay. I hear that the frontiersmen in Kentucky will come marching in and storm Washington."

"Much good it'll do them," Abel snorted.

"We'll see how much good it'll do," shouted the still-angry Charlie, "And if they march, I'll be with 'em. After I've knocked *your* block off, Abel Becker!"

Abel put his pipe down on the bench and pulled

himself to his feet. "How many times do you have to be reminded of a lady's presence?" he asked coldly. "If you're so eager for fisticuffs, I suggest we step outside. I'd take real pleasure in landing my fist on your beer-distended nose."

"Let's see ye try!" shouted Charlie, doubling up his fists.

"No, no, please," said Martin, getting up. "Come on, Charlie boy. John Junior and I will take you home. Calm down and come along with us."

But it took several minutes for them to drag the shouting, wildly gesticulating Charlie Lund from the shop. An embarrassed silence followed. Abel shrugged, bid Seth goodnight and left. Courtland White and Odell Senior followed. Papa, before taking his leave, walked over to the font cases to bid me goodnight. "No need fer you to look so scared," he said to me as he kissed my cheek. "These arguments ain't personal. Charlie'll forget it by morning."

The last to leave was Billy. "'Twas as good a ruckus as I've ever heard in this place," he said with a cheerful grin. "Goodnight."

Seth sank down in his desk chair with a groan and dropped his head in his hands. The disagreement might have been entertaining to Billy, but to Seth it was a symptom of what was dividing the country, and it worried him.

I came up behind him and put a hand on his shoulder. "'Tis only foolish male arrogance," I said, trying to comfort him. "I wouldn't take it seriously."

"This little fight doesn't trouble me," he said, lifting his hand to mine. "What troubles me is the country's future."

"You don't believe my father's prediction, do you?

That the Kentuckians will storm Washington?"

"They might. Or, may God forbid, there could be a legislative impasse, where the Congress would have to choose a president themselves. Or the Hamiltonians could find some trickster method of snatching victory from the jaws of defeat." He shook his head glumly. "This could be the end of the country. After such a promising beginning, 'twould be a damned shame."

That was how Seth was. He took the country's troubles very much to heart. Learning that about him endeared him to me, as so many things I was discovering about him did. Learning about politics, I thought, was not nearly as interesting as learning about this man I had married.

But what I did not know was that politics—this troublesome election, in particular—was about to change my life.

20

The early days of February, 1801, were gray and damp. Not cold enough for snow, the rain nevertheless chilled one's bones. The weather matched my mood. I was feeling a gnawing depression, for it was six months since my wedding, yet my relationship with Seth remained unchanged. Unfailingly kind and even affectionate, he never crossed over the line that separated friend from lover. I began to wonder if perhaps he'd ceased to love me, and if he no longer even desired to consummate our marriage. That thought undermined my confidence in my womanly attractiveness, leaving me fearful yet again to take the initiative to bridge that one large gap between us. My mother was already asking why I was not with child. How much longer, I wondered, could I pretend that nothing was amiss?

The gloomy weather matched Seth's mood, too. He, however, blamed his mood on the political climate. "'Tis as nasty as the weather," he told me. "I'd hoped, when the popular vote for Jefferson was so overwhelming, that matters would turn out well, but now they're worse than ever."

"Why worse?" I asked.

"It's this tie in the electoral college," he said.

"But it's what you expected, isn't it? I remember your saying that—"

"No, it's not a tie between Jefferson and Adams, the two presidential contenders, but between Jefferson and his vice-presidential choice, Aaron Burr."

"I don't understand," I said. "No one voted for Burr for president."

"'Tis a flaw in the Constitution, failing to allow the electors to discriminate between the votes for president and vice president. It simply provided that each elector should vote for two men and that the candidate with the greatest number of votes should become the president and the next greatest the vice president. Since the growth of political parties was not anticipated by the men who wrote the constitution, they didn't envision that the two names on each ballot would be a fixed pair, one presidential and one vice-presidential nominee from each party."

It was all too much for me. "I still don't understand," I admitted, utterly confused.

Seth, always patient with me, explained the details as clearly as he could. "Look at the totals," he said, showing me a sheet on which he'd listed them. "The electoral votes total 73 for Jefferson, 73 for Burr, with 65 for Adams, and the same for Pinckney. This means, of course, that although Adams and Pinckney have been defeated, Jefferson has not really won. Since there's a tie between Jefferson and Burr, the matter must now be determined by the outgoing House, and they still have a small *Federalist* majority."

"But they can't possibly vote for Mr. Burr, can they," I asked, "when everyone knows the voters intended Mr. Jefferson to win?"

"Who knows what they'll do? With each state having

but one vote, I'm afraid the Federalists will try to use their majority to accomplish their aims with any sort of legal trick they can devise. The House can, in the end, appoint anyone. Or no one. In another month, on March 15th, we're supposed to inaugurate a new president. I only wish I could anticipate who he might be."

By mid-February he began to learn the answer. The Congress, still Federalist in its majority, felt that anyone would be better than Jefferson, and had decided to vote for *Burr!* As Seth reported in his newspaper,

On February 11, in the new capitol on the Potomac river called Washington, the representatives had held their first individual vote. The total, astoundingly, was Jefferson 51, Burr 55. This, however, is not enough to make Aaron Burr the next president, since the rule is one vote per state. Thus the tally came to eight states for Jefferson, six for Burr. (The Maryland and Vermont representatives were split, so they had to abstain.) But to win, a candidate needs nine states. Several other votes were taken, but no one budged. At this writing, the tie persists.

As the news slowly dribbled in to New Castle, Seth seethed. Ten votes were taken . . . fifteen . . . then thirty . . . with not one change. Every night, a crowd of men huddled round the stove of the shop waiting for news. Because I knew how important this was to Seth, I was there, too.

"Damn Burr," Seth muttered when he learned that the thirtieth ballot had changed nothing. "Why doesn't he announce that he won't accept the presidency when everyone knows he was elected for the second position?"

"Because he's shrewd," Abel Becker responded. "If he keeps his mouth shut and stays incommunicado in New York, he might find himself president."

"I suppose you think that's right!" Seth snapped, jumping up and rounding on the lawyer with unaccustomed bitterness. "Do you really think such an outcome would be good for the country?"

Abel's eyes fell. "No, I don't."

Seth, taken aback, blinked. "You don't?"

The lawyer puffed thoughtfully at his pipe. "I think you're right about this, Seth. The people have spoken. Their will should not be ignored."

Seth dropped down in his seat, amazed. "Abel Becker, have I heard aright? Are you saying you've changed your position?"

"Guess so."

The answer was hailed with cheers from the others. The arch-Federalist in their midst had surrendered his position. "I'll be flimflammed!" Papa exclaimed. "I never thought to live to see this day."

"If ol' Abel can change," Martin remarked after the hubbub died down, "maybe that means some of the congressmen will, too."

"It certainly gives me some hope," Seth said with a wry smile, "and I haven't felt hopeful in days."

Billy Shupp, who'd been busily sweeping up the day's debris, paused in his labors. "If you could change Mr. Becker's mind, Mr. Trahern, p'raps you should go to the capitol an' try to change one o' the congressmen."

"Huh!" Seth snorted. "Very likely."

But Abel stared at the boy intently. "Out of the mouths of babes," he muttered. Then he rose and looked at Seth. "I think that's a damned good idea. You *ought* to go."

Seth gaped at him. "Who, me? Go to Washington and try to talk a delegation of Federalists into changing their votes? Don't be insane."

"I've never been saner. You don't have to convince a delegation, my boy. Only one man. Have you forgotten that our Delaware is the only state that has but one congressman?"

"Bayard!" Seth exclaimed, arrested.

"Exactly."

"But he's a staunch Federalist. Why should he listen to me?"

"Because you're good at convincing people," Papa offered eagerly.

"He's right, Seth," Abel said.

"But you, Abel, are better," Seth countered. "You're an advocate, after all, trained in argumentation. And you're of Bayard's party."

"Very well, then, I'll go with you. What do you say?"

Seth hesitated. "I hadn't ever considered . . . I don't think I'm—"

The other men crowded round him, urging him on. "Do it, Seth. Go! You don't want the government goin' to the dogs, do you?"

He only shook his head. "I'll think it over," he said.

"There isn't time," the lawyer urged. "I heard that the House members stayed up all night the other night, voting over and over again. Burr may be the president before we get there."

That was all I had to hear. I stepped forward out of the shadows and beckoned my husband aside. "I think you should go, Seth," I whispered. "If matters go awry in this election, you will never forgive yourself for not having tried."

He gaped at me for a moment, then took my hands

in his. "Are you sure, Rachel? I don't like leaving you alone. I'd be gone two or three days."

"That's not so long. If I'm lonely, I'll go to stay with Mama and Papa." I smiled up at him proudly. "Do it, Seth! Go to Washington and make Mr. Bayard do the right thing."

But it was to be more than three days. The two men left on Thursday, the thirteenth. On Saturday a message was delivered to me saying that they hoped to return early the following week but that they could not be certain. There was nothing else in the message to indicate what was happening. Nor was there a private word for me.

The days passed, but they seemed endless. There was no one to talk to but Frau Gruenwald, who was by nature a woman of few words—and many of those were not English. I chose to stay away from the shop, because I did not think it fitting to be there when Seth was not. Nor did I go home to Mama, for I wanted to avoid answering questions about why I was not with child. Besides, I wished to be on hand to greet Seth when he returned.

Sunday passed. Monday crept by. Tuesday was the most interminable day I'd ever spent. By evening I gave up my vigil at the front-room window and decided to go to bed early. I lit a branch of candles and placed them near the door so that Seth might have some light in the event that he returned during the night, and, lonely and despondent, I went upstairs.

I had just buttoned my nightshift when I heard someone at the door. My heart leaped up into my chest. "Seth?" I called, running barefoot to the top of the stairs.

"I'm home," he shouted.

I ran down to the staircase's turning and gazed down

at him. He was still in his cloak and hat, and, with the candlelight behind him, I could not read his face. "What happened?" I asked, all agog.

He took from his pocket a creased sheet of paper and cleared his throat. "Well, madam, let me read to you what the whole town will be reading on page one of the *Newcastle Register* tomorrow, as soon as we can get it into print."

"Seth!" I stamped my bare foot in impatience "Just *tell* me!"

"Hush, woman, let me read!" And he proceeded to do so.

Mr. James A. Bayard, the Congressional representative of Delaware, met with two of his constituents from New Castle on Friday the fourteenth of February. After talking with them for more than an hour, Mr. Bayard returned to the House and proposed that they adjourn until Monday. Meetings with all the aforesaid parties, in addition to the delegations from Maryland and Vermont, were held throughout the weekend. Rumors abounded, which this paper will not deny, that Mr. Jefferson himself attended one of these meetings. At Monday morning's vote—the thirty-sixth vote on the matter—Mr. Bayard changed his vote to Jefferson, taking the hitherto-tied Maryland and Vermont with him. Mr. Jefferson is now our duly-elected President, and the country can breathe again.

I squealed in delight. "Seth! You *did* it!" I raced down the steps and, before reaching the bottom, leapt into his arms. "You're a hero!"

My action caused his hat to fall to the floor. The

paper he'd been holding drifted from his grasp. But neither of us paid any heed. He tightened his hold on me and lifted me up onto his chest. "You look so beautiful," he whispered. "I missed you so."

"Oh, my dear," I sighed, nuzzling his neck, "not as much as I missed you."

I suppose being in his arms that way, it was natural for us to kiss. It took just the one kiss to open the floodgates of the passion we'd withheld so long. We couldn't seem to stop. We kept on kissing, hungrily, madly, for a long, long time. I could feel his heart beating through all his clothes. Mine was racing so wildly I knew he could feel it through my thin nightclothes. *Goodness,* I remember thinking in a brief spasm of shame, *I'm only in my shift.* But the feeling was immediately drowned in the overwhelming excitement of this uninhibited embrace. Shame had no place here, I realized in surprised delight. I could have been naked, and it would still have been right.

Without setting me down or even breaking the rhythm of our kissing, he started up the stairs. It was I who lifted my lips from his. I had to ask. "Does this mean you think I'm . . . ready?"

He grinned at me, his eyes alight. "And about time," he said as he carried me over the threshold of the bedroom and kicked the door closed.

21

*F*or me it was the loveliest of springs. Never had the budding trees displayed a fresher rebirth nor the sky a more beneficent glow. The very air carried a fragrance so heady I felt drunk just breathing. I was truly happy. Sometimes I found myself laughing at nothing . . . at the mere joy of being alive.

I felt as if I'd expanded somehow . . . a butterfly unfolded from the chrysalis of girlhood. It was for me a completely new way of living. Our nights were full of lovemaking, as if we were trying to make up for the six months of abstinence. In the mornings my body seemed to retain the sensations of the night; it recreated the feel of him between my legs. I felt no shame. This, I believed, was how life should be. Sometimes, while dressing, I looked at myself in the mirror and touched my breasts the way he did, bringing on a desire for him that clenched my muscles and stifled my breath. I could hardly wait for the night. If I then went to the shop to set type and caught him looking at me, I would blush. Hotly. Not from guilt, but only because I suspected, from the tiny little gleam that flared up in his eyes, that he could read my thoughts. The tiny little half-smile on his face at those moments brought a glow to my heart.

For the space of a breath, before we quickly looked away from each other, joy, like an arc of lightning, sparked between us.

Then one morning I felt ill. I knew what that sort of discomfort meant. It was too soon to be certain, but I would not be surprised to learn that I was with child.

The morning sickness did not return the next day or the next. A week went by before I felt it again. By this time I was sure. I decided that I would not tell anyone just yet—it was a wonderful secret to savor for a while. But that morning I luxuriated in bed for two extra hours, propped up on the pillows, indulging myself in daydreams about the little creature growing inside me.

When Frau Gruenwald came in to make the bed (for she was now permitted to do so), she took one look, gaped, grinned, and cried, "*Ach!*"

I tried not to smile back at her. "What, Frau Gruewald, do you mean by that *ach*?" I asked in mock innocence.

"*Nicht*. Nuttink," the woman said, but she chortled and clapped her hands together happily. "Stay dere long as you want. I bring you breakfast in bed today."

I couldn't help myself. I grinned at her. "Oh, Frau Gruenwald," I said in glowing admission of my secret, "I'm so happy!"

"Someone else will be happy, too," she laughed. As she backed out the door, a benign smile lighting her face, she added, "Is time, missus, you call me Clara."

I giggled contentedly and drifted off to sleep. A little while later, I was brought awake by a firm shake. I discovered Frau Gruenwald—Clara—standing over me with an expression on her face completely different from what it had been a few moments before. "A man downstairs asks for you," she said, frowning darkly.

"A man? Who?"

The housekeeper shrugged. "I tell him you come?"

"Yes, please. I'll be right down."

It must be Simon, I thought as I dressed. If it were my father, Frau Gruenwald—no, Clara—would have said. But I had no idea why Clara had looked so disapproving.

I hurried down the stairs. A man was standing in the front room, staring out the window. It was not Simon. The man was taller and slimmer than Simon, and his hair hung down to his shoulders like a frontiersman. "Yes?" I asked, a disquieting premonition making me uneasy.

He turned around. One glimpse was enough to cause my chest to constrict. It was Peter Mason.

My knees gave way and I staggered. He had to catch me in his arms to keep me from falling. "Peter!" I gasped.

"So," he said coldly as he set me back in balance, "you *do* remember me."

"Oh, God! It *is* you!" Unable to catch my breath, I stepped back from him and supported myself by leaning on the doorframe.

"Yes, it's me. I said I'd come back, and I did. You said you'd wait, and you didn't."

I stared at him, my head aswim. He was alive and well! He'd survived.

When the shock faded, I told myself I was glad for him. But I didn't want him here in this house. Not here where I'd been so happy, where I'd—it filled me with sudden shame to admit it to myself—where I'd forgotten him. "It's . . . it's been more than a year," I mumbled.

"Yes, a year of hell for me. But not for you, I see."

I had no defense, nothing to say. All I could do was

stare at him. I saw a man much changed. His face was
lean and weathered, with lines around the mouth that
had not been there before. Nevertheless he looked so
young! I hadn't remembered how young he was. He
was less than a year older than I, which meant he was
not yet twenty.

He was peering at me, too. I could see his frozen
expression softening. I took a step toward him. "Peter,
I'm very glad you're safe. But I—"

He shook his head to stop me. Then, letting his eyes
roam over me, he smiled that half-mocking smile that
had endeared him to me from the first. "You're even
prettier than you were before," he said. "I didn't think
that could be possible."

Now I knew it was time to stop him. I put up a hand
to ward him off. "You mustn't say such things. If you
found me here, you must know that I am wed."

"Yes, I know." He came up to me and grasped my
shoulders. "Damn it, Rachel, how could you do it? You
and I were *promised*!"

Tears sprang to my eyes. "I heard . . . I believed you
would never come back."

"How could you believe that? You knew how much I
loved you. Didn't I swear I'd come back and we'd be
married?"

"Yes, b-but—"

There was a sound in the doorway. I wrenched
myself free and looked over my shoulder. Frau Gruenwald stood in the doorway, glowering more darkly than
before. "You need me, missus?" she asked pointedly.

"No, she don't need you," Peter snapped.

But the woman would not take his word. "Missus?"
she asked again.

"It's all right, Frau—Clara," I said. "Mr. Mason is an

old friend. You can go." That was my first mistake.

The housekeeper glared at me before turning away with obvious reluctance. Peter went to the door and closed it.

"Peter, don't," I said in quick disapproval.

He leaned against the closed door and crossed his arms over his chest. "Damn it, Rachel, I know they forced you into this marriage. We have to talk about this. Without some old biddy listening in."

"They didn't force me, Peter. It was my own—"

He bridged the space between us in two steps and took my hands in his. "You don't need to lie to *me*, Rachel. This is Peter you're talking to. Do you think I forgot the last night we had together? You said that if they forced you to marry Mr. Trahern you'd die! Isn't that what you said?"

"I suppose I—"

"You *suppose*? Damn it, woman, those were your very words!"

"Very well, I said it. But I'm not the same as I was. I've changed."

"No, you haven't. You couldn't! *Look* at me, Rachel. Take a good look. I'm the fellow you wanted to run off with. It was *me* who said we couldn't. You didn't stop loving me! Admit it!"

His pain was apparent in his eyes. My heart ached for him. "Oh, my dear," I said gently, "don't you see? It doesn't matter whether I stopped loving you or not. It's too late for us."

"Oh, yes, it matters. It's *all* that matters." He gripped my arms so tightly I feared there would be marks. "Tell me when you stopped? After a month? Three months? Six? When?"

"How can I say—?"

"You can't say! Because you never stopped. And I can prove it!"

He pulled me to him and kissed me ruthlessly. I struggled against him for a while, pushing at his shoulders with both my hands, but it was useless. The muscles of his arms were like iron. I made a sound in my throat to indicate to him that I wanted him to let me go. It was, I thought, a pleading, trapped-animal sound. But what he heard was the sound of stifled passion. I know, because it sent a tremor right through him. When I felt it, I was touched by the depth of feeling it revealed. *Poor Peter*, I thought, and I relaxed my struggle. That was my next mistake.

Encouraged, Peter lifted his mouth from mine and placed his lips on my throat at a spot where he remembered I'd been particularly sensitive in the past. I felt my flesh react with a little pulse, and he knew his memory had not failed him. "You dearest, sweetest of girls," he murmured into my neck, "you can't know what holding you feels like to me. It's what I dreamed of through every rotten hour on shipboard."

I felt trapped. "Please, Peter, stop," I begged. "I'm sorry if you've suffered, you know I am, but we—"

"*Suffered*?" Peter stiffened, dropped his hold and stepped away. His face, his stance, his entire aspect had changed. He was beside himself with anger. "Damn it, woman, you say the word easy enough. But it's only a word to you, ain't it? You have no idea of what's behind it."

I was shocked by the rage in his face. "I didn't mean to belittle—"

"Of course you're belittling it. If I tell you impressment was hell, how can you believe me? How can you know? No one who wasn't there can possibly know! On a British ship you're a slavey. It's work, work, bone-breaking, boring work every minute of the day except for a few hours in the hammock. If you're too slow for 'em, they flay you with a knotted rope. And if you're caught dawdling, it's twenty lashes of the cat in front of the whole crew. So you don't even dare to cry out, even though the lash is cutting stripes across your back till the blood runs."

I wilted, nauseated by the scene he described. "Oh, Peter, dear boy, no! They didn't—!"

"Didn't they though?" Furiously, he ripped off his coat and threw it over on the settee. He followed this with his waistcoat. When I realized what he was doing, I tried to stop him by catching hold of his arm, but he flung me away. His neckcloth followed the rest onto the settee. Then he undid his shirt, almost ripping off the buttons in his haste, and turned to show me his bared back.

The sight made my stomach heave. His broad, muscular, once-beautiful back was not only marred by a shocking number of lumps and divots, but it was horribly disfigured by long, crooked scars and purple-white welts crisscrossing the whole of it from shoulder to waist. It was a sight that could not fail to move even a dispassionate observer, and I was far from dispassionate. Tears choked my throat and welled up in my eyes again. Shaken to my core, I stumbled over to him and let both my trembling hands brush softly over the dreadfully blemished flesh in some sort of vain attempt to soothe it. My third mistake.

At my touch, he swung around to me. The sight of my tears melted his anger. "You *do* love me," he whispered, wiping the wetness away with his fingers.

I couldn't answer. The sight of his back had undone

me. It would be cruel, I told myself, to tell him at this particular moment that he'd been superseded.

To him, my silence must have meant submission. He pulled me into his arms and kissed me again. Then, in one quick movement, before I could protest, he lifted me up, tossed my arms over his shoulders, and carried me to the settee. He threw me down right on top of his clothes. With his mouth on mine and his hold rigidly tight, I could neither speak nor move until he had me beneath him. As soon as he lifted his mouth from mine, I cried out, "Peter, let me up!"

But he did not believe I was sincere. I'd stroked his back, after all. The act was louder than my words. Ignoring those words, he looked down at me in a kind of amazement. "Do you know I've imagined us like this every waking hour of the whole hellish year? I don't know how I'd have stood it without the memory of you."

"Peter, please," I tried again, "you must let me up. I'm sorry if—"

"No, you have to know what you did for me." He lifted his hand and smoothed my hair, his eyes warm with tenderness. "In the worst times, when I was tied hand and foot to the grating, with the cat cutting bloody stripes across my back and the whole damn company lined up and watching for me to crack and scream for mercy, I'd close my eyes and conjure you up. In my mind's eye I'd see you looking just like you are now. And I'd try to imagine the feel of you . . . my mouth on your throat . . . your sweet breast under my hand, and the inside of your thighs . . ."

His lips and hands were obeying his words. And I couldn't stop him. All I could reach with my hands was his bare back, but I could not beat at him or scratch him there, not over his already mutilated flesh.

". . . and I could almost feel the softness of you . . ."

I squirmed beneath him to try to free myself, but that only inflamed him more. He tore the dress from my shoulder, and I felt his lips move slowly to my nipple. Then—and I cannot explain it to this day—I felt a spasm in my groin and my resistance died.

". . . and my desire for you grew so strong it took my mind from the pain," he was whispering.

His breath was coming in pants, and his fingers and mouth grew more urgent. To my everlasting shame, I felt myself slipping into a strange, dizzying miasma of confusion. It did not seem like passion, but I didn't know what it was. *Dear God*, I wondered, *do I still desire him?* His hand was moving up, up my thigh, his fingers reaching for the place he must not go. I knew I must not let him. In desperation, I took hold of his ears and pulled his head up. "Peter, *no!*" I pleaded urgently.

His face was flushed and his eyes unfocused. "Yes, you must," he said thickly. "I've waited . . . dreamed it . . . so long!"

"I *can't*—!"

He kissed me into silence. I was gasping for breath, and he responded by pushing his hips between my legs. The movement brought something inside me wide awake. I was not feeling passion, I was *not!* I knew at last that I did not want this man inside me, where Seth had been, and where his baby now was growing. What I was feeling was sheer, naked terror!

In a kind of hysteria, with a strength that came from deep within me, I shoved against him with all my strength. The movement managed to heave his body from mine. In relief, I brought myself upright. "Peter, we can *not* do th—"

"Rachel?" came a voice from the hallway. And before

either of us could move from the settee, hurried steps sounded outside the door. "Clara came running to the shop and said you—"

The door was flung open. Seth stood in the open doorway, his eyebrows raised in concern. For a moment nobody breathed. Seth slowly took in the scene . . . Oh, God, how often I've envisioned it from his point of view: his wife, red-faced and horrified, her lips parted, her gown torn from her breast; and Peter Mason, the man of his wife's dreams back from the dead, sprawled bare-chested over the settee, looking exactly like what he was, a man caught in the act.

I saw my husband's face turn white. Not till the moment of my death will I forget the look in Seth's eyes. I have never seen a man being fatally stabbed, but his expression seemed to me to be the look of someone who has just been knifed in the chest and instantly realizes he is taking his last breath. I remember staring at those eyes and thinking, *Oh, dear God, I have killed my husband.*

I think I choked out Seth's name. I know I lifted my arms and took a step toward him, in the desperate belief that I could protect him, staunch the wound somehow, hold him back from death. But he stepped back, away from me, as if my touch would infect him with some dire disease. A look of revulsion came into his eyes and mixed with the pain. It struck me dumb.

Before I could recover my voice, Seth turned and left. I opened my mouth to cry out his name, but my throat had clenched and no sound came. I wanted to run after him. I had to stop him. I knew the only way to hold on to what I'd had with him was to keep him there until I could make him understand. But I couldn't seem to make my legs move. Then came the sound of the outer door closing behind him. It was like a gunshot. I shuddered from the impact of it.

And then I knew—not in my mind where reason lived, but in my blood and bones, the residence of a woman's instincts, those alert informers always attuned to the advent of catastrophe—that my brief days of happiness were over.

22

I felt myself rising from a black void. I wanted to reach the light, but I felt a deep terror of it, too. Something in that light was going to hurt me. Slowly, fearfully, I opened my eyes. The first thing I saw was my mother's face. "Mama?" I asked thickly.

"Hush, dear, hush." Mama was holding a bottle of sal volatile under my nose.

I was confused. "Where—? What happened?"

"You fainted."

"Fainted? I've never—" Slowly, vaguely, some snippets of memory began to edge into my mind. *Peter. Peter came back.* Alarmed, and not yet knowing why, my eyes quickly took in my surroundings. I was in the bedroom, Seth's and mine. But only my mother was there with me.

Then the memory came at me in a rush. All of it, up to the moment when the sound of the door closing behind Seth had struck me with the impact of a bullet. I sat up and looked wildly about me, hoping it had been a dream, hoping I would see Seth here in the room. But he was not there. There were only shadows. Good heavens, it was night! How long had I been lying here?

I fell back against the pillows and let the cold finality of Seth's departure wash over me. Oh, God, it had really happened! It was not a dream. I'd killed Seth's happiness . . . and my own. And I'd lain for God knows how many hours in a dark stupor, doing nothing to salvage the wreckage I had wreaked.

Now it all began to come back to me. Seth had run out, and after an interminable moment, Peter had come up behind me and put a hand on my shoulder. "Don't look like that, sweetheart," he'd said softly. "It's for the best."

I remembered turning and gaping at him. "The b-best?" I croaked.

"Of course. Now he knows. We're saved hours of explanation and useless agitation. You can begin the standaway right now."

A standaway? Separation? The mere sound of those words set me trembling. Was that the inevitable conclusion to this nightmare?

I remembered peering dazedly at Peter's face. It had suddenly seemed the face of a stranger. Unquestionably handsome, and more boyish than I remembered, but unfamiliar and—what a moment in which to realize it!—callow. Had I really loved that face?

Peter had smiled down at me, a smile of relief, of self-satisfaction, of triumph, even. "Come, get your things together. We should leave this place."

"Leave?" I was stupidly echoing his words because my mind was numb. I hadn't thought of leaving, but of course a standaway meant that I'd have to leave. *Standaway . . . separation . . . leaving . . .* The words fuddled my brain; it would not accept the idea of separation. Peter's face blurred in my sight, and the walls of the room began to spin. The air around me grew dark, the spinning became dizzying, and I felt my knees give way. That was all I knew . . . until now.

Trying to still a growing hysteria in my breast, I

looked up at Mama. "Where is . . . Seth?" I asked, my voice high-pitched and desperate.

Mama only shook her head. She looked white-faced, and her mouth was tight, as if holding her pain in strict control. I knew that look. I'd seen it in court.

In that moment I learned what true misery was. "Mama," I begged, the tears beginning to fall, "you mustn't think I . . . I couldn't— I wouldn't—!"

"Hush, my love, not now," Mama murmured. She took me, trembling and weeping, into her arms and rocked me like a baby while I sobbed.

It was a long time before my sobs ceased. Then, exhausted, pale, and blurry-eyed from weeping, I looked up at my mother and took a hiccuping breath. "Mama, you must believe me!" I whispered brokenly through swollen lips. "You must believe I did not have criminal conversation with Peter. Not today. Not ever."

Mama stroked my hair gently. "Hush, child, I believe you. I know what your feelings are for Seth. I know."

"But . . . will Seth b-believe me?" I asked.

Mama shook her head. "How can I say?" she murmured sadly. "Kind and good-hearted as he is, he is but a man."

23

M ama had sent Papa to talk to Seth. He came back pale and tight-lipped, with but a meager message: that I could remain in the house until I'd made other arrangements. In the meantime Seth would sleep on a mat in the shop.

"Won't he speak to me?" I asked in despair.

Papa, frowning in a way I'd never seen before, shook his head. To this day, Papa has never spoken of the events of that day. He did not believe me as Mama did. And I sense that, deep within, he has not forgiven me. You should not rely on him to testify on my behalf. I think he would refuse you if you asked. I don't blame him. One such trial is more than enough for a father to endure in a lifetime.

Since I realized Seth would not be convinced to come home while I was there, and I could not in conscience keep him from his own home, banished to a mat in his shop, I went away with my mother. It was probably another mistake in judgment. If I had stayed we may have— No, I should not have written that. There is no point in dwelling on ifs and might-have-beens.

As it was, I went home to my parents. I waited in a

tense agony for some word—any word!—from my husband, but none came.

After enduring two days of silence, I knew I had to speak to him. Somehow, some way, I had to save my marriage. I waited till late in the evening, when I knew Seth would have closed the shop, and I went to his house. Clara answered the door. "Ah, missus!" she cried, her face expressing the most delighted relief. "Come in, come!"

But Seth heard her. "Close the door, Clara," he ordered from somewhere within.

She turned toward the sound. "But it's the miss—"

"I said, *shut the door!*" His voice held such implacable, icy authority that she had no recourse but to obey. Her face sagged, and with tears starting from her eyes, she slowly closed the door on me.

I went back home, devastated. I could not sleep. In the early morning, after hours of useless tears, I went down to the dining room, took down the inkwell and pen and paper from a shelf, and tried to write him a letter. But everything I wrote sounded unconvincing. I did not know how to explain my actions. I went up to bed again, utterly spent.

It was dawn when I fell into a stuporous sleep. Either that brief sleep or sheer desperation brought me an inspiration. Written words, I thought, always seem more convincing when they're printed. I decided I would print a letter to Seth on his press.

The next evening I followed Billy when he left work and prevailed upon him to give me his key to the shop. Late that night I stole in, and by the light of a candle I set type. I used only letters from the upper case for my message:

DEAR SETH:

    I AM NOT AS GIFTED AT WRITING AS YOU
ARE, SO I DON'T KNOW WHAT WORDS WILL
MAKE YOU BELIEVE ME, BUT I AM WRITING THE
TRUTH. I WAS FOOLISH TO SEE PETER
WITHOUT A CHAPERON, BUT THERE WAS NO
CRIMINAL CONVERSATION BETWEEN US. I
LOVE ONLY YOU. PLEASE FORGIVE ME AND
TAKE ME BACK. YOUR WIFE.

I put the printed page in an envelope, sealed it, wrote
his name on it with his pen, and left it on his desk. Then
I locked up the shop and went home to bed.

I waited on tenterhooks all the next day for a
response. At nightfall I heard a knock at the door.
Before Mama could even rise from her chair, I dashed to
answer it. It was Billy Shupp.

"I've come for my key," he said curtly. "I got a right
good tongue-lashing for what I done."

"I'm sorry." I took the key from my apron pocket and
handed it to him. "Is there any . . . message?" I asked
breathlessly.

"Message?"

"An answer to my letter. The letter I left on his desk."

The boy shrugged. "I seen him reading something
from an envelope. A printed thing, was it?"

My heart was pounding. "Yes. Didn't he write anything—or say anything—when he read it."

"No." Then he seemed to hesitate.

"What is it?" I prodded. "Was there . . . something
else?"

Billy shrugged. "He crumpled it and—"

"*Crumpled* it?"

"—an' he threw it in the stove."

My heart sank. I couldn't utter another word. After a moment, Billy turned and scurried off.

I was so crushed that the next few days were hellish to me. When I could no longer endure Seth's continuing silence, I decided to try one last time to reach him. I waited until Mama and Papa went to sleep, and then I slipped out again. I ran all the way to town, hoping Seth was still at work. When I saw that the print shop window still dimly glowed with light, I breathed a sigh of relief. He was there!

But when I peeped in through the window I saw that John Odell and Charlie Lund were there, too. Seth sat at his desk, doggedly writing. He was not taking part in whatever the discussion was between Lund and Odell. There was nothing for me to do but wait.

It seemed like hours, but it was probably not more than a quarter-hour before the two visitors came out and went their separate ways. I came out of the shadows and made my way to the door, but I was still a few steps away from it when Seth emerged. He shut it tight, clamped his tall hat on his head, and started off. I followed silently, several steps behind. Finally I worked up the courage to speak. "Seth," I ventured.

He spun around. For a moment he just stared at me. Then he asked, "What is it? Is anything wrong?" His voice was tentative, careful, reserved.

"Everything is wrong," I said, catching up with him. "Please, Seth, you must let me speak to you. You cannot wish for matters to go on this way."

He sighed as if in defeat. "No, I suppose I can't. But there is nothing you need to say to me. I told your father I would agree to a divorce."

The very word smote my heart. "I don't want a divorce," I said at once.

"Of course you do. You have your Peter back. Marriage with him was what you always wanted. You warned me of that quite clearly, right at the start."

"But that was before—"

"From my brief observation of the scene in my parlor, ma'am," he cut in coldly, "it seems clear that the feeling still survives."

His tone, and the inference behind it, cut me deeply. "You assume too much from that brief observation," I snapped back.

His mouth twisted into a scornful sneer. "I should hope that your action was the result of real feeling. Otherwise one would have to conclude that your behavior was nothing better than that of a wanton."

I gasped. It was a slap I had not expected of him. I could feel the blood drain from my cheeks.

He must have seen it, for he immediately retracted. "Sorry, I did not mean—" Then he regretted the retraction, for his expression hardened. "Damn it, Rachel," he said, "what did you expect? That I would pat your head and wish you well? That's asking too much of me. 'Tis enough I'm giving you back your freedom. You'll get no more from me. Not words, not friendship, not even kindness. Nothing more, do you hear?" And he walked firmly away.

I ran after him. "Please, Seth, you must believe me. My so-called wanton behavior was not what it seemed."

He laughed a sneering laugh but did not slacken his stride. "Oh, wasn't it?"

"No, it wasn't," I insisted, breathlessly trying to keep up with him.

Suddenly he whirled around and grasped me by the shoulders, his eyes burning with fury. "Listen to me, woman," he said between clenched teeth, "and listen well, for I shall not speak of this again. You have made me a cuckold, but you shall not make me a fool. I saw your beloved with his naked chest, and I saw you with that flush on your cheeks. Can you possibly believe I would not recognize that flush? Time, perhaps, may one day succeed in wiping from my memory the sight of you in the flush of passion, but nothing you say now—or ever—will succeed in doing it. So save your breath."

He had never spoken to me that way before. I felt as if he had taken a strap and beaten me with it. But it was not only his words that left me bruised. I was being pelted by my own guilt. He was right when he'd said he'd seen the flush of passion on my face. Peter *had* stirred up passion in me. It may not have gone as far as Seth supposed, but it had certainly gone far enough to make me see myself as unfaithful. How could my body have betrayed me so? Was I, as Seth had accused, a wanton? I held up my hands as if to ward off any more blows. "Please," I pleaded in helpless confusion, "please . . ."

I suppose I looked so pathetic that his anger abated. He shook his head in self-reproach. "I never intended to speak to you so, Rachel, but you insisted on this exchange. I can't pretend that I don't feel wronged. But in spite of all I said, I don't entirely blame you. You told me quite honestly that I was a second-choice husband. I married you knowing full well that your heart was not mine. It is my own fault for allowing myself to believe I could win it for myself."

"But you did win it," I cried. "You did!"

The angry look came back in his eyes. "Don't!" he snapped. "I cannot bear to hear *lies* from you. Nor can I bear your pity. You needn't concern yourself about me. I lived in adequate contentment before we wed, and God willing I shall do so again. There is but one thing you can do for me: go and live the life you desire and *let me be!*" And he stalked off without a backward look.

I did not follow. I had heard enough.

24

For several days I stayed secluded in my old room. Mama let me be. I believed I was thinking matters through, but it was not really thinking. My brain, thickened by a numbing despair, did not fully believe what my instincts knew: that whatever had been good in my life was over. Beside my overwhelming shame and the pain of Seth's disbelief and rejection, I was enduring a bout of the most blood-chilling fear I'd ever experienced. I was with child. What would become of the baby if I lost my husband?

During those nightmarish days I did not respond to Peter's attempts to see me. But when Papa broke the news to me that Seth was arranging for a divorce, terror for my child forced my brain to work. I knew I had better think seriously about the future. Peter wanted me, even if Seth didn't. In my need for some feeling of safety, I realized that, in extremity, I could use Peter to save my child from bastardy. He'd been calling at the house every day. When he next came, I went downstairs and met him. Though we spoke with formal politeness, always in Mama's presence, it was clear he expected to wed me. I did not disabuse him of that expectation.

Word spread through town like a flash flood . . . Seth and Rachel Trahern were having a standaway. I was not surprised. New Castle is a small, close-knit community, and I suppose my absence from the shop, the Trahern house, and even from town was immediately noticed. What was more surprising was how quickly the townsfolk learned that an action for divorce would be taking place within a fortnight.

I, of course, knew nothing of the gossip until I received a visit from Clara Gruenwald. It was evident that she wanted to speak to me privately, so Mama excused herself and left us alone in the parlor. Clara did not waste a moment on amenities. She pulled her chair close to mine and seated herself on the edge. "Is true, missus? You and Mr. Trahern will divorce?" she asked bluntly. "This is what I hear in the market."

"Already?" I exclaimed in chagrin. But since I knew the gossip was not Clara's fault, I did not pursue the subject. "Yes, it's true," I admitted.

Her lips began to tremble. "Please, missus, you know this is not a good thing," she said tearfully.

"No, it's not. But it can't be helped."

She clapped a shaking hand to her mouth. "Ach, Gott! Is my fault. I should not have run for him."

"Run for him?" I asked stupidly.

"For Mr. Trahern. That day the man comes. I thought the man frighten you. I run to Mr. Trahern for help." Her face seemed to collapse, and tears rolled down her cheeks. "Is my fault!"

"No, no," I mumbled, almost wishing for a moment that I *could* blame her. Anything would be better than bearing my own guilt. But I knew that Clara's act had not caused the rift between Seth and me. It was Peter's presence, which Seth and I would have had to face sooner or later. Clara had only made it happen sooner. "You did what was right."

She looked at me dubiously. "You mean it, missus?"

"Yes," I assured her. "Yes, I do."

She wiped her wet cheeks with the back of her hand, and for a moment we sat in silent thought. Then Clara took a deep breath. "Maybe, if you tell Mr. Trahern of the child," she asked hopefully, "it would make things right?"

I was horror-struck. "Child?" I began in immediate, instinctive denial, despite the fact that I knew she was privy to my secret. "Tell me, Clara, what makes you think—?"

She looked straight into my eyes. "I ain't blind, missus. I seen you in the mornings. I seen you smile. You know, and I know."

I sagged back against my chair. I knew it was pointless to deny it. The looks and the few words we'd exchanged that last morning in Seth's house had been a clear admission on my part. "Please, Clara, you must not tell anyone," I pleaded. "Even my mother does not know."

"Is not my place to tell such thing," she said, dismissing my alarm with a wave of her hand. "From my lips it will never come. But why *you* keep silent, missus? Is not right. Mr. Trahern should know."

Yes, I thought, *he should*. But under the circumstances I could not chance it. Since he hadn't believed what I'd tried to tell him about what happened with Peter, I feared he also might not believe that he was father to my child. If our marriage was to end, and I had to wed Peter, it would be better to let Peter believe the child his. "Seth must not know, Clara. Not ever."

"But why?" she asked again, her eyes showing true concern for me.

Her sympathy touched me deeply. She surely must have thought I'd betrayed Seth, yet she did not judge me. I reached across and squeezed her hand. "I can't explain, Clara, but I have reasons," I said firmly, though my voice cracked. "Good reasons."

"You sure, missus?"

I could only nod. If I had spoken, I would have cried.

She squeezed my hand in return and got to her feet. "No one will learn anything from me," she said. It was a pledge.

As she passed my chair on her way to the door, she smoothed back my hair. "I am sorry," she said.

"Clara?" I croaked as she crossed the threshold.

She paused and looked back at me. "Yes, missus?"

"Take g-good care of him."

25

Later that week a small group of people met in Mama's parlor to witness the divorce. I remember how Mama stood straight and stony-faced during the entire divorce procedure, while Papa stalked back and forth between the window and the doorway. Perhaps the fact that this was the second time they'd had to witness such a procedure made it so hard for them to bear. One divorce in a family is rare. Two divorces are unheard of.

The only other people present besides Seth and me were my brother Simon and John Odell as witnesses, and Abel Becker as, in his words, "an ex-officio observer."

I had ordered Peter to stay away.

Abel gave Seth a statement to read aloud. In a dead voice Seth read the words. They stated that he, Seth Trahern, and I, Rachel Weller Trahern, had agreed to wedlock on the mistaken belief that my true betrothed, unnamed, was dead. Since that unnamed betrothed was now known to be alive, and since Mr. and Mrs. Trahern had been living a standaway since the unnamed betrothed had reappeared, he, Seth Trahern, was willing for the marriage to be considered annulled.

Then I read a similar statement. The paper shook in my hand, and my voice was so choked that Abel suggested I read it again, louder, so that the witnesses would not be in doubt of what I said. I glanced round at Seth, but he was looking at the floor. I noticed that Mama had pressed a handkerchief to her mouth. Not wishing to prolong this agony, I read the statement again, as loudly and as firmly as I could. But when I came to the words "willing for the marriage to be considered annulled," my voice failed me. I choked them out, thrust the paper into Abel's hand, and ran from the room.

About ten minutes later, standing at the window of what had been my girlhood bedroom and was now my room again, I watched the visitors' carriages depart. Seth's was first. Abel's was last.

It was over. I was divorced.

26

*H*ow do you face the future when you know you've shattered your life? It takes courage, and as you've seen, that's a quality I sadly lack.

Fortunately, there's an inevitability to life. The dawn comes each morning whether or not one wishes to face it. With or without courage, one must live one's days. So I did. I mustered what little courage I had and rose from my bed every morning, dressed myself, greeted my parents, did my chores, made myself smile. And the days passed.

For the sake of my unborn child, I could not afford to let *too many* days pass. I had to take the necessary next step before too long. Therefore, within a month of my divorce, before the end of June, Peter and I were married. It was a small, somber occasion, though Peter did not seem to notice the lack of gaiety.

That was not all he failed to notice. We spent our wedding night in my old bedroom. The consummation of our nuptials, on my narrow girlhood bed, probably did not last long, but to me it seemed endless. Every muscle, every nerve and fiber of my body, tensed against the new, unwanted husband. I feared that Peter would sense my antipathy, but when at last it was over, he sighed and went contentedly to sleep. I lay awake, as far from him as the scanty bed allowed, and wondered if I would ever be able to endure these embraces—which for me would be, at best, dutiful—without the ache of comparing them with the joyful abandon of the passion I'd once known.

Peter and I moved out of my parents' house the next day. Aware that Papa could not abide Peter, I arranged for us to move in with Simon and Abby. It was agreed that Peter would help Simon with the plowing for a fair wage, a small portion of which would be deducted for our lodging. After a stay of less than a week, however, I realized we could not remain. Although Simon's wife and I enjoyed each other's company, and I tried to help her in her many tasks, I could see that the small rent we paid for our room did not compensate poor, worn Abby for this overcrowding. Simon's house was already too small for his growing family, and we occupied a bedroom they could not easily spare. In addition, I suspected that Peter resented taking orders from Simon. Something, I knew, had to be done.

One day when I was returning to Simon's house from town with a parcel from the butcher shop under my arm, I came face to face with Seth. He was walking with Courtland White, arguing something so earnestly that he didn't see me. It was Courtland who caught sight of me and stopped short. My heart, beating at twice its normal speed, jumped right up into my throat. Seth looked up, and I saw his face stiffen. Courtland tipped his hat and muttered an awkward how-de-do. I bowed but could not utter a word. Seth gave me a small nod, the mere edge of politeness, and passed by. Courtland, embarrassed, made a quick leg and hurried after Seth. Though trembling in every limb, I made myself walk on.

I could not eat that evening. Nor could I face spending the night with Peter. I pleaded a headache and sat alone in Simon's dark parlor until I was sure Peter would be asleep. *This can't go on*, I told myself in the darkness. I could not bear hurting Seth and myself in this way. I had to leave New Castle.

But where was I to go? There was no one I knew, no relative or friend, in any other place in the world . . . except . . . *Clarissa!* The moment my sister's name popped into my head I knew I'd found the answer. I would go to Canada, where my sister had gone before me.

It took very little persuasion to get Peter to agree. He was already chaffing under what he complained was Simon's short temper. Therefore, as soon as we could arrange it, we took almost all that was left of Peter's shipboard pay, bought a horse and wagon, packed up our few possessions (and they were few, for I would not take anything I'd acquired in my months with Seth, nor would I accept any chattel from Mama's house), and set off for the north.

Before we trundled off on the New Jersey road, I said my good-byes—to Annette, to Simon and his family, to Papa, to everyone I'd ever known. But two particular good-byes caused me more pain than I can describe. One was to Mama, who, after calmly bidding me good fortune and walking with me to the wagon, suddenly wrapped me in a trembling embrace and burst into tears. I had never seen her weep, and it overcame me. When we parted, I could not stop my own flow of tears. If I had known that I would not see her again in this lifetime, I could not have felt more heartsick.

The other good-bye was to Seth. On my last night in New Castle, after everyone in the family was asleep, I stole out of the house on stockinged feet, my shoes in my hand. I ran into town and straight to Front Street, praying that the print shop would not be closed. I had to get one last glimpse of him.

The window of the shop showed but the faintest glow; I was not sure anyone was still there. When I peered into the window, however, I saw him in the faint light of the tiniest remnant of a candle that flickered on his desk. He was sitting there, one elbow on his desk with the hand propping up his head and his other arm hanging down, a pen dangling loosely from his fingers. He was motionless, merely staring at nothing. The expression on his face was so completely bereft of feeling that even the reddish glow of the candle couldn't give it life. It was something beyond sadness. He was spiritless, as if enveloped by a weariness so great that he could not write, or stand, or even raise his head. *Oh, Seth!* something within me cried. *My love, what have I done to us?*

I would have given anything—even the heart from my chest!—to have been able to go inside, take that head in my hands and kiss away that look. But I, and circumstance, had made a wreckage so great that it was past mending. I was unable to do anything but skulk there in the dark until I could no longer bear to see those eyes. With that look imprinted on my soul, I crept away and went back to Simon's house and my new husband's bed.

27

Though the look in Seth's eyes and my mother's tears weighed heavily on my spirit the next morning, I set off on our migration trying to start my new life with optimism. There was a baby growing inside me. Despite a steady and permanent pain in my heart for the loss of Seth, I would have his child. Moreover, I chided myself, hadn't the Reverend Mr. Phillips said in a sermon that the capacity for love is infinite? Did that not mean a woman could love more than one man in a lifetime? I had loved Peter once. Why could I not do so again?

At the start I thought I could. Peter was very cheerful those first days of our travels. He even sang jolly songs as we bumped along the dirt roads of New Jersey, sometimes a bawdy ballad like "The Farmer's Daughter," and sometimes a more familiar tune to which he'd change the words very cleverly to apply to us, as he did one day with the old English "Barbara Allen." I actually laughed when he sang silly rhymes like this:

> It came upon a Martinmas Day
> When green leaves turned to yeller
> When Peter Mason o' Delaware
> Fell in love with Rachel Weller . . .

Yes, he could still reveal that boyish charm when his mood was good. But the trouble was that his mood often changed, and what most often affected his mood was work. During that extended migration, I discovered in Peter a quality that I'd not seen in any other man of my acquaintance: he did not like to work. Work is so much a part of every man I know that it had never occurred to me that there might be some who were not suited to it.

Since it was summer, a time when a farmer needs all the help he can afford, Peter easily found farm work at every place we stopped. But nowhere did the situation last. Sometimes he quit after two days; never did we stay more than a week.

At first I told myself he merely wanted to keep moving. Especially after I told him I was "expecting" (news which he took with sincere delight), he seemed eager to reach Montreal so that I might be with my sister when my birthing time came. But I began to notice that protracted employment always seemed to have a negative effect on his mood. By the third day of any hire, he would grow testy. He would leave me in the evening and not return for hours. When he came back, he'd smell of ale. "A man's entitled to a pint or two after a day sweating in the fields," he'd say if I remarked on his condition. No later than the fourth day, he'd begin to complain about his employer. First he'd accuse the man of being unfair, then of being a "backbreaker," and finally a "damned slave driver." By the time I'd heard those words for the third employer in a row, I began to wonder where the real fault lay. I couldn't help remembering how I'd found Peter asleep under a tree that day at my father's farm. But I had not the courage (yet again!) to suggest that perhaps his own tendency to malinger might be the cause of his difficulties.

I was in my fourth month of pregnancy when we finally arrived in Montreal. It did not take long for us to locate Mr. Hooper's Livery Stable and the neat white house alongside it in which my sister's family lived. Clarissa and Jacob greeted us with eager warmth, Clarissa and I embracing and laughing and crying all at once. "Good Lord, Rachel, look how you've grown!" my sister exclaimed lovingly.

I put her hand on my enlarged stomach. "In many ways," I laughed.

Jacob kissed me on both cheeks, like the true Montrealer he'd become. And Clarissa's three little children were so excited by the joyousness in the air that they danced around us noisily. The delight they all found in this reunion filled me with hope.

Later, when Clarissa and I had a moment alone, my sister studied me closely. "You've changed, my dear," she said, frowning.

"Of course I've changed," I said. "I was fourteen when you last saw me."

"I don't mean that. You had such happy eyes back then."

"Happy eyes?" I pretended I did not know what she meant. "What on earth are happy eyes?"

Clarissa shrugged. "I don't know exactly. But yours used to sparkle." She took my face in her two hands. "What is it, Rachel, my sweet? I think you have suffered in your life."

I felt tears gather in my eyes. "Hasn't everyone?" I said, trying to be flippant. But in another moment I was opening my heart to my loving sister, telling her all that had happened to me in the past year. I knew that if there was anyone in the world who would understand my pain, it was she. In the time that followed, it was a great relief to me to be able to share my innermost feelings with a sympathetic woman.

It was soon decided that Peter would go to work for Mr. Hooper and that we would lodge with them, at least until the baby was born. It was a fortuitous arrangement, for tending horses seemed a more congenial occupation for Peter than farming. Jacob was an easygoing employer. Noting that Peter preferred tending the horses to smithing and wheelwrighting, Jacob kept those latter chores for himself and his two apprentices, and let Peter do the work he liked. This kindness did much to improve Peter's moods. And the warmth with which we were treated by Clarissa and Jacob Hooper made Peter more inclined to remain at home during the evenings than to seek out a tavern.

The baby was born in January of 1802, two months before I claimed he was due. He weighed almost six pounds. Clarissa was wonderfully convincing when she exclaimed to everyone how lucky we were that our premature baby was so large and lusty. I bless her to this day for her support of my lie. She was ever loving and caring.

Peter was so overjoyed at having a son that he didn't object to my naming him Josiah after my father. And the first time he held the infant and studied his face, he said that the boy was the image of his own mother. Since that poor woman had died in Peter's early boyhood, his memory of her appearance was necessarily vague. I was glad of it.

And so little Joss entered our lives, as sweet-natured a child as ever breathed. When I held him in my arms, suckling him or rocking him to sleep, I knew a love unlike any other. It seemed to me that God had taken pity on me and given me this greatest of all gifts. With Peter settling down and my baby in my arms, I began to believe that I could find some contentment in my life.

But it was not to be, for Peter was not capable of contentment for very long. Soon he began to complain again. "My work at the stables was worth more than what Jacob's givin' me," he pouted.

"But my dear," I pointed out, "we've managed to save enough from that pay that, if we continue for another year, we might buy a house."

"A year's too long to have to endure working in the stables," he retorted, "or livin' with Clarissa's brats, who're always underfoot and in my way."

I did not say, though I wanted to, that perhaps Clarissa found *him* constantly underfoot and in *her* way.

I did, however, find us lodging of our own: two large, cheerful rooms in the house of an elderly widow, Mrs. Washburton, an acquaintance of Clarissa's who, though not needing the financial assistance that the rent provided, needed help with the cleaning and cooking, which I provided.

For several weeks, it proved a satisfactory arrangement, although it gave Peter an excuse for going out in the evening to the tavern to avoid Mrs. Washburton's company in the parlor. I did not object, for if he stayed at home, he spent the time complaining that Jacob was becoming a backbreaker.

One morning, early in May, I awoke to find Peter gone. On his pillow was a note which read:

> *Your brother in law is a slave-driver who I cannot bear to work for one day longer. I am going to the Ohio teritory which is rich with oppertunity for an enterprising man. Now that I have learnd what there is to know about*

the livery bizness, I intend to establish stables of my own out there in the west, where there is a growing need for them. I sure will miss you and the boy, but it is time for me to be a man. Do not forget me, Rachel, for I swear I will send for you as soon as I am financhully able. I am taking our savings, which I will need to start up an establishment, but I know you will not be destatute with your sister and brother in law to look out for you. Please believe that I am ever your loving husband, Peter.

A confusion of emotions flooded over me at reading those words, the strongest of which was rage. But I did not admit to myself that a more significant emotion surged underneath. I did not, at that moment, recognize that feeling, but I can tell you now that it was distinct relief!

With rage uppermost in my heart, I dressed Jossy and went to unburden myself to my sister. The moment she saw my face she knew something was amiss, but she waited until we'd gone to her kitchen and settled the baby in an old cradle before she asked what was wrong.

I told her flatly that Peter had left me. I was reluctant to show Clarissa the actual letter, because Peter had written those unfair words about her kind, generous Jacob, but when she asked for the details, I let her see it.

She read it over quickly. When she finished, she shook her head in disgust. "He's a fool," she said.

"A *dastardly* fool!" I stormed, letting my repressed anger loose. "How *dare* he do this to me after I gave up my happiness for him?" I paced about the room in a fury. "Haven't I been a good wife to him, enduring his moods and keeping silent about his ineffectuality as a worker?"

"Come, sit down," Clarissa said. "I'll brew some tea. It will calm you."

"I don't want to be calm," I cried. "I want to slap his face and give him a tongue-lashing such as he'd never forget! I wish I had him here just long enough to beat him with a stick!"

"Come now, dearest," Clarissa said, "you know you'd never do such a thing. You're not the sort to hurt anyone. Nor are you the sort to rant this way."

I was taken aback. Yes, I had been ranting. I took a deep breath and got control of myself. "No, of course I wouldn't beat him," I admitted, for in my mind's eye I saw Peter's scarred back. "I suppose the poor fellow has been beaten enough already." I sank down on a chair, my rage abated. "Perhaps," I sighed when Clarissa's tea and comforting words had had their effect, "I haven't been as good a wife as I ought to have been."

"Don't be silly," Clarissa said, refusing to believe ill of her sister. "Even Jacob admires your patience and understanding of Peter's moods."

I shook my head. I could not in honesty accept such praise. "No, I did not truly love him as I should have."

Suddenly awash with guilt for my own failings, I realized that I couldn't truly blame Peter for leaving. Perhaps, I thought, he instinctively guessed what I was just becoming aware of—that *I would not be crushed by his departure!* It was a surprising discovery. "You will never fathom," I said to my sister in amazement, "what a strange feeling I am experiencing all at once."

"I think I can," she said with a little smile. "You feel that a great weight has been lifted from your shoulders."

"Heavens, am I so transparent?" I exclaimed. "How did you guess?"

She shrugged. "You're not transparent, my love, but I've had time to become acquainted with your no-account husband."

We drank our tea in silence. Sitting there in Clarissa's kitchen, I took stock of my situation. I had nothing, no money (for Peter had stolen our savings) and no prospects. But there was only one thing that concerned me: my son. I had to make a life for him. Something inside me said I could do it. I was young enough and strong enough, I told myself, to find a way to care for him. I had not shown much bravery in my life before, but now, for little Joss's sake, I would find the courage I needed.

Clarissa, meanwhile, was rereading Peter's letter. "I always felt, Rachel," she said when she at last put it down, "that your Peter reminded me of someone. Now I know who."

"Who?" I asked.

"Who do you think? The one who deserted *me*. George Epps."

28

For two years I lived with Mrs. Washburton, who let me keep my rooms rent-free in exchange for taking care of the cooking and cleaning. For a while I had to rely on Clarissa for my other needs, but I soon found a way to earn some money by helping the schoolmaster of a little church school not far from where I lived. I taught the younger children reading and simple reckoning, while the schoolmaster taught the older ones more advanced studies, like multiplication and spelling and catechism. Clarissa was happy to look after my little boy (we called him Jossy) on those days when I was in school. She and Jacob loved him almost as much as their own.

I heard from Peter twice during those two years. They were brief letters, each one telling me he'd moved—first to the Michigan Territory and then to the Illinois. In each of the missives he claimed that the new move was a wise one. "This new location," he wrote each time, "will provide great oppertunities for a man of vision."

When showing the second letter to my sister, I remarked with a sigh, "'Tis quite like Peter to keep believing that better opportunities always exist just beyond the horizon."

"What bothers me more than that," Clarissa said, looking up from the scrawled page, "is that this deuced husband of yours never inquired, in either of his letters, about your health or Jossy's. Nor does he make the slightest inquiry about how you are managing to live."

"There would be no use in his inquiring," I pointed out dryly. "Since he hasn't given me an address, there's no method by which I can possibly answer him. But, tell me, Clarissa, why do you keep calling him my husband? He cannot be considered a husband if he deserted me, can he?"

Clarissa shook her head. "In a court of law, I think his letters would prove you haven't really been deserted."

The remark did not trouble me at that time. Whether or not Peter was still legally my husband didn't seem significant. Now, of course, it may mean a great deal.

At that time, there were other matters that troubled me. Every day that I looked at my beautiful little boy's face, I yearned to take him to New Castle (which I still thought of as home). I didn't let myself dream of showing him to Seth, but I ached to show him to Mama. He was already saying words and trotting about on sturdy little legs, babbling and smiling at everyone, as happy and sweet-natured as a child can be. Mama would burst with joy to see him, I knew. But the cost of traveling so great a distance was prohibitive; even though Jacob would let me have a rig and two horses, I'd have to pay a driver (for an unescorted woman with a baby needed a man for protection) and have enough extra funds to house us for four or five nights at inns along the way. I had managed a small amount of savings, but not enough for that. And although Jacob offered to give me the money I'd need, I would not accept such a gift.

One day, however, word came that made my dreams of taking Jossy to see his grandmother die aborning. Clarissa had a letter from Papa saying that Mama had had a heart seizure and had passed on.

It is not to our purpose here to describe my grief. Suffice it to say that my guilt for all the ways in which I'd failed my mother swept over me in a tornado of regret. Clarissa, too, suffered the blows of remorse, for she also had intended to take her children to meet their grandmother one day. It occurs to me now that we poor mortals like to fool ourselves into believing that we are as admirable as our intentions—we tell ourselves that we are good and generous because we fully intend *some day* to be so—but in the finality of death, all good intentions, all hopes for future atonements are swept away, and we must face the naked fact that it is too late to become what we thought we were. In the immutability of death the living recognize their inadequacy . . . and grieve.

But time does its work and eases the pain. When the anguish abated, Clarissa and I talked about Papa's needs in his altered circumstances, and we concluded that I and Joss should return to New Castle. "Why not you, too?" I asked my sister.

"It is too late for me," she said. "My life is here now. But, Rachel, to be honest, if I could live my life over again, I would not run away after the trial. I would stay where I wanted to stay, back home in New Castle, with my husband and family."

"But why? You are happy here, are you not?"

"Yes. But back then I wanted to live near my family, near Mama, near you. Leaving you brought me much misery and loneliness. It took a long time to learn to weather the loss."

"But if you'd stayed," I reminded her, "you would have had old biddies like the Widow Rowse calling you adulteress. And your children would have been called names, too."

"Yes, I know. That's why we left. But it was cowardly. Names are not stones, as the saying says. We would have endured, and in time it would have been forgotten."

"And the children? What about the children?"

"They can be strong, too, if their parents are. If I've learned anything in life, Rachel, it's that one shouldn't be cowed by other people's opinions. By fear of a bad name or a bad reputation. So long as you have a good opinion of yourself, you can abide the rest."

I thought for a long time about her words. I realized that I had married Peter only to keep a good name. Clarissa, in her new insight, would think it was wrong of me, but I was not sure. There was Jossy. I was not at all sure I should have subjected him to the stain of bastardy. Clarissa might believe that the children can endure, but I could not chance it. Not for Jossy. At a terrible cost to me, I had bought him a name. I told myself that my decision had been for the best.

Now that it was decided that I should return to Papa, I yearned to start out. Under these circumstances, I accepted Jacob's financial assistance and, as soon as I was able to make arrangements, my son and I set out for home.

29

With what a confusion of emotions I returned to New Castle! Seeing Papa again was itself both a gladness and an agony. He had altered a great deal in the almost-three years since I'd last seen him. He was stooped, grayer, and less surefooted. Mama's death had left its mark on him. How alone he must have felt when she died! I blamed myself for not having been there alongside him when he most needed me.

His emotions must have been equally confused by the sight of me. Though I could see in his eyes how glad he was to see me, his disapproval of my choices in life still lay there beneath the surface. My divorce from Seth he would never forgive, in spite of his gratitude that I had come to ease his loneliness.

But there was no confusion in his joy at seeing his grandson. He was so overcome with emotion at the sight of his little namesake that he actually trembled. I had taught Jossy to say "Hello, Grandpapa," which he pronounced Heyo, G'anpapa, and when Papa heard it he was completely overcome. He lifted Jossy in his arms, nuzzled his neck, and wept.

There was nothing equivocal in the affection with which I was welcomed by Annette. She was quite ecstatic, as I was, not only at the renewal of our friendship but at seeing our babies become acquainted. We had been girls together; now we would be mothers together.

My reunion with Simon and Abby was also unequivocally affectionate. Our first dinner together, with Papa and all the children around Abby's table, was a most happy occasion. The only difficult moment came when Simon managed to get me alone. I was carrying some dishes to the kitchen when Simon caught up with me in the passageway. "Little Jossy is a clever tyke," he said, trying to make the remark casual. "A lot quicker 'n our Benjy was at that age."

Sensing what was in his mind, I tensed. "Yes, he is quick, I think," I said.

"And Abby and me was noticing . . . that his eyes are . . . well . . ."

"Yes? What about them?"

Simon peered at me intently. ". . . that his eyes are such a light gray."

I raised my chin and looked straight into his eyes. "Yes, Peter says they're just like his mother's."

I brushed past him, and that ended the conversation, but I knew what he suspected. And I feared that my response had not convinced him that his suspicions were unfounded.

When Clara Gruenwald came to call, the pain again suffused the gladness. "You ought to tell him," she murmured when Jossy waddled over to her and allowed himself to be dandled on her knee. "Such a *suss kind!* The man deserves to be told."

God knows I would have loved to tell Seth he had a son he could take pride in, but I could not endanger the scheme I'd so carefully undertaken to ensure that my son had legal paternity. "Clara, you gave me your word," I reminded her. She pressed her lips together in disapproval, but she nodded. Clara was, like my mother, a woman of honor. She would not betray me.

Of course, Seth did not come to see me, although I let myself dream that he would. And if he would not come to see me of his own volition, I was too proud to see him on mine. On the rare occasions when I went into town and passed his shop (on my way to the cobbler's or the draper's, or when passing through on my way to Simon's place), I did not permit myself to look inside. I walked by quickly, with my eyes lowered.

But I did read his newspaper. It was foolish of me, I suppose, to continue to take pride in his writings when I no longer had any connection with him. But I couldn't help myself. My eyes took in every word, and my fingers sometimes moved involuntarily, as if they were itching to set the type. I even tried to read between the lines, to see if I could detect signs of how he was feeling. The subject matter of the paper became almost personal to me. When I read what he wrote about the election, for example, pointing out the differences between this one and Jefferson's first, it brought back a flood of memories. There was not a word in his editorial to indicate that the new improvements in the election law, separating the vice-presidential election from the presidential, were in some part due to him. He was in his writing, as he'd always been, as modest as he was insightful. How could I not be proud?

More than a year passed in this way. It was a year of relative contentment. I was among people I loved, I was useful, and my son brought sunshine to my life. When another letter came from Peter, forwarded to me from Clarissa, with the news that he was heading south to the Louisiana Territory (where, of course, there were better opportunities for a man of vision), it made little difference to my expectations or my peace of mind.

My son was providing my father with some contentment, too. Jossy followed Papa about all day, chattering comments and questions about everything he saw and eagerly attempting to lend his assistance to whatever chores Papa was occupied with. Papa would give him simple tasks to do and watch him accomplish them with a glow in his eyes that combined love and a bursting pride. Anyone could see that the child was a balm to Papa's wounded soul.

It was a time of peace for us. But I'd discovered by that time that there is no permanence to peace; turbulence always roils underneath, with upheaval imminent. I knew in my bones that upheaval was coming, and that it would involve Seth.

30

The first sign of that upheaval was when Jossy developed a high fever. When Papa and I noticed the boy's unusual listlessness and high color, we treated the fever with the herb tisanes we'd always used for illness. Then we tried the two patent medicines Papa believed in: Daffy's Elixir and Turlington's Balsam of Life. But the fever continued to climb. We tried cold compresses, but when this too was ineffectual, I became frightened. And when Papa (more frightened than I, if that were possible) muttered the words "scarlet fever" and suggested going to town to fetch Doctor Muncie, I was too terrified to wait. I picked up the boy in my arms, wrapped him in a blanket, and ran like a person crazed into town to the doctor's house. By the time I reached Front Street, I was puffing for breath. I must have appeared wild, windblown, and disheveled. After passing Seth's shop, his new printer's devil—a tall, gangling, bespectacled seventeen-year-old, very different from the garrulous Billy Shupp—came running after me and took the child from my arms. "I'll carry him for you," he said.

I was grateful, for his long, untired legs could make better time than mine. "To Doctor Muncie," I gasped. "Run!"

Doctor Muncie bled the boy and gave him a powder to make him sleep. And we waited. We spent the night in Doctor Muncie's dispensary. He bled Joss once more during the night. When he wanted to do so a third time, I objected, for I could not bear to see my little boy's blood flow again. I argued that the fever seemed to have somewhat abated, and the doctor (himself not convinced that another bleeding would have any effect) let me have my way.

It was an endless night. In the morning, Jossy opened his eyes and smiled at me, quite normal again. It seemed to me a miracle! Whatever it was that had ailed the boy, it had not been scarlet fever. I sank to my knees and thanked God for the reprieve.

Later, when we left the doctor's house, we found a small crowd gathered round his doorway. Word had spread of my wild dash to the doctor's, and caring friends had come to hear word of my little boy. Some had been waiting for hours. Annette was there, and Clara. And Papa, of course, with Simon and Abby. And I caught a glimpse of Seth, who turned and walked away as soon as we emerged. When I had time to think about it later, I realized that he must have seen me as I ran past his shop with Jossy in my arms and sent his apprentice to assist me. It touched me deeply that he showed such concern for the boy he thought was Peter Mason's child. But it worried me, too. Any affinity between Seth and my son seemed dangerous to me.

The second upheaval—a quite literal one—took place in February of this year, a cold, gloomy month of overcast skies and brutal winds. Jossy had just turned four and was not happy about being constrained indoors so much of the time. A few months earlier, I had made a passing remark to Reverend Phillips about my teaching chores in Montreal, and he had asked me to assist him in his small church school. He even offered a small stipend. Since the work required my presence a mere few hours in the morning, and in the winter months only, a time when Papa would be free to watch over Jossy, I agreed. Papa was quite willing, and the schedule had proceeded without problems for three months until that fateful occurrence in February.

It was the first time my presence was required at the church in the late afternoon. Reverend Phillips had organized a program of recitations and songs for the children to present to their parents, and, since some of the performers were my pupils, he wanted me to assist. Papa assured me he was as capable of keeping an eye on Joss in the afternoon as he was in the morning; I was to go along to church, he said, and not concern myself about them.

But (as near as I can piece together the circumstances) Papa must have fallen asleep in his chair while watching Jossy play with marbles on the floor near the fire. Perhaps the fire died down and the child grew cold. We believe he wandered into the kitchen, where I'd set a roast to cook on a spit for our supper, and tried to pull off a piece to eat. Something must have fallen over—the spit, perhaps, or a glowing log—and when he tried to right it, he burnt his hands. Hurt, and frightened that he'd done something naughty and would be scolded, he ran up to the bedroom and hid under the bed. By the time the smoke from the kitchen woke Papa, the kitchen was ablaze. In a terrified search for Jossy, he was overcome by the smoke.

Meanwhile, at the church, I was serenely enjoying the children's performance when suddenly Mr. Odell Senior came running in, his face red from cold and exertion.

"Fire!" he shouted, and dashed over to the stairway to the steeple to ring the bell. There was an immediate uproar, but soon the men in the fire brigade made it clear the fire was not here in the church but elsewhere, and they ran out to the tavern—their gathering place where their buckets and water barrels were stored. I was so busy trying to calm the frightened children that it did not occur to me to ask where the fire was. I was helping Mrs. Cochrane herd her four children out the church door when I saw two of the men of the brigade run by with their buckets and heard one of them shout, "It's the Weller place."

I remember gaping for a moment, thinking, *It can't be!* But I knew I'd heard aright, and I immediately ran after them, unshawled and unbonneted but with no sense of the cold. I think I was screaming. By the time I reached home, the whole house was in flames. The men were passing the buckets, but it was clear the effort was useless. Papa, his face black, was staring at the flames wild-eyed. "Joss!" I screamed. "Where's Joss?"

He turned to me, his eyes white in his black face, and crazed with agony. He couldn't speak, and didn't need to. I knew my boy was in that inferno. I ran toward the flames in utter hysteria. The men held me back, of course, though I struggled against them with all my might, screaming like a banshee. Then the kitchen roof fell in with a terrible crash. The sound crushed me; I fell to my knees and beat the ground. "No, no, *no!*" I cried hoarsely, my voice completely gone, "God would not do this to me!"

And then I heard a sound from the crowd like a sigh. I looked up and saw Seth emerging from round the far side of the house, stumbling forward, but carefully protecting something in his arms. I don't think I took a breath as I watched him come toward me. "He's all right," I heard him say before I was sure the bundle he carried was Joss.

Time stopped for me. The sounds in the air became muffled, and the movement around me became slow and vague as if this were happening under water. Seth came toward me slowly, swimmingly, as if in a dream. I saw that Joss was clinging to his neck with both arms, his little head buried in Seth's shoulder. Seth tried to loose the boy's hold and hand him down to where I still knelt on the ground, but Joss would not let go of him. Finally Seth got down on his knees in front of me. "It's your mother," he said to the boy softly. "You don't have to be afraid any more. It's your mother." And he handed the child into my arms.

I don't remember much of what happened next. I know that I clutched my child in my arms, rocking him back and forth and sobbing in convulsive relief, while the little boy tried to soothe his hysterical mother by murmuring over and over, "Don't cwy, Mama, don't cwy." When at last I'd gained some self-control and looked up to thank Seth for saving not only Joss's life but mine, he was gone.

Later that night, after we'd salved and bandaged Jossy's hands, after we'd gone to church and thanked God for the salvation we'd received, after we'd convinced Papa not to go back to the farm to sift through the smoking remains, when we were bedding down on counterpanes on the floor of Simon's parlor, with an exhausted Joss asleep upstairs in his cousins' bedroom, Papa and I talked about how to thank Seth properly for what he'd done. There seemed nothing that was adequate to express our inexpressible gratitude. We decided that we'd let Joss do it for us.

For the next two days, while Papa busied himself sifting through the debris of the farmhouse for anything useful that might be salvaged, I sat in Simon's parlor knitting a muffler for Seth with pearl-gray wool I had carded and spun thrice to make it as soft and fine as could be. I worked day and night, so it would be done quickly. When it was finished, Abby gave me a sheet of silver paper she'd been saving and helped me wrap it. Then we dressed Joss in clothes borrowed from his cousins, handed him the package and turned him over to Papa for his excursion to the print shop. Papa and I had agreed that it would make the situation awkward if I were present, so I stayed behind and waited eagerly for their return.

It was almost two hours before they came back, but they both looked happy. Papa reported that Seth had accepted the boy's shy thanks with his usual modesty. Jossy, tremendously excited by the visit, wanted to tell me about it himself. Words tumbled out of him as he described how Mr. Trahern had taken his hand and showed him around the shop and let him hold the handle of the "p'inting p'ess." He'd had the "bestest" time. And he added that Mr. Trahern had said he could come back any time.

"You should've seen how he gazed up at Seth as if he were some sort of God," Papa muttered a little jealously. "The boy's got himself a hero now."

"Did Seth like the muffler?" I asked. The answer was important to me, for the gift had been the only way I knew how to express my unfathomable gratitude.

"I guess he liked it," Papa said. "He unwrapped it and said his thanks and put it aside."

"Is that all he said? Thanks?"

Papa shrugged. "What else did you want him to say?"

I couldn't answer. What I wanted couldn't be put into words.

31

*P*apa was right that Jossy had found a hero. The child prevailed upon his Grandpapa to take him to visit Seth the very next day. Papa told me the boy followed his hero around the shop the way he once followed his grandfather, his eyes wide with admiration for everything Seth did. And poor Papa couldn't even permit himself to feel jealousy, for, after all, Seth had not only saved the child's life but saved Papa from having to spend his remaining years in punishing guilt for having fallen asleep that fateful day.

Seth was obviously taken with Jossy, too, for the boy's prattle inspired him to make Papa a most generous offer. Knowing that the rebuilding of our house could not be undertaken until the winter weather eased (which might not occur for at least three weeks), and realizing, from little remarks that Jossy made to him, that we were uncomfortably cramped in Simon's house, he offered us his home. He was quite insistent, Papa told me, claiming that he quite often slept on a mat in the shop. This refuge I refused. "He's done more than enough for us. I won't put him out of his bed," I said.

But Papa suggested that if he and Joss accepted the invitation without me, Seth would not have to leave his bed. Without the presence of a female in the house (this female in particular, though Papa did not say that), Seth could still sleep in his own home. And, of course, the crowding at Simon's house would be eased. Though I was reluctant to part with Joss for so many nights, I could not object. Papa's reasoning was sensible, and I would still be with my son during the days.

I worried, however, that too much of a liking between Seth and Joss might develop during that time. Little Jossy's adoration of Seth was already obvious, and I had no doubt that, with such proximity, Seth would grow fond of my sweet-natured son. Anyone would. But I felt uncomfortable at the prospect of a growing intimacy between them. I couldn't help wondering if this unexpected closeness might lead to trouble.

I did not have to wonder long.

The new house was not finished until midsummer, for construction had to wait for winter to pass and then for spring plowing to be done. Although it had been erected by the voluntary labor of several of the neighboring farmers, the required lumber and supplies had cost Papa every last penny of his savings. There was nothing left for the furnishings required to make the house fit to inhabit. That was when our friends came to our rescue again. They brought us gifts of some of their spare furniture—the necessities we needed to enable us to move in: two chairs, a table made by Simon, a battered old chest, a kitchen workbench, and a small wooden bed for Joss (from Annette, who insisted that her daughter had outgrown it, a claim that anyone looking at the tiny Nicole could see was pure nonsense. But it was a kind lie, typical of the generosity everyone was showing us). So we moved in and managed quite well. The only significant items of furniture we lacked were beds for Papa and me. We had to sleep on featherbeds on the floor.

Jossy is a good-natured boy and made no complaints when, after more than four months, he moved out of Seth's house into ours. But he made comparisons nonetheless. "Mr. T'ahern has a picture on the wall," he told me, "of a castle an' a waterfall."

"Does he, indeed?" I muttered, pretending uninterest to discourage him from dwelling on the matter.

"Why don't we have a picture on the wall?"

"Perhaps we will one day," I said.

The boy also told me about the cupboard with the glass doors with "lots an' lots of cups an' dishes," about the silver candlesticks, about the six chairs lined up in the dining room—"two of 'em *elbow*-chairs!"—and on and on until I was quite disgusted with him. "Well," I said at last, hoping to dismiss the subject forever, "Mr. Trahern is rich, and we aren't."

One morning, after Papa had gone out to the fields and Joss was feeding the chickens (one of the chores he could be relied upon to do without supervision), and I was trying to refinish the much-scarred top of the chest, I heard someone riding hurry-scurry up our path. I opened the door to discover Seth leaping from his horse. My heart jumped into my throat. We hadn't met face to face since my return two and a half years ago. In fact, I hadn't had a good look at him since that night, more than four years before, when I'd studied his face through the shop window. I noticed at once that his hair was streaked with gray and that his forehead had lines that had not been there when I'd last looked at him. And he was leaner than he'd been. I wondered if Clara was taking proper care of his eating. But my eyes drank him in as if they'd thirsted for the sight of him.

He, however, was not thirsting for the sight of me. As he strode toward me, I could see that this was not to be a casual visit. His face was white and his eyes burned with fury. "G-Good morning," I managed, my chest tightening in already fearful apprehension.

He did not answer but stomped past me into the front room. I shut the door and followed, my heart pounding. I am embarrassed to admit that, despite being completely discomposed, I was uncomfortably aware that I hadn't bothered to replait my hair that morning and that I was wearing an enormous, ugly, and very stained apron.

After a moment, during which he seemed to be trying to get himself in control, Seth whirled about and faced me. "Is it true, Mistress Mason?" he demanded, tight-lipped. "Is he mine?"

It was a question I'd long been dreading, yet I was completely unprepared for it. "Wh-what?" I stammered. "Wh-who—?"

"You know very well who. Little Joss."

"I don't know what on earth you're talking about," I said, the falseness in my voice reverberating in my ears.

"Yes, you do. Damn it, Rachel, I want the truth! Am I the boy's father?"

I had to be strong, I told myself. I had to brazen this out. "Is that what you think?" I asked, raising my brows in affected disbelief and trying to sound amused. "That you're Jossy's father? Whatever made you think such a—? Who would say—?"

"It's not important what or who brought it to mind. What I must know is if it's the truth."

I turned away so that he might not read my eyes. "It's ridiculous," I said.

"It's far from ridiculous. It's entirely possible. I've

been reckoning the months. It could well be."

Somehow the words made me angry, as if he, not I, were guilty of falsehood. I turned back and faced him. "Well, reckon again!" I snapped. "The boy's name is Josiah Mason. That should tell you who his father is."

"I know his name. I want to know his true paternity."

"How dare you, Seth!" I cried, fanning the anger that was rising within me. The anger, I realized, not only helped me conquer my terror but made me sound sincere. "You are calling me a liar. How dare you come barging into my home and insulting me with these groundless accusations!"

"I have grounds for them. Once the possibility was suggested to me, I thought of many grounds."

"What grounds? There are no grounds for imagining I would lie to you about such a matter."

"Yes, there are. Indeed, ma'am, there are. If I had made you pregnant just before Mason's reappearance, and you had wished to divorce me and wed him, you'd have a very good reason to lie to me."

I stared at him aghast, wondering how he could be so right and so wrong at the same time. "No," I said truthfully. "That makes no sense."

"Why not?" he demanded.

"Do you think," I asked in sincere wonderment, "that it would have made a difference to you, after what you saw—or thought you saw—in your parlor that day, if I told you I was carrying your child?"

He looked astonished by the question. "Of course it would! How can you ask it?"

I shook my head. "Don't you remember how angry you were? If I had told you I was with child, you would not have believed me. Just as you didn't believe anything else I said to you."

"That's nonsense!" he declared firmly. But in his eyes I read a shadow of a doubt. Then his expression changed, and he took a step toward me. "What are you saying, woman? Do you realize that by that statement you are admitting that you *were* with child then?"

"I am admitting nothing of the sort. We are merely speaking in suppositions."

"Then let us deal with the facts. Jossy told me his birthday is in January. I didn't think anything of it then. But once the suggestion was planted in my head, I did the reckoning. And I realized, ma'am, that you and Mason would scarcely have had time to manage a January birth even if you'd conceived him on my couch!"

I felt my throat close. My deuced fearfulness again. "He was premature," I mumbled. "Two months premature."

"Yes, of course," he said with quiet scorn. "Premature. The universal excuse of dishonest women."

I could not let my fear defeat me. This was too important. So I took a deep breath and spoke with all the fury I could summon up. "You may believe what you wish, Seth Trahern. I know better than anyone how impossible it is to make you change your beliefs once your mind is made up. I hope, however, that you don't intend to make those beliefs public. I have a son who has a legitimate name, and I shan't allow anyone to besmirch it. Do you hear me? Not anyone!"

Seth's breath caught in his throat, and his eyes widened. "He *is* my son, then," he said in a gasp of certainty. "You're admitting it."

"I'm doing nothing of the kind. I shall never—!"

Jossy came running in at that moment with the egg basket. "I on'y found eight this morning," he announced, handing me his cache. Then he saw Seth. "Mr. T'ahern!"

he exclaimed, dashing across the room and clutching Seth about the legs. "You came!"

Seth, though shaken, knelt down and picked the boy up. "Did I hear you say you counted to eight?" he asked the boy with a forced, yet proud, smile.

"I can count more'n that," Jossy bragged.

"Yes, of course you can." Seth's smile widened, but I saw him stare at Jossy's face for a moment before clutching him to his chest in a tight embrace. "He looks like my mother," he said to me over the boy's shoulder.

"Peter always said the same thing," I retorted.

Seth shook his head, dismissing my words. "You have made me lose four years. I won't lose any more." He set the boy down and turned to go.

I followed him to the door. "What do you mean?" I asked, my knees atremble.

Certitude having made him calm, Seth merely shrugged. "I mean, ma'am, that you lied to me in the most heinous way, a way which I cannot forgive. I do not yet know what I can do about it, but the boy is mine." And as he walked away from me to his horse, he said without looking back, "He is mine, and I shall have him."

32

*O*ne morning, a fortnight ago, I was surprised to see an old fall-back chaise approaching the Weller road. The top of the carriage was dropped back in spite of the cool fall weather, and as it drew near I recognized Abel Becker in the driver's seat. I had no idea why Abel should be calling, but I took off my apron and went to the door.

Abel heaved his bulk clumsily from the driver's seat and climbed down. "Good morning, ma'am," he called, walking toward me.

"Good morning to you, Abel. Did you wish to see Papa? He's in the barn."

"No, Rachel, my dear," he said, removing his hat, "'tis you I've come to see."

"Me?" I was surprised. There was a careful, almost wary expression in his eyes. I felt a premonition of disaster as I showed him in.

We sat down opposite each other at the dining table, and I offered him tea and a johnnycake, which he refused. "What I've come to tell you will not be pleasant," he said.

"Then say it straight out, please, Abel," I said, "for my innards are already tense as a bowstring."

"Well, then, here goes." He reached across the table for my hand. "Seth is going to bring a case of criminal conversation against you."

"Oh, God!" I felt my blood seep from my heart.

Abel explained as gently as he could that Seth wanted his son and that, in order to achieve his ends, he had to negate our divorce. "We both very much regret the necessity to do this, Rachel, but we see no other way."

Confused, I could only gape at him. He, though only the messenger, guiltily dropped his eyes from my face. I withdrew my ice-cold hand from his grasp. I could not speak a word. I knew that there must be a great deal I should be asking him, but in my dismay I did not know what to ask. Even if I could have framed the questions, Abel could not have answered. As he explained to me, he was Seth's attorney and as such could not discuss the matter with me.

When I found my voice, there was only one question that occurred to me. "Does Seth know you've come to tell me this?" I asked.

"He insisted on it."

I nodded, staring at my white-knuckled hands. It was hard for me to imagine that the Seth Trahern, who was so patient, loving, and kind to me when we were wed, and who so courageously saved my son from death by fire not six months ago, could be the same Seth who is bringing me to face the shame and humiliation of a case of criminal conversation, a shame that he knows, from our meeting after the court case he tried eleven years ago, is of all things the most dreadfully abhorrent to me. "He must hate me very much," I murmured, struggling to keep my voice steady.

"I don't think he hates you, Rachel. But he very much loves the boy."

"Does he, indeed!" The words burst out of me in a flash of fury. I sprang up from my chair, dashing away the tears that I could no longer keep back. "Well, the boy is not his, and he shan't have him."

Abel quietly rose. "I'm truly sorry, Rachel," he said with sincerity and started toward the door.

"I'll not succumb to this, Abel," I told him, clenching my fists. "I'll fight for my son to my last breath!"

Abel paused in the doorway. "If you truly intend to fight him, my dear, you must find yourself a lawyer."

"Yes, of course." I put a trembling hand to my pounding forehead. "But who?"

"I cannot in conscience recommend one to you under the circumstances," he said, "but if I were you, I'd take myself to Wilmington or, even better, Philadelphia, and find myself a good one."

That, Mr. Galliard, is why I've come to you. You now hold in your hands the sum and substance of my life. I assure you that everything I've written here is the truth, the whole truth, exactly as I remember it.

I do not understand the legal reasons for the course of action Seth Trahern has instituted, how it will avail him of what he wishes . . . that is, the custody of my son. It goes without saying that losing my son would be my life's greatest tragedy. I pray that these writings will inspire in you the necessary brilliance to win my case. But whatever happens, sir, please be assured that, for your efforts in my behalf, you have my everlasting gratitude.

PART II

Seth's Story

33

*D*oggone it, Abel, I don't see why you need me to tell you anything. You're my closest friend. You know the facts. The rest is all private stuff. Do the intimate details matter that much in a court of law? Yes, of course I know the information's privileged. Even so . . .

Very well, if you think it necessary I'll relate the whole to you as I remember it, though I feel like the damnedest fool relating matters that I've never spoken of to a soul. Especially since I hate like the devil having to bring this suit against Rachel in the first place. It'll break her heart. I swear, Abel, I didn't know I was capable of an act of such cruelty. I feel like a damned murderer. If the boy wasn't mine, and if I didn't have this . . . this terrible, deep feeling for him that, believe me, I don't understand and have no idea how it came upon me . . . I'd never . . .

Yes, you're right. If I'm to win this blasted case, I'll have to stop berating myself. Very well, then, herewith my tale . . .

34

I don't remember exactly when I first began to realize I wanted Rachel for my wife. It's strange, really, how I ever came to think of it at all. I'd always believed that the lovely Rachel Weller was beyond my reach.

I needn't tell you how every man in town used to goggle at her when she came along the street. Remember how we all would come to our doors and watch her pass? How the customers at Hansen's would crowd into his oriel window with their glasses in their hands and gape at her? And how Charlie Lund at the livery stable would freeze in the very act of swinging his hammer and keep staring with his arm up in the air? Up and down the street the men would pause in their activities and watch her go by. Rachel's passage. It was like a ship's, leaving a wake behind.

I couldn't really fathom it. Rachel was indeed lovely to look at, but in a quiet, unobtrusive way. She wasn't particularly elegant or distinguished, just a simple country girl, unpretentious and unadorned. So why did the mere fact of her passing by distract all the men?

It might've been the sweetness of the little half-smile that lit her face. Or the sparkling brightness of her eyes. Or the grace of her walk, that dance in her step—the way she'd swing her arms and shoulders, the slight sway of her hips—that couldn't be disguised even in those awful boots she used to wear. There was something so artlessly feminine in the way she moved that I myself felt drawn to watch her, despite feeling foolish when I did.

I recall one day when I looked up from my desk and saw Billy Shupp gaping out at her. I came up behind him to get my share of the sight of her, and the boy pressed his hands against his stomach and looked up at me with what I can only describe as agony. "Y'know, Mr. Trahern," he mumbled, "when I look at her it hurts right here!"

I knew just what the boy meant, for I felt the same way. Rachel would pass by and leave behind a kind of ache. As if one had experienced a wisp of a delicious dream that, on waking, one knew could never come true.

What remained in Rachel's wake was a hopeless yearning.

Of course, I didn't think of her for myself. I was too old for her, for one thing—almost thirty. And for another, this scar of mine . . . I thought it frightened the women off. I remember my own mother weeping and wailing about it when I came back from the war. I was but fifteen when I ran off to fight the British, and in my very first battle—the one at Hannah's Cowpens—I was slashed. The war ended soon after, but my face was pretty well healed by the time my mother saw the wound. Yet she carried on as if I were still bleeding. She took my face in her hands, tears streaming down her face. "My beautiful boy," she cried over and over in that Scottish tongue of hers, "what ha'e they *done* to ye?" It's no wonder I didn't think of myself as the answer to a female's prayers.

So trying to court a true beauty like Rachel Weller was out of the question for me. Nevertheless, I was always fascinated with her. And I realized, even years ago, that there was more to Rachel than being fair of face.

Now don't raise your eyebrows like that, Abel. I'm not the sort of fool who attributes depth of character to a woman because she has a pretty face, as some men do. You know Rachel, after all. I've even heard you say that she's different from the pretty girls who preen when you look at them. You've always remarked on the unusual modesty and sweetness she has about her. What I'd noticed—long before I had anything personal to do with her—was that she had this way of looking at people with a kind of intensity, as if she were trying to read their souls. Back in those days I noticed things about her that had nothing to do with her appearance. How she'd slip an arm around old Mrs. Magill's waist to help her up the church steps, or tend Abby Weller's baby when Abby came to town to visit the draper's. By God, just seeing her with that baby on her shoulder was enough to make a man want to be a father!

And I remember one summer, at one of the ladies' circle picnic suppers, when she truly won my admiration. I was playing chess with Courtland, and between moves we joked about the young girls who were strutting about and giggling to try to get the attention of the young men. I noticed that Rachel, who couldn't have been more than sixteen, was not participating in the flirting games but was sitting by herself watching the young children play. One of the children—Harry Simpson, who was probably about twelve at the time but very big for his age—was being hounded by one of the smaller ones. Harry was a head taller than the little teaser and tried his best to hold him off without hurting him, but the smaller boy kept tormenting him. Finally Harry lost patience and hauled off a good swat at the other boy, who immediately began yowling as if he'd been badly trounced. The mothers all ran over, and the Widow Rouse, jumping to conclusions as is her wont, began to beat poor Harry across his shoulders with her parasol, calling him a bully. Rachel jumped up, wrenched the parasol from Widow Rouse's grasp and made an impassioned defense of the boy. "Just because he's large," she scolded, "you needn't assume he's a bully." Widow Rouse was so surprised at being opposed, especially from so unexpected a source as the quiet Rachel, that her mouth fell agape.

Rachel stood there like an avenging angel and made the little boy apologize to Harry. The mothers, shamed, brought Harry a plate of peach pie and cookies. I think Harry Simpson fell in love with Rachel on the spot. And in truth, so did I.

But believe me, Abel, wooing her was the farthest thing from my mind.

35

I'm speaking the truth, Abel. Marriage was *not* of interest to me. There are wantons aplenty hanging about at Hansen's waiting to satisfy a man's appetites. And as you know full well, having sat in my shop a thousand nights arguing with me about politics, I was too preoccupied with the actions of the federal government to think about wedlock.

The time I'm speaking of was about a year before Jefferson's first election, and Adams had signed those nightmarish Alien and Sedition Acts. In our town everyone but you and Courtland thought Hamilton had lost his mind. In spite of my feeling of disgust at those acts, I'd written an editorial for the paper that week defending Adams on other matters, and all the Jeffersonians in town were furious with me. So when Joss Weller appeared at the door of my shop, I thought he'd come to berate me.

It had snowed the night before, and by morning a sharp drop in temperature had covered the ground with a crisp veneer of ice. I found it surprising that Joss Weller had battled the cold and the unpleasant conditions of the road just to argue about my editorial. But there he was, bundled up in that funny sheepskin-lined coat of his, with a cap tied onto his head with a long, knitted muffler. He was red-nosed and bone-cold by the time he reached my door, yet his greeting was unusually jovial as he stamped the snow from his boots. But so many fellows had come in to complain about what I'd written that I was on the defensive. "Listen, Joss," I said before the man had a chance to open his mouth, "just because a man's a Jefferson supporter doesn't mean he can't give Adams credit when credit is due."

Weller blinked in surprise. "What? I didn't come to—"

But I just ignored the interruption and went on with my diatribe. "I've written often enough against President Adams' closeness to the arch-Federalists who fill his cabinet and have his ear. But now he's averted a war with France. When this deed is coupled with other recent events, it seems to me Mr. Adams has regained the wisdom, moderation, and solid good sense that he showed in earlier days."

Weller wrinkled his brow. "Can't say I agree," he remarked. "You turnin' into a Hamilton man, Seth?"

I glared at him. "You know better than that. I can give the president credit when it's due without becoming a member of the Federalists, can't I?"

"Sounds wishy-washy to me." He rubbed his chin dubiously. "Don't know enough to answer you proper, but it sure goes against my grain to say a good word for the damn Feds."

"That's just the trouble with this country now," I said. "Too much partisanship. I tell you, Joss, the whole atmosphere's been poisoned by a cloud of dishonesty, disgust, despair, and doom."

Weller suddenly grinned. "You're sure a smooth talker when the subject's politics, Seth Trahern."

I immediately felt foolish for pontificating. "I'm only quoting what I just wrote for next week's editorial," I said, abashed. "Couldn't have said it so smoothly otherwise."

"Sure you could. I heard you do it lots of times."

"Only when I've downed a few." By then it began to dawn on me that he didn't seem to want to argue. In fact, it was suddenly apparent that he hadn't even *read* the controversial editorial. Now it was my turn to be puzzled. "But you surely didn't come out on a day like this to admire my oratory, Joss. Why did you come?"

"It's somethin' personal," Joss said, looking suddenly awkward. "Come with me to the tavern, and I'll tell you over a pint."

I blinked, completely at a loss. But I nodded and reached for the heaviest coat of the few hanging from the hooks on my wall. Then I turned to Billy. "When you've finished Frisch's notices, you can start on the folding."

"Right," Billy said, not looking up from the printing press.

So out we went into the cold. We had to lower our heads against the wind. Joss wrapped his muffler over his ears, but I had no head covering. I remember how my hair pulled from its riband and whipped about my face. We were unable to speak, for the wind would have torn the words from our tongues. We trudged silently down the street to the tavern. Once inside, we caught our breaths and ordered two brews. Hansen was leaning on the bar reading a much-handled newspaper. "What've you got there, Hansen?" I inquired.

"The Philadelphia *Gazette*. A traveler passin' through from the north left it yesterday. You c'n have it, Seth, though it's more'n a week old."

"Thanks," I said gratefully. "There's always something in a Philadelphia newspaper I can use. I'll take it when I leave."

"What do y'mean, something you can use?" Joss asked as we started across the taproom.

"For my paper," I explained. "I read every big-city newspaper I can get my hands on, looking for nuggets to pass on. It's one of the ways I find out what's going on in the world."

We took seats at a small table in a corner of the room in front of Hansen's large window. There was no need to worry about privacy; except for the portly, slow-moving Hansen, no one was there. "Well, what's on your mind, Joss?" I asked, full of curiosity. "You didn't come out today just to ask about the newspaper business."

"I'll come right out with it," Joss said. "I want to talk to you about my Rachel."

I was caught completely by surprise. "Rachel?"

"You asked me t'other day if she was promised to the Mason boy. Do you remember?"

"Yes, but—"

"An' I said 'over my dead body.'"

"Yes, I remember."

"Well, later, I asked Sarah about it."

I was utterly bewildered. "About *it*?"

"Him. About *him*."

"The Mason boy," I repeated, trying to understand.

"Yes, the Mason boy, of course!" Joss said impatiently. "See, I thought I ought to make sure there was nothing in it—in Rachel's interest in the boy—for me to worry over. And Sarah said it was only calf-love. Nothing . . . er . . . meaningful, if you get my drift."

I gave an affirmative nod, but I didn't know what he

was talking about. I kept searching Weller's face to find a clue to his intention. "I suppose, feeling as you do about Peter Mason, you're relieved," I remarked, just to keep up my end of the conversation. "But I don't see why you're telling *me* all this."

"I thought you'd be interested."

It was as if the man was speaking another language. "Why did you think that?"

"Because you asked me about Rachel and the Mason boy in the first place."

"Oh, I see." I didn't see a thing, but I felt a flush come up on my neck, and I shifted uncomfortably in my chair. "I suppose I shouldn't have asked," I mumbled. "Not any business of mine."

Joss looked miserable, as if the conversation was not proceeding at all in the way he'd expected. I, on the other hand, felt positively thick-headed. If he had a purpose in discussing the subject of his daughter with me, I had no idea what it was.

Poor Joss squirmed in his seat. "Since you'd asked," he said lamely, "I wanted to assure you that Rachel ain't serious about that slacker Mason."

I didn't see why Joss felt he had to assure me of anything. Yet, since he seemed so uncomfortable, I felt I had to say something. "Well . . . uh . . . thank you," I mumbled.

This took Weller by surprise. "Thank me? For what?"

"For telling me."

"That's all you have to say?"

I shrugged helplessly. "To be honest, Joss, I don't know what you're expecting me to say. In fact, I don't know what we're talking about."

Weller looked at me like a drowning man. He was struggling to find words but seemed unable to do so. I simply sat there and waited. Finally he cleared his throat and plunged ahead as if determined to complete his mission, whatever it was. "Well, see, we thought . . . Sarah and me . . . that—"

But Hansen chose that moment to waddle toward us with two mugs of porter, forcing a cessation of what I was beginning to guess was going to be some sort of delicate negotiation.

We exchanged the usual remarks with Hansen about the weather being bad for business. When Hansen finally left us, Joss picked up his mug and took a long swig before resuming. "To get back to what we were saying," he said, "Sarah and me, we thought your question about my girl showed that you were—how shall I put it?—*interested* in her."

But I still didn't grasp his intent. "Interested?" I asked bewilderedly. "In what way?"

Joss, his patience snapped, slammed down in his mug. "In what way do you think?" he barked. "In the way of marriage."

"*Marriage?*" I felt my face freeze in amazement. "Are you saying . . . Rachel and *m-me?*"

"Who *else* am I talkin' to?"

"That's . . . that's *ridiculous!*" It *was* ridiculous, I told myself, and I meant every word. But my voice, I noted, had been a croak. What was worse, my pulse had turned rapid. Why, I wondered? Was it merely from shock or . . . something else?

Joss gaped at me, as amazed by my reaction as I had been at the suggestion of marriage. "Do you mean to sit there and tell me you never thought of it yourself?" he asked after he'd recovered himself.

"No, of *course* not!" I said it firmly, although I felt the flush on my neck creep slowly up to my cheeks. "I wouldn't . . . I never . . ." I gulped so hard I could feel my Adam's apple wobble. I took a quick swallow of air. "Of course not."

Joss, not one for sensing undercurrents, heard nothing in this response but rejection. His temper flared up at once. "Why not? What's wrong with my Rachel? She's a fine girl, ain't she?"

"Well, yes, I . . . suppose she is."

"And clever?"

"As far as I know."

"And pretty, ain't she?"

I stared at him and then dropped my eyes to my brew. "She's the loveliest girl I ever laid eyes on," I said at last.

Joss's face immediately brightened with triumphant glee. "You said that in a voice you'd use in church."

I suppose I had. I'd given him a glimpse of so secret a feeling that even I hadn't realized how deep it was.

Though Joss was not usually a man to recognize subtleties, I suppose that glimpse was too plain to be missed. "Well, then," he said, leaning back in his chair, a smile suffusing his entire visage, "what are we sittin' here arguing about? You can't have any objections to weddin' the loveliest girl you ever laid eyes on."

The surprise now over, I could think logically again. "Yes, I can," I said with a sigh.

Joss rolled his eyes to heaven. "Damn it, man, you try my patience! What objections?"

"For one thing, I'm too old for her."

"No you ain't," Joss declared. "I don't think so, and neither does Sarah."

"What does *Rachel* think?" I asked pointedly.

That was a poser to Joss. He sat up and fiddled with the handle of his mug. "Well, I . . . we didn't discuss anything of this with her," he admitted. "Wanted to know your intentions first."

I shook my head. "I don't have intentions. Until you brought up the subject, I never thought of such a thing."

"Do you mean to sit there an' tell me you never gave a thought to the girl you say is so deuced lovely?"

"Not in the marrying way."

"In what way, then?"

I remember making an impatient movement with my hand, trying to fend off this barrage of impertinent questions. "In an admiring way," I said dismissively. "From a distance."

But Joss had had that glimpse of my insides, and the revelation gave him confidence. "And when you asked about her and Peter Mason," he taunted, "I'm supposed to b'lieve that was from a *distance?*"

I winced. "I never should have asked it, that much is plain. But you're making too much of it. I asked the question in simple friendship. I didn't think Peter was a good enough choice for her. It doesn't follow that I was offering myself in his place."

"Well, *I'm* makin' the offer. I'm inviting you to take my daughter in marriage. My sweet, fine, clever, lovely daughter. You ain't gonna turn me down, are you?"

I didn't answer for a long, long moment. The thought that I might truly wed the glorious Rachel began to sink in. It was music in my brain. How could I just ignore it?

Joss waited in silent suspense. "I don't know," I mumbled at last. I remember getting up, turning to the window behind me, and staring out at the snow-whitened, empty street.

Joss came up behind me. "Seth, my boy," he said gently, "you can't just say you don't know. You must tell me something. I think, from all the signs, that you care for the girl. Am I right about that?"

"I lied, Joss," I heard myself saying. "I *did* think of her in a marrying way. Every time I saw her I thought of it. When she passed by my shop window with that dancing step of hers—light as a dandelion seed, even in her brother's clumpish boots—I thought of it. Or when I caught a glimpse of her bent head at church, with her shiny thick braid hanging down her back, I thought of it. But it was really more a dream than a thought. It's a damn foolish thing for a grown man to admit, but, yes, I sometimes did let myself dream of wedding Rachel Weller."

"Aha!" Joss cried in triumph. "So say the word, and the dream'll come to pass."

It's strange, Abel, but when I turned to answer him, I felt more like a man who'd lost a battle than one whose dream was about to come to pass. "I'll be honored to wed your daughter, Joss," I said quietly. "But only if she wants me."

As it turned out, she didn't want me at all.

36

I tell you she didn't! I'd be flattered, old man, by your insistence that I'm such a catch except for my awareness that an old bachelor like you has not the least notion of what a young, lovely creature like Rachel wanted in a man. You may safely take my word that it was not I she wanted.

I learned that soon enough. Not two days after Joss made his bid to me, Sarah Weller invited me to dinner for the express purpose of giving me the opportunity to make my offer, but from the moment I arrived I could see that Rachel was opposed to the idea. She was cold and formal and barely said a word during dinner. I tried to tell myself that she was just nervous, but it wasn't the blushing, shy kind of nervousness one would expect from a girl who was looking forward to a proposal of marriage. It was more . . . well, glowering. A kind of ill temper that one can't hide when one is forced to do something against one's will.

And afterwards, when Sarah pushed us both into the parlor and promptly disappeared, it became harder and harder for me to fool myself. The girl just didn't like me. And I couldn't blame her. Not only was I years older than she and not nearly as good-looking as Peter Mason (who I knew was still in her memory), but I was behaving like a tongue-tied gawk. In spite of my ability to write thousands of words a day, I could think of nothing to say to her. I mumbled all sorts of nonsense, which she promptly and sensibly dismissed.

As I grew more unsure of myself, she grew more confident. She teased me unmercifully about my lack of conversation and actually challenged me to flirt with her. I told her I had no talent in that regard. She retorted that it didn't take talent, only the ability to pay her compliments, even if I had to invent them. Any fool would have had the presence of mind to say there was no need to invent compliments for so lovely a creature as she, but instead, like a pompous ass, I said, "In my newspaper, ma'am, I deal with facts, not invention."

She burst into laughter. "Then is there nothing to admire in the 'facts' of me?" she taunted.

Well aware of how stupid I was being, I nevertheless reacted with anger. I suddenly wondered what I was doing there. . . Why I was allowing myself to be a victim of this female torturer. I hadn't wanted to do this in the first place; Joss had pushed me. I wasn't even sure, at that point, that I cared for the girl at all. All I knew was that I wanted to make a quick retreat. I made some sort of excuse and stalked out—not without stumbling over the doorsill first. Blast! What a great gawk I was!

Sarah and Joss stopped me at the door, quite overset by what was obviously the complete failure of their plan. I told them that the suggestion of matrimony between myself and their daughter had been grossly misconceived, and I went out with all the speed I could muster.

I felt humiliated, degraded, misused. I determined never, never to subject myself to such an experience again. Ironically, however, I did. Within a month. But with another woman.

37

I denied to myself that I'd found Rachel's rejection painful, but I fell into a deep dejection nevertheless. I suppose Joss had raised my marital expectations so high that the fall was a blow. You will probably not remember, Abel, that you yourself sensed my despair and asked me what was wrong. I admitted to you that I'd offered for a girl who'd rejected me, though I did not name her. "Damnation, Abel," I remember saying, "I've always thought of myself as a reasonable man, and it's not reasonable to become so dejected after what is really nothing more than a minor incident."

"Proposing to a female for the first time in one's life is hardly a minor incident," you said, trying to console me without prying into the details.

"Yes, it is," I insisted. "I don't know why I did it. Before I embarked on this foolish business, I never thought of wedding anyone. I was perfectly content with my life."

"And when you shake off this mood," you assured me, "you will be so again."

But days went by, and my dejection remained.

It was at this low point that I received an invitation from my aunt, my favorite of my mother's three sisters, to visit her in south Delaware to celebrate her sixty-fifth birthday. Aunt Parry is a tiny but very hardy woman with a great enthusiasm for living. She'd already outlived all her siblings and two husbands, and she'd recently been wed to her third, Mr. Horace Fillmore, a distiller of hard cider. The thrice-wed Aunt Parry liked, more than anything else, to entertain guests in her home.

Her invitation seemed opportune. I believed that a brief escape from my surroundings into Aunt Parry's cheerful domain would lift me from the depression that had become my constant companion. I promptly closed the shop and told Billy Shupp to take a week's holiday. Billy could hardly believe it. He was quick to point out that, for the first time in the history of the *Newcastle Register*, the weekly issue would not appear. I assured him that the town would survive. Then I packed up my Sunday coat and some clean linen, hitched two horses to my trap, and rode off on the four-hour journey south.

In the innocent way of bachelors, I had no idea of my aunt's true purpose in inviting me to her birthday celebration, but it didn't take long for me to learn what it was. Immediately after she'd greeted me with effusive embraces, Aunt Parry whispered to me that her new husband's niece was also visiting. "All the way from New York City," she added excitedly. Then she took my arm and almost dragged me to the parlor. Before I was permitted even to nod to the other guests, she led me to a strikingly handsome young woman seated on the window seat. "Nancy, dear," Aunt Parry gushed, "here at last is my adored nephew, Seth Trahern, whom I've spoken of so often. And Seth, my love, make your bow to Miss Nancy Fillmore." And if that were not evidence enough, by the time I'd endured Aunt Parry's machinations at dinner that evening (where she made certain I was seated right beside Miss Fillmore), I had no doubt that matchmaking was her object.

I didn't really mind. Miss Fillmore had dark, abundant hair, brilliant black eyes, and the pronounced, shapely features of an actress. And she was no simpering miss. She had strong views on everything from house furnishings to politics and expressed them very readily and with firm conviction. Her manner was so confident that I could hardly believe she was but twenty. I could only deduce that living in New York City gave a young woman an air of worldliness. I was quite impressed with her. I liked the way she strode into the room, I liked the directness with which she asked how I'd gotten my scar, I liked the way her eyes flashed when she defended Alexander Hamilton against my attacks. I began to wonder if the companionship of the engaging Miss Fillmore could drive Rachel from my mind.

Nevertheless, later that evening, when Aunt Parry showed me to my bedroom, I accused her of blatant trickery. "Don't deny it, ma'am," I said. "Your birthday party was just a ruse to hoodwink me."

She responded with a hearty laugh. "True, my boy, too true. But 'tis for yer own good."

There were still traces of the Scottish brogue she'd spoken in her childhood on her tongue. The sound reminded me of my mother and added to my feeling of affection for this little woman, despite her managing ways. But I would not let the delicious brogue keep me from delivering a much-deserved scold. "It's always the excuse of the interfering females to declare that their machinations are for their victims' own good."

"Oh, victims, pish-tush," Aunt Parry retorted. "Time ye were wedded. Past time, if ye'd ask me. If yer mother were alive, she'd've had you leg-shackled long before this. So, since ye won't do somethin' for yerself, the matter is left to me."

"But I have done something for myself," I admitted ruefully. "I've made a girl an offer."

"Have ye? *Truly?*" Aunt Parry clapped her hands together, as happily excited as a child. "Then why didn't ye tell me at once that y're bespoke?"

"I'm not bespoke. She refused me."

Aunt Parry's face fell. "No! I'll not believe—! Who *is* the foolish chit?"

"It doesn't matter. You haven't met her."

"Oh, ye poor dearie," she said, wrapping her arms about my waist in motherly affection, "but it doesn't matter a fig, for I've picked out the perfect partner for ye. Y're taken wi' the girl yerself, I'll wager. I saw the way ye were watchin' her at the table."

"Yes, I suppose I was. But 'tis a mark of shallow feelings, is it not, to turn so promptly in pursuit of this woman after offering for another just a sennight since?"

"Nay, lad, don't trouble yer mind. It ain't shallow feelings. In my eyes, it shows ye have courage."

My aunt's response seemed to be mere empty words, but later, lying awake in the unfamiliar bed, I turned them over in my mind. Perhaps Aunt Parry was right, I thought. Perhaps pursuing a second woman so soon after being humiliated by the first was taking a risk— the risk of a second humiliation. When looked at in that light, the act *could* be considered brave. It was a comforting thought.

Nothing happened on the second day of the visit to disillusion me about the exciting Miss Fillmore. Aunt Parry, delighted to see me getting on with Nancy so well, encouraged me to take charge of her attractive

guest—to take her walking in the morning and riding
in the afternoon. It turned out to be a most pleasant day.
In the evening, the whole company—the hostess, her
new husband, and several other houseguests—repaired
to Aunt Parry's parlor after dinner, where Miss Fillmore
entertained us all by singing lively ditties while accom-
panying herself on a beribboned guitar. "Isn't she
enchanting?" Aunt Parry asked me repeatedly, beaming
at me in fond expectation.

"Charming," I agreed, my eyes fixed on the dark-
eyed singer.

For the next two days I tried to convince myself that
Nancy Fillmore was indeed enchanting. I told myself
that, compared to a certain young lady in New Castle,
she was in many ways more desirable, to wit:

- Miss Fillmore read newspapers and knew about
  politics, which Rachel didn't;
- Miss Fillmore sang and played the guitar, which
  Rachel didn't;
- Miss Fillmore liked me, which Rachel didn't.

I felt suddenly quite cheerful. I basked in the illusion
that I'd conquered my feelings for Rachel Weller. I truly
believed I was entirely heart-whole again.

By the fourth day, however, my cheerfulness began
to dissipate. After listening to Miss Fillmore repeatedly
interrupt Uncle Horace's political remarks to express her
own, after finding her nightly concerts growing longer
and less pleasing (for the young woman seemed to
demand more and more praise for her efforts), and after
having once too often found it necessary to fend off her
less than subtle coquetry, I was ready to admit the truth,
to wit:

- Miss Fillmore was rude, which Rachel wasn't;
- Miss Fillmore was peacocky, which Rachel wasn't;
- Miss Fillmore was a flirt, which Rachel wasn't.

I realized that the wisest course was to cut the visit short. "I must get back," I told my aunt. "You see, Aunt Parry, I would not be playing fair with my subscribers if I fail for two weeks in a row to put out an issue."

"But ye can't leave now," Aunt Parry cried, "with nothing settled between you and Nancy."

"Nothing to settle," was my brief response.

"But ye . . . ye *like* the girl! Ye liked 'er from the first moment ye set eyes on 'er. Ye told me so."

"Yes, I did. But to be honest, Aunt Parry, I changed my mind."

My tiny aunt glowered at me. "What do ye mean, changed yer mind? One day she's charming an' the next she ain't?"

I was sorry to have misled my aunt into believing her matchmaking scheme had a chance of success. "I'll admit this much," I said awkwardly, "I am sometimes hasty in making judgments. In all probability Miss Nancy Fillmore is neither so attractive as I imagined her at first nor so distasteful as I find her at last. It's plain she'll make someone a more than satisfactory wife. But not me." I leaned down and kissed my aunt's cheek. "Sorry, my dear. You made a good try."

But in truth I wasn't sorry. I no longer wished to pursue Miss Fillmore. It was Rachel I wanted. All other women would fail in comparison.

Aunt Parry knew enough about human nature to refrain from insisting, although she said to me at my departure that she was greatly distressed to see me go. If

Miss Fillmore was distressed as well, she had too much pride to show it.

On the ride home I came to a decision. I would make no future attempt to take myself a wife. I was a bachelor by nature, and a bachelor I would remain. The moment I made that pledge, I felt a wonderful peace of mind.

It did not last, of course. The very next time Rachel passed by the shop, the same old depression overwhelmed me. I would be a bachelor, that was true, but I'd always have an ache inside that, clearly, no one but Rachel could ever ease.

So how is it that I managed to wed her after all? Simple. She came and asked me.

38

*B*elieve me, no one could have been more startled than I. Months had gone by. Except for one occasion when she'd asked me to try to discover what had become of Peter Mason, Rachel and I had not exchanged a single word.

On the day she made me the proposal, Billy Shupp was outside washing the shop windows when he saw her heading in our direction. He dropped the washcloth into the bucket and ran into the shop. "She's comin' again!" he exclaimed excitedly. "I swear to God I think she's comin' again."

I was brushing ink onto a pair of leather inkpads, holding both pads by their handles in one hand and the inkbrush in the other. "Who?" I asked while carefully painting the rounded ends of the pads with the thick black ink.

"Her! Miz Weller!"

I spun around, my heart jumping about like a schoolboy's. My elbow knocked the inkpot to the floor, and a small black puddle began oozing out. I ignored it, blinking at the shadow that had just appeared on the opaque glass of the doorway. Completely unnerved, I hurriedly placed the inkpads on their stand on the worktable. The inking-brush was still in my hand, however. I made a hasty and bumbling attempt to pick up the pot and place the brush in it, but the ink was all over the outside of the pot and not only left thick black smears on the table but on both my hands.

The doorhandle turned. I gulped, put a hand to my forehead to brush away this bushy hair of mine, and immediately realized that I must have made a black smudge across my forehead.

The doorbell jingled, and she came in.

She seemed to bring a breath of spring into the shop with her, though it was a gray, chilly day, more like February than April. I can still see her. She looked as clean and fresh as the daffodils that were bursting into bloom in front of the shop. Her face was shiny and just-scrubbed, and her hair was tied back at the nape of her neck with a blue ribbon, like a schoolgirl on her first day of Bible class. She was wearing a shawl with flecks the exact color of those daffodils, over a blouse whose collar was pristine in its starched white smoothness. And a smell of lilacs wafted in with her. It made me dizzy.

She looked from my streaked face, my blackened hands, and the mess on the floor to Billy Shupp's wide-eyed expression. "Oh, dear," she exclaimed in embarrassment, "have I come at . . . at an awkward time?"

"No, not at all," I assured her. "A little carelessness on my part. It happens all the time."

"Huh!" Billy sneered, for he'd never known me to slop the ink, much less drop an entire inkpot on the floor. I tend to be scrupulously neat and strict about the cleanliness of the shop. "How can the printed sheets be clean if your tools and your hands aren't?" is something I always point out to my apprentices.

But I didn't pay any mind to Billy. I was too busy trying to hide my inner turmoil from public view. Though "inner turmoil" is a completely inadequate phrase to describe what I was feeling on seeing Rachel in my shop again. I swear my damn heart was thumping so hard that I actually wondered how I could keep it from exploding. "Is there something I can do for you?" I managed to croak.

"Well, I . . ." She glanced at Billy again.

Not taking my eyes from my visitor's face, I put a dirty hand in my pocket, pulled out a quarter-dollar, and told Billy to take himself off to Hansen's for a mobby.

"Don't you want me to mop up that mess first?" Billy asked, hoping he'd be able to stay around and overhear.

"No," I said, and I made a firm head-gesture toward the door.

The boy, knowing what was good for him, left at once.

"Won't you sit down?" I asked Rachel, indicating the bench near the stove.

She shook her head, somewhat uneasily I thought. "May as well say what I've come to say standing up. So if I'm refused, I can run away faster."

"I won't refuse you anything," I assured her, trying to sound as kind as I could, though I feared that I might heave something heavy through my window if she asked me to find out anything more about Peter Mason.

"Thank you for saying that," she said. "But I wouldn't wager on it if I were you. You see, I've come to . . . to ask you . . . a . . . a very *intimate* question."

"Indeed?" I sounded to my own ears like a fatuous uncle. "It's not often that young ladies come in here with intimate questions." And I told her to ask me flat out whatever it was and get it over with.

She agreed. She squared her shoulders and said, "Mr. Trahern, what I want to know is . . ." She expelled a nervous breath and then proceeded in a rush. ". . . do you still want to wed me?"

I couldn't believe my ears. "What?" I asked stupidly.

She seemed to take that as a refusal. Her face clouded and her lower lip began to tremble. "There, you see? There *are* some things you'd refuse me." She took a backward step and turned to run away.

But I wouldn't permit her to go . . . not just yet. I'd heard enough to want to hear more. I grasped her hand and pulled her back. "Wait!" I demanded, utterly bemused. "What, exactly, have I refused?"

"My proposal," she said flatly, seeming to find it easier to admit now that the matter was out in the open. "I asked you to marry me."

"Did you?" I remember shaking my head in disbelief, though I'd heard her well enough.

She looked down at the hand I held, now marked with a black smudge. "Perhaps I didn't say it very well."

I looked, too. "Oh, drat, look at what I've done to you," I muttered.

"'Tis naught."

"'Tis not naught," I insisted, playing for time. I needed to get my wits in order. "You'll have to scrub that dirt with lye soap. Just my luck to be covered with ink the one time in my life a beautiful young lady makes me a proposal."

The corners of her mouth turned up in a small smile. "You do look a sight," she said, and she put a timid finger on the smudge on my cheek.

It's wonderful how a man can be soothed by a woman's touch. I felt a warm glow spread right through me. I grasped that hand, too, and peered down at her earnestly. "Are you certain you mean this, Rachel? I thought you found me a bore."

"I never said such a thing. And if I did, I was a stupid child to say it." She smiled at me ruefully. "If you're going to throw all my foolish remarks in my face, Mr. Trahern, we shall never get to the point."

"But it *is* the point. I told your father I'd be the happiest man in the world if I could wed you. But only if you wished it. *Do* you wish it, my dear?"

She dropped her eyes from my face. "Why else would I be here?"

"Because your parents sent you, perhaps?"

"They don't know anything about this."

"Then look at me, Rachel, and tell me to my face that you wish it."

She met my eyes. For a long time she studied my face. I don't know what she read in my expression—maybe it gave her an inkling of how much I loved her—but whatever it was, I could see a glow come into hers. "I wish it, Seth," she assured me. "Truly."

I don't know, Abel, confirmed old bachelor that you are, if you can imagine what I felt. A palpable shiver of joy ran right through me. A dream that seemed completely beyond my reach was suddenly on the verge of becoming a reality! It was too much good fortune to be believed. In fact, I suddenly wondered if I *should* permit myself to believe it. I was old enough to know that when fortune is too good to be believed, it shouldn't be. I knew better than to surrender too easily to foolish euphoria. Besides, there was something between us—something crucial—that was still unspoken. How could I let myself feel euphoric when I knew full well that I was avoiding a matter that should be discussed? On the other hand, how could I bear to spoil this moment by bringing the matter up?

She saw the change in my expression and seemed

stricken with fear. "My wishing it is not enough then?" she asked.

I dropped my hold on her hands and turned aside. "Before we go further," I said, not looking at her, "there's something I ought to ask."

"Ask, then."

So I did. Bluntly. "Does this mean you've outgrown Peter Mason?"

"*Outgrown?*" She stiffened as if I'd shot her. "You are presuming that my feelings for him were childish," she said in furious offense. "The truth is that there was nothing childish about them."

I felt as if two hands had clenched my throat. "You still love him, then?"

Rachel bit her lip. I think she was thinking of how to answer me. I suppose she thought that if she answered truthfully, she'd lose me. "I won't lie," she said. "I think I will always love him."

Of course she would. I knew the answer before I'd asked. But even knowing it, I felt the joy seep out of me like the air from a punctured balloon. "Then, for God's sake, woman," I burst out angrily, "why are you here?"

She shrugged, unable now to say anything but the truth. "I believe he's surely dead. I am ready to begin a new life."

I winced. "That's not what I wanted to hear," I mumbled miserably.

"I know," she said. "I'm sorry. I would like to say I love only you. Perhaps, one day . . ." She looked at me with frightened eyes. "But that's a poor offering, I suppose. Shall I consider myself refused?"

I stared at her, so lovely, so innocent, her eyes clearly revealing her fear that she'd spoken too much truth.

Well, I have as much pride as the next fellow, and, my word on it, Abel, I wanted to reject her. But I could not. Not with her eyes peering at me in that vulnerable way. "How can I refuse?" I admitted. "I was able to walk away from you once, but not now."

Her relief was palpable, but she couldn't accept it without asking, "Why is it different now?"

It was the strangest moment of the whole strange interview. What I felt was both this enormous pain and a gentle, forgiving affection. "Because you came here to me, all by yourself, offering yourself to me. No one else made you do it. That's too precious a gift to be refused." But I couldn't help adding, "even if you must hold some of it back."

She did not resent the afterthought. "Thank you, Seth," she said, "that was . . . kind."

I didn't feel at all kind. I felt as if I'd been in a battle, and I was losing. But I couldn't explain it to myself, much less to her. "I feel more confused than anything else," was all I could think of to say.

"Yes, I know," she said, her voice warm with sympathy. "Me, too. But do you mean you'll *do* it, then? *Marry* me?"

"Yes," I said. "Yes, I will." It was a sort of surrender.

A deep sigh escaped her. She knew she'd won, but she was too fine to gloat. "I hope, Seth," she said, choked, "that you'll not come to regret this."

Having surrendered, I let myself be happy. I smiled at her. "How can I feel regret? What I feel most of all is fortunate. More fortunate than I ever expected or deserved." I wanted to take her in my arms. It was so strong an urge that it clenched my insides. But I was so besmirched with ink that I couldn't touch her. "You realize, don't you, that these inky hands are the only reason I am not crushing you in my arms," I said in self-disgust.

She came up to me, stood up on tiptoe, and kissed my one clean cheek. And that was the way we sealed what I suppose was the strangest betrothal in history.

39

I woke up on my wedding day feeling distinctly uneasy. What was I doing, I asked myself, marrying a woman whose heart ached for another? I was a good man, solid, reliable, sober, honest. I deserved better. I was sorely tempted to forswear it all and run.

I knew I wouldn't. I am not the sort to renege on an obligation. But the feeling of dismay did not leave me all day. By the late afternoon, dressed in my Sunday best and standing in the Wellers' parlor receiving good wishes from the few guests, I was so downcast I almost did run.

To make matters worse, the weather that day was unbearably hot. All the guests looked red-faced and uncomfortable as they sweltered in that airless room in the choking summer heat. And I probably looked more miserable than all of them; I could feel the sweat running down my back, and my mouth was so dry I didn't feel capable of saying a simple "I do."

And then my bride walked into the room.

Do you remember, Abel, how Rachel looked the day of our wedding? Yes, breathtaking is the word. She was slim as a reed in that soft, dove-colored dress that draped so sweetly over the curves of her. And I'd never seen her hair falling loose that way, with those little pink flowers woven in. They were just the color of her cheeks, and they gave her the perfect bridal air. I thought that never since Homer's Helen had there been so beautiful a creature on this earth. I forgot every misgiving that had filled my mind. When I took her hand as we stood before Reverend Phillips, I felt almost joyful.

Then I noticed Rachel glancing at the door. At first I thought nothing of it. But when she did it for the third time, it occurred to me that she might be hoping for a last-minute rescue, dreaming, perhaps, that the missing Peter Mason would burst in and wrest her from my arms. The thought effectively killed my joy in the occasion. Every time she looked over her shoulder, it was a blow to my innards.

I must own, Abel, that I was not a little disgusted with myself. What sort of man was I, my mind kept asking, to accept being someone's second choice?

But then, all in a moment—it was when Reverend Phillips was saying those words about entering the married state not blindly but advisedly and reverently—everything changed again. She glanced up at me with those eloquent, innocent eyes and smiled. It's a smile I grew to know well—that small, rueful smile she has when she's unsure of herself, an expression filled with a self-effacing charm. With that one look, my feelings of resentment and rebellion dissipated like dew in the sun, and I understood the truth: that I wanted her so badly I would take her on whatever terms I could get her. Second choice, third, *tenth*! What did it matter so long as she was mine at last?

It was humbling to discover I was so lacking in pride. But I consoled myself by swearing that I would one day win her full heart. I'd be so gentle, so protective, so loving, that in time she would forget Peter completely and care for me with an intensity that equaled my own.

We were strangers at first, I admit that. But I didn't press her. I let matters develop naturally. It took several months, but by the end of the year I truly believed I'd accomplished it. She'd grown to love me, I was convinced of it. Her face would light up whenever I came home. She even came to the shop to work, though God knows I never asked her to do it. It seemed to me that we could hardly bear to be apart from one another, day or night. She seemed so happy, so fulfilled in every way a wife can be. Yes, Abel, don't bother to ask. In *that* way especially! Damn it all, even now it's hard for me to believe I was fooling myself.

Those months when Rachel and I grew close to each other were paradise to me, fool's paradise though it was. I had never known such contentment, not before and certainly not since. But I should have been prepared for a catastrophe. Earthly paradises always have their snakes.

40

My joy came crashing to an end in one nightmarish day. Rachel had not come to the shop that morning. I had the impression she was not feeling well. I was working at my desk when Clara Gruenwald came running in. My heart immediately clenched in terror, for Clara had never before done such a thing. I stumbled to my feet, the blood draining from my face. "Clara? What's—?"

"Go home!" Clara wheezed breathlessly.

"Why? What's wrong? Has something happened to Rachel?"

"There's a man!" the woman said, sinking down on the bench and trying to catch her breath. "A no-good man. Go! Hurry!"

It made no sense, but I ran out at once. I ran all the way like a man demented, frightened almost witless without knowing why. I burst into the house and cried out her name. I heard a noise in the parlor and turned toward it. The parlor door was shut, a most unusual condition. I ran to it and flung it open. I know I was saying something, but the words died on my lips. I seemed to freeze in place. My eyes were taking in a scene that my brain was refusing to interpret. It took a moment to understand that my wife, my beloved, adored wife, was standing in the middle of the room with an expression of horror on her flushed face, her chest heaving, and her hand covering a naked breast. And on the sofa, sprawled in the classic position of a man interrupted in the midst of the act—bare to the waist, trews undone, and breathing hard—was Peter Mason.

I don't know if I can describe to you what I felt. I was like someone who's strolling contentedly along on solid ground when it suddenly gives way. You feel yourself falling down, down into what seems a bottomless pit, the winds whistling about your ears and the sunshine blotted out by an impenetrable darkness. As you fall, you sense certain things at once: that your days of happiness are over; that no matter what the outcome, life will never be the same; that you are a helpless mote in the stormy currents of chance, unable to affect any change, unable to steer a course in any direction other than the downward one that fate has swept you into. It's akin to descending into hell.

I barely remember the next few days. I don't even remember feeling pain. I was benumbed. I left the house, I know that. I slept at the shop until I learned that her mother had taken her home.

The next few days passed in a blur. I remember trying to reason out what had happened (strange how one clings to reason when one's world goes askew), to understand what Peter's return must have meant to Rachel. It was her girlhood dream that had amazingly come true. Agonizing though the admission was, I had to admit what was obvious: that no matter how much she'd cared for me, with the reappearance of Peter Mason I was once again relegated to my position of being second choice.

After some time, her father came to me and, teary-eyed

and miserable, discussed terms of a standaway. I agreed to everything he said, though I don't believe I heard a word.

Then, one night, when I left the shop to return to my starkly empty house, Rachel appeared out of the shadows and pleaded with me to reconsider the business. She said she had not asked for a standaway. I knew that she had not intended to hurt me, but I was in no mood to endure her misguided attempt at kindness. She was quite sincere, I think, in her feelings of loyalty, but I would have none of it. Her attempts to convince me that she wanted to remain my wife fell on deaf ears; second fiddle was no longer a part I wanted to play. I said some angry, hurtful things, reminded her that I'd seen what I'd seen, and I actually called her a wanton. Nevertheless, she persisted in her denials until I said flatly that I wanted neither her lies nor her pity, that she should take for herself the life she'd always dreamed of, and that I was perfectly capable of returning to my previous bachelor existence. Then I stalked off and left her standing there alone in the dark, feeling, I suppose, relief.

I did not see her again until the day you arranged the dissolution of our marriage.

I was glad that she and Peter went away. I don't know if I could have borne their continued proximity. I tried to forget her. I tried to refrain from asking Joss about her when he (infrequently now) came to the shop. I even tried to interest myself in courting someone else. Yes (don't look at me with that leer!), I did! Lucy Harper. I started out one evening to take her walking. But I didn't go through with it. It would have set up expectations I knew I could not in the end fulfill. I knew I would love Rachel all my days. I couldn't let an innocent woman learn the pain of being second best, at least not from me. I knew all too well that the price of being second choice was much too dear.

41

I know you think me a good sort of fellow, Abel, and so I used to think of myself. But I changed in the three years that Rachel was away. A dark side of me—one that I didn't know was there—began to grow. An anger, like the dark smoke of burning refuse, permeated my soul. You see, I'd become the most ludicrous figure a man of pride could be: a cuckold. When I went to church and people greeted me, I wondered what scorn was lurking behind their smiles. It seemed to me that the men who came to the shop to discuss politics had less respect for my views than they'd once had. I was uncomfortable with people and miserable when I was alone. I was so curt and gruff with everyone that Billy Shupp took it upon himself to lecture me on the subject. I knew he was right, but I didn't know how to change.

And I refused to take any blame for my actions. That my life had plunged so abruptly into despair was no fault of mine, I told myself. Rachel had done it to me. She'd used me shamefully when it had suited her and discarded me without a qualm when I'd become an inconvenience. She'd made a fool and a laughingstock of me. The thought of what she'd done became more unforgivable with every passing day. What had once been an unconditional adoration for the woman became a cesspool of resentment. I hated the very thought of her.

I tried to throw myself completely into work. My newspaper had always been my source of pride. I added four more pages to the size and spent every waking hour trying to fill them. You'll probably remember how I immersed myself in the Republican cause in the congressional election of 1801; we certainly had enough heated arguments about it. But when the Republicans eked out a mere twenty-vote plurality against the Federalists, it was scarcely enough of a triumph to bring me any satisfaction.

There was no satisfaction, either, in the fact that the number of my subscribers was stagnant. The population of the county was growing, but the *Newcastle Register* was not growing with it. New newspapers were starting up all around—new *Gazettes* and *Tribunes* and *Couriers* springing up wherever one looked. True, they printed all sorts of nonsense and gossip, carrying advertisements for dozens of foolish items from ladies' corsets to Jones's Chicken Water for curing gout, all the while trivializing the news that was important. But these newspapers were entertaining reading, and the competition among them was fierce. I knew it would not be possible for so many publications to survive. When I saw the number of my subscribers begin to decline, I feared I'd be among the failures. I had no wife, no children, and my assets were dwindling. I was on the verge of losing everything that had made living worthwhile. It was the lowest point of my life.

Obviously, life has improved for me since then. I credit the curative effects of time and a bit of good fortune for the gradual improvement of my circumstances. When the *Philadelphia Gazette* reprinted my editorial on extending the voting franchise beyond the propertied class, they appended a note declaring my writing to be "a prime example of the best of thoughtful journalism." Don't ask me how it happened or who it was at that newspaper who did it, but it changed my fortunes! When I first heard of it, I was pleased at the praise, of course, but I never expected word of it to spread as far abroad as it did. It was amazing! Subscriptions began to come in from as far away as western Pennsylvania, New Jersey, and Maryland's eastern shore. I felt an overwhelming gratitude to that unnamed Philadelphia editor when my subscription list began to grow again. What an enormous relief it was to realize that my newspaper would survive!

There was another circumstance that was balm to my wounded self-esteem. I've never told anyone about this, Abel, for fear of sounding like a braggart over a very minor triumph. A publisher from Philadelphia, who happened to read those encomiums about my writing, came to see me one day. He offered me a position as the editor of his newspaper at a very flattering salary. It's a large paper, with a circulation a hundredfold larger than mine. For a while I was tempted to accept the offer. I thought that perhaps, if I separated myself physically from New Castle, I might be able to put all my unpleasant memories behind me. But when I considered further, I realized that I never could. Those memories are as much part of me as this scar on my cheek. If I left here, I'd be taking my memories with me and losing my friends, my paper, my home, whatever was still good in my life. So I rejected the offer.

The Philadelphia man still asks permission every once in a while to reprint one of my editorials, for which he pays a tidy sum. You won't believe this, Abel, but my views on Mr. Jefferson's purchase of the Louisiana Territory—which you, if you remember, did not think very highly of—were reprinted from the Philadelphia paper to publications in both Boston and New York. And my diatribe against Aaron Burr after his shooting of poor Hamilton brought me letters from as far away as Kentucky and Maine.

I admit that the income from these writings is not impressive, but you yourself suggested another source of income for me. Do you remember your suggestion, that I invest in the new paper mill that Odell Senior was building? It was good advice, which I am glad I took. The mill's been paying off handsomely, and I must admit that there's nothing more nourishing to a fellow's self-esteem than the knowledge that he's becoming a man of financial substance.

With this improvement in my circumstances, you might expect an improvement in what I've been describing as the black side of my nature. But the miasma that filled my soul whenever Rachel came to my mind did not lighten. Even my last visit with Sarah Weller did little to ease the festering animosity that had become part of me.

Sarah, when she came down with the influenza, had a premonition that the attack would be her end. I suppose the illness was so debilitating—even at first, before it settled into her lungs and became pneumonia—that she knew she would not recover. A few days before she sank into the feverish stupor that led to her death, she sent for me. Joss, when he led me through to her bedroom, apologized for taking me out of my house on such a cold, blustery night, explaining that his wife had insisted on seeing me at once. I told him that no apology was necessary, that I was glad to have the opportunity to see her, but I couldn't help asking if there was any particular reason that made this visit urgent.

"Not as I know of," he said. "She won't tell me." He looked up at me, his eyes tearful. "She's goin' down fast. Dr. Muncie fears the good Lord'll be takin' her before the week is out. Don't be too much taken aback when ye see her."

I *was* taken aback. When last I'd seen her, a fortnight before at church, she'd been as strikingly imposing as ever. Though her hair had grayed since Rachel left, she was still sturdy and strong, sitting in the pew in that straight-backed way of hers, with her chin high and her hair braided round her head like a crown. Now, two weeks later, she seemed to have aged a decade. She lay back against the pillows, coughing feebly, her cheeks gaunt and greenish-white, her gray hair wild and lying loose around her head, her cheeks sunken, and her eyes unfocused. It was not until I sat down beside the bed and took her hot, dry hand in mine that her old alertness returned to her face. She looked at me closely. "Seth, my dear boy," she breathed hoarsely, "thank you for coming."

"I should have come sooner. I didn't know how ill you are. Is there something I can do for you, Sarah?" I asked.

"No, not for me. For you," she said between small spasms of coughing. "Joss, leave us for a bit."

When he'd gone, she struggled to lift herself higher on the pillows. I tried to help her, but she motioned me away. "Do you believe in the truth of deathbed pronouncements?" she asked suddenly.

I was surprised at the question. "I never thought about it," I admitted.

"Well, think about it. When someone realizes he's

soon to stand before his maker, he's not going to lie, is he? A deathbed statement, then, is likely to be trustworthy, is it not?"

"I suppose that's so," I said.

"Well, I'm about to make one to you."

"A deathbed statement?" I had to smile. Despite its hoarseness, her voice had had a touch of her old energy, so I could not believe she was at death's door. "Listen, woman," I said firmly, "you can't make me believe you're dying."

"'Tis God's truth, whatever you believe," she insisted.

"See here, Sarah, what is this nonsense? You don't have to make any deathbed declarations to me. I believe whatever you tell me, dying or not."

"Good, then," she said, "for you didn't believe it before, when Rachel told you, but perhaps you'll believe me now."

I winced. "If this is about Rachel, ma'am, I'd rather not—"

"Hear me out, Seth. 'Twill be healing for your soul to listen to me." She paused for a spell of coughing and then proceeded, her voice perceptibly weaker. "I know what you think happened that day . . . that day when the Mason fellow came back. But I know Rachel better than you. I went to her that day, saw her, talked to her, took care of her. She spoke the truth." She grasped my arm in a painful grip and spoke urgently. "*There was no criminal conversation between them.*"

I shook my head. "Sarah, *don't!*" I said, easing my arm from her hold. "What is the point now? She's married to him. There's no longer any relevance—"

"I'll go to my grave happier if I know you believe it." She lifted herself up on her elbows and fixed her eyes on my face. "Do you believe me, Seth?"

I had to meet her eyes. How else can one acknowl-
edge a deathbed declaration? "I believe you, Sarah," I
lied. "Of course I do."

She sighed and sank back against the pillows.
"Thank you for that. I hope the day will come when you
can tell *her* you believe it. Then she can die happier,
too."

I did not believe her, despite the obvious fact that she
believed it. I could not. I had seen the evidence that
Sarah had not.

Besides, there was nothing—not a deathbed declaration, not a substantive improvement in my finances, not
the success in my newspaper, nothing!—that could
erase the blackness that had lodged itself inside me.
Although the circumstances of my life had improved,
the part of me that remembered Rachel remained as
dark as ever. Any sort of forgiveness was an impossibility.

42

No one in town told me that Rachel had returned to her father's house, not Hansen (who always kept me informed of such items for the newspaper), not my housekeeper, not even you, Abel. I suppose you all wanted to protect me from pain. 'Tis humiliating to realize that you all thought me too pathetically fragile to be told.

It was Tom Dagget who brought the news to my attention. Tom had become apprenticed to me just a few months earlier (after Billy'd left for West Virginia), and having come here from Wilmington, he'd never known Rachel. He was also completely ignorant of our pasts. One day he chanced to look out the window, and something or someone caught his eye. He gave a long, low whistle. *"My!"* he gasped. "Who's *that*?"

Since Tom's a lot more serious-minded than Billy, I was curious to know what had impressed him so greatly that it had called forth a whistle, so I got up and looked. And there was Rachel passing by. Rachel, back from Canada and walking down Front Street as casually as if the three years since she'd last done it had not even happened.

To say that the sight of her shocked me would be an

understatement. I truly believe my heart stopped. But what else I felt besides shock is hard to say. Did I hate her still? Yes. Was my anger and resentment as strong as ever? Yes. Could I stop gaping, turn my eyes from her, and walk away? No. Not at all.

I must have gawked like a schoolboy. I couldn't stop drinking in the sight of her. I saw at once that she'd changed. She was older, not a girl any more. Sterner looking, too, I thought, not quite so ready to smile. And her walk was different—firmer, somehow, and less . . . less buoyant. But she was, if possible, more beautiful than ever. Womanhood had only enhanced her. There were lines in her face that strengthened her, and a depth and fullness about her that weren't there before. It was no wonder that sober-sided Tom had whistled.

I don't know how much pain the sight of her gave me, because it was nothing when compared to the twist in my belly when I caught sight of the little boy she held by the hand. Rachel had a *son*! In the months of our marriage, I'd yearned for us to have a child, and now she had one. But not mine.

I've never known such jealousy as I felt toward Peter Mason at that moment. Not only was he the father that I'd wanted to be, but he and Rachel had made a perfect child. I watched the boy as he hop-skipped alongside his mother on strong little legs. He was as sturdy and comely as one could wish, his back straight, his mop of thick, tawny hair bouncing, his cheeks chubby with health, his light eyes bright, taking in everything. The mere sight of him overwhelmed me; I was enveloped in an avalanche of longing. If the accursed Peter Mason had only remained at sea, I thought, those two beautiful passersby could have been my family!

I slowly became aware of Tom eyeing me curiously. I

wondered what outward signs I'd exhibited of my inner turmoil. All I was aware of was the trembling of my fingers. I stuffed my hands into my trouser pockets and tried to get hold of myself. "That's Rachel Mason," I said, my voice sounding peculiar to my own ears. "Joss Weller's daughter."

Tom must have noticed something strange in my response. "Seems like you know her," he remarked, peering at me through his spectacles, head cocked questioningly.

Shrugging, I turned back to my desk. "Well," I mumbled in an attempt to sound indifferent, "I *used* to know her. Once."

43

Sometimes I stood at the shop window and wished she'd walk by with the boy, just so I'd get a glimpse of them. At other times, I wished they were back in Canada, so that I might possibly be able to banish them from my thoughts and find some peace. But a year or more went by without abatement of this ambivalence and discomfort. Fortunately for my sanity, I was able, during working hours, to put Rachel and her child from my mind. At least while writing my newspaper, my mind was occupied with other matters.

One day, when I was actually not thinking of them at all, Tom again brought them to my attention. What was occupying my mind at that moment was an editorial about the upcoming election, and how different this one would be for Mr. Jefferson from the confusion of his first presidential campaign four years before. "This time," I remember writing, "President Jefferson will surely have so large a majority of electors that there will be no suspense in the matter at all. Not only are the voters happy about the Louisiana purchase and the control of federal spending, but they positively cheer whenever there is any mention of his abolishment of the excise tax on whiskey . . ." Thus engrossed, I was able to put personal matters very far from my thoughts.

Tom, who'd been waiting for me to finish so that he could set the editorial into print before going home, was standing at the window. Suddenly he gasped. "Something's amiss out there," he said. "Mrs. Mason's running down the street with her little boy in her arms!"

I ran to the window. I knew at a glance what the situation was—the boy was ill, and she was rushing him to Dr. Muncie's. She'd evidently run all the way from the Weller farm, for she was panting from the exertion and her feet seemed unsteady. "Go out to her, Tom," I said, "before she stumbles and falls. Carry the child for her."

Tom did so, and when he returned he told me what he'd learned, that the child might have the scarlet fever. I felt a chill run right through me. I knew that scarlet fever is a quick killer of children. But, in truth, I didn't understand my attack of fear. After what his mother had done to me, why should I care? Who was her child to me that I should so greatly fear for his health? Nevertheless I did, and I was unable to concentrate my mind on anything else all that night. I could only stand at the window and watch the street for any sign of activity at the doctor's office.

Word of the boy's illness somehow spread through town. By dawn, a small crowd had gathered in front of the doctor's office. The usual busybodies were there, of course, but there were some who really cared: Simon had come with his wife Abby (who herself had lost a sister to scarlet fever); Joss Weller had followed his daughter in from the farm; Annette Knudsen, always a loyal friend to Rachel, had left her child under Martin's care and come; and my housekeeper Clara was there, too. I couldn't help myself—I joined them and listened while they speculated on the various frightening possibilities.

"If the boy is truly infected with scarlet fever," Annette whispered to me, "he may not last the day."

"Poor little Jossy," Abby Weller said tearfully. "The fever comes so quick . . . and so furious."

"And if he lives through the fever," one of the biddies added, "he might still succumb in the aftermath, when the skin peels."

"Or he might live through it and be deaf the rest of his days," Joss muttered worriedly. "Though I'd settle fer deafness an' a leaky ear, if only the good Lord'd let him live."

"Amen to that," said Clara and Abby both.

"What can Dr. Muncie do for him?" I asked.

"Bleeding or blistering, puking or purging," Simon muttered in despairing disgust. "That's all they know to do."

So we all waited and silently prayed. Just after sunup the door opened, and Rachel appeared in the doorway. One only had to look at her face to know that the boy didn't have scarlet fever after all. He'd had one of those childhood fevers that rage alarmingly high for a night and then decline in the morning without apparent reason. He was much better, Rachel told the waiting friends. The doctor said she could take him home.

I felt a flush of relief so strong it was as though I were the father. Even while in the throes of these feelings, I didn't understand any of my strange emotions. What I *did* understand was that I didn't want Rachel to know that I had in any way concerned myself with her welfare and that of her son. My pride would not permit it. So I edged away from the crowd before she could see me.

What puzzled me even more than my own confusion

was the mystery of the continued absence of Peter Mason. Where the devil *was* he? Why hadn't he been here as he should have been, suffering through the night with the rest of us? Why wasn't he here offering protection to his wife and son? How could he bear to go gallivanting off, leaving Rachel so alone?

Those questions occurred to me again at the time of the fire. You remember the Weller house fire, Abel, don't you? Since you were there, I needn't go into the details of it. But I remember asking myself, as we raced up the road to the house and saw the flames starting to lick the roof, *Where is the damnable Peter Mason when he's needed?*

I shall never forget that day. The smell of the smoky air, the strange, reddish darkening of the afternoon light, the sound of crackling timbers, the horrible fear in the pit of my stomach as I looked at Joss Weller's blackened face and guessed that someone was trapped inside—those things still haunt my dreams.

The whole fire brigade knew from the start that the Weller house was doomed. Because of its distance from town, we knew we would not be in time to save it. But we tried our best. Remember how we decided that the pump would slow us down, so we just grabbed up the buckets, ran up to the house, and set up the lines from the well?

By the time I arrived, the line was forming. The whole kitchen wing was aflame, and the fire was spreading along the roof. I immediately became uneasy, because I didn't see any of the family members standing about. I was about to ask where they were when I saw Joss totter out, his whole face black. My stomach dropped to my shoes in sheer terror. Whatever hatred and resentment I had stored up toward Rachel did not any longer exist. Nothing existed for me but the need to know that she was not in that house. I ran over to Joss and grabbed at his shoulders. "Where's Rachel?"

"She's in town," he wheezed, his voice choked by smoke. "But oh God, oh God, I can't find Jossy."

Jossy! I knew whom he meant, for I'd learned the boy's name from Abby Weller during that terrible morning in front of Dr. Muncie's dispensary. I didn't wait to hear more but ran in the door to find him.

The whole house was thick with smoke. Flames had already burned through the wall that abutted the kitchen, consumed the lower stairs and were climbing steadily upward. I yelled the boy's name but heard nothing but the crackle of the flames. Keeping low, I stumbled through the three rooms, peering through the smoke and trying not to breathe, but I found no sign of the boy. And there was no way to get upstairs.

Feeling the worst sort of desperation, I ran out again and motioned for the first man I saw to follow me. It was Odell Junior, a fortunate choice, for he's a strong fellow with a cool head in a crisis. We rushed round to the back of the house, where I assumed there was an upstairs window. There was, but flames were already licking the roof above it. I climbed onto Odell's shoulders, and he heaved me up. I used my elbow to break through the panes of glass and hauled myself in, something I never could have done if desperation weren't driving me.

The smoke was not quite as thick here as down below, but black clouds of it were pouring up from the burning stairwell. It would very quickly become unbearable. And I was very much aware of the flames above my head. How long, I wondered, would the roof timbers hold?

The room in which I stood was a bedroom with one single bed and a child's crib. I saw no sign of the child. I ran quickly to a second room, but it seemed to be nothing more than a storage room. I stood there help-lessly, not knowing where to turn. The fear that little Jossy had been trapped in the kitchen became a sicken-ing possibility. I couldn't bear the thought of it—it made me retch. If the mere possibility did that to me, I wondered with horror what the reality of it would do to Rachel.

Then I heard a sound. It seemed to come from the bedroom. I dashed back. "Jossy?" I called. "Jossy, are you in here?"

For a heart-stopping moment there was no sound. Then I heard a whimper coming from under the bed. I knelt down and peered under it. And I saw the whites of his eyes.

It took a moment for my eyes to adjust to the dim light under the bed. What I saw then wrung my heart. The boy was cowering against the wall, crouched down on his haunches, elbows tight against his sides, and both hands held out as if pleading, with palms up. Even in the dim light I could see that they were seared by flame. They must have been giving him dreadful pain, but even that could not fully account for the sheer terror in his eyes. The look awoke a protective desire in me that I'd never before experienced, an urgent need—so strong it surprised me—to ease that child's pain.

"Oh, Jossy! Thank God!" I breathed, and held out my arms to him.

He did not move.

"I'm a friend," I said. "I've come to take you outside."

He didn't respond. I slid my head and shoulders under the bed and started to wiggle toward him, but he edged away. "No, no," he murmured, trembling.

"You must come to me, boy," I insisted gently. "We have to go at once."

"No, I was bad," he said. "Bad."

I didn't understand him. "Bad?"

"The fire. I d-dropped the l-log. It's my fault."

"No, no, it's all right," I said. "I swear to you it's not your fault. Please come."

He stopped edging away. "I hurt," he said, tears tumbling from his eyes. And he held out his hands to me. They were trembling. I will never know how he'd borne that searing pain for so long.

"Yes, I see," I said. "Come with me, and we'll make those hands better."

He studied me for a moment, and then, apparently deciding he could trust me, he leaped at me, throwing his arms about my neck. Holding him tight, I began to wriggle out, legs first, but before I'd gotten very far a burning beam fell down across the bed, setting the bedclothes aflame. The boy screamed. I sheltered him with my body, but the bed did not collapse. I squirmed out as quickly as I could while holding him fast. There was nothing overhead now but burning beams. The child gaped up at them, and I could feel his heart racing in terror. I said some reassuring words as I carried him to the window. When I looked down, I saw Odell and three other men standing there below, peering up at us. "Here!" I shouted. "Catch him."

But little Jossy wouldn't let me go. "No, no," he wailed. "Hold me!"

I couldn't help it; I had to wrench him loose. Holding him off from me, I leaned out and let him drop, screaming, into Odell's waiting arms. Then, as the roof caved in behind me, I leaped from the sill.

It was not a particularly perilous jump. The only injury I sustained was to my ankle, which had twisted under me. I paid it no heed, for little Jossy was still screaming, although he was safe in Odell's hold. Seeing how he held his arms out to me in pitiful despair, I took him back in my arms. He nuzzled my neck wetly, his arms holding onto me as if for dear life. I rocked him thus until his sobs subsided. Odell grinned at me. "I think, Seth, old man, you've made a friend for life," he said.

I don't think I can describe to you, Abel, what I felt when I held that child on my shoulder. It was another new emotion . . . a tenderness so strong it made me shake at the knees. That my holding him could ease his sobs gave me an unfathomable joy. He'd embraced me with a faith so complete that I could not, for my life, fail him. There was, I felt, nothing in the world he could demand of me that I would not do for him.

By this time the house was almost completely enveloped by flames, so Odell and the others moved us away from the heat. As we rounded the building (I limping on my swollen ankle and letting Odell support me so that I wouldn't trip and endanger my precious bundle), I saw Rachel. She was kneeling on the ground, beating the earth with her fists in a wild hysteria. But a cry of relief from the crowd made her look round. When she saw me, she seemed to freeze, her fists upraised, her body stiff, even the look in her eyes tentative, as if she were afraid to hope. That look, that posture, didn't change until I brought her son to her and laid him in her arms. Only then did she collapse, rocking him convulsively and weeping, while the little fellow tried to soothe her, telling her through his own tears not to cry.

I wanted to do that, too, to rock her in my arms and tell her not to cry. I wanted it so much it ached me. But my awareness of that ache made me furious with myself. What sort of weakling was I to feel this way after all she'd done to me? I should not have this desire to soothe her, not any more; she herself had estranged me and made any sympathy I might have for her a travesty. So, *the devil with it*, I said to myself, and I limped off, took up a bucket, and joined the line of men who still continued their hopeless labors to control the fire.

But something had changed in me. Though my resentment of Rachel still remained, from that day onward that little boy was unshakably dear to me. I didn't know how or why, but I knew with utter certainty that I loved, fiercely and completely, another man's son.

44

It never occurred to me that the boy could be mine. In such matters I must be incredibly thick-headed, for there were certainly clues I should have seen. Even Simon must have suspected, for he tried to give me a hint: he once remarked that the boy's eyes were just the color of mine. I gave the remark scant attention, dismissing the matter of eye-color as mere coincidence. Only later did Simon's casual observation take on a deeper significance.

At first I thought nothing of the boy's paternity but that it was as Rachel claimed: Jossy was Peter Mason's son. Nevertheless, I took great pleasure in the little lad's visits to my shop. I showed him how I set type, and I printed some childish stories especially for him, always with his name up at the top, sheets of print that he truly treasured. I taught him the letters, and when he showed some evidence of reading, I thought I'd burst with pride.

When he came to visit, it was always in the company of his grandfather. Rachel never came. I think she avoided me in thoughtfulness for my comfort, understanding that a meeting between us would be awkward. I knew how grateful she was to me; her father so repeatedly expressed her heartfelt thankfulness for my saving her son that I was embarrassed by the unnecessary reiterations. But, you see, I didn't want to hear her words of thanks. I'd taken her gift—the muffler she'd knit for me—and stuffed it in a drawer. I wanted that muffler no more than I wanted her damned gratitude. Though it was a fine muffler, soft and warm. Whenever I opened the drawer to feel it, I thought it smelled of her.

One day Jossy presented me with a gift of his own—a drawing he had made with charcoal. It was a rudimentary representation of my shop. He'd drawn a desk, a misshapen, overly large printing press, and two stick figures, one small and one large, apparently holding hands. He informed me proudly that the little one was himself and the large one was me. I thanked him with sincere pleasure and took it home with me that evening. Clara, when she brought me my supper, saw it and beamed. "Such a *klug kind*," she exclaimed. "So clever. Like his papa."

"Huh!" I sneered. "I never noticed anything particularly clever about his 'papa.' I thought Peter Mason a jack-pudding from the first, and nothing I've heard that he's done since has caused me to change my mind."

"No, no, I not mean Mr. Mason," Clara said with a dismissive wave of her hand. "Iss you I meant."

I didn't take it in. "What are you babbling about, Clara?" I asked, concentrating on the steaming bean porridge she'd set before me.

She gasped and clapped her mouth with her hand.

That gesture caught my attention. "What?" I asked again.

With what seemed like an effort, she took a deep breath, crossed her arms firmly over her chest and said, "The papa iss you, mister. You."

I didn't miss it this time. Stiffening, I put down my spoon. I gaped at my housekeeper as if I'd never seen her before. "What are you saying?"

"You hear right."

I glared at her. "Don't be ridiculous, woman. I hope you've not been repeating such nonsense to anyone else."

"I don't say this to nobody else. Not another soul. But nonsense it ain't."

"Of course it is. If I were Jossy's father, wouldn't I know it?"

"Not if your missus didn't tell you."

"But she told you, I suppose."

"No need she had to tell me. When I seen her—how you say?—smiling like sunshine in bed that morning, I know."

"What do you mean?" I asked stupidly. "What morning?" My head was swimming. I didn't know what I felt. There was something in Clara's manner that reeked of sincerity. It was impossible to doubt her. Yet I kept on doubting. "What morning?" I repeated.

"It was the morning before Mister Mason come, I tell you that. She was, I bet, a month *schwanger* by then. That morning I guess it, and I ask. She laughs and nods her head, so happy she iss."

"*Schwanger?*" I gulped. "Pregnant?"

"Yes, pregnant. By a month."

"*Before* Mason—?" I got to my feet, hardly noticing how my knees were shaking. "Then Jossy's my son? *Mine?*"

I was scarcely able to take it in. I stood there staring at nothing as this bombshell exploded in my brain. Finally, I turned to Clara again. "Then, God damn it, why didn't she *tell* me?" I demanded.

Clara merely shrugged. "Don't ask me. Already I say too much." With that she turned and walked out.

I could neither eat nor sleep. I prowled the house all night long, remembering, wondering, counting months. Simon's look when he'd made the remark about Jossy's eyes . . . had he known? And what about Peter? Did he know who the real father of Josiah Mason was? Had he discovered it? Was that knowledge the reason he was not with his wife?

And above all, there was the mystery of Rachel. If I were truly the father, why had she not told me?

The thought that she'd lied about this put me in an uncontrollable rage. The next morning I galloped over to the Weller farm like a man possessed, stormed into her house, and demanded the truth from her. Of course she would admit nothing. She would not allow the paternity of her son to be questioned. She declared that intention with a firmness I had not known in her before. I could not help but admire it.

Nevertheless, the actual wording of her answers was evasive. I came away convinced that Clara's information was correct. And Rachel herself provided me with a possible explanation for why she'd failed to tell me about her pregnancy. She did not think I'd believe her. And under the circumstances—with the arrival of Peter Mason on the scene at just that time—she was probably right.

So here we are, Abel, at the point where I need your advocacy. I want custody of my son. I want to raise him, to feed and clothe him, to educate him, to love him openly, to have him know his father. I must be able to claim him as my own. It means more to me than I can say.

I know that according to law the father is the natural

guardian of his minor children. You've explained that what is meant is the *legal* father. And the legal father is Peter Mason. Therefore my only hope is to deny the legality of the divorce and Rachel's subsequent marriage. If her marriage to Peter is illegal, she is still my wife, and the boy is legally my son. So proving the illegality is what we must do.

Believe me, I'm aware of what that will do to Rachel. I'll be tainting her with the accusation of adultery. I know what pain that will bring her, for I remember as clearly as if it were yesterday how she reacted to her sister's trial. She, like poor Clarissa, will be accused of criminal conversation. She will be unbearably shamed. And I will be the means.

Don't look at me in that reproachful way, Abel! Blast it all, I refuse to be deterred by feelings of guilt! She took her happiness without considering the cost to me. Why, then, is it wrong for me to snatch a bit of happiness without reckoning the cost to her?

I suppose you're thinking that this is an act of revenge, that my hatred still rages, that the dark side of me is still in control. Damn it, man, don't you think I've asked myself a hundred times what my motives are?

Yes, I wonder if I am really so depraved as to wish Rachel to feel some of the agony I felt. And I ask myself if I wish to get back at her for making me a cuckold. I think the answer is no. Yet how can I be sure? I don't believe I care any longer about being thought a cuckold. I've become so accustomed to everyone's knowing it about me that it means nothing now. I don't think I'm seeking any sort of revenge. I don't believe I hate her now. I'm not sure I ever really did. Perhaps the hatred was only pain. How can I be accused of hatred any more? When I put the boy in her arms that day, was I not overjoyed for her joy? My feelings toward Rachel are not at all clear to me.

The one thing that *is* clear is this: the boy means everything to me. I want to be his father more than I ever wanted anything in life. If it means causing suffering to Rachel, I am sorry. But by lying to me, she brought it on herself. By God, this is something I must do. Don't try to dissuade me, Abel. I've made up my mind.

PART III

The Trial

45

*J*ossy had worn his britches out at the knees, as boys
will. Rachel was patching them by the light of the
dining-room fire, when her father came in the front
door, bringing in a great blast of cold air. She looked up
at his wind-reddened face. "Ah, Papa," she said, getting
up and putting her sewing aside, "come, sit here at the
fire and warm yourself. You look frozen through."

She helped him untie the muffler he'd wrapped
around his ears and slipped his heavy coat from his
shoulders, keeping herself from asking him anything
about his visit to town. He'd gone on one of his now-
rare visits to the print shop. Rachel guessed that it was
the news in this week's *Register* that had drawn him—
the news that the Non-Importation Act against Britain
was finally being enforced. He'd probably wanted to
hear what the Tories had to say about it. But Papa rarely
mentioned Seth and the newspaper to her these days.
With the trial so close at hand, he seemed to think that
anything having to do with Seth was a sore subject to
her.

He sat down and held his hands toward the warmth.
"Yer lawyer's come," he said abruptly. "I heard that he
an' his clerk bespoke rooms at Hansen's."

"Good," Rachel said as she hung up his things. "I wasn't expecting him for a day or two."

"What's good about it? The trial don't start till Monday."

"There are several matters I'd like to ask him about before the trial starts." She perched on the hearth and picked up her needlework.

"What matters?"

Rachel began to answer and then hesitated. "Are you sure you want to talk about this, Papa? I told you that you don't have to involve yourself with the trial."

He glared at her. "Don't talk such rubbish. Don't y'think that what happens to Jossy matters to me as much as to you?"

"I know it does. But this whole business is going to be very upsetting. You can keep yourself out of it. You've been through enough already in your life."

"I can deal with it. I ain't so feeble that I can't stand by my daughter at such a time."

Rachel heard the affection he tried to hide under the gruffness of his manner. "Thank you, Papa," she said softly.

"Never mind thanks. What are the matters you want to ask yer lawyer about?"

"Well, you see, when I saw Mr. Galliard in Philadelphia, he explained to me that he couldn't contrive a strategy for the case until he'd received a 'pleading' from Abel."

"A pleading?"

"Yes. It's a statement to the court giving the plaintiff's arguments—"

"The 'plaintiff.' That's Seth, right?"

"Right." Rachel smiled at her father's determination to understand. It was warming to her soul to have some-

one on her side. It was also helpful to her own understanding to explain things to someone else. "He's also
called the complainant—the one making the complaint."

Papa nodded. "I see. Go on and explain about the . . .
that other word."

"The pleading. That's a statement giving the plaintiff's reasons for making the complaint and the legal
basis that makes the complaint actionable."

"Actionable, eh?" He threw her a proud grin. "Good
God, woman, you sound like a lawyer yerself."

Rachel laughed. "Not much of one. You've now
heard the entire extent of what I've learned."

"But what is it y'want to ask this Galliard fellow
about the—what did y'call it?—pleading?"

"I want to ask him what it says. You see, Mr. Galliard
told me that until he knows how the plaintiff will plead,
he can't devise a plan of defense."

Her father sighed and wearily pulled himself to his
feet. "I sure hope," he muttered, "that he devises a good
one."

Rachel watched him leave, noting with a little clench
of her heart how stooped his back had become. When
she resumed her mending, her father's last words rever-
berated in her mind. *Was* there a good plan? Back in
Philadelphia her lawyer had told her outright that her
case was weak. She remembered that she'd asked him
why.

"You must understand, ma'am," he'd said, "that under
common law women have very limited legal rights to
their children. Children are the property of their fathers
until they are twenty-one years of age." He'd warned
her that she'd best be prepared for the worst. "In cases
of separation and divorce," he'd intoned at the last, "the
child is inevitably given to the father, even if that father

is guilty of gross misconduct. If Mr. Trahern can prove he's the legal father, we *cannot* win."

She remembered how she'd stiffened at those words. Her muscles were tightening now, at the mere recollection! But she'd managed to ask Mr. Galliard *how* Seth could prove he was the legal father. "After all," she'd said, "I am married to someone else—to Mr. Mason—and I was so when my child was born. Doesn't that make *Mr. Mason* the legal father?"

"Yes," the lawyer had granted, "unless Mr. Trahern can convince the jury otherwise."

The memory of those words made her hands tremble so much she had to put down her sewing. *Could Mr. Trahern convince a jury otherwise?* she asked herself. If anyone could do it, it was Seth. He was the most convincing person she'd ever known!

How could her life have come to this pass? That Seth was the man she had to oppose in court was too great an irony to have to face. Seth, who'd always been generous, kind, and good. It was hard to believe he could do this to her.

The door to her father's bedroom opened, and he emerged, dressed in his nightshirt and cap. Rachel, surprised, watched as he crossed, barefooted, through the dark parlor and stopped in the dining-room doorway. "Y'know, Rachel, I can't stop thinkin' about it," he said, shaking his head in bewilderment. "Seth Trahern is the finest man I know. How can he be doin' this to us?"

"Strange, papa," Rachel said sadly, "I was just thinking the very same thing. He's not the sort . . ." She turned away and stared for a moment into the fire, as if she'd find an answer there. "He must have a good reason."

"I'd never've guessed there was so much hate in him."

"It's not hate, Papa. It's love."

"Love?"

"Yes, love. I'm sure of it." She looked over her shoulder at her father. There were tears in his eyes, just as there were in hers. "'Tis most certainly his reason. He must love our Jossy very, very much."

46

M r. Galliard and his clerk called on Rachel the very next afternoon. They had both evidently enjoyed driving out to the farm in their rented curricle. Galliard in particular seemed cheerful and brisk. "Lovely day, ma'am," he greeted. "Much warmer than yesterday."

"Yes," she said, taking their coats and hats, "the wind has died."

While Harry Ferguson, the clerk, set out the papers on the dining-room table, Galliard kept up a flow of polite conversation. "I strolled about New Castle this morning. Charming town. After the noise of Philadelphia, it was very pleasant to experience the sense of quiet amiability that permeates the atmosphere. Don't you agree, Harry?"

Harry shrugged. "I didn't see much of the town," he reminded his employer. "You had me occupied this morning taking notes on the pleading."

"Yes, so I did," Galliard acknowledged. Rachel noticed that a tiny specter of annoyance crossed his face, but he quickly covered it. It was as if he were determined to exude good cheer. "I quite admired the flash of the river one can glimpse at the east end of every cobbled street," he went on, "and the modest houses that cluster so neatly along the main thoroughfares. So many of them have shutters and doors painted in bright colors."

"Yes," Rachel said, "the Swedish settlers started the practice a hundred years ago."

"Did they indeed? Imaginative of them, I must say. But Mistress Mason, what I most enjoyed was the scent of the air. Clean and fresh and tinged with the faint musk of woodsmoke. Delicious! I wish we had air like this in Philadelphia."

"In Philadelphia," Harry muttered, so absorbed in sorting out his pages of notes that he was hardly aware he spoke, "we have to grow accustomed to the smell of horse urine and rotting garbage."

"Harry!" Galliard snapped. "Watch your blasted tongue!"

"Oh!" Startled, poor Mr. Ferguson blinked up at Rachel. "Sorry, ma'am," he mumbled, reddening to his ears. "Forgot myself."

Rachel waved away the apology. "May I offer you gentlemen some tea?" she asked.

Mr. Galliard shook his head. "I think we should get right to the business."

Rachel thought Mr. Ferguson looked disappointed; the smell of baking bread emanating from the kitchen was probably tempting to him. However, knowing that he'd already spoken out of place, he kept silent.

Just as they were about to take places around the table, little Jossy appeared with a basket of baby rabbits in his arms. "Look, Mama, Delilah's given us some new bunnies," he clarioned from the doorway.

"Yes, Delilah Rabbit is most generous," Rachel said dryly. "But Jossy, we have guests. Come in and say your how-de-dos to Mr. Galliard and Mr. Ferguson, and then go to Grandpapa in the barn. He'll help you to feed the bunnies."

Jossy said a shy how-do-you-do, shook their hands with manly dignity, and left. Galliard looked after him, smiling. "Loveable child," he said when Jossy had closed the door behind him, "with his mother's sweetness of expression."

"Thank you," Rachel said. "I wanted you to have a glimpse of him. It will help you to understand how much this case means to me."

Mr. Galliard's cheerful expression changed to one of lawyerly seriousness. He sighed and turned to the papers. "With your permission, Mistress Mason," he said, frowning down at them, "Mr. Ferguson will take notes. Will you sit there opposite me?"

"Please, sir," Rachel said as she took the seat, "I'm not comfortable with so much formality of address. Can you not call me Rachel when we're not in court?"

"Of course I can," he assured her as he sat down.

Harry slid some of the papers over to Rachel. "It's the pleading," he said, and they waited silently while she read it.

When she looked up with a questioning frown, Galliard explained that the argument the plaintiff intended to use—as described in the pleading—was an attack on the validity of the self-divorce. That said, he cleared his throat. Rachel surmised that it was his way of preparing to deliver unpleasant news. His earlier high spirits, she realized, had been nothing more than a ruse to conceal his concern. But now he looked directly at her, his worry apparent in his eyes. "I know you will wish me to be blunt about our chances for a favorable outcome, Rachel," he began, "so I shall say at once that they are worse than I thought."

She felt herself grow pale. "Are they?"

"Yes. The opposition is not arguing paternity, as I had hoped they would. Instead, they are attacking the legality of your divorce from Seth Trahern, where we are quite vulnerable. If they can prove Mr. Trahern is still your legal husband, then the child becomes his, *ipso facto*."

"*Ipso facto?*"

"It means 'by that very fact.' In other words, the very fact of his being your legal husband would be so strong it would override all other considerations, regardless of right or wrong. A legal husband, as I told you, is by law the father of the minor children and holds all rights over them."

"Oh, dear," was all she could say.

"I wish they'd gone for paternity," Galliard sighed.

"Why, Mr. Galliard?" she asked in confusion. "I thought that the question of paternity would surely win for them. You must be aware, after reading my story, that Seth is Jossy's real father."

"Yes, but they don't know that."

"Seth knows."

The attorney shook his head. "He suspects. He can't know. Paternity is very difficult to prove. ''Tis a wise father who knows his own child,' as the saying goes."

"But all they need do is ask me in court. I could not lie under oath."

"They cannot ask you. There is something called the Rule of Exclusion. It says that wives and husbands cannot testify for or against each other."

"But I am not his wife."

"That, my dear, is the very thing they are trying to disprove."

She shook her head, her brow wrinkled. "Does that

mean I will not be permitted to speak at all in my own behalf?"

"No, nor will Trahern be able to speak on his, so that evens the score a bit." Galliard got up and looked again at the plaintiff's pleading. "I suppose," he said, half to himself, "they chose the divorce issue instead of the paternity issue because they can't be certain they can prove his paternity."

"Seth seemed *very certain* when he accused me of lying to him," Rachel said.

"No man is *ever* certain he is the true father of his children," Galliard declared. "Never has been in all of history! That specific insecurity in males has been the basis for half of all common law and most of the rules of wedlock."

That concept gave her pause. "Indeed?" she asked in surprise.

Ferguson nodded in agreement. "It's all because of property, ma'am. Man has made all sorts of laws to insure that the offspring who inherits his property is of his own blood. But all the laws in the world can't make him sure."

"I suppose they can't," Rachel murmured thoughtfully. "I never considered such things."

She pondered what they'd said, but her lawyer did not give her many moments to dwell on the matter. He began to ask about the characters of the various witnesses they might call for their defense. Then he encouraged her to speculate on the nature of those witnesses the other side would call. After an hour of this sort of speculation, he got to his feet. "Well, ma'am, that is all we can do until the trial."

The clerk collected his notes and gathered the other papers together. Before leaving, Mr. Galliard turned to Rachel with a sigh. "I hope you understand, my dear, that if Mr. Trahern's lawyer can convince the jury that your divorce was, for any reason, not binding, we shall lose and have no other recourse."

"None, ever?" she asked, alarmed.

"I fear not."

Ferguson, who'd been watching her closely, jumped to his feet. "You mustn't worry, ma'am," he said. "Mr. Galliard won't fail you. He's the best."

"Adrat, man, be still!" Galliard swore at him. "Can't you see she must be warned?"

"Sorry," Ferguson muttered, reddening again.

"And there's *more* to warn her of." Mr. Galliard faced Rachel and went on, his voice quite gentle, considering what he was saying. "There are other ramifications as well that you must face if the finding goes against us. In addition to the pain of losing the custody of your child, such a finding would mean that, in living with Mr. Mason, you were guilty of criminal conversation." He lowered his voice and dropped his eyes. "Adultery, you know."

"Yes, I know. But I don't give a fig for that." She turned her face from him and stared out of the window. It was true, she thought in some surprise. She was not a fourteen-year-old. She had changed. She was no longer afraid, at least not about unimportant things. "I care not what people will think of me, or what names they will call me," she told the men watching her, "so long as I have my child."

"But if Mr. Trahern should win," the lawyer persisted, coming up behind her and turning her about to face him, "you will not have a choice of one or the other. You will have lost both your child *and* your good name."

"Then, Mr. Galliard," she said firmly, meeting his eyes, "we *must not lose*."

"Easy to say, ma'am. You must try to see the difficulties. The fact remains that yours was what is called a self-divorce, a practice that, though not uncommon, has little legal standing. All they need do to invalidate the divorce is to convince the jury that Trahern was an unwilling party to the act."

"Yes, I'm aware of that. But we have one major point in our favor. You must imprint it on your brain." She fixed him with a level look, her eyes flashing and her elbows akimbo. "'Twas Mr. Trahern *himself* who instigated the divorce," she said. "And it was his attorney, Mr. Abel Becker, who arranged it."

Galliard smiled at her with real approval. "Very good, Rachel" he said. "You remind me of one of those Amazonian females of myth, a warrior ready to do battle." He started for the door with his clerk close behind. "Your point is indeed a favorable argument for us. And you may rest assured I shall use it to good effect. One thing to keep in mind, however, is that the opposition is aware that their case has this weakness."

Rachel followed them to the outer door. "They may be aware of it, but 'tis a fact they can't change, is that not so?"

Galliard merely shrugged and kept walking. "Yes, but as they are aware of it—and, believe me, they are *very much* aware of that weakness—you can be absolutely certain they are planning a defense against it."

"What defense?" she asked nervously, following them out to their two-wheeled curricle.

"I wish I knew," he said as he heaved himself up the carriage steps. "We shall learn soon enough."

47

*S*eth was sitting at the bar at Hansen's, drinking a tankard of home brew with Charlie Lund, when he glanced up from his drink and caught sight of Simon in the mirror behind the bar. He turned around to greet him, but when Simon saw who it was, his color rose. He nodded at Seth curtly, turned on his heel, and stalked out.

Seth went after him. "Simon," he called, "come back, please."

Simon halted but did not turn. "I can't . . . I won't speak to you. Not these days."

"Your father was in the shop just the other night. If he can speak to me, so can you."

Simon shook his head and continued to walk away. "P'rhaps Papa is more forgiving than me," he said over his shoulder.

Seth loped after him, caught his arm, and pulled him round. "Come back inside, Simon. You came in for a brew. I don't want to keep you from it. I won't try to speak to you, if that's what you wish." Then, seeing Simon hesitate, he smiled ruefully. "Come on, man. I can't argue much longer. I'm freezing out here."

Simon, noting that Seth was indeed in shirtsleeves,

shrugged and went back with him to the tavern. For a while, they stood side by side at the bar, drinking but not speaking. Charlie Lund, wisely sensing the tension, finished his tankard in one good swig and put on his heavy coat. "If I go," he whispered in Seth's ear, "maybe you two'll work things out."

"Huh!" Simon sneered as soon as the blacksmith left. "Charlie's whispers're loud enough to wake the dead."

"He was trying to be tactful," Seth said.

"Maybe, but he could just as well've stayed. Whether he's here or not, you and me ain't gonna work things out."

"I don't blame you," Seth sighed. "I don't like myself very much either, these days."

Simon blinked at him. "Then why the devil are you doin' this terrible thing?"

"You know why. It was you who put the whole matter in motion."

Simon looked truly amazed. "Me?"

"Yes. You said something to me about Jossy's eyes. It started me thinking. That led to my discovery that he's my son."

"I never said he's your son," Simon declared angrily, though he was careful to keep his voice low.

Seth gave him a level look. "No, but you know it's true."

"I ain't sayin'. That's somethin' no man ever knows for sure. But even if he *is* yours, that don't excuse what you're doin' to my sister."

Seth dropped his eyes. "No, it doesn't. Blast it, Simon, I hate it, too! I just don't know any other way to get my son."

"Why're you so damn determined to take him? Don't you care how much you're hurtin' my family?"

"Yes, I care. But Simon, try to understand. You have three children and may yet have more. Jossy is the only son I'll ever have."

"You can't be sure of that. You may marry one day."

"I shall never marry again."

Simon heard something in Seth's voice—a tone of finality tinged with pain—that touched him. "I wish that goddamn Peter Mason had never been born," he muttered.

Seth gave a mirthless laugh. "Yes, so do I."

They drank in silence. When Simon's tankard was drained, he put it down and glanced at Seth from the corner of his eye. "Goodnight," he said, turning toward the door.

Seth understood just what Simon was indicating with that one word: We cannot be as we were while this battle is going on, but in my heart you are still my friend. He looked up at his former brother-in-law gratefully. "Goodnight, Simon," he said. And he put out his hand.

Simon hesitated for a moment. Then, with an intake of breath he shook the proffered hand and went quickly out the door.

A few moments later, Seth himself rose to leave. He was shrugging into his overcoat when Abel came into the tavern, accompanied by another man. "Ah, Seth," Abel said jovially, "we are well met. This is Mr. Galliard, Rachel's attorney from Philadelphia. Mr. Galliard, meet the complainant, Seth Trahern."

The two men shook hands, and Abel helped the visitor off with his greatcoat. Seth studied Galliard with interest. He was a stocky fellow, although by no means as large and full-bellied as Abel, with a round face and small, shrewd eyes. His formal attire—neckcloth carefully folded, vest elegantly embroidered and sporting a chain with a gold fob, hair neatly curled above the ears—immediately identified him as a city gentleman. Abel, with his wrinkled collar, loosely tied neckcloth, and old-fashioned britches, made a decided contrast. Seth, cocking an eyebrow, looked from one to the other. "'Tis strange for two opposing attorneys to be rubbing elbows socially, is it not?"

Abel laughed. "We're not conspiring, if that's what you're suggesting," he said. "Galliard has some questions about Delaware court procedure. I invited him to meet me here so that we can talk over a drink. You're welcome to join us and listen in, if Mr. Galliard has no objections."

"It would be my pleasure," Galliard assured Seth with a gallant little bow.

Abel shouted to Hanson to bring them some mulled ale laced with arrack, and the three men made their way into the taproom. Abel had no sooner settled himself at the table than he drew out a long-nine. "Would you like to join me in a smoke?" he asked the visitor.

Galliard shook his head, a faint expression of disapproval passing over his face. Abel, ignoring it, lit up the cigar and drew in a deep, hungry breath.

Seth winced. "Dash it, Abel," he said in amused rebuke, "you might ask our visitor if he objects to your blowing smoke at him."

Abel's eyebrows rose in affected innocence. "You don't *mind* my smoking, do you, Galliard? Long-nines are a treat for me. They're a harmless enough pleasure, don't you agree?"

"I suppose so," Galliard said a little reluctantly, "I'll try not to be disturbed by it."

"Right," Abel said cheerfully. "Live and let live, eh?"

After the drinks were brought, Galliard cleared his throat and turned to Seth. "I would normally avoid ask-

ing questions of my opposition," he explained apologet-
ically, "but there are no other attorneys in town whom I
may consult."

"I have no objections," Seth assured him, "if my
advocate does not object."

"I don't know why I should," Abel said, "since there's
nothing illegal about exchanging information not related
to the case. What is it you want to know, Galliard?"

"Well, you see, I've never had a case in Delaware
before. Are there any special characteristics of Delaware
court procedures that might surprise me?"

Abel shrugged. "No, you'll face few problems with
the Honorable Thorwald Andersen, the judge who'll be
hearing our case," he said. "Judge Andersen, although
fond of quoting the maxims he learned at his mother's
knee on every possible and several impossible occasions,
is more informal in his courtroom practice than many of
Delaware's Britishly hidebound judiciary."

"That's fortunate for me," Galliard said. Seth noticed
that he looked relieved.

Abel took a long pull on his cigar. "Equity or Chancery
might have given you a few problems, but General Ses-
sions won't be very different from what you'd find in
Pennsylvania," he assured his colleague. "Our way of treat-
ing our juries may surprise you, however."

"Oh? How is that?"

"They're sent upstairs to the jury room and locked in.
They get neither food, water, nor candles until they've
decided."

"Good God! What's the point of that?" Galliard
asked in horror.

Abel grinned. "The point is to get a verdict quickly.
You may be sure that, in those circumstances, there's no
shilly-shallying."

"A quick verdict is not necessarily a wise one," Galliard demurred.

"No jury verdict is necessarily wise," Seth put in dryly, "so it may as well be quick."

"I can't disagree with that," Galliard said, laughing. "In my time at the bar, I've heard a good number of foolish verdicts issued after long deliberation."

The men finished their drinks in good spirits. All Mr. Galliard's questions had evidently been answered, but none of the three men made an effort to bring the conversation to a close. Seth was vastly entertained listening to the two lawyers question each other in an effort to take each other's measure. Galliard managed to discover that Abel, although older than he, was content with a much less active law practice than his. "You seem almost *boastful* of the fact that you don't spend a great deal of time at your work," he said to Abel in surprise.

Abel laughed at his evident disapproval. "You needn't look down your nose," he said. "I'm an easy-going sort. Lazy, you know. Besides, unlike you, I'm a bachelor and have no wife or daughters to support."

"But not so lazy," Seth put in pointedly, "that you won't do your all to win this case."

"No," Abel grinned, "not so lazy as all that. Galliard, you can count on a stiff opposition."

"You don't have to tell me that," Galliard said, rising. "If you think, Mr. Becker, that you can lull me into complacency, you have the wrong fellow."

Bidding his host and Seth goodnight, Galliard gave a hearty handshake to each of them, and he took himself upstairs to his room.

Abel and Seth remained at the table. After some moments of thoughtful silence, Seth remarked, "Very pleasant fellow, that."

"Yes," Abel agreed, frowning as he put out what was left of his long-nine. "He's a jovial, generous fellow who made a delightful companion in the taproom, but . . ."

Seth looked at his friend curiously. "But . . . ?"

"He may be much less delightful in the courtroom. I'm not sure, but I felt he was hiding his light under the proverbial bushel; a good lawyer, like a good poker player, doesn't reveal his hand. I suspect he will make a formidable adversary in court."

Seth rose and smiled down at his friend. "Don't worry, Abel," he said, pressing the older man's shoulder affectionately, "I doubt that he's as formidable in court as you."

But later that night, before sleep came, Seth reluctantly admitted to himself that Rachel had chosen her lawyer well. As far as legal talent was concerned, Abel Becker would be meeting his match.

48

Rachel woke on the morning of the first day of
the trial to the *pit pit pat* of rain thrumming on
the windows. The sound depressed her. Although she
did not consider herself superstitious, she harbored the
foolish instinct that says a sunny morning is a more aus-
picious foretoken of success than a rainy one. It was the
dark side of the saying, 'Happy the bride the sun shines
on.'" *Well*, she thought with wry amusement, *if the sun is
lucky for a bride, maybe the rain is lucky for an adulteress.*

Seth awoke to the same sounds and the same misgiv-
ings. He stared out of the window of the bedroom he'd
once shared with Rachel and sighed deeply. He'd been
dreading this day, despite the fact that it was his own
doing. Watching the rain run down the panes, he
remembered that it had rained the day of Clarissa's trial.
If Rachel was remembering it as he was, she was probably more depressed by the weather than he. *Poor Rachel*,
he thought miserably, *what a discouraging omen this morning's rain must be for her!*

Seth set out for the courthouse on foot, for it was
only a short walk. He came upon Abel on the way. It
was a fortunate meeting, for Abel had had the sense to
take an umbrella. When they arrived at the courthouse,

they were not surprised to find a large crowd milling about. "Damnation," Seth swore, "even the rain hasn't kept them away!"

"Don't blame them," Abel said. "A court battle like this is as good as a play to them."

"I suppose it is," Seth muttered under his breath, "but it goes against my grain to be the one providing the drama in their lives."

The attorney hustled his client through the crowd, ignoring their curious stares, and the two slowly made their way toward the door of the New Castle court-house. It was a building that Seth passed every day on his way to the shop, but it seemed altered to his eyes this morning. He peered up at it as if he'd not seen it before. It was more than a century old, a tall, boxlike brick structure topped with a steeply angled roof and a cupola. Seth had always found it solid and modestly imposing, perfectly appropriate for a public building. Today, however, it seemed stodgy and oppressive. How is it, he wondered, that he'd not noticed before that it resembled a garrison . . . or a prison?

They passed through the entryway into the large courtroom. Seth had not been inside for many years. Abel guided him to the table where they would be seated throughout the trial. Seth took his assigned place, his heart beating rapidly and every muscle tensed. He kept his eyes fixed on the green baize covering of the table for several moments.

When his pulse became somewhat steady, he lifted his eyes and looked about him. Every aspect of the large room, except for one, seemed a satisfactory setting for the drama to come: the Judge's banc, a dias of dark, carved oak, was situated impressively high on the rear wall—quite center-stage; the space before it, where the lawyers performed, was raised about a foot above the courtroom's cobblestone floor; the jury box was on the judge's right, separated from the place of action by white-painted railings like the loge of a theater; the witness box at the judge's left was also clearly demarked by painted rails; and—most helpful for the spectators observing the drama—the high windows (four of them, two on each side of the wall opposite the judges' banc) and a hanging chandelier provided the light. The exception, which tied a knot in Seth's chest, was the dock, the place for prisoners. It was in front of the lawyers' tables, raised almost as high as the witness box, and horridly visible to everyone. That was where Rachel would have to sit. The thought of having to see her there made him wretched.

Mr. Galliard and his clerk were already in place at the defendants' table. So was the prothonotary, who would be recording the proceedings. But Rachel had not yet arrived. Seth wondered if she'd be making the trip in from the Weller farm in their wagon. As far as he knew, she had no other means of transportation. She'd be drenched when she arrived. *Damn it*, he thought, *I wish I had a way to provide her with a carriage. Perhaps if I made a secret arrangement with Charlie—*

Before Seth could finish the thought, a stir among the spectators caused him to look up. Rachel had entered on the arm of her father. Rain-soaked, just as he'd feared. Fortunately, she'd worn her shawl over her head and shoulders. He watched as she removed the wet shawl and handed it to her father. Joss, he noticed, squeezed his daughter's hand before sliding into a seat among the spectators.

Mr. Galliard and his clerk hurried down to greet her, Mr. Galliard smiling broadly, evidently in approval of her appearance. It seemed to Seth that every eye in the room was examining her with approval. She was wearing a high-waisted dress of soft gray homespun, topped modestly with a white tucker, and her hair was properly restrained in a neat, ruffled cap. Despite her severely puritanical garb and her extreme pallor, she was still utterly lovely to look at. And the sweetness of expression that had captured him from the first was very much in evidence. Seth was stricken with guilt. She was too fragile—and too innocent—to be tainted with the accusation of criminal conversation. What on earth was he doing, instigating this nightmarish court battle?

As Galliard led Rachel down the aisle past the gawking spectators, Seth kept his eyes fixed on her. She seemed calm and contained, but he knew by her clenched fingers that she was inwardly terrified. Her lawyer led her to her seat and then joined his assistant at his table. As soon as he left Rachel's side, Seth saw, dawning in her eyes, an awareness of where she was. It was a look of horror that she was in the dock, the place where thieves and murderers were made to sit in full view of the onlookers. He saw a flush of humiliation suffuse her cheeks. *Good God,* he thought with anguish, *this is my fault. I've put her on the stage, the center of a vulgar melodrama!*

At that moment, their eyes met. Their glances held for a moment, and a flash of something—pain? reproach? regret?—flashed between them. It was Seth who dropped his eyes.

Filled with guilt and self-loathing, Seth leaned forward toward Abel and stretched out his hand. He would stop this thing. He could not subject Rachel to this torture. But then a vision of Jossy's face appeared before his eyes. Jossy. His son. The charming, sweet-faced child whose first four years had been denied him. Had he not the right to raise the boy, to read to him, to laugh with him, to bind his cuts, to soothe his tears, to tuck him into bed at night? Seth's jaw tightened, and he withdrew his hand. The court case would proceed. He would not draw back from it, no matter what expressions he read in Rachel's eyes. And to keep from weakening, he would try, as much as possible, not to look at her.

Rachel, on the other hand, kept her eyes on him. Seeing him sitting there so implacable, so unforgiving, stiffened her spine. She would not show him how frightened she was. She pulled back her shoulders, smoothed her skirts, folded her hands in her lap and lifted her chin, all the while repeating to herself a phrase she'd once read that she'd been rehearsing in the wagon: *If thou art afraid of wounds, go not near the battle.* The words strengthened her spirit. Every time she said them, it was like making a pledge. She would not run from the battle, she swore, no matter what the wounds might be!

The appearance of the judge at the side door caught everyone's attention. The action was about to begin. The judge, the Honorable Thorwald Andersen, a small, wiry man with a head of bushy white hair and a hooked nose that held a pince-nez, made a grand entrance. Rachel was favorably impressed with him. Though his manner was formal and reserved, he had kind eyes. She watched him intently as he took his seat and signaled the prothonotary to swear in the jury.

This done, Abel Becker rose to make his opening statement. Though delivered with real panache, it was substantially the same as the pleading Mr. Galliard had given her to read:

"Mr. Trahern, who is known to you all as a man of unimpeachable character, is here seeking justice. He asks for custody of his minor son, called Josiah Mason, the opportunity for whose rearing was most cruelly removed from the rightful father for the four most delicate and impressionable years of the child's life. And why? Merely because of a legal *mishap*, an informal separation from his wife by a procedure called self-divorce, said divorce being procured through grievous error. What you, the jury, must understand, is that a self-divorce has no legal standing unless both parties *willingly* agree to it. We will prove, in the course of this trial, that Mr. Trahern was *not* willing, and thus the divorce was not legal. He therefore not only *deserves* but by right *ought to have* the child given into his lawful custody."

Rachel, her pulse racing nervously, leaned forward as Galliard rose to counter. His manner was less emotionally grandiose than that of his learned opponent. He had told Rachel that he would start by being calm and reasoned, saving the emotional bombast for the trial's more climactic moments. "Despite Mr. Trahern's unimpeachable character," he said quietly, "his claim is false. We will prove to you that, since he himself had instituted the divorce proceeding against Mistress Rachel Mason and had agreed to the terms of it in full view of at least a half-dozen witnesses, he was a *willing* partner to the divorce, a divorce which was believed by the defendant, Mistress Mason, to be—and must *still* be considered to be—a lawful and permanent arrangement. It is the defendant's contention, therefore, that her present husband, Mr. Peter Mason, although not present in court at this time, is *ipso facto* the legal father of the boy in question."

That ended the morning session. When they returned to their places that afternoon, the rain had stopped, but the sky was as heavy and dark as it had been earlier. Mr. Becker called his first witness: Courtland White. Rachel had already told her lawyer that he was a man of substance, good education, and a close friend of the plaintiff. She now noted that Galliard was leaning forward, listening intently, for he'd told her that this witness would give him the key to the direction Becker intended to take.

The prothonotary swore the witness in, and Mr. White took his seat in the witness box. After the preliminaries, Becker asked, "Did you know the plaintiff before he intermarried with Rachel Weller?"

"Yes, we were schoolboys together," said Courtland White.

"And you were close friends, were you not?"

"I would say so, yes. Even though we never agree about politics." This last was said with a grin thrown to Seth. Rachel noted that Seth did not respond with even the slightest smile. His grim expression remained as unchanged as the sky.

Abel proceeded. "But you are familiar with his nature, his character?"

"Yes, I think I am. I know him as well as anyone."

"Then tell us, Mr. White, did you notice any change in his character after the marriage took place?"

"Not in his character, perhaps," Courtland said, "but certainly in his spirit."

"Can you describe that change?"

"Yes, I can. There was a . . . a shine to him. He was happy. There's no other way to describe it. In all the years I've known him, he never was so happy as during those months of his marriage."

"I see." Abel let this information sink in by pausing in his questioning and taking a turn round the table. Then, when he stood a good distance from the witness, he resumed with dramatic intensity. "Think carefully about this next question, Mr. White," he intoned. "Did you *ever,* in that time that Mr. Trahern was married, notice anything—any sign, any word, even the slightest incident—to make you suspect that he wanted a divorce from Mistress Trahern?"

Courtland answered promptly, "No, never."

"You're certain?"

"Oh, yes. We always teased Seth about having snared the prettiest girl in New Castle. He'd grin and say 'New Castle? Don't you mean the whole country?' I swear, Abel . . . I mean, Mr. Becker . . . we all thought—and Seth did, too!—that he was the luckiest fellow in all Christendom."

"Then, when you heard he'd had a divorce, you must have been quite surprised, were you not?"

"Surprised? I could hardly believe my ears."

"Then how do you explain this sudden about-face in his marital status?"

"I can't explain it."

"Do you think he voluntarily agreed to it?"

"No. It can't have been voluntary. I can only conclude that he must have been . . . well, coerced into it."

"Objection, your honor," Galliard interrupted. "Mr. White's conclusions do not have validity."

The judge upheld him.

Abel barely blinked. He promptly rephrased the question. "But it *is* your contention that he must have agreed to the divorce unwillingly?"

"Yes. Very unwillingly."

"Objection," Galliard repeated.

"Sustained," the judge said.

"But you have a *basis*, have you not," Abel persisted, "for believing that Mr. Trahern was unwilling to divorce?"

"Yes, I have. His mood was miserable afterward. Completely miserable. If he was happy before and miserable after, that seems to me a sound enough basis for concluding that he was unwilling."

"It seems so to me, too. Thank you, Mr. White," Abel said, turning away. "Your witness, Mr. Galliard."

Galliard rose and approached the witness box. "Mr. White," he began, "you said, I believe, that you and Mr. Trahern are good friends, is that right?"

"Yes, sir."

"Good friends despite the fact that you never agree about politics?"

"Yes, sir."

"Did you ever manage to change his mind about political matters . . . to agree with you about any of them?"

Courtland smiled in fond recollection. "No, sir, I never did. He was always strong-headed about politics."

"Ah! *Strong-headed*, eh? So strong-headed you couldn't tease, cajole, coax, or coerce him into changing his views?"

Courtland, realizing what the lawyer was getting at, stiffened. "Well, er . . . no, I couldn't. Not about politics, anyway."

"But if he's so strong-headed, to use your own word, isn't he likely to be strong-headed in other matters?"

Courtland White, a bit disconcerted, shifted in his seat. "I . . . I suppose so."

"Therefore he's not the sort to be easily teased, or cajoled, or coerced into doing something he was unwilling to do?"

The witness, cornered, glowered at the lawyer. "I suppose," he said reluctantly.

"Yes or no, Mr. White. Is he the sort to be coaxed into doing what he's at heart unwilling to do?"

Mr. White sighed in defeat. "No, he's not," he admitted.

"Thank you, Mr. White," Galliard said, returning to his seat. "That's all I wanted to know."

Two more witnesses followed: John Odell Junior and Charles Lund, both of whom testified in a manner similar to Courtland White, and both of whose testimony Galliard weakened in the same way.

By this time the courtroom was almost dark, the candles of the wall sconces quite inadequate in the high-ceilinged room. Since days are short in October, and the heavy sky only worsened the matter, the judge recessed for the day. Galliard and his clerk escorted Rachel out, one on each side, forming a protective phalanx against the ogling crowd.

Although Galliard seemed optimistic about the day's proceedings, Rachel was troubled. "I don't understand what they're doing," she exclaimed when they were out of hearing of the crowd. "Why aren't they bringing up the *reason* Seth wanted the divorce?"

"I wondered about that myself," Harry Ferguson said in agreement.

"Are you referring to the matter of the supposed adultery with Peter Mason?" Galliard asked.

"Yes," she said, her mouth tightening.

"They won't bring it up. It would do their side no good to bring it up," her lawyer said.

"Why not?" Ferguson asked.

"Heavens to Holland, boy, when will you learn to think like a lawyer?" Galliard scolded. "They are trying to prove the illegality of the divorce by claiming he was *unwilling*. If the jury hears that Trahern's wife was unfaithful, might they not believe him not only *willing* but *eager* to divorce her?"

"Oh, I see. Then why don't *we* use it?" he asked.

Rachel thought it a very sensible question. But Galliard evidently did not. He glanced over at Rachel to see how she was taking this frank discussion. She looked back at him calmly, trying to show him that she was not upset. "Don't worry about me," she assured him. "I'm keenly interested in everything you say and think about this case."

Nevertheless the lawyer shook his head. "I would rather not go into the matter of adultery unless we must," he said. "We'll see." He walked on a few steps, deep in thought. Then he paused and smiled at his client in a way that Rachel thought was meant to be comforting. "There's another reason they're avoiding the subject of criminal conversation," he said quietly in her ear. "I think Trahern must have instructed Becker to avoid getting into it."

Rachel turned to him in surprise. "But why?"

"To protect you, my dear. I think he cares about your feelings."

"My feelings about the *adultery*? What nonsense! Everyone knows—or they think they know—about that. I have no reputation left. And I have no feelings left on that subject to protect."

"But perhaps Seth doesn't realize that," Galliard suggested as they crossed the Market Street square and approached the wagon that had brought her. Her father was already seated in it, waiting for her, so Galliard lowered his voice again. "The only explanation I can think of for the mild direction of their argument is Trahern's desire to be as kind to you as possible."

"*Kind?*" She threw her lawyer a look of scorn. "If he's so kind about my feelings, why does he want to take my son?" In a spasm of anger, she spurned his attempt to hand her up and climbed into the conveyance on her own. "My feeling toward my son is the *only* feeling that requires his kindness. As for any other kindnesses, he can spare himself the trouble."

Galliard sighed. "You're right. And if he's determined to win this fight, he won't be able to be kind for long. Things are bound to turn unpleasant. You'd best be prepared."

"I'm prepared," she said, taking the reins from her father and snapping them smartly. "I assure you I'm fully prepared." And with a nod of dismissal, she drove off into the deepening twilight.

49

*T*he sun shone brightly the next morning. As an omen, however, Rachel was to discover it was completely untrustworthy.

Her difficulties began as soon as court resumed. The first witness Abel Becker called was a surprise to almost everyone in court: William Shupp. Mr. Galliard asked the court's indulgence and went over to the dock to Rachel to ask who he was. "Goodness, it's Billy!" Rachel exclaimed under her breath. "He's come all the way from West Virginia for this!"

"Billy? Who is—?" Then he remembered. "Ah, the fellow in the shop. Seth's apprentice."

"Yes. He has his own printing business now. But, Mr. Galliard, I don't know why would he come all this way—?"

Being unprepared for this witness and uneasy about what he might say, Galliard turned to the judge and objected to his presence. "I have not," he declared, "been notified of his appearance."

"Sorry, your honor," Abel said in rebuttal. "Mr. Shupp is a substitute for a witness—Mrs. Clara Gruenwald— who has disappeared."

"Disappeared?" Judge Andersen asked. "What do you mean?"

"She's gone out of the state, Your Honor. I've been unable to locate her. I intend for Mr. Shupp to replace her."

Galliard cleared his throat. "While I sympathize with my learned colleague's predicament," he said with exaggerated politeness, "I nevertheless believe I should have been notified of the replacement, should I not?"

Abel made a small bow in his direction. "I do apologize to the learned counsel and the court, your honor," he said smoothly, "but Mr. Shupp has come from so great a distance that the trip took three days. When I sent him a communication requesting his attendance—a mere week ago, when I learned of Mrs. Gruenwald's disappearance—I had no certainty that it would be received, much less that he would respond affirmatively. Since I doubted that he would arrive in time to testify, I didn't think it necessary to provide Mr. Galliard with his name."

The judge, although frowning at Abel in disapproval, nevertheless expressed his willingness to accept the explanation if Mr. Galliard had no further objection. Mr. Galliard asked for another moment to confer with his client.

Rachel and he had a hurried exchange "Why would they have sent for him from such a distance?" he asked her worriedly.

"I don't know, but surely Billy is unlikely to have any information the other witnesses don't have."

Galliard seemed somewhat relieved by her assurance. "If you feel that this new testimony probably will not be more damaging than what we've already heard," he mumbled, "then no doubt I can handle it." Rachel believed he was even more encouraged by Abel's admission that Clara Gruenwald was not available; he'd often expressed concern that Clara's testimony would prove more damaging than any other. She, after all, was the only witness who had actual knowledge of the boy's true paternity. Shupp was, from Galliard's point of view, a good exchange for Gruenwald.

Mr. Galliard, therefore, announced to the judge in his most magnanimous manner that he would withdraw his objection to this witness despite the lack of warning of his appearance.

Billy Shupp was then produced and sworn in.

Rachel observed the now-grown Billy with interest as he took the stand. Now in his mid-twenties, his red hair was still his most noticeable characteristic. The greatest change in him was his air of self-confidence, an air more suited to someone twice his age. In a fellow so young, Rachel thought, it might have seemed cocky. In his case, however, she suspected that it was not cockiness so much as a strong belief in his own competence, a characteristic that Seth used to say he'd often observed in men who ran their own businesses, a quality that he believed bred particularly well in the new, entrepreneurial American climate.

Billy Shupp leaned back in his chair and smiled at Seth, who threw a small smile back at him. It was the first time Rachel had seen Seth's expression soften.

"What is your relationship to the plaintiff, Mr. Shupp?" was Abel's first question to the witness.

"I was his apprentice in the printing shop for eight years," Billy said. "Seventeen-ninety-six to eighteen-aught-four."

"Would you say you knew him well in those years?"

"Oh, yes, very well. Mr. Trahern was like a father to me."

"How would you describe him?"

"I think the best word I'd find for him was fair. He was always fair. And kind. But not easy, mind you. He always expected good work. Firm as a rock about that. He'd never accept slovenly work. A high stickler, he was."

"Before his marriage to Mrs. Trahern, what would you say about him. Was he moody? Disgruntled? Hard to please?"

"No, I wouldn't say that. He was steady, y'know. Eventempered. Reliable. You knew what to expect from him."

"Did this change at all after his marriage to Mrs. Trahern?"

Galliard jumped to his feet. "Your Honor, I object to Mr. Becker's repeated reference to my client as Mrs. Trahern. Her name is Mason."

"That's just what we're trying to disprove, your honor," Becker countered.

"Really, gentlemen," the judge snapped, glaring down at them both in disgust, "this is too petty a matter to take seriously. As my sainted mother used to say, 'Small bickerings lead to large battles.' I refuse to arbitrate the point. Each of you may call the lady whatever name you choose. We shall know whom you mean. Continue your questioning, Mr. Becker. You, Mr. Galliard, *sit down!*"

Abel Becker winked at his adversary in amused triumph before returning to his witness and repeating his question: "Did Mr. Trahern's character change at all after his marriage to Mrs. *Trahern?*"

Billy laughed at Mr. Becker's emphasis of the name. But when the judge pounded his gavel, he immediately turned serious. "No, not really," he responded, "except that he was happy."

"Did he *say* that? That he was happy?"

"No, but he didn't need to. I could tell."

"How?"

The witness snorted. "Wasn't hard. There were signs. Like he whistled a lot when he cleaned the press, and he walked with a kind of swing, that sort of thing."

"One expects that sort of euphoric behavior from newlyweds. It usually passes rather quickly, doesn't it?" Abel asked.

Galliard boldly made another objection. "I believe Mr. Shupp is a bachelor. Is his view of such marital matters to be taken as expert testimony?" he asked in his dryest tone, winning a satisfying titter from the listeners.

The judge, unimpressed, overruled. "In that sort of observation of wedded couples, one needn't be necessarily be expert," he commented. "As my sainted mother used to say, 'You don't have to be swimming in the ocean to know when the waves are rough.' You may answer, Mr. Shupp."

Galliard leaned over to his clerk and whispered something in his ear. Rachel, seated near them, thought he said something about wanting to removing His Honor's pince-nez and taking a swing at his hooked proboscis. She clearly heard him add, "Him *and* his sainted mother."

Meanwhile, Billy Shupp was obediently answering. "I suppose in most cases the couples cool, but in the case of the Traherns, well, it seemed to me that they grew even closer and happier as the weeks passed."

Abel feigned astonishment. "Are you saying, Mr. Shupp, that in all the time of his marriage, Mr. Trahern *never* showed signs of discontent? Of regretting his married state in any way?"

Billy snorted. "Regretting it? Never! I ain't never seen a man so contented. When the Missus used to come to the shop to set type, I'd see them exchange those little looks, y'know, like they had this happy secret between them no one else could share. Like lovebirds, y'know. You may take my word he never regretted it fer a second."

Rachel couldn't help herself. She darted a glance at Seth. But he'd put a hand up to shield his face.

"Then how do you account for his agreeing to divorce her?" Abel went on.

Harry Ferguson leaned over to Galliard and whispered in his ear. Rachel suspected he was asking why Galliard wasn't objecting. Even she could understand that the answer would be Shupp's conclusions, which wouldn't be valid. But Mr. Galliard shook his head. Perhaps he wanted to hear Billy's answer.

"He did it for *her* sake," Shupp said, looking directly at Rachel for the first time.

"Her sake? Mrs. Trahern's?"

"Yes, sir. He didn't want no divorce. *She* did."

Abel threw Galliard another triumphant leer. "Thank you, Mr. Shupp," he said and took his seat.

As Mr. Galliard passed the dock on his way to face the witness, he warned Rachel in an undervoice, "This may become unpleasant."

She raised her chin. "I told you I'm prepared," she whispered back.

Galliard approached the witness. "Mr. Shupp, may I commend you for coming all this way to testify for Mr. Trahern? You must be a very loyal friend."

Billy shrugged. "Well, he deserves it. He taught me a lot more than just printing. He taught me to be a man."

"Did he? That is a fine thing to say of someone. Tell me, Mr. Shupp, did he do that by talking—lecturing you on behavior, say? Or did he do it by example?"

"By example, for sure. He ain't the type to lecture a fellow."

"He didn't lecture you? Then did he perhaps pass the time in the shop talking to you about himself?"

"No, the shop is a place of business. And I was just his devil . . . only a boy, y'see. He didn't talk about his private life to me."

"Then I can't help wondering, Mr. Shupp, how you can be so sure about something as private as a man's relationship with his wife as to claim he didn't want the divorce."

"He didn't have to talk about it. I could tell."

"How could you tell?"

"By his mood. His misery. After."

"If he didn't speak of private things, how can you be sure that the misery he showed wasn't due to some other facet of his life?"

"Because there wasn't any other facet of his life to get miserable about. Business was good. Politics was good. What else would make him miserable?"

"I'll ask the questions, Mr. Shupp, if you don't mind. The fact remains, does it not, that you have no direct knowledge of what Mr. Trahern had on his mind when he divorced his wife?"

"I may not have been in his head, sir, but I sure saw the mood he was in."

"Yes, you told us that already."

Rachel thought Galliard had sounded waspish. Was he finding Billy a hard nut to crack?

Galliard took a deep breath and went on. "And you are explaining your employer's bad mood by saying that it was Mrs. Mason, formerly Trahern, who wanted the divorce?"

"Yes, I said that, and I'll say it again. Mr. Peter Mason came back from the dead, and she wanted to wed him."

There was a loud murmur from the audience, but Galliard quieted it by speaking over it. "Did she tell you that?" he asked.

"Well, no, but I knew it. Lots of folks knew it."

"How did you 'know' it if you never heard her say so?"

"For one thing, she used to go walkin' out with Mason before he went to sea and disappeared. And for another, she up and married him right after he came back. Seems like pretty good proof to me."

There was a noticeable snicker from the onlookers. Billy Shupp looked quite proud of himself.

"It may be pretty good proof to you, Mr. Shupp," Galliard said in annoyance, "but I presume the jury won't find it adequate."

The judge rapped his gavel. "That will be enough of that, Mr. Galliard," he reprimanded. "We don't make presumptions about the jury, as you should know." He leered down at Galliard in a repugnantly superior way, as if the Philadelphia attorney was an idiot schoolboy. "He that knows *least* presumes *most,* you know."

"A saying of your sainted mother?" Galliard muttered irritably, an utterance he immediately regretted.

Abel, however, gave a snort of amusement. The judge snapped sharply at attention, his leer abruptly vanishing. "What did you say, Mr. Galliard?"

"Nothing, your honor."

"Mr. Becker, what did Mr. Galliard say that made you laugh?"

"Nothing, your honor, I assure you," Abel said with bland innocence. "I only coughed."

The judge (wisely, Rachel thought) let the matter drop.

Galliard was relieved. Nevertheless, he was obviously not happy at the way the exchange with Billy Shupp had gone. He took a moment to gather his thoughts. "Mr. Shupp," he said after a long silence, "is it your opinion that Mrs. Mason somehow convinced Mr. Trahern to divorce her in spite of his own desires, purely in order to allow her to be free to wed Mr. Mason?"

"Yes, that's exactly what I think."

"How do you suppose she could do that? By threats? By coaxing?"

"No, nothin' like that."

"No, of course not. It does seem unlikely, especially after you yourself explained how firm Mr. Trahern was in everything he did. Do you think a man as firm as you say Mr. Trahern was could be pushed, coaxed, or cajoled into divorcing his wife if he didn't wish to?"

"Yes, I do, in this case," the fellow said adamantly.

"Why in this case?"

"'Cause it wasn't a question of being firm or not being firm. It was a question of Rachel's happiness. Seth divorced her to make her happy."

Galliard pounced. "Then, in order to make her happy, he divorced her *willingly*, did he not?"

Billy was taken aback. "Willingly?" He looked over to the plaintiff's table as if for help, but there was no help coming. "I wouldn't call it willingly, exactly," he muttered at last.

"Wouldn't you? Then let's see what you *would* call it. You claim that to make his wife happy, Mr. Trahern sacrificed his own happiness. Would you call such an act generous?"

Billy looked at Galliard suspiciously. "Yes. Of course."

"More than generous, wouldn't you say? Magnanimous? Noble, even?"

"Yes, I would," Billy said belligerently. "Noble is *exactly* what I'd call it."

"Sacrificing one's own wishes for someone else's happiness *is* noble, I agree. But to do it, to do a noble act, one must be *willing* to make the sacrifice, mustn't one?"

Billy looked like he'd bitten into a fruit he didn't know was sour. "I wouldn't say that, necessarily," he mumbled.

"You wouldn't? But the very definition of that sort of nobility implies willingness, does it not? We can't call an act noble if the act is done *un*willingly, can we?"

"Objection," Abel snapped. "The witness is being asked to compose definitions. Is the learned counsel expecting the witness to be a lexicographer?"

"Overruled," said His Honor. "You don't have to be a lexicographer to know what 'noble' means." Then he threw Galliard a glinting look through his pince-nez. "And that was not a quote from my sainted mother. You may answer, Mr. Shupp."

Billy looked miserable. "What was the question?" he asked.

"I asked if you could call an act noble that was made unwillingly."

"I don't know," he said belligerently, his self-confidence shaken but by no means slain. "All I know is Seth didn't want to divorce his wife. And you can't put words in my mouth that say he did."

"But the words were your own, Mr. Shupp," Galliard pointed out gently. "You said yourself that Mr. Trahern did a noble act. I'm sure the jury knows, as you do in your heart, that an act, to be called noble, *must* be done willingly."

"But, I—"

Galliard cut him off. "Thank you, Mr. Shupp," he said, turning away. "No more ques—"

The witness ignored the dismissal. "Just one minute here!" he burst out. "You can't call it willingly if he was *tricked* into it, can you?"

"Tricked into it?" Galliard turned back and faced him. Rachel wondered if he was heading into a trap. "I don't understand, Mr. Shupp," the lawyer asked. "How was he tricked into it?"

Billy glanced over at Abel Becker as if for reassurance. Rachel followed his glance and saw Abel give him a blink and an almost imperceptible nod. Then the witness said, "By her not telling him she was expecting."

There was a gasp from the onlookers. Rachel felt her heart leap.

Galliard eyes brightened. "Expecting?" he asked.

"You know," the fellow said, disgusted by Galliard's feigned ignorance. "Expecting a baby."

Mr. William Galliard took a deep, relieved breath and threw Rachel a look of triumph. There it was, out in the open, the grounds on which he'd planned from the first to fight this case. The paternity issue.

50

*W*ith the paternity question now open, both lawyers took quick glances at their clients to see how the principals in the case were taking this disclosure. Rachel's head was high and her face frozen in an expression both proud and impassive. Trahern, on the other hand, sat with his shoulders slumped and his head lowered, his hands on the table clenched tightly. One could see at a glance how miserable this very private man was being made by the open display of the dirty linen of his life.

Galliard turned back to Billy Shupp. "How can you make that claim? Did Mrs. Mason tell you she was 'expecting'?"

"No, sir, she didn't tell me. Far as I know, she didn't tell no one. I learned about it later."

"How much later?"

"In February of aught-two. After the boy was born."

"But the boy was born in Canada. How did you learn of it?"

"From Rachel's own brother, Simon Weller. He told me."

"He told you what?"

"That Rachel had just had a son."

Galliard raised his brows in contempt. "And you concluded from *that* that she was pregnant before the divorce?"

"Well, she had to be, didn't she?" Billy countered, unperturbed by the derision in the attorney's voice. "It was only seven months from the time of her wedding to Peter Mason."

"Counted the months, did you?" Galliard sneered. "Like any gossiping busybody?"

The judge's gavel pounded. "Mr. Galliard!" he shouted in angry disapproval at the same moment that Becker cried "Objection!"

"I withdraw that remark," Galliard said quickly. "But since this witness cannot possibly have direct evidence in the matter of my client's pregnancy, I have no further questions for him."

Becker indicated that he had no redirect, so the Honorable Thorwald Andersen called a recess. The hubbub from the crowd as the principals and their attorneys fought their way out was louder than it had ever been before.

Abel Becker steered his client around the corner of the courthouse, where, partially screened by a leafy elm, they could discuss the morning's events in some privacy. Seth spoke his mind at once. "Damn it, Abel, what are you doing? You know I want the case tried on the illegality of the divorce."

"Yes, I know you do. But you see, don't you, how Galliard has been weakening the supporting evidence? I had to let Billy say it. His testimony would have been a complete waste otherwise."

"But this paternity thing . . . did you see Rachel's face?"

"Yes, I did," Abel answered, "and I think she's holding up remarkably well. Sits there straight as an arrow, head up, taking it all as bravely as a soldier."

"You didn't look in her eyes." Seth shook his head ruefully. "As *my* sainted mother used to say, ''Tis of little good to the unfortunate to be brave.'"

"See here, Seth, I did warn you that this would happen, that we cannot win without bringing up matters that are bound to be painful to hear."

This was not a bit soothing to Seth. "But you said you'd try to keep Rachel's pain to a minimum."

Abel, who, as a friend of Seth's, was also trying to keep *his* pain to a minimum, sighed helplessly. "You do want to win, don't you?" he asked. "If you do, you have to accept the blows. I'm afraid, my friend, that you must learn an axiom of our profession, a precept that sooner or later I must make all my clients accept: There are no gains without pains."

Galliard, meanwhile, was steering Rachel toward the river in an attempt to find a place of relative seclusion. While they walked, he tried to assure the tight-lipped woman that Billy Shupp's testimony had not been as damaging as she might have feared. "He brought up the pregnancy business because he knew he'd lost the 'willingness' argument," Galliard explained. "And in raising that issue, he did us a favor. We wanted the case to be argued on the paternity issue, after all."

"*You* wanted it," Rachel reminded him. "Not I."

Galliard only shrugged.

They reached Front Street, where they could see the river. She stared out toward the water. "The ways of the law are very strange," she murmured to herself, shaking her head in bewilderment.

"In what way, ma'am?" Galliard asked.

"If our case is an example, the whole business is based on lies, not truth."

Galliard, who took great pride in his profession, drew up in offense. "We do not lie! We may omit some of the truth in order to get justice, but we do not lie."

"Don't you? Everyone, it seems to me, is lying. Seth's side is claiming he was unwilling to divorce me, when it was really *I* who was the unwilling one. And we are claiming I was not pregnant at that time, when you and I both know I was. Can you deny that we are lying on both sides?"

"I do deny it. We do not actually lie. By emphasizing some points and avoiding others, we shape the truth to our advantage. You do want to win, don't you? Does not justice triumph if you are allowed to keep your son? Even if the truth is a bit bent along the way?"

Rachel peered at her attorney dubiously. "Yes, I suppose so," she said at last, "but what if we did what we swore to do when we took the oath—told the truth, the whole truth, and nothing but the truth? I can't help wondering what would happen then."

51

*R*achel tried not to reveal her agitation as she went about her household chores that evening. Worn out by the strain of the trial, she wished nothing more than to go to her bed. But Jossy and her father had to be given their supper, and Jossy had to be washed and put to bed. She took off the Sunday dress she'd worn to court, slipped on her old homespun and an apron, and set about preparing the simplest meal she could—barley soup that she'd made earlier in the week, salt pork, and hominy. With that and a bit of appleleather for after-sweetness, they would have to be content.

It was quite dark by the time she'd set the table and heated the food. She'd just called her father and Jossy to come to the table when they heard a horse gallop up to their door. Ordering them to start their soup while it was hot, she went to the door and opened it. There was a man standing there, a man she did not recognize in the dim light emanating from the candlelit dining room. "Who is it?" she asked, peering out.

The man laughed heartily and seized by her waist. "Don't you know yer own husband?" he asked, lifting her up and swinging her about.

"*Peter?*" She felt faint. "Oh, God," she gasped, struggling to keep herself from slipping into the tempting escape of a swoon.

Holding her high, he looked up at her. "Still the prettiest woman ever," he grinned.

She stared down at him, aghast. He was recognizable now that her eyes had become accustomed to the dimness. He was older, heavier, somewhat shaggy, and sporting a new, large moustache. It was that facial addition that had kept her from recognizing him. He was in many ways unchanged, but now that his youthful looks were gone, his face revealed more of what he really was: a self-indulgent, shallow braggart. An instant revulsion swept over her, followed by an almost overpowering rage. "Put me down!" she ordered.

He set her on her feet and tried to take her into an embrace, but she held him off. "I suppose," she said, breathing hard, "that you must . . . come in."

He crossed the threshold with a swagger, his heavy boots making an unfamiliar clumping on the wood floor. Joss, gaping, got slowly to his feet. "What on God's earth—?"

"Aye, it's yer son-in-law," Peter grinned, putting out his hand.

Joss refused to take it.

Peter turned to the little boy who was staring up at him. "And is this Jossy?" he cried. "You sure have growed! Come here, boy, an' give yer Pa a big bear hug!"

Jossy, instinctively wary of this too-hearty stranger, slipped from his chair and backed away until he could clutch at his mother's skirt.

"Leave him alone," Rachel ordered coldly, stepping protectively in front of the child. "We are at supper. If you're hungry, you're welcome to sup with us."

"Sure I'm hungry," Peter said. "I been in the saddle since sunup."

"Then sit you down. But, understand, Peter, that you will not be welcome after the meal."

"Hey, now, is this the sort of greeting to give yer man after three years?" he said, trying to put an arm about her.

"We'll talk about that after Jossy goes to bed," she muttered, eyeing him in stern reproof as she pushed him away.

She set the food before him, and they began to eat in silence. Rachel gave her attention to her son, who, staring at the intruder with eyes wide with alarm, had to be coaxed to eat. For several minutes no words were exchanged, but Peter soon broke the silence by asking "Don't you care to know where I been?"

It was not Rachel but her father who answered. "Go ahead and say, if ye're bound to tell."

It was all the encouragement Peter needed. He launched on an account of his travels that had finally taken him to the Mississippi Territory, where he'd managed to buy some land. "When the gover'ment purchased Louisiana," he boasted, "the value of my land went way up." He looked around at them, expecting some interest if not admiration. They gave him neither; they did not look up from their plates.

Rachel hurried her son through the meal and took him up to bed. The child said little as she washed him and dressed him in his nightshirt, but it was plain that he was troubled. When she was tucking the blankets around him, he burst out with what was on his mind. "That man said he was my Pa."

Rachel drew in a deep breath. "Well, he isn't, so don't trouble your head about it," she said as casually as she could.

"Then why did he say it?" the boy asked.

"Because he wishes he was." She leaned over him and, with a comforting smile, tousled his hair. "Because you're such a fine fellow, any man would want to be your father."

"Oh, Mama," he objected, giggling in relief, "that's silly."

"I don't think it's silly," she said, "but silly or not, you can forget about that man downstairs. He'll be going away in a little while, and we won't see him any more."

She came downstairs in time to hear her father shouting, "You have damn brass, Peter Mason, to sit there eatin' my Rachel's cooking after braggin' as how you *married two other women*!"

She stopped short, surprising herself by giving out a snort of amusement. So he had other women, had he? Somehow the news was a relief to her. Her rejection of him would therefore not be painful to him. Feeling calm for the first time since her husband had arrived, she walked into the room. "Is that true, Peter?" she asked bluntly. "Two other women?"

Peter smiled sheepishly. "Aye, it's true. One in Missouri and one in Mississippi. But it don't mean nothing. You were always the only wife for me. That's why I came back. I want to take you out west with me."

"Really?" She smiled almost admiringly. "You are quite a fellow, Peter Mason. You must be without peer in your ability to fool yourself. Did you really think that you could desert me for more than three years, after having stolen our savings and leaving me penniless, and then expect to resume relations as if nothing had happened?"

"I know I acted wrong," Peter said, "but things're different now. I'm pretty well off these days. That's why I waited all this time, to have something to offer you."

"Then what'll ye do with your two other wives?" Joss snorted.

Peter ignored him. "You well know, Rachel, what you've always been to me."

"But now you have two others to take my place," she said. "Let them suffice."

"They don't count, I swear. I know we've had some bad years, you an' me, but it will all turn out for the best, you'll see."

"No, Peter. It'll turn out for the best only when you leave here."

"Ah, come now, girl!" He got to his feet, a coaxing smile on his face. "You don't mean it."

"Oh, yes, I do." The fellow's arrogance—his obvious expectation of her capitulation—made her furious. "I want you to leave."

"Let's not be hasty," he said, still smiling. "Let's go to bed an' talk about it in the morning."

"I said I want you to leave," she said through clenched teeth. "*Now!*"

He heard a firmness in her tone he'd never heard before. There was no mistaking her intent. "All right," he yielded, "I know I surprised you. I'll go and give you some time to get used to the idea."

She said nothing more as she led him to the door. But when he'd crossed the threshold she spoke her last words to him. "Listen to me, Peter, and believe what I'm saying. I will not go west with you. I will not go any-where with you. I do not consider myself your wife any longer. Nor are you welcome in this house. Papa keeps a shotgun in the shed. If you try to put one foot over this threshold again, as God is my witness, I swear I will take it out and shoot you myself."

And she shut and latched the door.

52

*T*he next day being Sunday, there was no court. After church, Rachel invited Mr. Galliard and his clerk to come out to the farm to dine with them. Although Peter's shocking return had left her discomposed and not really in a state to wish for company, she couldn't help pitying her lawyer and his assistant, who would surely be lonely at the inn on the Sabbath, so far from home and family. Harry Ferguson, unaccustomed to being asked to join his employer in social affairs, shyly shook his head and refused the invitation, but Rachel insisted. "You must come, Mr. Ferguson. We are having roasted goose. Stuffed with plums."

The awkward fellow lifted his hat, blushing from neck to hairline as he always did when a female paid any heed to him. Mr. Galliard slapped his clerk on the back and thanked Rachel for both of them. "You can have no idea how grateful we are," he told her. "A home-cooked dinner is always much appreciated by travelers. Especially roasted goose."

Joss offered to take Mr. Galliard up in the wagon, but since all four could not fit upon the benchlike seat, Galliard told Harry to go off and hire a gig from Lund's stables.

"I can walk out to the farm," Harry offered in his bashful way. "I don't mind a good stroll."

"No, no," Mr. Galliard insisted. "Hire the carriage and follow us out there. That way we needn't require that Mr. Weller drive us back to the inn when dinner is over."

Harry set off at once to do his bidding. In the wagon, Rachel—squeezed between her rotund father and her substantially built attorney—handed her father the reins. "I'm too atwitter to manage the horses," she said, twisting her fingers together.

"Out-and-out miffy, I'd say," her father agreed, whipping up the horses. "Not as I blame you, after all the tribulations you've endured."

"Tribulations?" Galliard inquired. "Of course the trial must be worrisome to you, but you've been behaving with great dignity and restraint. Has it truly been a tribulation to you?"

"Of course it has," Rachel admitted with a rueful smile, "but I think Papa is referring to something else."

"Something else?"

"Yes, something else has happened," she said, "but I don't like to discuss it with you on the Sabbath. You are entitled to a day of rest from legal matters."

"If the matter is connected with the case, ma'am," the attorney assured her, "I prefer to have the information as soon as possible, even on a Sunday. You must tell me at once."

"Well, then, sir, here it is," she said without further apology. "Peter Mason has come back."

Mr. Galliard was surprised but, lawyerlike, tried not to show it. He only said a careful "I see."

Rachel gave a quick account of what had happened. Her missing husband had appeared at their door the evening before, she told him. The shock had been great. She'd wanted to slam the door in his face. So had her father. But the boy was watching, so they'd controlled themselves. "We tried not to make a to-do in front of Jossy," she explained, feeling embarrassed at having to speak of it.

"Damned whiffler!" Josiah Weller muttered, snapping the reins.

"I take it you don't like him, sir," the lawyer said.

"*Like* him? Not by a long shot," the old fellow replied bitterly. "Never did."

"He told us he'd been living in the Mississippi Territory," Rachel went on, "where he'd managed to buy some land and make a great profit on it."

"So he claimed," Josiah said, "but I don't believe a word of it. Truth may sometimes come out of the devil's mouth, but never out of Mason's."

"It doesn't matter if he's speaking the truth or not," Rachel said to her father. "I wouldn't go west with him even if he'd become the richest man on earth."

"Is that what he wanted?" Galliard asked. "For you to go west with him?"

"Me and the boy."

"Did you ever hear the like?" Josiah flung out. "He had the damn cheek to make that proposal while sittin' there eatin' my Rachel's cookin', after braggin' as how he'd *married two different women*! But a'course, he swore he never considered anyone but Rachel as his real wife! Huh!"

"Don't excite yourself, Papa. It makes no difference to me what he does or whom he weds." She was sure of the absolute truth of those words. But there was something else worrying her, something that had troubled her from the moment she'd slammed the door on Peter.

She turned toward her lawyer uneasily. "Tell me, Mr. Galliard, if it should somehow get out in court that he takes wives as easily as he buys a new coat, would that destroy the argument that I am his legal wife?"

"No, I don't think so. But it would complicate things. Did you tell him about the trial? Will he be coming to court?"

"No, I said not a word about it. I wished only that the man would leave. When I showed him the door after dinner, I told him quite firmly that it was my intention not to let him cross my threshold again."

"And he agreed?"

"He was sullen, but he went away. It was only afterwards that I wondered if I'd been hasty . . . if you might think his presence in court could be a help to our case."

"It has crossed my mind once or twice that having a loyal husband sitting beside you might make the jury more likely to believe in your marriage, but—"

She winced, alarmed. "Do you truly think so? Good heavens, have I done the wrong thing? But perhaps we can find him. I have no idea where he's gone, but he can't have gone far in one day!"

"No, no, be tranquil," Galliard assured her. "I don't really want him. For one thing, he does not appear to be the sort of fellow to whom a jury would take a fancy. And for another, I decided long ago that a woman alone, as you are, is more likely to win sympathy from the jury than a woman accompanied by a man, even a likeable one."

Rachel expelled a long, relieved sigh. "Thank goodness. I would dread having to endure any dealings with Peter Mason. I don't want to see him again in this life. Not ever. And if God will forgive me my sins, I won't see him in the next life either."

53

The light emanating from the print-shop window shone late Sunday night. Seth was at work. Having to spend his days in court, he had to find time for his work whenever he could. The paper had to be printed on time, no matter what else was occurring in his life. He was, therefore, standing at the composing table setting type, despite the fact that it was past midnight. Outside his window, everything was dark and still. The whole world seemed to be sleeping. When the doorbell suddenly jangled, it startled him. He wheeled around to find Abel coming in. "Why are you still up at this hour?" he demanded inhospitably. "I hope you're not here to talk about the case, Abel. I don't want to even *think* on it the one day we're not in court."

"No, you clunch, I'm not here to discuss legal matters," Abel said cheerfully, seating himself on the bench and taking out one of his long cigars. "I was on my way home from Hansen's and saw your light. Just came in to keep you company."

"Oh." Seth felt somewhat abashed at his rudeness. "Don't know why you bothered," he muttered, keeping his eyes fixed on the type. "I'm not very good company these days."

"No need to tell me that," his friend laughed. "I'm well acquainted with your moods." He opened the stove, set a rolled-up strip of paper aflame and lit his long-nine with two puffs. "You don't have to speak at all, as far as I'm concerned. I'll just sit here and smoke and watch you work."

Seth grunted and resumed his typesetting. To his amazement, the bell jangled again. Charlie Lund entered, carrying a large wrought-iron frame. "Good heavens, Charlie," Seth greeted, "I didn't expect you to mend that chase for me on a Sunday. And so late!"

"I knew ye'd be needin' it," the blacksmith said. "I didn't mind doin' it tonight."

"What on earth *is* that thing?" Abel inquired.

"It's called a chase," Seth explained. "It frames the composing sticks that contain the type, like this one I'm holding, and it locks the page of print in pla—"

The bell jangled a third time. Astounded, they all turned to the door. Two men burst in. One of them, who appeared to be in a terrible temper, was a stranger. The other, an unshaven vagrant in a shabby pea coat, carrying a large, flat wooden box, was instantly recognized. "Timmy Styles!" Charlie cried in surprise. "What the hell're you doin' here?"

Abel's eyebrows also rose. Timmy Styles, who'd come back from the sea two years before but had never settled down to steady work on land, was now known as the town drunkard, supporting his craving for drink by taking odd jobs and the charity of kind housewives. "Yes, Styles. Why aren't you at your usual place, at Hansen's bar?"

"Ask him," Styles muttered, pointing to his companion.

Seth was studying the stranger closely. There was

something familiar about him. He was dressed in high style, with a striped velvet waistcoat and narrow trousers tucked into a pair of topboots in a mode affected by young bucks. *This fellow is past the age to indulge in such foppery*, Seth thought. The stranger's outlandish appearance was enhanced by his moustache and his long hair that, instead of being tied back, hung over his shoulders frontier style. *Frontier style.* The moment those words crossed his mind, Seth gasped. "By God, it's Peter Mason!"

"*Mason!*" Abel's cigar dropped from his mouth.

"Yup, it's Mason alright," Peter said belligerently, stomping with his heavy boots across the floor and thrusting his face into Seth's. "What's this I hear about you trying to steal my son?"

Seth stared back at him coldly. "I'm glad that you found *something* important enough to bring you back to your wife's side."

Mason grasped Seth's neckcloth. "I asked you a question."

Seth thrust him away so roughly that the intruder stumbled. Before he could recover his balance, Abel stepped between them. "Why don't you go out to the Weller place and ask your wife?" he said.

"I don't have to ask her," the enraged fellow said.

"Why not? Have you *seen* Rachel?" Seth couldn't help asking. "Does she know you're back?"

"No, I ain't seen her, not that it's any business of yours," Peter snapped.

"Then why don't you just go and ask her about all this?" Abel suggested, trying to urge the fellow out the door.

"I don't have to ask her." Mason pushed the lawyer aside and confronted Seth again. "I ain't gonna leave this place until you swear, in writing in yer newspaper, that you have no claim on my son."

Seth eyed him with contempt. "Don't be a fool."

"Fool, am I?" Mason sneered. "We'll see about that."

"Look here, Mason," Abel said reasonably, "this matter is just what we're arguing in court. Why don't you calm down and wait until the jury decides who has claim to the child?"

"I ain't gonna calm down. He can call me a fool, but I ain't stupid enough to believe that anyone can win in a New Castle court against the oh-so-great Seth Trahern."

"You may take my word, Mason," Abel tried to assure him, "that the trial is completely fair."

"I ain't takin' anyone's word. I know who counts in this town. I ain't movin' from here until he says in writing that I'm Jossy's father."

"An' tha's final," Timmy Styles put in. It was clear from his slurred speech that he was drunk.

"Since I will not write anything of the sort," Seth said, shrugging and turning back to his work, "I assume you will be taking up residence here. Make yourself at home."

Peter followed Seth to the composing table. "I figured you'd be stubborn about this," he said, "so I have another way to settle this."

"Have you, indeed?" Seth asked mildly, bending over his work.

"Show them, Timmy," Peter ordered.

Timmy obediently opened the box he carried and showed the contents to Charlie and Abel. "What're those?" Charlie asked in alarm. "*Dueling* pistols?"

Abel examined the two long-barreled pistols resting on a velvet pad. "So they are." He looked over at Mason with a sardonic smile. "What do you want to do with them? Fight a duel?"

"Just so," exclaimed the belligerent Peter Mason. "With a duel we don't need a court case or a newspaper announcement. We can settle this whole business once and for all."

"You're out of your head," Charlie declared. "Why'nt you be sensible and wait for the trial to be over before you go berserk."

"I can't wait for the trial. I'm going west tomorrow. Besides, I already told you what I think of the damn trial."

"Well, you're wrong about that," Charlie insisted. "Rachel is liked in New Castle as much as Seth, and prob'ly more than Abel. So the jury'll be fair."

"Liking has nothing to do with it," Abel said in disgust. "Juries don't vote on popularity. If there are one or two of the twelve who are foolish enough to wish to, the others soon set them straight."

"Well, I ain't going to chance it," Mason insisted. "And I ain't going away having everyone thinking I ain't the father of my boy. I have my honor. And if Trahern don't accept my challenge, he has none!"

This drew objections from both Abel and Charlie, and everyone began shouting at once. Only Seth stayed removed from the fray. But after listening for a few minutes to the angry disorder, he stepped in among them and held up his hand for silence. "Enough. If a duel will end this harangue, I'll meet him. Let's go down to Upton's Glen right now and do it."

"You're mad!" Abel exclaimed in horror.

"Perhaps. But I've made up my mind. Will you be my second?"

"Only if you can convince me that you haven't dispensed with your sanity."

"I'm sane enough. It just occurred to me that the outcome—either way—will have certain advantages. Whether I kill him or he kills me, it will bring the blasted trial to an end."

When Seth finally convinced Abel that he meant to go through with the ridiculous plan, the lawyer felt compelled to make appropriate arrangements. He sent Charlie Lund to roust Dr. Muncie out of his bed at once. When the bewildered doctor arrived, dressed only in a heavy woolen robe that he'd thrown over his nightshirt, he also tried to reason with Mason. He gave up only after he realized that Seth was giving him no support.

"Very well," Abel said, in a voice resonant with disgust, "I suppose we may as well start out. We're as ready as we'll ever be. Charlie, you act as referee."

"Nothing doing," Peter objected. "Lund is a friend of Trahern's. He won't be impartial."

"But there's no one else here," Abel said.

"Then get someone."

"Who can I get? Whoever I might choose will be a friend of Seth's."

"True," Dr. Muncie said. "So let's call off this ridiculous charade."

"I know someone whom Mason would accept," Seth suggested. "Mr. Galliard."

"Who's he?" Peter wanted to know.

"He's the lawyer from Philadelphia arguing against me. Will he be impartial enough for you?"

Abel glared at Seth. "You *are* mad! You can't ask him to get up in the middle of the night for a thing like this."

"Sure you can," Peter said, pleased to have someone on his side. "Just tell him it'd be an easy way to win his case."

Abel threw up his hands in surrender.

Fifteen minutes later, Charlie led a confused, sleepy-eyed Galliard into the shop. Seth, who'd been staring out the window, turned and nodded to him. The Philadelphia lawyer, whose attire in court was always impeccable, now looked very different. He'd put on his breeches, but his shirt was not tucked in, and he wore no vest or neckcloth. "What am I doing here?" he asked, peering bewilderedly at each of the men seated round the stove.

Abel was perched on the edge of Seth's desk, swinging his pocket-watch by its chain. "Ah, Galliard!" he greeted. "Thank you for coming. We are in the midst of a serious contretemps, which I am hoping your good sense will manage to alleviate. But first, let me introduce you to the members of this assemblage: Seth and Charlie you know, of course. But you haven't yet met New Castle's medical man, our Dr. Muncie, standing there in his *robe-de-chambre*. It will surely interest you to know that the good doctor is the very one who refused to be called to testify in our trial on the matter of premature births, since he felt his testimony might harm Rachel."

"How do you do?" Galliard said, reaching out and shaking the doctor's hand. "It's a pleasure to meet a man of integrity."

"Huh!" The sarcastic grunt came from Seth. The doctor's refusal to testify had been a bone of contention between those good friends. Seth's scornful reaction to Galliard's praise made the doctor laugh. It was the only time anyone in the room had laughed.

"And there on the bench," Abel continued, "is the instigator of this meeting, none other than hitherto-missing Peter Mason himself."

Peter didn't bother to rise but only nodded at him.

"Yes, I guessed as much," Galliard muttered.

Seth Trahern wheeled about and stared at him with pained surprise. Abel was taken by surprise, too. "How do you guess that?" he demanded.

"Rachel . . . Mrs. Mason . . . told me he was in town," Galliard admitted.

Seth winced. "She *knows*, then," he said, his throat and his fists tightening. "Has she . . . *seen* him?"

"Yes, of course," Galliard said.

Seth wheeled about to Mason. "You damn liar," he snapped, "you said you hadn't seen her!"

Mason looked sullen. "You can believe whoever you wish."

Seth turned to Galliard. "She *told* you she'd seen him?"

"Oh, yes," he replied. "She sent him packing."

Seth took a deep breath, and his fingers relaxed. That Rachel had rid herself of this scoundrel was the best news he'd had since the trial began.

Abel Becker returned to the matter at hand. "The last gentleman present is Mr. Mason's old friend, Mr. Timothy Styles. He is here as Mr. Mason's second."

"Second?" Galliard asked, stupefied.

"It seems," Abel said dryly, "that Mr. Mason has challenged Mr. Trahern to a duel."

Galliard gaped. "Did I hear aright? Did you say *duel*?"

"You heard right enough," Dr. Muncie said in disgust. "It's already arranged. Timmy is Peter's second, and Abel is Seth's. Timmy, the fool, has actually brought pistols."

Mason jumped to his feet. "That's right. We brought pistols. No man is going to say I ain't father to my son and go unchallenged."

"Enough!" Charlie Lund crossed the room and

pushed Mason back down on the bench. "We heard you say it a dozen times already."

Galliard looked from one frozen face to the next in disbelief. "Are you men serious? I know dueling is a popular sport in modish southern climes like Charleston and Savannah, but is this sort of thing still countenanced in Delaware?"

"It ain't against the law," Charlie said. "Don't you have duels in Pennsylvania?"

"I've not heard of any," Galliard said. "Not in the two years since Aaron Burr killed Mr. Hamilton. There were one or two disputes that came close, but they were settled amicably before shots were fired."

"I've been trying to settle this, if not amicably, at least sanely," Abel said, "but there's no appeasing Mr. Mason. He's determined to make use of his friend's pistols."

"What is it you expect to prove on the dueling field, Mr. Mason?" Galliard asked him.

"I have my honor," Mason declared stubbornly. "I ain't going to leave this town having everyone saying I ain't the father of my boy. Either Seth says, in writing, that he ain't the father, or I shoot him dead."

"But that's just what we're arguing in court," Galliard said. "I myself am arguing your side. Why don't you leave town as you planned, and let me do my job in your behalf? When the jury brings in a verdict in Mrs. Mason's favor, you'll have been vindicated."

"Will I?" the fellow sneered. "Either you're a damned looby or you're taking me for one. No jury in New Castle is going to find for a Philadelphia lawyer against Seth Trahern and Abel Becker."

Timothy Styles, who'd nodded off, shook himself awake and jumped to his feet. "No man's gonna say Peter Mason's a looby. Not in front of me!"

"Shut up, Timmy," Mason muttered, pulling him back down on the bench. "No one said I'm a looby."

"You *are* a looby, Peter," Charlie Lund said bluntly. "I don't see how bullets can prove what the courts can't."

"Look," Mason said, rising, "I ain't gonna change my mind. I've said all I'm going to." He turned his back on them. "You know my position."

His 'second' also got to his feet. "You know Peter's posi . . . posi . . . tion," he said, his tongue thick. "He has his—"

"We know, we know," Charlie Lund interrupted. "He has his honor."

There was a moment of silence. Then a clock on the wall behind the press—a large, hexagonal timepiece with a small pendulum—struck five. When the fifth bong had sounded, Seth turned around. "It's useless to continue this verbal wrangling," he said. "It'll soon be light. Let's go and get this over with."

Abel nodded and got to his feet. This signaled Peter Mason and his second to pick up their pistol-box and start out. The doctor, after viewing all of the others with a look of utmost scorn, muttered something indistinguishable and followed them. Then Charlie made for the door. The shop was quickly emptying.

"Wait a moment," Galliard called out. "What am *I* doing here?"

Abel paused on his way to the door. "Oh, didn't I explain? We needed someone fair and impartial to be referee. Seth suggested you." And off he went.

Galliard glared at Seth. "I suppose I should be flattered."

Seth gave a little laugh. "Yes, you should, Mr. Galliard, you should. It isn't often that a man in my position shows such respect for his enemy in court."

"Does choosing me to referee a duel show *respect*?" Galliard asked scornfully.

"It does indeed. The truth is, sir, that Mason would not trust the position to anyone in town, convinced as he is that he's disliked here. But I knew that you, an outsider and the one person arguing for his paternity, would be instantly acceptable to him."

"So it wasn't your respect for me but my acceptability to Mason that made you choose me," Galliard pointed out sarcastically.

"It was my respect for you that made you acceptable to *me*," Seth countered, his smile broadening. He put a friendly arm about Galliard's shoulder and marched him to the door. "Come along, man."

"Just a moment, Mr. Trahern," Galliard said, pausing at the doorway. "Although we are enemies in court, I have a liking for you. I don't want to be party to your demise. Damnation, don't you realize you may be dead within the hour?"

Seth threw the Philadelphia attorney a rueful smile. "Don't look so alarmed, Galliard. I doubt there will be blood shed. We shall probably delope. A couple of shots in the air and this whole ridiculous charade will be over, costing us nothing but a few hours' sleep. Isn't that how duels are fought these days?"

54

The street they followed—Thwart Street—angled sharply north. At its end, they followed a path down a thinly wooded slope. At the bottom was a grassy clearing almost entirely surrounded by woods. "'Tis a depressingly suitable spot," Galliard remarked to Seth, who was walking beside him.

"So it is," Seth said dryly. "This is not the first time Upton's Glen has been used for this nefarious purpose. I think my paper reported a duel here about a decade ago."

"Oh? And what was the outcome?"

"Not very newsworthy. The antagonists deloped."

"I earnestly wish that tonight's outcome will be the same," Galliard said worriedly, "but I hope, sir, that you will take care. Mr. Mason seems to me the sort who is out for blood."

Charlie Lund called for Galliard to pace off the space. While he did this, Peter and Seth removed their coats. "Are you truly going forward with this farcical activity?" Dr. Muncie asked. Receiving no response from the duelists, he shrugged and placed himself in the center of the measured-off area and watched the activity, his arms folded over his chest in a stance of disapproval and his lips moving in muttered deprecations.

Then Charlie—the only one among them with no specific role assigned to him—took it upon himself to check the weapons. By the time the ground was measured, and they'd all returned to the center area, Charlie was satisfied that the guns were primed and ready. "You should check them over yourself," he whispered to Galliard as he presented him with the box.

"I know nothing about pistols," Galliard told him. "Unless Mr. Becker or Mr. Styles has an objection, I shall take your word for their readiness."

Mason selected his weapon first. When Charlie objected that they should have drawn lots, Seth said it didn't matter. The duelists took their weapons and went to stand back-to-back in front of Galliard, lifting their pistols up before their faces. With Becker's prompting (for Galliard had no training for these duties), the "referee" instructed the duelists to take their full ten paces. "You must turn *after* my count of ten and fire at will," he said. The word "after" was strongly emphasized.

Galliard's voice trembled as he counted. Seth mentally counted along with the referee, marching forward with long steps. ". . . seven . . . eight . . . nine . . . te—" But before the last digit could roll fully from Galliard's tongue, Mason whirled around and fired. He had not even taken his last stride.

Seth, who'd not yet turned, felt a sharp pain in his side and staggered forward. He heard Dr. Muncie curse. Abel, who'd been standing close by, flung himself toward Seth, catching him in his arms just in time to keep him from falling. Seth tottered against him, his pistol still in his right hand. He lifted his left and tried to touch the place on his right side, about six inches below his armpit, where he could already feel blood flowing.

"Damn you, Mason, you yellow-belly, you were *early*!" Charlie Lund shouted.

Styles, sobered by the gunshot, kept Mason from moving. "Damn it, Peter, you didn't play straight. Now you have to stand pat."

"Exac'ly right," Charlie loudly agreed. "See, you lily-liver, even your own second is shamed at yer dishonor."

The doctor, meanwhile, ran up to Seth and tried to examine him, but Seth waved him away. Freeing himself from Abel's hold, he now stood erect. "Yes, Mason, stand still," he said in a low, threatening voice. "I'm not dead. I have yet to take my shot."

Mason paled. Styles backed away. Seth steadied himself, elbowed Abel away and slowly, deliberately, raised his gun.

Mason set his pistol down and raised his hands, palms up, in a kind of surrender. "All right, Trahern," he said, his knees quivering. "You win. I'll concede. You can delope."

Seth said nothing. His eyes narrowed coldly as he carefully took aim.

"You can't shoot now," Styles cried. "It'd be like murder."

Mason nodded in agreement. "Murder," he echoed through white lips.

"You can't call it murder," Abel declared. "It's his right."

Galliard, the referee, promptly agreed. "He still has the right to fire—at will."

"Go ahead, Seth, *shoot* the miserable coward," Charlie Lund urged. "He asked for it. He's always asked for it. He's never been anything but trouble."

Seth tightened his finger on the trigger.

"Please, Seth, don't!" Styles begged.

"I conceded, didn't I?" Peter asked, his attempt at belligerence weakened by the terror trembling in his voice. "You got no call to shoot now."

Seth merely steadied his aim.

"Oh, God," Mason muttered, shutting his eyes.

"Go ahead, Seth," Abel said. "Shoot."

Even Dr. Muncie urged it. "Go on," he said, "he deserves it."

"Yes, Trahern," Galliard said in quiet agreement, "no one would blame you if you shot the poltroon dead."

Seth stood there pointing his pistol at the abject Mason for several seconds, during which no one but Mason moved a muscle. Mason, eyes still shut, was shaking at the knees. Seth, remembering a certain scene in his parlor, felt a grim satisfaction in the prospect of putting a bullet into the chest of the wretch standing twenty paces in front of him.

"Please!" Peter begged in gasping whisper.

With a reluctant sigh, Seth surrendered to the promptings of his better nature, lifted his gun, pointed it toward the sky, and, grimacing with the pain the act of raising his arm caused him, deloped.

55

Against Dr. Muncie's express orders, Seth went to court the next morning. It was a session he could not miss, for Abel had told him there would be a surprising development. Though his wound ached dreadfully from the pain of the freshly sewn sutures, he took his place with a feeling of excited anticipation. As he looked about him, it seemed to Seth that only the most perceptive onlookers could have guessed that anything was amiss. He'd worn a bulky coat so that no one could detect that it was hiding a tightly bandaged wound. And he was sure no one could see that Abel and Galliard were tired from lack of sleep, for they showed no outward signs of it. In their attempt to hide their exhaustion, they were, if anything, brisk.

Galliard briskly rose to begin his parade of defense witnesses, but before he could call the first one, Abel briskly rose and asked the indulgence of the court. "One of my witnesses—Mrs. Clara Gruenwald, the one who's been missing—has suddenly returned. Since her testimony is very significant, I would like to call her as my final witness before my learned opponent begins his defense."

Seth stiffened. If Clara had indeed returned, his case

was won. Clara had information about Jossy's paternity no else possessed. Seth knew that Clara had left town for Rachel's sake, but he did not know why she'd returned. Whatever the reason, it was a boon for his cause but a blow for Rachel. Seth's eyes flew over to Rachel, to see how she was taking it. To his surprise, she seemed unperturbed. She was merely looking down at her hands, which were folded on her lap.

Galliard, however, was evidently quite startled by this development—he seemed noticeably shaken. He looked toward his client questioningly, but she did not lift her eyes. Even his pointed clearing of his throat did not prompt her to look up. She showed not the slightest sign of alarm.

Well, Seth told himself, it was not his place to be concerned. He was her accuser, not her advocate. Let her lawyer handle these eventualities.

Galliard, who probably could find no good reasons to object to the intrusion of this witness, nevertheless made the routine objections: the witness was introduced too late; counsel had already concluded his presentation; defense had not been informed. The judge summarily overruled each one.

Clara Gruenwald was called and sworn. She made a pleasing, motherly appearance, her form matronly ample, her gray hair pulled tightly back from her face and covered with a lace-trimmed cap, and her dress of brown homespun very much in keeping with the dignity of her carriage. As she took her seat in the witness box, the seriousness of her expression and rapid blinking of her eyes were the only signs of her inner nervousness. Seth recognized that nervousness because it exactly matched his own.

He glanced over at Rachel again and was again surprised at how calm she seemed. Surely she knew that Clara Gruenwald could devastate her case!

Abel sailed right in with his questioning. "You are Mr. Trahern's housekeeper, are you not?"

"Ja, I am," Clara said in her thick German accent.

"And were you the housekeeper when Mr. Trahern brought Rachel Weller home as his bride?"

"Ja, I was."

"Would you say that you and Mrs. Trahern were friendly?"

"Maybe not so much at first, but later we came to be friendly."

"How did that come about?"

"She was . . . is . . . a good, kind lady. We grow to like each other, so we become friendly."

"Would you say you were *intimate* friends?"

"No, I would not." She fixed Abel with a look of disdain. "Friendly is not friends. I was her housekeeper, not her friend."

(This stiff-necked response surprised Seth. Both lawyers, too, showed surprise. Galliard jotted a note to himself. Seth suspected he would try to probe this matter. If he could show that the housekeeper felt friendlier to her employer than to Rachel, he might show prejudice and thus weaken Clara's reliability.)

"But didn't Mrs. Trahern often talk to you about personal matters?" Abel prodded.

Mrs. Gruenwald shrugged. "I would not say often. Sometimes she did."

"Did she ever speak about her marriage?"

"Sometimes."

"Was it your impression it was a happy marriage?"

"Ja."

"Very happy?"

"Ja."

Abel paused dramatically before delivering his coup. "Did a time come, ma'am," he asked slowly and pointedly, "when Mrs. Trahern told you she was expecting a child?"

Clara, hesitating, glanced over at Rachel before replying. But when she did answer, she spoke firmly. "She don't have to tell me. I know."

"How could you know if she didn't tell you?"

"A woman knows. Mornings she was lazy in bed. Smiling always, even when she cannot keep down the breakfast."

"Did you tell her you knew why she was acting this way?"

"Ja. I tell her that I guess it. We was, how you say, like laughing together on it."

"Do you mean you teased her about her condition?"

"Ja. Teased."

"Now this is important, Mrs. Gruenwald. Was this before or after Peter Mason came back from the sea?"

"Before. Ach, ja. It begins many days before."

"Then it is your opinion that the father of Mrs. Trahern's child is Seth Trahern?"

"Is not opinion. Is fact. She tell me so."

"She told you in so many words that Mr. Trahern was the father?"

"Ja, she did."

Abel smiled. "Thank you, ma'am. Your witness, Mr. Galliard."

Galliard requested permission to confer. With this granted, he went to the dock and leaned over the rail. Seth watched him carefully. It seemed to him that Galliard was arguing with her. But Rachel kept her eyes lowered and did not respond. Finally she lifted her head and said two words to her attorney. Seth could not hear, but he thought she said, "Ask *her*."

Galliard turned away slowly. Seth could see his mind working, trying to get some sense of how to deal with this destruction of his case. The look of dismay in his eyes was plain to read.

Nevertheless he approached the witness box with as confident an air as he could assume and cleared his throat. "Mrs. Gruenwald," he began, "I believe you said that Mrs. Mason didn't actually *say* she was expecting, is that right?"

"She say, if not in words."

"Not in words. Do you expect us to believe that the information was relayed merely by smiles and laughter?"

"I no expect anything, mister. But I know what I know."

Galliard frowned at her. "I've been hearing a great deal of that sort of knowing. But we need specific information so the jury can know what it knows."

"Objection!" Abel snapped. "Is that a question, Mr. Galliard?"

The judge, of course, upheld him. Galliard rephrased. "Did the defendant, Mrs. Mason, ever actually tell you—in so many words, mind you—that she was expecting?"

"Ja," the witness said stolidly. "She did."

"When was that?"

"After."

"After what?"

"After the standaway."

The defense attorney's eyes brightened with hope. "That means when she was no longer living with Mr. Trahern. How can you therefore be certain that it wasn't *Mr. Mason* who was the father?"

"I'm certain."

Her unshakable certitude was impressive. Galliard did not seem able to move her. Seth himself was wondering why Clara had turned on Rachel this way, betraying the very woman she'd just described as being so good and kind. Was she trying to hurt Rachel, to revenge herself on her for some unsuspected misdeed? *Ask her*, Rachel had said. Perhaps she was right, he thought. Perhaps her lawyer should probe the reason the housekeeper went away, and, more important, why she came back.

Galliard had evidently had the same thought. "Is it true, ma'am, that you ran away when you thought Mr. Becker might ask you to testify in court?"

"Ja. Is true. I went to stay with sister-in-law in New Jersey."

"Why did you do that?"

"I know the missus would not wish me to say these things. And I wish not to bring hurt to her."

"So you went away."

"Ja. Far away. Another state."

"And yet you came back and agreed to testify. If you don't wish to hurt her, why did you do that, Mrs. Gruenwald?"

"Because she ask me to."

Seth stiffened in shock. Had he heard her aright?

Galliard too was startled. "She? *Who?*" he asked, ignoring the hubbub among the spectators.

"Her. Rachel. The missus."

The hubbub was becoming an uproar, but Seth barely heard it over the confusion in his brain. Mr. Galliard, too, seemed not to believe what he'd heard. "You must have misunderstood me, ma'am," he insisted. "You can't mean Mrs. Mason, the lady sitting right there in front of you."

"I not misunderstand you, mister. I understand perfect. Is *she* who ask me to come here."

The judge was pounding his gavel to no avail. Seth turned toward Rachel in amazement. Did you really do that? his eyes asked.

Galliard was still refusing to accept what the witness was saying. "No, ma'am, you can't be right," he insisted. "Mrs. Mason *wouldn't* . . . she'd have no *reason* to . . . and no *way*—"

The woman in the witness box shook her head. "Look here, mister," she said earnestly, pulling a folded paper from the bosom of her dress, "here is letter. She write and beg me to come. You can read for yourself."

Galliard took the paper she held out and stared at it in disbelief. The court fell silent as he read, holding its collective breath.

Seth leaned across the table to his lawyer. "Abel—?"

Abel merely nodded to him and got to his feet. "Your honor," he said, "if that letter supports Mrs. Gruenwald's claim, I request that it be submitted to the court as evidence."

Judge Andersen agreed. Galliard, throwing Rachel a glance of reproach, reluctantly handed the note to the judge. He read it quickly and then handed it to the waiting Abel Becker.

Seth watched as Abel read it, the lawyer's expression changing from impassivity to utter astonishment. Then he handed it to Seth.

The words on the page seemed to jump out at him:

Come back at once . . . it's time for truth to be told . . . answer everything they ask . . . if nothing else will heal this rift, perhaps the truth will . . .

Seth still could not believe what he was seeing. He turned and stared at Rachel. Can you really have done this? he silently asked. Purposely destroyed your case? Admitted to criminal conversation? Lost your son?

But Rachel did not look up from her intent contemplation of her folded hands.

Seth slowly rose, his face white, his eyes wide with torment and fixed upon the woman sitting before him in the dock. "*Rachel?*" he asked aloud, holding the letter out to her. The word was a cry of bewilderment.

Rachel glanced up at him—quickly, guiltily—for one moment, but then she immediately returned to her contemplation of her fingers. However, she couldn't hide the flush that crept up from her neck and suffused her face. A flush of admission. A flush that said *yes, yes, I did it!*

Seth stood staring at her while all the spectators held their breaths. Then he turned to his attorney, whose mouth was still agape in astonishment. "Stop this damn proceeding, Abel," he said quietly. "I can bear no more." And he turned, stumbled down the stairs and ran from the room.

56

Rachel, like every other person in the courtroom, watched Seth go. When the doors closed behind him, the uproar resumed. Rachel, however, remained seated quietly in the dock. For the first time since she'd sat in that seat, her breathing was even, her pulse quiet, her heart calm. Things were happening just as she'd hoped they would.

The judge hammered his gavel but without conviction. Ignoring the noise, Abel rose and approached the bench, signaling Galliard to follow. He requested a postponement in order, he said, to permit his client to fully consider the new evidence. Galliard concurred. He had nothing to lose by concurring; his case was lost no matter what the judge might decide.

"Very well, I'll grant it," the judge said. "As my sainted mother used to say, 'We hate delay, but it makes us wise.'" Then he hammered his gavel and loudly adjourned.

Rachel came down from the dock to where Galliard stood waiting for her. He suggested they remain where they were until the spectators had dispersed. While they waited, he asked the question she expected him to ask: "Why on earth, ma'am, did you do something so foolish as to write that letter?"

"Can you not guess?" she asked, giving him a small smile.

"No, ma'am, I can't." He rubbed the bridge of his nose bewilderedly. "You women can sometimes be a complete mystery to a man."

"Do you remember, not so many days ago, when we talked about lies and the law?" she asked him.

"Yes, I do. And I told you that bending the truth was acceptable when it helped to win."

"Yes, but do you remember what *I* said?"

His brow furrowed. "You said you wondered what would happen if we told the truth, the whole truth, and nothing but." He gaped at her in sudden understanding. "Is *that* what you were trying to do? See what would happen if the truth were told?"

"Yes."

He threw up his hands. "Well, now you know. You lost us the case!"

"Perhaps," she said. She would not say another word. Ignoring his glare, she walked out the door.

Mr. Galliard followed. As they came out of the court-house, they discovered that a number of people were still loitering about. Among them were Abel Becker and Seth Trahern, who were waiting more eagerly than any-one else for Rachel to emerge. Rachel turned to her lawyer. "What happened in court today evidently has made no more sense to them than it has to you, Mr. Gal-liard," she whispered.

Abel was approaching. Mr. Galliard stepped protec-tively close to his client. "Do you wish me to explain to him—?" he asked her.

But Abel was already there. One could almost *see* the questions on the tip of his tongue. As he pulled Galliard aside, intending to query him privately, Seth strode up to Rachel and grasped her shoulders. "For God's sake, Rachel, *why*?" he demanded furiously.

She lifted her eyes to his. "If you don't know why, Seth Trahern," she said, "you are as stupid as you were five years ago." With that, she thrust his hands from her and, head high, marched pridefully down the street.

"Rachel, *wait*!" he cried and made as if to follow her. She'd not gone very far, however, when she heard a frightening sound. It was a sharp intake of breath, so sudden and agonized that she wheeled around and saw that he'd stopped and was clutching his side. His face had turned ashen. "Seth!" she cried, "What—?

"Abel," he gasped as he doubled over in pain, "come . . . quick—!"

As Rachel watched, frozen to the spot, Abel ran to him, reaching him just as Seth fell to his knees, still doubled over. Abel knelt before him. "Good God, what is it, Seth?" he asked.

"What is it? What's happened?" the onlookers were asking.

Seth shook his head and slipped an exploratory hand inside his coat. When he withdrew it a moment later, it was covered with blood.

Rachel's hands flew to her mouth in terror. Someone among the loiterers screamed. Abel reached out his arms, and Seth tumbled into them. "Abel, can you get me . . . to Dr. Muncie?" he managed between gasping breaths. "I think he'll . . . have to . . . stitch me up . . . again." And with that he fainted dead away.

57

*T*he door to the inner room of Dr. Muncie's dispensary was kept closed for more than two hours. Rachel, Abel, and Galliard were the only ones Dr. Muncie permitted to remain in his outer room; all the rest of the crowd that had followed when the wounded man was carried to the dispensary had long since been dispersed.

"You needn't look so alarmed," Dr. Muncie had assured Abel before disappearing into his dispensary. "I told you last night that Seth was not mortally wounded. Mason's bullet didn't come near a vital organ." He now believed, he explained, that the pressure of the events in court that morning had caused Seth to strain himself and rip open the stitches with which he'd sealed the wound the night before. The weakness that had caused Seth to lose consciousness was probably the loss of blood.

While the two lawyers and Rachel waited for the doctor to give them further news, Rachel looked from one to the other. "What did Dr. Muncie mean by the words 'Mason's bullet'?" she asked.

"Shall we tell her?" Abel asked Galliard.

"I think she should know it all," Galliard said without hesitation.

Abel nodded in agreement and, after urging Rachel onto one of the doctor's wooden chairs, related the events of the night before. She listened to the account with growing horror. That Peter Mason was the cause of Seth's wound shocked and distressed her. She sat unmoving for several minutes, trying to still the upheaval in her breast. She felt sick with misery and guilt. Would there *never* be an end to the damage her ill-considered marriage to Peter had wrought? she asked herself.

When she at last recovered a semblance of calm, she looked up at Abel. "Will Peter be arrested and bring further shame on us?" she asked.

"No, he's taken himself off," Abel assured her. "By this time he's probably put a good distance between himself and the New Castle constabulary. Making his way back to the Mississippi Territory, I'd wager. I'm sorry to have to say this, Rachel, but after his dastardly performance last night, I don't think Peter Mason is likely to show his face in these parts again ever."

"You needn't be sorry, Abel," she said quietly. "Distance is exactly what I want from him."

Abel Becker took hold of another chair and pulled it up in front of hers. "I don't understand you, Rachel," he said, taking one of her hands in his. "If you wanted distance between you and Mason, why were you trying so hard to prove in court that your marriage to him is legal?"

"You know why. I wanted to keep Jossy."

"Then will you please explain," Galliard cut in irritably, "why you sent for Clara Gruenwald and purposely destroyed our case?"

She looked from him to Abel and back again. "Can neither of you guess? Did you not see what Seth did when he realized I'd let him win the case?"

Abel peered at her for a moment, brows knit. "He ordered me to stop it. And he walked out."

"Yes. Exactly," she said.

"Are you saying he wanted to *lose?*" Galliard asked, utterly perplexed.

Rachel threw him a tiny smile. "Perhaps not at first," she explained gently. "He adores Jossy, and when he realized he was the boy's father, he was torn apart with new feelings—with the desire for his own son, and with anger at me for having deprived him. So he brought me to court."

Abel cocked his head dubiously. "Come, come, Rachel," he said, "you're not suggesting, are you, that he never really wanted to win?"

"Don't you know the man at all?" Rachel removed her hand from his hold, stood up, and looked down at him. "Seth would never, in the end, have taken Jossy from me. He would never hurt me in that way."

"If you believed that," Galliard promptly asked, "why did you go all the way to Philadelphia to hire me to fight him?"

"When I first learned of the suit, I didn't think clearly. I was frightened and desperate. I knew only one thing: that I could not . . . would not . . . give up my son. So I came to you. But then I watched Seth in court. He was sorely troubled every time something was said that he thought was painful to me."

"Yes, he was," Galliard admitted. "I noticed that, too."

"You'd have been blind not to notice," Abel agreed ruefully. "He himself was my greatest obstacle. He tried to prevent any attempt I made to disparage you."

"It reminded me of his true nature," Rachel went on. "He is a good man, Mr. Galliard. Truly kind. Kindness is almost the essence of the man. I don't know how I could have forgotten that! Once I remembered it, I knew that he would not take my son from me, no matter who won in court."

"That still does not explain why you sent for Clara Gruenwald and destroyed our case," her lawyer grumbled. "If I could have won it, you would have had your son and, with your marriage to Mason upheld, you would *not* be found guilty of criminal conversation with Peter Mason."

"I think I'm beginning to see the answer to that," Abel said, a broad smile breaking out on his face. "She finally realized that she'd win by losing. Isn't that right, Rachel?"

"Something like that." She came up to Galliard and put a hand on his arm. "I have used you shamefully, Mr. Galliard," she said in soft apology, "and for that I am very sorry. But once I realized that I would not lose my son, I began to see that I could use the trial to attempt to win something very precious to me."

"Something you might win by *losing* the trial?"

"Yes. You see, five years ago, when I failed to convince Seth of my innocence, I withheld the fact of my pregnancy and married Peter because I was too frightened of losing my reputation and my son's good name. But in the intervening years I've learned not to care about those things. I've paid too high a price for a good name." She had to pause, for her throat was tightening with tears she would not let herself shed. "After all, what good is preserving a good name if it must go along with a bad life? You know my story, Mr. Galliard. You know what I feel for Seth. Sitting there in court, seeing him suffer even more than I over the things being said, I suddenly realized that by sending for Clara, I could prove something to him that I'd not been able to make him accept before—the truth. If by Clara's testimony he could see the truth at last, it would mean much more to me than my reputation. It would mean I might earn his forgiveness."

"You have my forgiveness, Rachel," came a voice from the inner doorway.

"Seth!" Rachel looked up over Galliard's shoulder, her heart thumping. She did not know which of the two emotions churning inside her was strongest: deep embarrassment at being overheard, or wild hope that matters between her and this man she loved were about to change.

Seth stood in the doorway, his hair disheveled, his bloody shirt ripped open, and his chest encircled by an enormous bandage. Dr. Muncie hovered behind him. "He'll do fine if he'll only agree to rest," the doctor informed them.

Neither Seth nor Rachel paid him any heed. They were staring at one another, transfixed. But as Rachel's eyes searched his, the hope that had burst into bloom inside her died. What she'd hoped to read in his eyes was not there. "You heard?" she asked, shaken.

"Yes."

"All of it?"

"Enough."

Her heart sank. "And that's all you have to say? That I have your forgiveness?"

"What else do you expect?"

Her whole body stiffened. "More," she said. "Much more."

He put a weary hand to his forehead and leaned against the doorframe. "You have your son. You have my forgiveness. What more can you want?"

"Damn it, Seth," the doctor cut in, "you're too weak

to be standing about. Come back inside and lie down."

"Be still, Muncie," Abel Becker ordered, his eyes fixed on Seth's face. "Let's you and I and Galliard go into your dispensary and permit these two to speak to each other alone."

Rachel took a backward step and shook her head. "We can speak later. He should rest."

"No!" Seth said. "Let's finish this." He stepped away from the door and let the lawyers pass by. When they'd closed the door, he dropped his eyes from hers. "What more do you want of me, woman?" he asked coldly.

"I told you five years ago what I wanted," Rachel said.

He sighed like a man too long beset. "I've forgiven you for *that*, too. You warned me in advance that you loved Mason, so I can forgive you for . . . for what happened. And I commend your bravery in admitting in court that Jossy is my son. But, sorry as I am to say it, if you believe that admission proves you to be innocent of criminal conversation in my eyes, you are mistaken."

Rachel felt the blood drain from her face as she listened to those cruel words, each one of them a whiplash to her soul. When he finished, she swayed slightly. She wanted to swoon. A swoon would be an escape from this pain. But when he made a step toward her, as if he wanted to catch her, she stiffened her spine. She would have none of his help, not after what she'd just heard. She would be steady on her feet no matter what it cost.

Seth, himself dizzy from pain, weakness, and the emotional upheaval of the last few days, hated himself for what he'd just said, truth though it was. He could see he'd hurt her deeply. She was staring at him as if he were some sort of monster. "Rachel, I . . ." he began. But he couldn't go on. He really had nothing else to say.

"And I said you were *kind*," she said bitterly.

They continued to stare at each other for what seemed to him only a heartbeat of time, but it must have been much longer. Then she waved her hand before her eyes as if she were brushing away a nightmare, turned her back on him, and stalked to the door. But before leaving, she threw a quick glance at him over her shoulder. "It has taken me five years, Seth Trahern," she said in a voice more icy than he'd ever heard her use, "to realize what a fool you are!" And with a slam of the door behind her, she was gone.

58

*S*eth leaned his head against the doorframe and groaned. It was a sound that came from deep inside him. It must have been louder than he thought, because the inner door burst open, and the doctor and the two lawyers came running out. "Are you all right?" Dr. Muncie asked.

"Of course he's all right," Abel said, looking his friend over carefully. "He's only groaning because he knows Rachel's right. He *is* a fool."

"Good God," Seth said in disgust, "you *listened*!"

"The door isn't very thick," Muncie said with an apologetic shrug.

"Even you, Galliard?" Seth shook his head at the visitor from Philadelphia. "I'm not very surprised at Abel here, for as we all know, his ethical standards are no better than most. And the doctor will probably excuse his eavesdropping by saying he was concerned for my health. But I didn't expect such behavior from *you.*"

Galliard gave an abashed smile. "'Tis asking for moral restraint beyond the human to expect us not to have listened."

"Morals be hanged," Dr. Muncie declared. "I can see

in your face, Seth, that you're in pain. Come, Abel, help me get him back to bed."

Gingerly, so as not to put additional strain on the wound, they helped the unprotesting patient into the inner room and sat him down upon a narrow cot that had been placed against the farthest wall. The bed-clothes on the cot were still stained with blood.

Abel lifted Seth's legs onto the bed while Dr. Muncie piled up several pillows and lowered Seth upon them. Seth closed his eyes for a moment, while the three other men stood there surveying him. When he opened them, and saw three pairs of eyes studying him with various lugubrious expressions of concern, he snorted in rueful amusement. "You look like three owls," he muttered. "Well, go on! Say what you want to say."

None of them said a word.

"Go on, Abel," he urged again. "I know that look. You called me a fool. You want to castigate me."

"Yes, I do," Abel said. "Rachel offered herself to you, and you spurned her. If that was not the act of a fool, I don't know one."

"And you agree with him, I suppose?" Seth threw at Galliard.

"Yes, I do. I do indeed."

Seth turned slightly on his pillows in order to look up at the doctor. "And you, too, Muncie? Are you going to join this chorus?"

Dr. Muncie held up his hands. "Don't look at me. I hold no opinions concerning your marital life—"

"—or the lack thereof—" Abel put in.

"Or the lack thereof. I only suggest that, in your con-dition, this may not be the best time to discuss subjects that agitate you."

"There is nothing to discuss, agitating or otherwise,"

Seth insisted. "My marital life was a farce and is unworthy of discussion."

"Your marital life was as ideal as is possible in the always-perplexing relations between the sexes," Abel said, "and if you had an ounce of sense, you could make it so again."

Seth raised himself up on an elbow, wincing in pain as he did so. "Are you demented, man?" he demanded. "The woman made a cuckold of me! You heard me forgive it, but am I expected to *forget* it?"

"There, you see?" the doctor cried, urging him back down. "You've stretched your arm. I tell you, Seth, I won't have you destroying my work again! Another tearing of those sutures and I won't be responsible for the consequences."

"I'm fine," Seth assured him. "Well, Abel, can you answer *that*?"

Abel frowned down at him. "If it were me, *I'd* forget it."

Seth snorted. "Hah, very likely! This from a man who hasn't spoken to his own brother for twenty years because the fellow cheated him of a twenty-five-pound inheritance."

"There's something I'd like to say," Galliard said. "I'm hesitating because I'm but a recent acquaintance who has not earned the right to interfere. Long friendship, like that between you and Abel, permits him to express opinions on intimate matters freely, but from a brief acquaintance like me, perhaps expressing such opinions will be considered impertinent."

"Oh, go ahead, man," Abel urged. "Be impertinent."

"Shall I, Trahern? I can't help having opinions in this matter. And I admit that I've become quite strongly attached to all the parties in this dispute."

"Yes, we've become quite a close-knit family, have we not?" Seth said dryly. "Hardly an intimate detail we haven't shared. So go on, Galliard, say your say."

"Very well. I have only a question. What if you were wrong?"

"Wrong?" Seth asked, not understanding.

"What if you've *misjudged* the lady's guilt?"

"Yes!" Abel cried, clapping Galliard on the shoulder. "My learned colleague has spoken with the wisdom of our profession. Perhaps you misjudged her. Give the lady the benefit of the doubt."

Seth closed his eyes, both to show his disgust and to shut them from his view. "Oh, go away," he said dismissively. "The wisdom of your profession, indeed! You lawyers make me tired."

"Why?" Abel demanded. "Because you have no good response to our reasoning?"

His opened his eyes. They flashed with anger. "Because there is no cause so ill you will not argue it. Because you like to turn white into black and black into white. As in this case, where you are asking me to doubt where there *is* no doubt."

"There is always doubt," Galliard proclaimed pompously.

Seth fixed his irate gaze on him. "Not always, Galliard, not always. Not when one has seen the evidence with one's own eyes."

"Even then," Galliard insisted. "And I believe I can prove my words."

"What?" Seth gaped at him, puzzled by his sudden air of conviction. "How can you—?"

"Let me get my briefcase. Fortunately I did not give it to my assistant after court. I have it with me." And he turned on his heel and marched into the other room.

When he returned he carried with him a sheaf of pages tied with a wide black ribbon.

All three watched him curiously. Seth in particular was eyeing him with dubious suspicion, but Galliard made no explanation or apology. He merely tossed the beribboned bundle on the bed near Seth's hand. "Here," he said. "Read that."

It was a thick pile. There were words on the top page, but they were largely hidden by the bow of the ribbon. "What is it?" Seth asked, eyeing it as if it were likely to explode.

"Read it and you'll know."

"Now?"

"No," Galliard said. "I think you should read it at home. In private. I think you'll find it worth your time."

"Very well, I'll go right now."

The doctor, although muttering objections, helped Seth button his tattered shirt and put on his coat. Seth put the parcel of papers under his arm and, with a nod to the others, went out.

As he closed the outer door behind him, he realized that he hadn't asked Galliard how soon these mysterious papers had to be returned. He turned back and opened the door. As he put one foot over the threshold he heard Abel's voice. "If those papers are what I think they are, Galliard," he was saying, "you've done something much more unethical than eavesdropping."

Seth stood where he was and listened. If they could eavesdrop, so could he.

"Yes, they are just what you suspect," Galliard said. "Her own words in her own hand."

"Damnation, man, aren't they privileged communication?" Abel exclaimed. "Where's your conscience?"

"I know quite well it's an ethical infraction. But I

hope that the end will justify the means."

"What are you talking about?" Dr. Muncie asked. "What sort of papers have you given him?"

"Can't you guess?" Abel said. "It's the information he received from Rachel to supply background for the case. Rachel's papers."

Seth stepped backward over the threshold and closed the door quietly. He took the tied pages from under his arm and stared at them. Rachel's papers. There appeared to be a couple of hundred pages. What on earth was he holding in his shaking hand—a treasure or a torment?

59

A pale sun was setting as Seth left Dr. Muncie's office. Despite the cold December air, he walked slowly. This unusual pace, so different from his usual long stride, was not caused by the pain of his fresh sutures but by the weight of the parcel he carried. Not the physical weight of it but the moral one. It was a worrisome burden.

Rachel's papers. Abel had said they were privileged communication, meant to be read by her lawyer and no one else. He had no moral right to read those pages, none at all. But Galliard had said they would prove something . . . prove that he'd been wrong in his judgment of his once-upon-a-time wife. Could that possibly be true?

He shifted the parcel to his wounded side and used his left arm to raise his coat-collar against the cold. This simple act made the packet of papers a physical problem as well as a moral one. When carried under his right arm, it created a painful pressure against his wound. He shifted it back to the other side, but it was still a troublesome burden. He ought to get rid of it, he told himself. He ought to return it to Galliard unread. No good would come of his reading it. After all, what did Galliard really know? His assertion that the papers contained some new proof was a ridiculous one. Seth had seen what he had seen, and he'd heard all Rachel's denials many times over. There was nothing she could have written in these pages that would change his mind.

He turned back toward Dr. Muncie's office. He might still catch Galliard there. If he returned the papers—and without even so much as undoing the ribbon—he would save both himself and Galliard from committing what the Philadelphia attorney had called "an ethical infraction."

The decision made, his step lengthened. He arrived back at Muncie's office in half the time it had taken him to leave. But Muncie was alone. The two lawyers had already gone.

The doctor eyed Seth worriedly. "I thought you'd be home by this time. You should be abed, not gallivanting round town!"

"I shall be there soon, I promise. But I must find Mr. Galliard. Did he say where he was going?"

Muncie shrugged. "No, but I assume he went back to his rooms. I hope, Seth, that you don't intend to follow him there. Go home to bed! Whatever it is you must see Galliard about can wait."

Seth did not argue. He merely nodded and departed. But he had no intention of obeying the doctor. He would follow Galliard to Hansen's. There was no harm in doing what he'd determined to do. Muncie was a mother hen. The new bandage was strong and tight. It would hold him together.

He had to pass his shop on the way to Hansen's, so he stopped there to give Tom Dagget instruction for the next day's print run. Tom reminded him that he'd not yet finished writing the editorial. There were five inches of space he still had to fill. With a sigh, Seth sat down at his desk, put the parcel aside, and went to work.

For twenty minutes he concentrated on the editorial he'd begun to write two days earlier. It was about Aaron Burr, whose attempt to start a separate republic in the Southwest had caused President Jefferson to have him arrested. His trial for treason was to begin in the new year. Seth wrote feelingly in support of Jefferson's action. Burr was ever a troublemaker.

By the time he'd finished, his right side ached painfully. The act of writing had not been soothing to his wound. He looked at the parcel lying at his elbow. He should, he supposed, take the damned thing over to Hansen's as he'd intended, but he yearned for bed. He'd take it home with him after all. There was no real harm, was there, if he returned it to Galliard tomorrow?

It was almost five in the evening when he returned home. The sun was setting, throwing long shadows across the road. He felt oddly depressed. And he was not cheered at the sight of Clara waiting for him in the doorway, her brow furrowed with worry. "Ach, mister," she cried, running down the front steps to meet him, "I been expecting you an hour or more."

"I didn't want you to come to work today, Clara," he said as they entered the house. "Go home to your husband."

"I go soon. I must give you dinner first."

"No, no, I'm not hungry," he said wearily. "I just want to rest now."

Her eyes swept over him suspiciously. "You feelink no good?"

He put a hand over the part of his shirt collar not covered by his coat, hoping there was no sign of blood on it. "I'm perfectly fine," he assured her. "Go on home."

She saw it was useless to argue. She threw her shawl over her shoulders and wished him goodnight. He crossed to the stairs, taking the parcel of papers from under his arm.

Clara lingered in the doorway. "I would like only to ask you—"

"Yes, Clara?" he asked absently. He was staring at the parcel as if spellbound.

"In court today. Did I do bad thing?"

He turned. "A bad thing?" He shook himself from his trance. "No, no," he assured her, "you did excellently well. You brought the truth to the proceeding, and the one who speaks truth, you know, is the one who can sleep well at night." Tucking his bundle back under his arm, he came over to her, leaned down and kissed her cheek. "So go home and sleep well."

After the door had closed behind his much-relieved housekeeper, Seth made his way up to his bedroom. He placed the papers on a table before a window through which a little daylight still shone. But he had no intention of reading it. He intended to take off his coat and torn, bloodied shirt, pull on his nightshirt and go to bed. He'd only brought the papers up with him to be certain he'd remember, in the morning, to return them to Galliard.

As he gingerly removed his coat, his eyes again found their way to the table. What were the words on the covering page, he wondered? He undid the ribbon, just to see. *Narrative, Testis Unus, By Mistress Rachel Mason, Philadelphia, November 2–3, 1806,* he read. His mind played with the words. *Testis unis,* he thought. *Doesn't that mean one witness?* In other words, there were no corroborating witnesses to this document. How could Galliard have claimed this could be proof of anything?

Rachel could have said anything, invented anything, written any sort of lie.

Except, of course, that Rachel did not lie, not ordinarily.

He threw his coat on a chair and again moved toward the table, slowly this time, his eyes fixed on the tied sheaf of pages. He did not want to touch them . . . some outside force was pushing him. Without quite deciding to do it, he found himself bending over the table . . . turning over the covering page . . . taking in the words "Even now, I can shut my eyes and see myself . . ."

From then on, he was never aware of taking his eyes from the writing. At some point—he did not know when or how—he pulled a chair up to the table and sat down. At some point he took down a candlestick from the mantelpiece and lit a candle. At some point he pulled the counterpane from his bed and wrapped it about him. At several points he got up from the chair, chest heaving with emotion, and had to pace back and forth around the room before he was able to sit down again and resume reading.

But when he'd turned over the last page, exhausted and drained, he did something he hadn't done for eleven years—not since the death of his mother. He dropped his head down upon his arms and wept.

60

Rachel sat in her rocking chair before the fire, staring into the flames. She'd used the last of ounce of her strength to keep up a cheerful facade for her father and son. Now that they were both safely asleep, she could permit herself to sink into misery. She wanted only to weep. Why, she wondered, was she sitting here so dry-eyed? Perhaps she'd been pushed beyond tears.

She had experienced, in her life, a great many hurts and disappointments, but it seemed to her that Seth's words that afternoon had cut deeper than any other. No matter how many times she'd turned them over in her mind, she could not find in them the least possibility of hope. His declaration—*If you believe that admission proves you to be innocent of criminal conversation in my eyes, you are mistaken*—had a cutting finality about it. In the five years of their separation, he'd erected so strong a wall between them that no effort of hers could ever breach it.

The sound of an approaching carriage interrupted these depressing thoughts. She went to the door to discover Abel climbing down from his curricle. "Good evening," she called out, trying her best to sound cheerful.

He doffed his hat and came in. "Good evening, my dear," he said. His tone was not happy.

She tried to stifle her feeling of alarm. What, after all, could he tell her that would be worse than what she'd already endured? Nevertheless she couldn't help murmuring, "I hope you are not the bearer of bad news."

"I'm here in Mr. Galliard's place. He wanted me to convey to you some final information regarding the case."

"Then please give me your hat and sit down. Shall we sit here at the table? There's no fire in the parlor."

He nodded and took a chair. "Your attorney sends his apologies. He wanted to come himself, but we were held up in court all afternoon, and he and his clerk just barely had time to catch the evening stage to Philadelphia."

"But why were you in court?" she asked, sitting down opposite him. "I thought Seth had withdrawn his complaint. Doesn't that stop all legal action?"

"When Galliard and I returned to court this afternoon," Abel explained, "it was to present a *nolle prosequi*—a statement that the complainant is unwilling to pursue the matter—but Judge Andersen said we were too late. The jury, he said, had heard enough to make a decision. He'd already issued his instructions to them. Well, as you can imagine, after hearing Clara's testimony, the jurymen's minds were made up. In less than half an hour they came down and found for Seth. They awarded him custody, declared your marriage to Mason void, and fined Peter Mason one hundred and seventy pounds." He gave a snorting laugh. "Seth can collect it if and when he can manage to find the poltroon."

Rachel gulped. "Never mind that. Did you say they awarded Seth *custody*?"

"Yes, but you know it's meaningless. Seth doesn't intend to claim the boy. He said as much to you today. And Seth's a man who keeps his word."

"True," she said with a sigh of relief.

"That's the long and short of it, Rachel. Galliard said to tell you how sorry he is that things did not turn out more satisfactorily."

"He has nothing to be sorry for," she said. "He did as well as possible for me in court. It was I who made a confusion of things. But it's all past. And I do have my son. That is what matters most to me."

"I know that," Abel said. "We're all glad it's over. The case was hateful to all of us." He fell silent and looked down at his hands, his lips compressed.

Rachel studied him curiously. "There's something else, isn't there?"

Abel cleared his throat. "Galliard asked me to tell you something that I fear you will not like. It was an impulse that he says he could not resist at the time. But it was a most unprofessional act, and he regrets having to take leave of you without making a full confession of it."

Her brows lifted in surprise. "Heavens, Abel, this sounds serious."

"It is, I think."

"Goodness, you are frightening me!" she said, half in amusement, for she did not quite believe that her attorney was capable of doing anything truly hurtful. "Tell me what it is at once, or I shall die of suspense."

"It seems that you wrote some papers—an account of your marriage that you prepared in Philadelphia and turned over to him. Do you remember them?"

"Yes, of course. How could I forget?"

"He brought them with him from Philadelphia along

with all the other papers pertaining to this case. There are times during a trial, you see, when a lawyer may have need to check some small detail . . ."

"Yes, of course. I quite understand that the papers might be useful." She gave him a small, uneasy smile. "He didn't lose them, did he? I should not like to think of them flying loose throughout the world."

Abel rubbed his cheek uncomfortably. "He did worse than lose them, Rachel. He *gave* them away."

Rachel had an immediate premonition of what he was about to tell her. It was a jolt that turned her pale. "Gave them away? Oh, *God*! *Not* to . . . to—!"

"Yes," Abel said in embarrassment. "To Seth."

"No!" Her fingers began to tremble and something in her chest clenched. Slowly, unsteadily, she rose from her chair. "How *could* he, Abel? He said those papers were *privileged*! Just between us!"

"And so they were. It was a most unethical, heinous act on his part. He said to tell you he was very sorry—"

"*Sorry?*" she cried, aghast. "Does he know what he's *done?*" She pressed her hands against her mouth, and a shudder of revulsion shook her entire body. "He's stripped me bare! Left me without a shred of *pride!*"

Abel blinked up at her in surprise. "That is a somewhat extreme reaction, Rachel, is it not? He only wanted to help. He thought there was information in those papers that Seth ought to know."

She glared at him as if he were completely deficient in understanding. "Don't you *see?* There *are* no facts in those papers that Seth doesn't know. All the facts have been revealed in court. But there are my *feelings.* The full extent of my foolish feelings that I have never revealed to anyone else! I would not wish anyone to know them, especially Seth." Her voice cracked with a tearless sob.

"Now I have nothing . . . nothing with which to cover my . . . my nakedness."

Abel felt utterly helpless. "Is there something I can do?" he asked. "I know Galliard would want me to do anything that might make amends."

Her head came up. "Yes," she said. She dashed around the table to him, grasped his lapels, and pulled him to his feet. "Go to him. Go at *once* and get the papers back!"

"I'm so sorry, Rachel, my dear," he said, patting her shoulder to try to comfort her, "'tis too late, I fear. He's surely read them by this—"

A pounding on the door silenced him. Rachel froze, for she knew with an eerie certainty who was out there.

"Rachel!" They could hear the urgency of his voice even through the door.

"Shall I send him away?" Abel asked.

She shook her head. "No. Let him in. Please."

"Shouldn't you do it?"

"No." It was a whisper. "I can't . . . move."

Abel went to the door and opened it. Seth was standing there in the wind, hatless, his hair untied and disheveled, his face pale, his eyes darkly circled, his coat undone. Rachel noticed, with horror, that he was still wearing the ripped and bloody shirt he'd worn at the dispensary. The pages Galliard had given him were crushed in his hand. He glanced at Abel without a spark of recognition, his eyes darting around wildly until he saw Rachel standing before the fire. "Rachel?" he called uneasily.

How weary he looks, she thought.

"Go in," Abel said.

Seth strode past him and did not stop until he stood right before her. "Rachel, I—"

She had recovered herself. Lifting a hand to stop him, she took a backward step. "You should be home," she said in a dry, distant voice. "In bed. Pampering your wound."

"I'm well enough. Muncie strapped me so tightly this time that nothing can possibly disturb his sutures. Rachel, I must tell you—"

"Are those my papers?" she asked, coldly cutting him off again. "Give them back to me, please."

"Yes, of course," he said in surprise, handing them to her. "But don't you want to—?"

"I don't wish to speak of them. The matter is past. The trial is over. There's no need for them now." And before Seth or Abel suspected what she had in mind, she turned and tossed them into the fireplace. The flames flared up at once, and the papers curled into black ash while they stared.

Seth smiled ruefully. "It doesn't matter that you've burned them. They are inscribed in my brain."

"Then I would be obliged if you forget them," she said testily.

"I shall never forget them."

She rubbed her forehead with trembling fingers. "Seth, this has been a most upsetting day. I need some peace. Please go away."

"Rachel, blast it all, just hear me out for a moment! I must . . . I need to . . ." He paused, as if he could not find the words he wanted. In that pause, he became aware of Abel's presence, a looming shadow on the other side of the table. "Damnation, Abel," he cursed softly, "can't you see this is private? Go home."

"No, Abel, stay!" Rachel ordered. "'Tis Seth who is leaving."

"Very well, then, let him hear me," Seth said. The

wild energy that he'd brought in with him seemed suddenly to seep out and leave him drained. He sank down on the nearest chair. "Damnation, woman," he cursed softly, "can't you see I'm in agony?"

"I see that you look ill. Go home."

He caught her hand. "Let me stay. I must talk to you."

She pulled her hand away. "I've had enough of your talk."

"Please," he begged, rising and grasping her shoulders, "give me just a moment. I only want to tell you that you were right today. Everyone knew it but me. Abel knew it. Muncie knew it. Even Galliard knew it. I have been the greatest fool. You must permit me to ask for your forgiveness."

She shook her head. "You've given me back my son. Twice. I owe you much for that. Therefore, I have nothing to forgive."

"Yes, you have," he insisted, his voice hoarse with the emotions he was trying desperately to control. "Please, Rachel, let me *say* this. Let me make my apologies."

With a reluctant sigh, she relented and nodded an assent.

He drew in a breath and went on. "You had never lied to me in all the time we were together, but when it was most important that I believe you, I would not. It was my life's greatest error, I know that now. Everything that's happened since is my fault. But I'm so great a fool that I didn't realize it until I read your words on those pages."

She would not let herself be moved by his distress. "You are not saying, are you, that you've changed your opinion of my truthfulness—something that you so firmly *disbelieved* this very afternoon?" she asked in cold disdain.

"Yes, of course that's what I'm saying!"

It was too momentous a change for her to accept. "Dash it, Seth," she cried angrily, "I don't understand you. How is it you so readily accept my *written* words as truth but refused to believe the *spoken* ones? They are essentially the same words, are they not? They tell the same tale."

"Yes, but, you see, when you spoke them, my understanding was blocked. I kept seeing the scene from one narrow viewpoint—mine. Always from the doorway of that damned room. When you spoke the words to me, I heard them through my own pain. But when I *read* them today, I heard them through *yours*."

"Oh," she said. It was a small sound. She didn't believe she'd heard aright. Had he actually said he believed her? Was he rescinding the dreadful words he'd spoken just this afternoon? She stared up at him, wide-eyed. Then, almost against her will, a louder "Oh!" issued from her throat.

Seth said nothing. He was waiting tensely for something more.

As the significance of what he'd said burst on her, Rachel hands flew to her mouth, and her breath quickened. "Good heavens," she said, her blood beginning to bubble in her veins, "it seems I owe a debt of *gratitude* to Mr. Galliard rather than a heap of blame."

Seth did not understand. "Gratitude for what?" He peered at her intently. "For giving me the papers?"

"Yes." She took a deep breath to steady herself. "Yes." She gave a little laugh. "I think I must write him a letter of thanks!"

Seth, even in his state of agitation, could tell that her mood had changed. "Does that mean you're forgiving me?" he asked, hope springing into his eyes. "If you are,

Rachel, please *tell* me. After five years of torment, I need to hear a kind word from you."

Rachel shut her eyes against the intensity of the eagerness that lit his face. When she opened them and saw in his eyes a light that had been gone from them for five long years, something inside her gave way. The hurt that had seemed permanently lodged in her breast began to dissolve. She reached out a hand and touched his cheek, tears spilling down her own. "I have wanted nothing more, all these years," she said, "than to tell the father of my son that I love no other man. And to have him believe me."

"Oh, God!" he breathed, sinking to his knees before her and clutching her tightly to him with his one good arm. "Believing you is the first real joy I've felt since you left me."

The only response she made was a tiny sob deep in her throat. She could feel, from the trembling of his arms, that he was as overcome as she. She bent down and gently urged him to his feet. When he stood erect, he drew her to him. She slipped her arms around him and dropped her head on his shoulder. She could feel his cheek caressing her hair. She did not move. She would have been happy to remain forever in this tender embrace.

But a sound made her lift her head. It was Abel, she realized in surprise. She'd forgotten he was there. Undoubtedly embarrassed by the intimate scene he'd just witnessed, he was edging his way to the door. "'Tis Abel," she whispered to Seth.

"Good God, man, are you still here?" he asked, keeping his eyes fixed on Rachel's face.

"Yes, but I—"

"I'm glad you are. I need some lawyerly information.

Since I withdrew from the case, does that mean Rachel is still legally tied to that dastard Mason?"

"Well, no. Judge Andersen did not let you withdraw. We won the case."

Seth looked around at that. "Did we, indeed?" he asked, smiling at his friend. "Does that mean that Rachel's marriage to Mason is null and void?"

"Yes. Your so-called self-divorce no longer has legal validity."

"Then she is still my wife?"

"Yes, she is. Although 'twould be advisable to remarry."

"Good," Seth said. "You have greatly relieved my mind." Although he turned back to Rachel and tightened his clasp on her, he continued to address his attorney. "But tell me, old man," he asked, "don't you have some papers to draw up to that effect?"

"No, I do not," Abel declared, laughing. "But I take no offense at your tactful dismissal. I shall depart at once."

"Good then. Goodnight to you."

"Yes, goodnight, Abel," Rachel's said, unable to keep her voice from quivering. "Thank you for coming."

When they heard the door close, Seth took her face in his hands. "Can it be true that this beautiful woman, whose love I've denied myself all these empty years, wishes to marry me again?"

"Yes, it's true. She does."

He kissed her then. It was a gentle kiss, but he did not release her from it for a long, long time. When at last he did, she looked up at him and brushed his hair back. He took her hand to his lips. "I should go," he murmured.

"Yes, I suppose you should. You look terribly pale. Are you in pain?"

"I am. This damnable wound of mine smarts like the very devil. But I hate to leave you now. We've been apart so long. I don't ever want to be parted from you again."

"Then stay."

It was a very tempting offer, but he shook his head. "I shouldn't. It would do your reputation no good if it were discovered I'd spent the night here."

She laughed. "My *reputation*? My dearest fool, a jury has just found me guilty of criminal conversation, yet this is the happiest day of my life! Of what importance, therefore, is my reputation?"

He held her off at arm's length and stared at her. "I think, my love, you are much changed from the girl I found crying on the rain barrel all those years ago."

She colored under his admiring scrutiny. "And from the frightened girl that I was on our wedding night."

He took her back in his arms. "I would never have believed, that night, that I could love you more than I did then," he said softly, his lips on her hair.

"You'll stay then?" she asked, hiding her face in the safety of his shoulder.

He lifted her chin and made her look at him. "If I may."

"Of course, this house is not like yours," she said, a blush rising up from her throat. "My bedroom is but an attic room, and my bed is very narrow."

"Is it?" He was unable to keep from grinning. "I believe, however, that we can manage to be comfortable."

She smiled and led him to the stairway. Seth paused at the foot and watched her climb. As his eyes drank in the womanly grace of her step, he marveled at the woman she'd become. Still lovely, she was no more a girl. The sufferings of life had deepened her, strengthened her. Rachel's passage. It was a miracle that the passage had led her back to him.

She turned to see what was keeping him, smiling down at him with that sweetness of expression that had always wrenched his heart. "Seth?" she called softly and held out her hand to him.

He went up and took it in his. "I think, Rachel, my love," he said as he followed her, "that, first thing tomorrow, I shall sit down and write a thank-you to Mr. Galliard, too."

PAULA REID is a writer of historical novels, most of them set in the early nineteenth century. Under the penname Elizabeth Mansfield, she received an award as the best writer of Regency fiction. She has also received awards for several of her plays and musicals. A teacher of literature and drama, she lives in Annandale, Virginia with her husband, a metallurgical engineer. She has two children.